The PURPLE EMPEROR

The PURPLE EMPEROR

BY HERBIE BRENNAN

SCHOLASTIC INC.

New York Toronto London Auckland Sydney
Mexico City New Delhi Hong Kong Buenos Aires

ISBN 0-439-80835-9

12 11 10 9 8 7 6 5 4 3 2 1   5 6 7 8 9 10/0

Printed in the U.S.A.   40

First Scholastic printing, September 2005

This one for Steve.
With love and thanks.

One

Mr Fogarty's house was at the end of a short cul-de-sac. The front windows were partly boarded up, which gave it a deserted, derelict appearance. But Henry knew they'd been boarded up while Mr Fogarty still lived there, so the neighbours wouldn't notice any difference. And nobody with any sense would try to visit him. Mr Fogarty had broken his last visitor's arm with a cricket bat.

Henry had a full set of keys, but he avoided using the front door and walked around the back. It was gloomy there as always – Mr Fogarty had erected an enormously high fence to stop the neighbours spying on him – and there wasn't much to see: just a grey, mossy patch of lawn and the garden shed beside the buddleia bush where Henry had first met Pyrgus. He walked down to the bush – it was one of Hodge's favourite haunts – and called out, 'Hodge! Come on Hodgie, suppertime!'

Hodge must have been lurking in the undergrowth, because he emerged at once, tail up, and polished Henry's ankle. 'Hello, Hodge,' said Henry fondly. He sort of liked the old tomcat, even though he'd made the place a killing field for rats, mice, birds and rabbits.

Henry walked towards the back door, taking slow,

careful steps on account of Hodge making figures of eight between his feet. When he unlocked the door and pushed it open, Hodge ran in ahead of him, eager for his pouch of Whiskas. Mr Fogarty had always fed him some foul-smelling stuff that looked like puke and cost less than 25p a tin. Hodge ate it under protest, but liked pouch Whiskas better. He'd never smooched Mr Fogarty the way he smooched Henry.

Henry opened the cupboard, took out two pouches and Hodge's special tin plate.

'You're ruining that cat – you know that,' a voice growled from the shadows.

Henry was so startled he dropped the plate, which clattered loudly on the kitchen tiles. Hodge squawked in protest and bolted for the door.

Two

'Scaredy-cat!' sniffed Her Serene Highness, Princess Holly Blue.

'I'm not a scaredy-cat!' Pyrgus protested. 'I just want to see exactly what he'll be doing.' He leafed ostentatiously through the pattern book. Lavish animation spells caused the butterfly illustrations to writhe and stretch their wings.

'You *know* exactly what he'll be doing,' Blue said fiercely. 'They're traditional designs – they haven't changed in years! And you saw them often enough on Daddy.' Her eyes clouded. 'While he was alive.'

'I know, I know,' said Pyrgus. He turned another page.

'Well, what are you waiting for?'

Pyrgus mumbled something under his breath.

'What?' asked Blue sharply.

'Don't like needles,' Pyrgus mumbled just a little louder.

They were in the Emperor's private quarters – Pyrgus's private quarters now – in the Purple Palace. The Royal Herticord had been waiting outside for nearly an hour.

'I know you don't like needles,' Blue said, not unkindly. 'But you have to have it done. And you have to have it done now, otherwise they'll still be itching at your Coronation. You can't have the new Purple Emperor scratching through the ceremony – people will think you have fleas.'

'I could use a healing spell,' Pyrgus said.

'You could pull yourself together,' Blue told him shortly. 'You've sent that poor man away twice already. Just grit your teeth and get it over with.'

'Oh, all right,' Pyrgus said with bad grace. He nodded to the footman standing like a statue by the door. 'Show him in.'

The footman swung the door open with a flourish. 'Sir Archibald Buff-Arches,' he announced loudly. 'The Royal Herticord.'

The man who strode in reminded Blue a little of her old enemy Jasper Chalkhill. He was overweight, and had a taste for extravagant clothing – he was wearing a shot-silk robe woven with illusion spells so that misty nymphs swam through its folds. But that's where the resemblance ended. His eyes showed he was no Faerie of the Night, and he walked with purpose. Two wiry helpers manoeuvred in a trolley spread with multi-coloured pots, several bottles and a tray that displayed Pyrgus's dreaded needles.

The Herticord bowed formally to Pyrgus. 'Your Imperial Majesty,' he acknowledged. He turned to Blue and made a lesser bow. 'Your Serene Highness.' She noticed he had very delicate hands. They were rather beautiful.

'My brother's ready for you,' Blue said quickly before Pyrgus could change his mind.

Pyrgus gave her a dirty look, but had obviously decided to go through with it. He turned to Buff-

Arches with exaggerated dignity. 'I'm in your hands, Herticord. Let's get it over with.'

The two helpers were busying themselves opening jars and bottles and laying out a range of gleaming instruments beside the needles. Blue saw Pyrgus turn a little green. The trolley looked as if they were preparing for major surgery.

'I expect His Majesty would like to know his options,' Buff-Arches said briskly.

Pyrgus stared at him and Blue's instincts told her that if her brother was going to chicken out at all, this would be the moment. But all he said was, 'Options? Yes, I'd like to know my options.'

'Traditionally,' said Buff-Arches, 'the tattoos are done without anaesthetic or magical intervention of any sort, save for a small transfusion should royal blood loss exceed two pints in any single hour –'

'Blood loss?' Pyrgus squeaked. 'Two pints an hour?'

'Oh, it seldom reaches anything approaching that amount,' Buff-Arches said easily. 'Unless, of course, one happens to sever an artery when preparing the Royal Transposition.'

'The Royal Transposition?' Pyrgus echoed. Blue moved nonchalantly a little closer in case he fainted.

'A deep tissue sample used to gauge the effect of the dyes. A safety precaution in case of allergic response. I tattoo the sample first – with a picture of a bee – then, if there is no reaction, we proceed with the formal illustration of Your Majesty's body. The tissue sample is normally taken from the royal buttocks.'

Blue fully expected Pyrgus to protest. *She* certainly would have – a tissue sample of that sort meant you couldn't sit down for a week. But all Pyrgus said was,

'Why a bee? Why do you tattoo the sample with a bee?'

'I haven't the slightest idea,' Buff-Arches said. 'It's simply the specified picture – specified by tradition, you understand.' He watched Pyrgus for a moment, as if expecting further questions, then said abruptly, 'But I was explaining your options. As I say, the traditional way involves no anaesthetic or magical intervention, but one of your illustrious ancestors, Emperor Scolitandes the Weedy, decreed that henceforth all Purple Emperors might elect to have their official tattoos carried out under general or local anaesthetic –' he gestured towards some bottles on the trolley '– these herbal tinctures here. Or, alternatively, that the candidate might light a spell cone that would render him temporarily immune to pain.' He paused expectantly, then added, 'Perhaps your Imperial Majesty would care to tell me the option of his choice?'

Pyrgus was staring at the tray. 'What are those instruments for?' he asked. 'The tissue sample?'

'Oh no, sire. Your Majesty will recall that my secondary duty as Herticord is to shave Your Majesty's head in the Royal Tonsure. The tools look a little off-putting, but that part of the procedure is quite painless, I assure you. Unless Your Majesty has a twitch, of course.'

'Do we have to do the shaving thing?' Pyrgus asked. He was a bit vain about his hair.

Buff-Arches nodded briefly. 'Yes, we do. Your Majesty is titular head of the Church of Light, so the tonsure is wholly appropriate. But if Your Majesty wishes, I can retain the shaven hair and have it made into a little wig for Your Majesty to wear when he is not engaged in State occasions.'

'Yes,' Pyrgus said quickly. 'Yes, you do that.'

'And Your Majesty's options? The anaesthetics, the spell cone ... ?'

'What did my father do?' Pyrgus asked.

For the first time Buff-Arches's expression softened. 'Your father, sire, opted for the traditional approach – no spells, no anaesthetics. He didn't even require my assistants to hold him down.'

Blue felt herself tense. It was only weeks since their father was murdered – and murdered horribly with an Analogue World weapon that had destroyed most of his face. But Pyrgus and their father had seldom seen eye to eye. It had got so bad at one stage that Pyrgus had left home and lived in the city as a commoner. Would he follow his father's example now?

'Then I shall do the same,' said Pyrgus grandly. He began to unbutton his breeches.

Blue left discreetly. She was proud of her brother, delighted with his choice. But she had no desire to be there when they took the tissue sample from his bottom.

There were still a million things to do before the Coronation. Gold leaf for the Cathedral, spell candles for the nave, gifts for the congregation, musicians, the celebratory games, rabbits for the Official Distribution, the Honour Guard, the clerical bribes, the State Barge, the seven conjuration troupes, the Endolg Chorus, the Male Companion – Pyrgus wanted Henry for that and Blue wasn't even sure Gatekeeper Fogarty had contacted him yet – the Female Companion, which would be Blue herself, except she still hadn't had her fitting for the dress, the Grand Salute, the new statue in the Great Square, the reception menu ... the list went on and on.

And all of it was down to Blue since Pyrgus wouldn't take it seriously.

She was hurrying towards her own rooms and the dreaded *To Do* list when she decided on impulse to get the fitting over with. She turned down a steep flight of narrow stairs that led to the servants' quarters. It wasn't an area of the palace she normally visited – when the Princess Royal needed something, servants came to *her* – but tradition had it that the gown worn by the Female Companion should be woven from the finest spinner silk *with no spell reinforcement.*

Ridiculous, but that was tradition for you. Everybody knew spinner silk was the most fragile substance in the world until it set. Afterwards, of course, it was the strongest. The trouble was, to get the astonishing form-fitting folds that made spinner dresses so desirable, you had to try the garment on before the fabric set. You had to try it on *carefully.* At least, you had to try it on carefully when you weren't allowed to use a stasis spell. If you were lucky, the whole thing didn't fall apart and you had the most wonderful gown in the realm. If you weren't, the Silk Mistresses made up another one (at hideous expense) and the whole process began again.

Most clients, even nobles, visited the Mistresses in their trading lodges above the spinner pits. It was only by a very special concession to the Princess Royal that her Coronation gown was being constructed in the palace itself. Blue would have been happy to give the Mistresses a state apartment, but they insisted on setting up their workshop in the servants' quarters. Blue discovered the reason when she entered it.

'Why's it so cold in here?' she demanded, her breath frosting.

One of the Silk Mistresses glanced up from her bench. If she was impressed by the sudden appearance of the Princess Royal, she didn't show it. 'The fabric is unworkable at higher temperatures,' she said.

Blue shivered and hugged herself. 'I've come for the fitting,' she said shortly. 'Is everything ready?'

The Mistress stood up and walked towards her. She was a tall, elegant matron with waist-length hair and her own gown was divine. That was the great thing about spinner silk. It made any woman look wonderful; any woman who could afford it, that is.

'Of course, Serenity. Please follow me.'

Blue allowed herself to be led across the workshop. The Mistresses had moved their entire operation into the palace, to judge from the garments they were creating. Blue hoped they hadn't moved their spinners in as well. She liked arachnids – she even owned an illegal psychotronic – but silk spiders were the size of terriers, too large even for her.

The Mistress opened a door to a second room, smaller than the first and empty of workbenches. There was a stunning purple and gold gown draped over a wooden form and illuminated by a gentle glowglobe. The fabric shimmered as if enchanted.

Despite herself, Blue sucked in her breath. 'It's ... amazing.'

The Mistress smiled lightly. 'Indeed, Serenity.'

On impulse Blue said, 'What's your name, Silk Mistress?'

'Peach Blossom, Serenity.'

'It's the most beautiful thing I've ever seen, Peach Blossom,' Blue said sincerely. She took a step closer to the garment. Although the temperature of this room was perhaps a degree or two higher than that in the workshop, her breath was still frosting. 'Do I have to undress to try it on?'

'Yes, Serenity. It will fit, of course, but your body heat will set the material to conform to your figure now and for ever. Assuming you don't tear it as you put it on.'

'I'll be careful,' Blue promised.

The material felt … elusive. Not quite slippery, yet somehow distant, as if it belonged in another dimension. Blue desperately wanted to put it on quickly – the room was so cold she was already shivering – but forced her numbing fingers to move with slow deliberation. The gown slid over her head and down her body like a slick of perfumed oil. She felt warmer at once and sensed the catalytic process as the spinner threads began to set.

'Well, done, Serenity!' Peach Blossom said. 'You may move now – it's quite safe.'

Blue moved and the gown moved with her. She was suddenly energised, as if someone had lit a euphoria cone.

'You look wonderful, Your Highness,' Peach Blossom said. 'Please come through and show the other Mistresses.'

Although Blue had never thought much about her appearance, she thought about it now. She felt graceful. She felt beautiful. She felt as elegant as the Silk Mistress herself. Her movements were a dance. No wonder the Mistresses could command such high prices for their designs: the effect of wearing one was quite extraordinary.

There was a burst of spontaneous applause as she walked back into the workroom. Several of the Silk Mistresses even stood up, smiling their delight. Blue smiled back in sincere appreciation, but at the moment of triumph an unexpected thought occurred: *Just wait until Henry Atherton sees me in <u>this</u>!*

Three

The man who stepped out of the shadows was tall, thin and wearing an ankle-length indigo toga embroidered with electrical and planetary symbols. He fixed Henry with a gimlet eye. 'You know they put dope in that stuff, don't you? Cat dope. Little twits get addicted and won't touch anything else. That's what makes it so expensive.'

Henry glanced at the pouch of Whiskas in his hand, then back at the scowling figure. 'Mr Fogarty! What are you doing here?'

'I live here,' Fogarty said sourly.

'No you don't,' Henry said. 'At least not this month.' There was a sudden excitement flowering in him. 'How's Pyrgus? How's the Realm?' He tried to sound nonchalant. 'How's, ah, Princess Blue?'

Fogarty bent down to open the cupboard underneath the sink. He extracted a tin and searched the kitchen drawer for an opener – the tin was so old it didn't even have a ring-pull. 'Pyrgus is a mess. Kid doesn't live in the real world, so how do you expect him to run an Empire? The Realm – well, that's what I want to talk to you about.' He caught Henry's expression and added, 'Your little girlfriend's fine.'

'She's not my girlfriend,' Henry said, flushing.

Fogarty ignored him. He took a small knife from the drawer and used it to transfer globules of grey slime from the tin into Hodge's metal dish. Hodge, now recovered from his fright, had returned to the kitchen and was watching with beady interest. Fogarty said, 'It's all fine on the surface. Nighters are generally behaving themselves. Hairstreak's gone quiet. There are rumours the Hael Realm's collapsed – don't believe it myself, but the portals are certainly closed, so the demons aren't giving any trouble. Lot of talk about hands of friendship, doves of peace, all that sort of crap. Trouble is, nothing's really changed.'

He set the dish on the floor and waited. Hodge trotted across, sniffed it once, then walked away and sat down with his back to them. 'What did I say?' Fogarty exclaimed triumphantly. 'That's an addiction! He won't touch normal food – he wants his fix.'

'Mr Fogarty, he doesn't *like* that cat food,' Henry said. 'It smells awful and it looks like –'

'Always ate it for me,' Fogarty cut in airily. ''Specially when he was hungry.' He stared intently at Henry and sniffed. 'Might as well give him the pouch now – you've turned him into a junkie.'

Henry decided he wasn't going to get into all this. He binned the puke food, rinsed the dish and squeezed pouch Whiskas into it. Hodge's tail went up and he began to eat at once.

Fogarty pulled out a chair and sat down at the kitchen table. 'Couple of things. Before I forget, Pyrgus wants you to translate for his Coronation.' Henry looked at him blankly, thinking of his last language exam, then remembered *translate* was the word Pyrgus used for travelling to the Faerie Realm. 'There's something called "Male Companion",' Fogarty went on. 'Sort of like best man at a wedding. He wants you to be it. Involves dressing up like a prat.'

Henry glanced at Mr Fogarty's own attire, but said nothing. There was a grin spreading over his face. He wanted nothing more than an excuse to go back to the Faerie Realm. It was such a brilliant place to be. I mean, he was a sort of a hero in the Faerie Realm. He'd been on adventures, saved Pyrgus from Hell. Be nice to see Pyrgus again. And Blue. Especially Blue. Not in the bath, of course. Not like he'd come across her before. But it would only be polite to call on Blue. Male Companion, eh? Mr Fogarty's idea of dressing like a prat probably meant something colourful and heroic, so Blue would see him really at his best, not wearing the sort of rubbish he'd had on the last time they met.

'When is it – the Coronation?' he asked.

'Two weeks – it's a Saturday here. The celebrations last three days, but you'll need to come on the Friday for a rehearsal.'

Henry's excitement popped like a balloon. He might get away from his mum overnight, arrange with his friend Charlie to pretend he was staying there for the night, but four days was out of the question. 'I can't get away for four days.'

'You doing something, or just worried about your parents?'

'No, I'm not doing anything. I mean, if I was I'd put it off. It's my parents – well, just Mum, actually. I don't see that much of Dad.' He realised suddenly that with being away so much Mr Fogarty wouldn't know his circumstances. 'I'm just living with Mum now – Dad has his own place. She'd want to know where I was if

I disappeared for four days.'

Fogarty shrugged. 'No problem – we'll use a lethe.'

Henry blinked. 'What's a lethe?'

'Makes you forget. You just swan off when you need to, crack a cone under her nose and she won't even remember she *has* a son until you come back. Anybody else in the house?'

'My sister Aisling,' Henry said, his eyes wide. He'd seen spells worked in the Faerie Realm, but it had never occurred to him he might actually use one himself.

'I'll get you a box: never know when they come in handy. You'll have to use one for each of them. Just be sure to hold your breath until you're out of the room.'

'Thank you,' Henry said. There was a warm feeling in his stomach at the thought of hexing his sister.

'So I tell Pyrgus you're coming?'

Henry nodded enthusiastically. 'Yes.'

Fogarty said, 'OK. The second thing is, I've decided to stay on permanently.'

'Here?' Henry asked. He had mixed feelings, but overall it was mostly relief. Since Pyrgus had made Mr Fogarty Gatekeeper of the Faerie Realm – hard to believe that was only a few weeks ago – the old man had split his time between the Purple Palace and his own home. While he was away, Henry kept an eye on the house and fed Hodge. But lately, Mr Fogarty had taken to spending longer and longer periods in the Realm and Henry didn't know how he was going to manage when he went back to school in September. As it was, things were tricky enough: his mum didn't approve of Mr Fogarty.

Fogarty shook his head. 'No, in the Realm. Like I

said, everything's fine on the surface, but nothing's changed underneath. Hairstreak still has his own agenda, however much he talks about building bridges. Pyrgus isn't any good at politics – doesn't have the interest. And he's a trusting soul. Thinks if somebody tells him something it's usually the truth. If he's going to survive as Emperor, he needs me to look after him. Far as I can see, that's going to be a full-time job.'

'Yes ... ' Henry nodded thoughtfully. Mr Fogarty was probably right. Apart from anything else, Pyrgus was terribly young to be an Emperor – much the same age as Henry, in fact. Then he caught Mr Fogarty's expression and said, 'There's something else, isn't there?'

Fogarty sniffed. 'Not as stupid as you look, are you, Henry?' He sighed. 'Yes, there is. I'm not getting any younger. If it's really three score years and ten, I'm well past my sell-by date. I've arthritis in my knuckles and I couldn't run fifteen yards from a copper without getting winded these days. Been thinking I might last another five years, maybe ten if I'm lucky, but I found out they've got treatments in the Faerie Realm that could give me thirty – *and* get rid of the damn arthritis. Except they don't work if I keep popping back and forth. Differences in the two environments, or something. Thing is, once you start the treatments your tolerance to this world drops. I've started the treatments. Longer I'm here, the more dangerous it is for me. So, when I go back this time, I'm staying.'

Henry said, 'But what are you going to do about the house, Mr Fogarty?'

Fogarty looked thoughtful. 'That's what I came back to sort out.'

four

For some reason, the gown helped Blue put things in perspective. Although she'd taken it off now and was wearing her familiar blouse and britches, she was no longer feeling nearly so frantic about the Coronation arrangements. Admittedly there was still a lot to do, but there were still two weeks to do it in. And it wasn't really fair to say Pyrgus didn't care. It was just that the whole thing upset him. He'd never wanted to be Emperor and he didn't want to be Emperor now, so he avoided thinking about it. And maybe that was all to the good – Pyrgus was capable of making a mess of nearly anything. Better to leave the arrangements to her – she was good at organisation. It wasn't as if she didn't have as much help as she needed. There were –

She turned a corner of the corridor and walked into her half-brother, Comma. There was something on his lips, something he'd been eating, that had turned them bright scarlet. He'd put on weight quite noticeably since their father died.

'Sorry,' Comma muttered. He glanced behind him as if afraid he was being followed, then gave Blue a forced half-smile. 'You're in a hurry, Sweet Sister,' he said.

She hated it when he called her 'Sweet Sister' and her annoyance made her sharp. 'I've a lot to do.' Comma had been no help at all with the arrangements, and while she was prepared to forgive Pyrgus, all Comma did was make her furious.

'There's somebody waiting for you in your bedroom,' Comma said.

Blue blinked. 'How do you know?' What she really wanted to ask was, *What were you doing in my bedroom?*

Comma shrugged infuriatingly and started to walk on.

'Who is it?' Blue demanded.

He waved to her without looking back. 'I expect it's one of your clever *spies*,' he said.

'What have you been eating?' Blue shouted. 'What were you doing in my –' But it was too late. He was already turning down a side corridor.

Seething, Blue stamped off towards her quarters.

There was no one in her bedroom except her cleaning maid. She turned to leave, swearing vengeance on Comma for wasting her time, when a tickling in her mind caused her to pause. Blue's eyes flickered round the room and a tingle of fear crawled down her spine. There was something wrong. For a moment she had no idea what, except it felt like something was out of place.

She mentally checked the furnishings. Nothing seemed to have been moved. She looked across at her dressing table. Everything was neatly in its place. Except for the jewel case that held her psychotronic spider which she'd slipped into a drawer, as she always did before the maid came in to clean – Princess Royal or not, psychotronic spiders were illegal, and fearfully dangerous. They could carry your mind so far from your body that you never got it back again.

So nothing different about the dressing table. Blue let her gaze travel around the walls, checking the pictures, lingering on the portrait of her father, feeling the well-spring of sorrow as she looked into the painted eyes. But nothing had been moved. Nothing had changed at all.

And yet something was out of place …

Suddenly she had it. The antique chair that sat beside her bed had disappeared. Blue stared for a moment, then said quietly to the maid, 'I'd like you to finish off some other time, Anna.'

'Yes, Your Royal Highness.' The girl dropped a curtsey and hurried out.

Blue moved cautiously towards her dressing table. There was a dagger in one of the drawers. Not that she was likely to need it. There were always guards close by in these troubled times. But close or not, they would take time to reach her and it was always as well to take responsibility for your own protection.

'You can show yourself now,' she said aloud.

There was a shimmering beyond the bed and Blue's chair reappeared. An extraordinary woman was sitting in it.

'Madame Cynthia!' Blue exclaimed.

'My deeah, you must forgive the invisibility – so ill-mannered of me. But I felt it best not to show myself while the servant remained.'

'Yes, of course,' Blue nodded. Cynthia Cardui, the Realm's famous Painted Lady, was a major contact in Blue's private espionage network, but it was astonishing to see her here in the palace. Madame Cynthia was elderly now, long retired from the stage, and seldom ventured far from her Cheapside apartments. 'Are you alone?'

'I fear so. Kitterick is visiting his relatives, otherwise I might have entrusted him with the mission. He's back tomorrow, but I decided I must undertake it myself. The matter is urgent.'

'Urgent?' Blue echoed. She felt an uncomfortable chill.

'My deeah,' said Madame Cardui, 'you must steel yourself. There is a plot afoot.'

Blue walked across and sat on the edge of the bed. She trusted Madame Cardui more than almost anyone else in the world. The old woman was snobbish and eccentric, but her contacts were legendary and her loyalty absolute. If she said something was going on, Blue was prepared to believe it.

'A brutal conspiracy, my deeah,' Madame Cardui went on. 'One would imagine with Lord Hairstreak routed, Brimstone in hiding and that dreadful creature Chalkhill behind bars, one would have nothing to worry about.' She sighed theatrically. 'Alas, no. I have received information of a plan to kill a member of the royal household.'

The unease Blue had felt since she saw Madame Cardui flowered into chill fear. But she held her voice steady. 'Which member?' she asked.

A look of distress crossed the Painted Lady's face. 'That's the problem, I'm afraid – we don't know.'

five

It was bone gruel again.

Brimstone stared into the cracked bowl and felt his lips dry out. The liquid had the consistency of dishwater, a thin, greyish fluid curdled with lumps of corpse-white gristle that smelled worse than the open sewer outside his window. He looked up at the toothless old crone and scowled.

'It's good for you,' Widow Mormo cackled. 'Keeps your strength up – my late husband swore by it.' She set a dirty spoon beside the bowl and a wedge of rough brown bread beside the spoon. A cockroach scuttled across the rickety table and Brimstone squashed it with his thumb.

'Your late husband probably died from it,' he muttered sourly.

'No need to be like that,' Widow Mormo said sharply. 'I'm a poor woman and I does the best I can on the pittance you pay me.'

Brimstone was paying her a groat a day, which was indeed a pittance, but meals were extra and bone gruel gave him diarrhoea. He'd planned to lay low in these miserable lodgings for at least six months, but now he was wondering if he could survive another six days. Even the threat of a demon prince paled beside Widow

Mormo's bone gruel.

The old sow muttered something he didn't catch. 'What?' Brimstone demanded crossly. 'What?' Without a spell to reinforce it, his hearing was going. But the spell he needed was one of the ones he'd been forced to leave behind and he didn't dare go out and buy another. A magical supply shop was the first place Beleth would think of looking for him. Probably had every one in the city staked out by now. A demon prince had huge resources.

The trouble was, it wouldn't end with loss of hearing. Brimstone was ninety-eight years old. Without magical reinforcement, his body would soon start to fall apart. Even with it, he knew he looked his age.

'I said there might be a way to make things a bit more comfortable for you,' Widow Mormo repeated slyly. 'Better food as well.'

'I'm not paying any more,' Brimstone told her promptly. These might be cheap lodgings, but most of his cash fortune had been stolen and all of his assets were beyond his reach. He had a substantial amount of gold about his person, but he'd no idea how long it might have to last. Demons had long memories. He might have to stay in hiding for years.

To his intense discomfort, the old bag pulled up a chair and sat beside him. He wrinkled his nose. She seemed to be wearing some hideous perfume, but she still smelled mainly of pee.

Brimstone shifted his own chair backwards. 'Widow Mormo –' he began.

'Maura,' said the old bag. 'Call me Maura.' She lowered her eyes. 'And I shall call you Silas.'

'You'll call me nothing of the sort,' Brimstone

snapped. Lower classes never knew their place when you were short of cash.

'What I was thinking of, Silas,' said Widow Mormo, not at all put out, 'was a little … arrangement.'

'What sort of arrangement?' he asked suspiciously. Anything that got him better food without paying more had to be worth listening to. But she'd want *something* in return, of course – people always did. Probably his help with an illegal spell. He'd told her nothing, but he knew he had the scent of sulphur about him and she was as shrewd as she was hideous. Chances were she'd put him down for a sorcerer the minute he'd walked through the door. It'd be an illegal spell all right. But how bad could that be? He'd dealt with demons all his life and his last contract with Beleth had called for human sacrifice. Nothing the crone came up with was likely to be in the same league.

'I'm a widow woman, Silas,' she said softly. 'Have been since my Stanley died.'

'What's that got to do with me?' Brimstone snapped.

'Thought we might get married,' Widow Mormo told him coyly.

Brimstone stared at the old bat in astonishment. Even in her younger days she must have been the ugliest woman in the country. Now, without teeth, warty, wrinkled, rheumy, balding, smelly, dirty, badly-dressed and flatulent, she'd have been more appealing as a corpse.

'You want me to marry you?' he said.

'Get you out of here,' Widow Mormo sniffed. 'I got a place of my own in the woods – log cabin with mod cons, a full cabinet of spells and a nice comfortable double bed. Keep my money underneath the mattress.

Nobody ever goes there. Nobody even knows about it.' She smiled seductively and gummily. 'We could slip away for our honeymoon.'

Brimstone frowned. A nice isolated log cabin could be just the thing he needed. Not to mention Widow Mormo's money and the spells in her magic cabinet. He cracked a wintery smile. He could cut her throat when they got there and bury her body in the woods.

'Yes, all right,' he said brightly.

Six

The Great Keep of Asloght was an imposing sight as it rose against the stark backdrop of the Nikure Barrens, but most of its structure was actually underground. The eighteen-hundred-year-old fort was built with a warren of subterranean chambers for food storage. Now prisoners were the only things that rotted in the gloomy cells. For more than three centuries, Asloght had been the Realm's main jail for recalcitrant criminals and political dissidents.

Harold Dingy was having trouble with the Governor of the Keep.

'I'm not saying these papers aren't genuine,' the Governor said. 'I'm not saying that at all. I'm just saying the sealing wax is red, and in my experience it should be pink.'

'Red ... pink ... what's the difference?' Dingy asked. He was a big man, not altogether used to being questioned. Especially the way he was dressed just now.

'Shade,' said the Governor. 'A shade of difference, you might say.' He looked up and smiled manically. 'And a shade of difference might make all the difference.'

Dingy didn't smile back. 'You know the prisoner these papers refer to?'

The Governor glanced at them again. 'Oh yes. Oh yes, indeed.'

'Scum, would you say?'

The Governor nodded. 'Of the lowest sort.'

'Deserving of the penalty the papers lay out?'

'Penalties are not my business,' the Governor said primly. 'My business is to detain – and where necessary torture a little – those placed in my charge. But since you ask, I believe this prisoner is deserving, very deserving, of the penalty laid out. Too good for him, in my view. Purely a personal opinion, of course.'

Dingy frowned. 'Too good for him? It's the ultimate penalty, isn't it? Can't get more ultimate than death.'

'Indeed not. But what *sort* of death? That's what I would ask.'

'What sort would you want?' asked Dingy, suddenly curious.

The Governor leaned back in his chair and made a steeple of his hands. He rolled his eyes heavenwards, or at least as heavenwards as the ceiling of his office allowed. 'Well, we could gradually starve him, or crush his feet and put him on a treadmill, bleed him to death, beat him to a pulp, feed him a slow-acting poison, remove his vital organs one by one, transplant his brain into the body of a rat, insert red-hot needles into his ears, nail his feet to the floor so he can't reach his food (which is starving him, I admit, but more stylishly), bake him in a slow oven, stampede a herd of elephants over him, force him to eat an endolg, staple his mouth and nose shut so he can't breathe, drown him in a cesspit, burn off his skin, drop an anvil on his head, stretch him between dray horses, feed him to hounds, electrocute him with an eel, drop him from a high tower, inject him with soapsuds, have him eaten by mosquitoes, make him stab rocks with a Halek knife, change him into a mouse and bring in the cat, bury him in snow until the spring, send him to the ink mines, drill holes in his head and pour in acid –' He waved an airy hand. 'This warrant only specifies hanging.'

Dingy glanced at the papers. They did seem a bit unimaginative. 'How about I duff him up beforehand?'

'Be a help,' the Governor said.

'So what about the sealing wax?'

The Governor shrugged. 'Red ... pink ... what's the difference?' He stood up. 'Put your hood up. I'll get somebody to show you to his cell.'

The basic cell in Asloght was a twelve-foot cube with a run-off for the water that seeped down the stone-block walls. Furnishings were confined to a heap of damp straw in one corner and a bucket. There were no curtains at the windows because there were no windows. Prisoners were issued with one stubby candle per week.

Jasper Chalkhill's quarters were rather more luxurious, thanks to a small fortune spent on bribes. He had more space, for one thing, a pink carpet on the floor, a proper bed in one corner, glowglobes set into the ceiling, an easy chair, a dining chair, a bookcase, a table and a small refrigerator filled with sticky snacks and drinks. Even compared to prison staff, Chalkhill was probably the most comfortable man in Asloght.

But that didn't stop him complaining.

'It's not what I'm used to,' he told the orderly he'd hired at huge expense to be his valet. 'I do so miss my little spells. They won't allow me any magic here, you know.' Which wasn't strictly true – a weekly absorbent spell took care of the damp – but there were certainly no magical luxuries.

The orderly, a patient Trinian named Clutterbuck, was engaged in light housework while Chalkhill reclined prostrate with boredom on the bed. 'I don't suppose I could tempt you to a little mahjong?' Chalkhill asked. 'We could play for sweeties. Anything to ease this dreadful *ennui*.' He drew the back of his hand theatrically across his forehead to give the suggestion emphasis, even though he suspected he knew the answer before he asked the question.

'Sorry, sir, don't know the game at all,' Clutterbuck told him briskly. 'Besides, sir, with respect, sir, gaming isn't in my contract. Just the basic Four Cs – cooking, cleaning, conversation and clothing. Four Cs, sir. Doesn't run to gaming, I'm afraid, on account of that being a G.' He began to set out the cutlery for Chalkhill's next meal.

'How would it be –' Chalkhill stopped. 'What's the matter?' The Trinian had moved abruptly to the door of the cell and was now pressed against the wall beside it, sniffing furiously.

'Danger, sir. Approaching us at walking pace.'

Chalkhill sat up in bed. 'How do you know?'

'Can smell it, sir – I had the training.'

Chalkhill swung his feet on to the floor. He was a fat man with a taste for flamboyant clothing, and although his opportunities to indulge it now were limited, he still managed a lime-green robe with jewelled pumps.

'Will you protect me?' he asked curiously. Then, before Clutterbuck could answer, echoed, 'Not in the contract – I know, I know.' He stood up. 'My, my, danger coming – this *is* exciting!'

'That's one way of putting it, sir. Now, if there's nothing more you need me for, I'll leave you to face it.'

'No, you run along, Clutterbuck. Thank you.' Chalkhill's eyes were fixed on the door and he licked his lips in some anticipation. Almost anything would be better than the endless, dreadful *sameness* of his prison days.

Clutterbuck unlocked the door and opened it to slip out. As he did so, a tall figure slipped in. Chalkhill's pleasurable expectation drained through the soles of his feet. The creature wore a black robe with a hood that covered its entire face except for two glittering dark eyes. It carried the large, sharp scythe and ceremonial oakwood hour-glass of a State Executioner.

'My God,' said Chalkhill in sudden dread. 'They've sent you to kill me!'

Seven

The Executioner seemed in something of a hurry. He swept down the corridors of the Great Keep like a herald of doom, dragging Chalkhill behind him.

'Steady on,' gasped Chalkhill breathlessly. At this pace he'd be dead before the man could hang him.

The Governor was waiting for them at the main gates. 'Where exactly are you taking him?' he asked the Executioner.

'That's something you don't need to know,' the Executioner told him flatly. 'Let's just say it's somewhere nobody will see what I plan to do with him.'

'Excellent!' the Governor exclaimed. He gave a signal to the guards and the gates swung slowly open.

There was a black coach outside, drawn by four black horses. A hunchbacked coachman in a black cloak and black three-cornered hat gripped the reins with claw-like hands. To Chalkhill's surprise, there were no bars on the windows. The Executioner bundled him inside and, to Chalkhill's even greater surprise, climbed in beside him. The coach lurched off violently the moment the door closed.

Chalkhill watched through the window, wondering if he could safely jump. But the Executioner pushed the hood back to reveal a moon-shaped face that was curiously familiar. 'Harold Dingy,' he said, grinning. 'Lord Hairstreak sent me to get you out.'

Chalkhill stared at him in astonishment. He'd spied for Lord Hairstreak for years, but he knew the drill well enough – any spy who got caught was on his own. Black Hairstreak would deny his existence and let him rot. Which was exactly what he had done since Chalkhill was jailed. 'What about the execution papers?' he asked suspiciously.

'Forged, of course.' Dingy caught his expression and smiled. 'Don't worry – he's got a job for you.'

A job? That would explain it. Chalkhill found himself beginning to relax. 'I don't suppose you know what this job is?' he asked.

'Course I do,' said Harold Dingy, still grinning broadly. 'He wants you to stop young Pyrgus Malvae becoming Purple Emperor.'

Eight

Blue found Pyrgus (at last!) in the throne room. 'Where on earth have you been?' she hissed. He was gawping at the Imperial Crown, an amethyst and gold headpiece that crackled with purple fire even in its protective case. In two weeks' time he would have to submit himself to the energies that coursed from it through his body, transforming him from Emperor Elect to Emperor. Before he had time to answer, she snapped impatiently, 'Doesn't matter – I need to talk to you.'

Pyrgus turned like a sleepwalker and stared at her blankly.

'In private,' Blue said.

Pyrgus blinked slowly. 'There's no one else here.' His mind was clearly miles away.

'Oh, for heaven's sake, Pyrgus!' The throne room was designed for public pronouncements, with acoustic galleries that carried every whisper into the winding corridors outside. It was the least private chamber in the entire palace.

He seemed to snap out of it a little and looked at her directly. 'All right, Blue,' he said mildly. 'We can use our father's quarters.'

They were *his* quarters now, had been since he became Emperor Elect. What was *wrong* with him?

What was he doing mooning about in the throne room in the middle of the night? But at least his suggestion was sensible. The Emperor's quarters were permanently spell-protected.

They walked together in silence, scarcely acknowledging the saluting guards. Blue felt the familiar sense of dread as they approached the suite. Every time she entered, she remembered. It was as if she could still smell the sickly scent of her father's blood. But nothing showed on her face as she pushed the vivid images aside.

Pyrgus closed the door. 'What is it?' he asked.

'I can't find the Gatekeeper,' Blue said.

That dreamy look again. 'Is that all? Mr Fogarty's gone home to the Analogue World. He'll be back tomorrow morning.'

'No, that's not all!' Blue said angrily. Curiosity got the better of her and she added, 'What's he doing in the Analogue World?'

'I asked him to invite Henry to my Coronation,' Pyrgus said. 'I want him to be my Male Companion – I told you that.'

'Why's he away until tomorrow?'

'Henry?'

'No, Pyrgus – Mr Fogarty! What's *wrong* with you?'

Pyrgus shrugged. 'He had some personal business to attend to.'

'What sort of personal business?'

'I didn't ask him.'

Blue closed her eyes briefly, seething with frustration. Pyrgus never seemed to care what was going on around him, not even when it concerned as important an official as the Gatekeeper.

Pyrgus said, 'Look, Blue, I'm a bit tired, so if that's all you wanted me for I think I'd –'

'Of course it's not all. Somebody's trying to kill you.'

It still didn't jerk him out of it. All he said was, 'Who?'

'I don't know who. If I knew who I'd have said, *Lord Hairstreak's trying to kill you* or *the Duke of Burgundy's trying to kill you*, wouldn't I? Actually, I don't even know for sure it *is* you, but you're the most likely.'

Suddenly Pyrgus was his old self again. He frowned. 'Back up, Blue. I want to hear this properly. What exactly have you heard and who did you hear it from?'

Blue took his arm impulsively. 'Oh, Pyrgus, I thought all this would stop when we put down the Nighter rebellion. But it doesn't stop, does it? And now we don't have Daddy to look after it.'

An odd expression flickered across Pyrgus's features. He tugged his arm free gently and put it round her shoulders. 'No, Blue, it doesn't stop. I don't think it will ever stop. But it may get better. Tell me what you heard.'

'There's a plot to kill a member of the royal family. I suppose it must be you – I don't see who else it would be.'

'You,' Pyrgus said. 'Or Comma.'

'You're Emperor Elect,' Blue said.

Pyrgus nodded. He removed his arm and went over to sit down in the comfortable leather wing chair his father had loved so much. He yawned. 'Sorry, Blue, I've had a long day.' He nodded again, thoughtfully. 'You're right, I suppose – it's most likely to be me.' He looked up. 'And you have no information on who's behind it?'

Blue shook her head. 'No. Not yet.'

'It'll be Hairstreak's doing, I imagine.'

He didn't just sound tired, he sounded old. Sitting in the wing chair with his stocky build and curly red hair, he looked so like their father. Blue said quietly, 'I'd think so too.'

Pyrgus brought his head up, another gesture that was a painful reminder of their father. 'Is your source reliable?'

'Madame Cardui,' Blue said. She didn't often reveal her sources, but she had no secrets from Pyrgus.

'The Painted Lady? I trust her.'

'So do I.'

'She's trying to find out more, of course?'

Blue nodded. 'Yes.'

Pyrgus stood up stiffly. 'Not much more we can do at the moment. I'll order extra guards and a heightened security alert. Then I have to get some sleep. We'll discuss the situation with Gatekeeper Fogarty when he comes back in the morning.' He paused at the door. 'I love you, Blue.'

Despite their problems, Blue smiled. 'I love you too, Pyrgus,' she said.

Nine

Gatekeeper Fogarty didn't come back in the morning.

Blue found Pyrgus pacing angrily outside the Gatekeeper's lodge. 'Where is he?' he demanded the moment he saw her.

'How should I know?' Blue asked shortly. 'You're the one he talked to. When did he say he would be back?'

'Dawn,' Pyrgus grunted. 'That was hours ago.' There were dark rings under his eyes as if he'd been up all night. Blue wondered if he hadn't slept – he certainly hadn't gone to bed *that* late.

'Maybe his valet or his housekeeper might know something,' Blue suggested.

'He doesn't *have* a valet or a housekeeper,' Pyrgus said crossly. 'He doesn't have any servants at all. Won't trust anybody with him in his lodge. You know what he's like. I can't even get in with the Emperor's master key – he's done something to the locks.'

The Gatekeeper's lodge was a tight conglomeration of tiny towers and spires within sight of the Purple Palace, but quite separate from it. It was set in formal gardens against the backdrop of the island forest where their father Apatura Iris, the last Purple Emperor, had once enjoyed hunting boar. Pyrgus stared thoughtfully towards that forest now.

Blue said, 'Perhaps his personal business took him longer than he expected.'

Pyrgus said abruptly, 'Madame Cardui – what exactly did she say to you?'

Frowning, Blue said, 'That there was a plot to kill a member of the royal family.'

'Royal family or royal household?'

Blue hesitated. After a moment she said, 'Household.'

'Are you sure?'

Blue nodded. 'Yes. You're right – she said *household*. I'm certain.'

Pyrgus dragged his eyes away from the forest. 'You see, if it's royal family, that means you and me and Comma and – well, you know: limited options. But if it's royal *household*, that includes the noble families in service and dignitaries like Mr Fogarty.'

'I know,' Blue said soberly. She stared at Pyrgus. 'You don't really think –'

She stopped. There was a priest running towards them from the direction of the palace. Running priests spelled trouble, as she knew from long experience. From the corner of her eye she saw small movements in the bushes near the forest's edge – Pyrgus had remembered the heightened security alert all right – but the hidden guards must have recognised the priest since they did not emerge.

Blue recognised him herself now. His name was Thorn, a member of the Dentaria, the Realm's most ancient Funereal Order. He was in charge of the vigil on the body of her father and would pray daily for the late Emperor's soul until Pyrgus was crowned. To her astonishment, he flung himself to his knees before Pyrgus and herself.

Thorn was not a young man and it was a moment before he caught his breath. 'Majesty,' he gasped finally, 'Serene Highness, your father – your father – the Emperor, your father – Majesty, your father's body has disappeared.'

ten

Brimstone rose early on his wedding day and pulled back the bedroom curtains with a flourish. Things were looking up already. The narrow street and open sewer outside his old lodgings had been replaced by flower beds and a well-manicured lawn. Widow Mormo was a superstitious woman. She believed it would be bad luck for bride and groom to sleep under the same roof the night before their marriage, so she'd arranged for Brimstone to stop over with her brother, who certainly kept a far more comfortable establishment than his smelly sister.

Brimstone stretched luxuriously. With a well-stocked cabin in the forest, he could hide from Beleth for months. He walked to the bathroom, brushed his teeth, then popped them into his mouth. The magical residue locked them in place with an audible squelch.

By the time he'd finished in the bathroom, some silent servant had slipped into his quarters and laid out his wedding suit. Brimstone put it on, admired himself in the mirror, then, humming a catchy little tune, went down to breakfast.

Widow Mormo's brother was already at the table.

'Morning, Graminis,' Brimstone said cheerfully.

'There's eggs,' Graminis grunted. 'Poached, fried or

scrambled.' He had the same tattered look as his sister, but nicer eyes.

'Poached eggs would be just dandy,' Brimstone said. Hell of a lot better than bone gruel, anyway. 'Two please – one hard, one soft.'

Graminis signalled to some half-visible servant lurking in the gloom of an archway and she scuttled off to fill Brimstone's order. 'Public prints?' asked Graminis, pushing the newspapers towards Brimstone. 'Find out what else is happening in the world this morning?'

This was the life all right. Brimstone tilted his chair back and unfolded the paper. It was full of the forthcoming Coronation, just two weeks away now, give or take. Public holiday had been declared, processional route was being painted, invitations had gone out. There was a special feature on the dress chosen by the Female Companion, the Princess Royal. Little brat had splashed out on spinner silk, sort of thing you did when you were funded by the public purse. The Male Companion was somebody called Iron Prominent, a name new to Brimstone – probably some hideous Hooray Henry with a receding chin. Emperor Elect Pyrgus was described as *looking forward to being of service to all the peoples of the Realm, irrespective of creed or race*', a sentiment so sugary it made Brimstone want to puke.

He started to turn to the section that gave news of Faeries of the Night when another Coronation paragraph caught his eye. It was no more than a passing mention of security arrangements at the ceremony. *'Since the new Emperor wishes to maintain contact with the common people, security provisions are to be kept to a minimum, a situation made possible by the continuing closure of all Hael Realm portals.'*

The continuing closure of all Hael Realm portals ... Brimstone frowned. 'Graminis, it says something here about Hael portals being closed.'

Graminis glanced up from his porridge. 'Didn't you know? Old news now. Hasn't been a functioning Hael portal for ... oh, must be ... must be weeks now.'

'You mean we can't evoke demons?' He could tell from Graminis's eyes that he was a Faerie of the Night like himself. Nighters had cat's eyes – very light-sensitive. That was why they kept their cities gloomy and most of them wore trendy shades. It also gave them an affinity with demons that the Lighters never had. Demons liked the dark as well.

'Not so much as an imp,' Graminis said. 'Plays hell with the servant problem.' He giggled suddenly. 'Get it, Silas? Portals closed *plays hell* with the servant problem.'

'Very droll, Graminis,' Brimstone acknowledged. 'How did the Lighters close them?'

'They didn't, not as far as I know. Just happened. Talk is Hael's collapsed.'

'What, all of it?'

'So they say. Seems their Prince of Darkness made a doomsday bomb and the damn thing went off in his face.'

Brimstone felt a rising excitement. If the Hael portals were down, he was free. Without the portals, there was no way Beleth could get to him, except by making the trip the hard way, in a vimana, and that would take years! And if Graminis was right, Beleth might actually be dead. It was incredible.

'Are you sure all the portals are closed?' he asked.

'Course I'm sure. Talk of the Realm just after it happened. And believe me, there've been a lot of sorcerers tried opening them again, but ...' He shrugged. 'Take it from me – anybody gets one working and you'll read about it. Headline news, I'd say.'

Graminis was right. It *would* be headline news. So Brimstone could come out of hiding now. He could go anywhere he liked and Beleth couldn't touch him even if he *were* still alive. All he had to do was keep an eye to the public prints for any announcement that the portals might be reopened. If that happened, he could hide again until somebody confirmed whether Beleth had been killed. Meanwhile – his heart leaped at the thought! – it was business as usual. He could cancel the wedding and go back to his glue factory. He could contact Chalkhill again. He could return to his comfortable lodgings in Seething Lane. More importantly, he could go back to his spell books and his gold. He could –

A thought occurred to Brimstone like a dousing of cold water. He'd tried to sacrifice the young Emperor Elect Pyrgus to Beleth. That wasn't the sort of thing the boy was likely to forget. Now he was going to be Emperor, he might just want a little vengeance. Emperors were notoriously vindictive. Maybe it would be better if he *didn't* return to Chalkhill and the factory just yet. Maybe it would be better if he kept a low profile and scouted things out before making any public moves. Maybe it would be better to let the marriage go ahead, kill the Widow Mormo as planned, and use her cabin as a base. It was perfect!

Brimstone found he had actually begun to smile.

'You're looking happy for a man who's about to get married,' Graminis remarked cynically.

Eleven

Lord Hairstreak had two main residences in the Realm. One was on the edge of the capital, where he'd housed his golden phoenix until Pyrgus Malvae had stolen it. The other, newer and much grander, was surrounded by three thousand wooded acres in the heart of Yammeth Cretch. The forest was full of haniels and sliths, so unwelcome visitors seldom got half a mile before being eaten or poisoned. There was a haniel crouched on a branch overlooking the sweep of formal lawn, its wings half furled as if about to leap and glide. Chalkhill eyed it nervously.

'Shouldn't worry,' Harold Dingy said. 'They don't come near the house.'

They waited at the bottom of the broad stone steps until a white-gloved, bewigged footman teetered down in high-heeled boots. 'His Lordship will be pleased to see you now,' he announced, staring out a little way above their heads. He handed Dingy a luminous green labyrinth coin and stepped aside. 'Go on! Go on!' he said impatiently. 'You know His Lordship hates to be kept waiting.' He gave Chalkhill a sidelong glance and smiled.

Dingy favoured him with a sour look, but flipped the coin. It hung in the air for a moment, then moved away up the steps. Dingy and Chalkhill followed hurriedly.

The great oakwood doors swung open at their approach. As they stepped into the entrance hall, there was a surprised squawk behind them. The doors were closing again, but they just had time to see the footman carried off in the haniel's claws.

Chalkhill looked at Dingy.

Dingy frowned. 'Never saw that happen before,' he said.

They followed the labyrinth coin through a warren of corridors until they reached an antechamber hung with silken drapes. The coin dropped to the ground with a muffled thud.

Chalkhill found the room vulgar. The drapes were indigo with a narrow scarlet trim and the illusion of leering demons. Why people used demons as art was quite beyond him. Fearfully ugly creatures. If he'd been decorating this room, he'd have used cherubs. Sweet little naked cherubs, all pink and cuddly.

'It's been a while since I saw His Lordship,' Chalkhill said by way of conversation.

'Hasn't changed much,' Dingy grunted.

Nor, when he arrived, had Cossus Cossus, Hairstreak's Gatekeeper. His head still looked too small for his body and he walked as if there was a ramrod up his back. 'Jasper,' he acknowledged, nodding briefly towards Chalkhill.

'Cossus,' Chalkhill nodded back. Neither of them smiled.

'I trust you're in good health?'

'Mustn't complain,' said Chalkhill. He sniffed, then added, 'Despite the prison food.'

'Not what you're used to, I suppose,' Cossus said sympathetically. He waved an airy hand at Dingy. 'Go away now, Harold – you've done your little bit.'

Dingy gave him a glare that would have withered grass, but walked off mumbling just the same. Cossus took Chalkhill's arm in an unusually friendly gesture. 'Now, Jasper, His Lordship wants to see you *privately*. He's waiting in the little Briefing Room.'

The little Briefing Room was a book-lined study with seven layers of permanent privacy spells that gave it the smell of old leather. Chalkhill had been there only twice before – once when he joined Lord Hairstreak's service, once when Hairstreak required him to kidnap Holly Blue, the Princess Royal.

Cossus left him at the doorway. 'Your ears only,' he murmured cheerfully. Then, surprisingly, 'Good luck.'

Lord Hairstreak was staring intently through the window, but turned the instant Chalkhill entered. 'Sit,' he said sharply. He was a small, slight man, dressed as always in black velvet.

Chalkhill sat. Despite his claim that they were bosom friends, he was actually terrified of Black Hairstreak. The man oozed ruthlessness from every pore. Chalkhill folded his hands in his lap and waited. Beyond Hairstreak he could see through the window what His Lordship had been watching – his footman being devoured by the haniel.

'You failed me, Jasper,' Hairstreak said quietly. 'You allowed that stupid child to beat you.'

Chalkhill felt his body chill. The 'stupid child' was Princess Blue, of course, who'd certainly got the better of Chalkhill in the past. He opened his mouth to voice a few excuses, then closed it again. It was safer to let Lord Hairstreak do the talking.

'I should have left you to rot in jail, you incompetent

crud,' Hairstreak hissed furiously. 'Your bungling cost me much.'

With an enormous effort of will, Chalkhill stopped himself from trembling. There was a chance Hairstreak had brought him here to torture him to death, but he was inclined to believe Dingy's reassurance that there was another job. Or was that just wishful thinking? Would Hairstreak trust him with another job when he'd failed in the last? Outside, the haniel took off from the lawn, carrying the remains of the footman's body. At a height of fifteen feet, the head dropped off and rolled under a rose bush.

Black Hairstreak's demeanour changed suddenly. He straightened his back and glanced towards the bookshelves. Chalkhill followed his gaze. He seemed to be looking at the twenty-seven volumes of Maculinia's *Dreams of Empire.*

Hairstreak said, 'I've decided to give you an opportunity to redeem yourself.'

Chalkhill said, 'Thank you, Lord Hairstreak.'

'Oh, don't thank me yet. It's a dangerous mission.'

Chalkhill said, 'Yes, Lord Hairstreak.'

'If you fail, you die.'

Chalkhill said, 'Yes, Lord Hairstreak.'

'But you won't fail this time, will you, Jasper?'

Chalkhill said, 'No, Lord Hairstreak.'

'Good, Jasper, good. Do you know anything about this mission I have for you?'

Chalkhill licked his lips. 'Your –' He hesitated. What the hell was Dingy's title? He wracked his brains, but nothing came. 'Your, ah, man, mentioned you might not, ah, want young Pyrgus Malvae to become Purple Emperor.'

Hairstreak rounded on him, eyes glittering. 'I want young Pyrgus Malvae dead – that's what I want! I want him assassinated. I want to make an example of him, Chalkhill. I want him killed publicly and horribly. I want it to happen at the moment of his greatest triumph, just before the Archimandrake crowns him at his Coronation. I want the world to know what happens to those who stand against Lord Hairstreak – and steal his valuable birds. That's what I want, Chalkhill. The question is, are you the man to give it to me?'

He wanted Pyrgus killed *in the middle of his Coronation*? That was a suicide mission. Kill the Emperor Elect in the Cathedral with all his guards around him and ten thousand people watching? It might just be possible, but getting away afterwards certainly wasn't. The killer would have a score of swords thrust through him before he took three paces. No way! No way!

Gripped by those glittering eyes, Chalkhill said, 'I'm your man, Lord Hairstreak!'

'What's this, Your Lordship?' Chalkhill asked hesitantly. It looked like a bubble wand, but he didn't imagine it really could be. Black Hairstreak was a serious man, and a bubble wand was little more than a child's toy.

'It's the weapon you will use to kill Prince Pyrgus,' Hairstreak told him grimly. 'It's called a blowpipe – I had it brought in specially from the Analogue World. Looks a little like a bubble wand, doesn't it?'

'Yes, it does, Your Lordship.' Chalkhill handled the artifact cautiously. It seemed no more than a short, wooden tube with primitive poker-work designs along its surface, but he wasn't familiar with Analogue magic and didn't want to set the thing off accidentally.

'That's the point,' said Lord Hairstreak. 'We need something that will pass unnoticed through Cathedral security. What better than an innocent bubble wand? Sparkling spheres to celebrate the Coronation of a brand new Emperor. I expect quite a few members of the congregation will be carrying them.'

Chalkhill looked at the tube. 'But this isn't a real bubble wand?'

'No.'

'It's a weapon of some sort?'

'Yes.'

It was terribly short and had absolutely no feel of a magical charge. Chalkhill said, 'How will I get close enough to the Emperor Elect to use it, Your Lordship?'

For the first time Hairstreak actually smiled. 'Ah, Chalkhill, faithful Chalkhill, you actually think I'm sending you to your death, don't you? Some sort of suicide mission, is that what you suspect?'

'No, Lordship, of course not!' Chalkhill protested. 'Nothing could have been further – I wouldn't – Lordship, it never occurred –'

Hairstreak's smile broadened. 'You're a trained operative,' he said. 'My master spy and soon to be my most effective assassin. Would I waste such a valuable resource?' He strolled casually back to the window. There was no sign of the haniel and a small team of servants was clearing up the mess of the footman. One of them dropped his head into a large brown paper bag. 'Do you want to know how I propose to get you out alive, Jasper?'

Despite a deep mistrust of Hairstreak, Chalkhill felt just the barest tingle of relief. 'Yes sir, I do. Yes, definitely. That's something I would like to know!'

'Here's the plan,' said Hairstreak briskly. 'First, the blowpipe. It's not a wand. It's not a magical implement of any sort, Faerie or Analogue. It's a simple weapon. So simple I guarantee no one in the Faerie Realm will recognise it for what it is. The thing's actually quite harmless in itself. But with these –' He took a small box from his pocket and handed it across to Chalkhill, who glanced questioningly at Hairstreak, then opened it. Inside were six tiny feathered darts on a bed of velvet. 'Don't touch the tips,' Hairstreak cautioned. 'They're soaked in spider venom. The smallest prick will kill you.'

Chalkhill snapped the lid shut hurriedly.

'It's an interesting end as well,' Hairstreak went on thoughtfully. 'Agonising, but interesting. First, paralysis. Then the skin turns blue. Then the pain starts. You scream yourself to death within four minutes. I tried it on one of the servants. Astonishing to watch – his face peeled off.' The pensive look left his eyes. 'You bring the blowpipe into the Cathedral quite openly as a bubble wand. You bring the darts in as part of the ornamentation of your hat. Now this is the clever part. When you want to kill the Emperor Elect, you simply take a dart from your hat – you'll be surrounded by my men, so no one will notice what you're doing – you take a dart from your hat, slip it into the pipe, then blow down it sharply.'

'Blow down it, Your Lordship?' Chalkhill echoed.

'Blow down it, Jasper,' Hairstreak repeated. 'It's the force of your breath that propels the dart towards anything you're aiming at!' He paused to look at Chalkhill with glittering eyes.

Chalkhill looked at the pipe, then at the box of darts. He looked back up at Hairstreak and gave an involuntary shiver. 'How delightfully ... *primitive*,' he said.

'Primitive but effective,' Hairstreak nodded. 'Our young friend Pyrgus will scarcely notice the wound. At most he might take it for an insect bite. There are three minutes before the paralysis sets in, a further four before he's dead – ample time, would you not say, for a getaway?'

Chalkhill examined the plan. If one ever dared to admit it, Hairstreak was an appalling little creep, but there certainly didn't seem to be any hidden agenda. Or flaws for that matter. Except possibly one ...

'Your Lordship –' He hesitated. 'There does seem to be one small problem ... '

Hairstreak scowled at him. 'Which is?'

'Sir,' Chalkhill said, 'you must appreciate that I am no longer what one might call an *undercover* agent. I mean, I thought it an absolutely *splendid* idea to try to kidnap the Princess Royal, but it did mean my secret identity as your, ah, master spy, was and is for ever exposed.' *And I was thrown into that dreadful, smelly jail,* he thought, but it was probably not the time to bring it up. He leaned forward earnestly. 'By which I mean, sir, that my face is known now. I have a certain ... notoriety. I'm afraid the Emperor's security people will never allow me to so much as *set foot* inside the Cathedral.'

'Ah,' said Hairstreak. A malicious little half-grin crawled up one side of his mouth. 'Ah-ha. You think I haven't thought of that? You think I haven't thought of something so *glaringly obvious*?'

'No, sir. No indeed. I didn't mean at all to suggest –'

But Hairstreak ignored him. 'That's the best part of the whole plan! You see, my dear Jasper, I shall not attend the Coronation.'

'You won't?' Chalkhill asked, wondering what that had to do with anything. 'But won't it be ... *expected* of you?'

'Of course it'll be expected of me, you cretin! Expected and politically expedient. Which is why I'm having a special illusion spell crafted.'

'Illusion spell?' Chalkhill repeated. He seemed to be repeating a lot of what Lord Hairstreak said in this conversation.

'You're going in my place,' said Hairstreak. 'As me.' He smiled openly again. 'I told you you'd be surrounded by my men. They'll be your bodyguards.'

Twelve

When a Purple Emperor died, tradition decreed that his body be dressed in the formal robes of his office, then placed under a stasis spell for display in the Cathedral until the day of his successor's Coronation. Four uniformed members of the Imperial Guard stood like statues at the corners of the bier while loyal subjects filed past tearfully to pay their final respects.

But the last Purple Emperor, Apatura Iris, lost most of his face when he was murdered and no amount of reconstruction spells seemed capable of putting it together again. There was no question of public display. Thus the body lay in stasis in the palace crypt, ministered to with hourly prayers by the mortuary priests.

'It was like this when I arrived,' Thorn said miserably.

They stood staring at the empty bier. There was no sign of vandalism, no sign of damage, but the body was no longer there. Blue said, 'Who conducted the last prayers? Before you?'

'Brother Sinapis.' Thorn hesitated. 'Serenity, I spoke with him. All was in order when he withdrew.'

'The guards?' There were guards at the entrance to the crypt, ceremonially dressed to be sure, but they would still have noticed anyone trying to enter.

'They saw nothing, Serenity.'

Blue said crisply, 'I want to talk to Brother Sinapis myself. And each of the guards. Please arrange to have them brought to my quarters, starting with Sinapis. They are to be isolated from each other before I speak to them – I don't want any discussion between them until I hear each individual story. I want you to –'

Pyrgus, who'd said nothing at all since Thorn had appeared before the Gatekeeper's lodge, now said sharply, 'Just a minute, Blue.' She looked at him in surprise. There was a note of command in his tone she'd never heard before. And a stern, strained expression on his face. 'We need to discuss this –' he gave her a warning look, '– and other matters with Gatekeeper Fogarty.'

'Mr Fogarty's not back,' Blue said unnecessarily.

Pyrgus lowered his voice, as if this would somehow prevent his being heard by Thorn, who was standing beside him. 'I don't want to trust any of this to servants. Blue, I want you to translate to the Analogue World and bring Mr Fogarty back at once – his personal business will have to wait. I'll speak to Sinapis and the guards myself.' He turned and his voice sharpened. 'You, Thorn, will personally organise a security search of the crypt. Tell the Captain of the Watch you have my full authority. I want the area swept for any clues, however small, to what has happened. Spare no expense – and that includes the cost of extracting impressions from the stonework, although I imagine whoever did this would have been cloaked.'

Blue stared at him in astonishment. This was a Pyrgus she'd never seen before – decisive, in charge … imperial. He glanced round at her. 'Are you still here,

Blue? You really must make arrangements to translate at once – the situation is both serious and urgent.'

'Yes, Pyrgus,' Blue said meekly.

Blue found Chief Portal Engineer Peacock bent over a basin in an anteroom of the chapel, scrubbing his hands with a stiff brush. 'Something I can do for you, Serenity?' he asked.

Blue nodded, her lips suddenly dry. 'Is the portal functioning?'

'Yes, of course, Serenity.'

'No, I mean is it functioning properly? You fixed it after the sabotage attempt –' the *successful* sabotage attempt, carried out on Lord Hairstreak's orders, although they'd never prove it, '– the, ah, business with my brother?' She didn't really want to spell it out, didn't really want to remember. Pyrgus had almost died when he went through it then.

Peacock looked bewildered. 'Ages ago, Serenity.'

'And it's working … ? It's working … well, properly … no problems now, are there?'

'No, Serenity.'

'How long does setting it take?' Blue asked.

'Setting the directional indicator? For where you want to go?'

'Yes.'

'Not long.' He was staring at her now. 'You just feed in the coordinates. Ten, fifteen seconds, say. Less. Less, probably. Do you want to use the portal, Serenity?'

There it was, all laid out in a single question. Blue said tightly, 'Yes.'

They walked together into the main chapel. The place was full of uniformed guards armed with stun

wands and there was a charged security fence surrounding the House Iris portal, both grim reminders of
the sabotage that had nearly cost her brother his life.
The portal itself had been reinforced – there were
heavy metal casings on the pillars, while the nearby
controls had been rehoused in impermeable obsidian.
The whole chapel had a sombre, military-camp appearance. The blue flames between the pillars seemed like
an inferno.

Blue frowned. 'It's in use?'

Peacock shook his head. 'We keep it running permanently now.' His face softened. 'Orders of your poor
father after ... after the business with Prince Pyrgus.
Makes it easier to detect any interference. Not that
there could be any now,' he added hurriedly.

'I see,' Blue said. She licked her lips again. 'How long
will it take to set it to translate me to the Analogue
home of Gatekeeper Fogarty?'

'Known coordinates,' Peacock said. 'Can have it
ready for you any time you want to go, Serenity.'

Blue said, 'I'd like to go now, Mr Peacock.'

He looked around, clearly searching for her
entourage. When he didn't find one, he said, 'You're
not going alone, are you, Serenity?'

The trouble was – she *was*. Mr Fogarty would want
to know what was happening and she had no intention
of talking in front of servants. Best to find him, brief
him, bring him back, tell no one else anything they
didn't need to know.

'Yes, I am.'

Peacock said uncertainly, 'This is your first time,
isn't it, Ma'am? Your first translation to the Analogue
World?'

'Yes.'

'Would you like me to go with you?'

'No, thank you,' Blue said firmly. She moved towards the security fence and one of the guards hurried to unlock the gate and let her through. 'I take it I simply step between the pillars, Mr Peacock?'

Peacock had entered the enclosure immediately behind her. Now he walked quickly towards the controls. 'Once I've made the settings, Serenity,' he said. 'I'll tell you when.'

Blue waited, a step away from the pillars. Her heart was thumping wildly, but she held her face impassive. It would never do to let anyone see how a princess of House Iris felt about something as simple as translating. It was perfectly safe – everyone knew that. She couldn't feel so much as a hint of heat, which was what it said in all the reference books: cold flame.

'The portal's ready now, Serenity,' Chief Engineer Peacock told her.

Sweating with fear, Blue stepped between the pillars without a moment's hesitation.

Thirteen

Brimstone hoped Graminis would get him to the church in time. 'Can't we go any faster?' he asked testily.

They were travelling in a clapped-out ouklo that looked older than God. It was an open carriage in funereal black with upholstery that smelled of grave mould, probably because Graminis was too mean to hire a proper wedding carriage. The spell charge was almost gone, so that instead of floating at a respectable height, the ouklo kept sinking lower and lower until it scraped on the road; at which point it shot up again like a startled rabbit to begin the sinking process all over again. The movement was making Brimstone positively seasick.

But at least the traditional wedding notice was displayed prominently across the back:

This Man Is Getting Married.
Pray for Him.

Graminis giggled. 'Don't you go upsetting yourself, Silas – Maura will wait. Waited for the last five, didn't she?'

Brimstone blinked. His bride-to-be had gone

through *five* previous husbands? He knew she was a widow woman, but five was ridiculous. Perhaps she ate them after mating, like a spider. Or murdered them for the insurance money. He'd have to watch that. Watch what he ate or drank in particular. Chances were she'd poisoned them.

The ouklo scraped and bobbed its way through narrow streets until the church spire hove into sight. The vehicle reached the graveyard and stopped. 'Have to walk the rest of the way,' Graminis said. 'Sorry about that – it's set for funerals.'

The church was as small as he'd expected – wedding hire was costed by the square foot – and built to the traditional squaring-the-circle design. Tiers of pews looked down on the altar. The carpeting was moth-eaten and threadbare.

There was a scattering of down-and-outs in the pews, doubtless hoping for a witness hand-out, and the central fire was already lit. As he and Graminis entered, half a dozen skinny nymphs began to dance listlessly around it.

The priest emerged from a trapdoor in the floor, which suggested things might get underway before too long. He was a squat, toad-like Faerie of the Night wearing the elemental yellow robes called for by the occasion. He favoured Brimstone with a bleak smile and Brimstone favoured him with a bleak smile back.

'The bride's here!' Graminis hissed.

Brimstone looked up towards the entrance arch that now framed the scrawny figure of his bride-to-be. She was wearing a tight black mini-dress split up one side and carrying a cactus.

Her legs looked like second-hand pipe cleaners.

fourteen

Bright sunlight caught Blue unawares, so that it took moments for her eyes to adjust. She seemed to be in an enclosed space, a cramped little garden of some sort. Quickly she reached around and felt between her shoulder-blades. No wings! At least the filter had worked properly. She gave a sigh of relief. All the safety texts told you to check for wings. If you shrank, you grew wings – that always happened. It's what happened to Pyrgus when the House Iris portal was sabotaged. And while it was sometimes difficult to decide on your size in a strange environment – the question of scale was always relative, the texts insisted – you either had wings or you hadn't. She hadn't, therefore she hadn't shrunk either. One hurdle crossed.

The next hurdle was whether or not the portal had remained open. She glanced behind her and there it was, a smaller area of flame at this side and no sign of the pillars, but definitely there. She didn't want to think about going back through that blue inferno, but at least the way was open.

Now, was she in the right place? Everybody said the portals never varied. You set the Analogue coordinates and that's where they took you. But there was always the possibility of sabotage or human error. She didn't think there was much chance of sabotage now, not with all the security in place, but human error could happen any time. So was she at Gatekeeper Fogarty's Analogue World home?

The shrivelled little lawn was a far cry from the lush gardens that surrounded his lodge at the Purple Palace, and the house beyond looked mean and gloomy – somebody had actually stuck brown paper to the lower windows. But she remembered both her father and Pyrgus remarking on the peculiarities of Mr Fogarty's Analogue lifestyle.

Blue gave a strangled squawk. Something warm and hairy had just rubbed against her leg. She looked down and saw an overweight tomcat polishing her ankles. He stared at her with luminous eyes and gave a little *whirr*.

Blue relaxed at once. Of course it was Mr Fogarty's home – this had to be the famous Hodge. 'Hello, Hodge,' she said quietly, and he *whirred* again. 'Are you going to show me where Gatekeeper Fogarty is hiding?' As if he understood, Hodge trotted off in the direction of the back door. Blue followed him with a little smile on her face.

'Mr Fogarty!' she called as she pushed the door open.

There was somebody inside, but it wasn't Mr Fogarty.

'Henry!' Blue exclaimed.

Henry jumped visibly. He'd been staring at something in his hand, a funny little black device with rows of numbered buttons on it. Now he glanced at her in surprise and what might have been delight.

'Blue,' he said breathlessly. 'What on earth are you

doing here?'

'Looking for Gatekeeper Fogarty,' Blue told him simply.

Henry's eyes went back to the device in his hand. 'They've put him in jail,' he said in a small, astonished voice. 'He's just called me.'

Blue blinked. 'Who's put him in jail?'

Henry looked at her blankly. 'The police. He went out to make some arrangements about his house and now they've put him in jail.'

'They can't put him in jail,' Blue said imperiously. 'He's a Gatekeeper of the Realm.'

'Over here he's just an old-age pensioner who used to rob banks. They can put him in jail all right. He's in a cell at Nutgrove Police Station.'

'I don't have time for this,' Blue snapped. 'We'll have to get him out.'

Fifteen

Henry stared around him miserably.

'Well, where is it?' Blue demanded.

'It must be round here somewhere,' Henry said. They were in Nutgrove Street, for heaven's sake. Nutgrove Police Station had to be in Nutgrove Street.

'Henry,' Blue hissed. 'I have to find Mr Fogarty. I have to get him back to the Realm.'

'Yes, I know,' Henry said.

What he didn't know was what they were going to do when they found Nutgrove Station. Blue seemed to have the idea they would just march in and demand Mr Fogarty's release.

'Let's try down there,' he suggested.

'We've already *been* down there,' Blue said. But she followed him as he moved off.

'Blue,' Henry said, 'what's happened?'

Blue's tone softened. 'I don't really know yet. But something's going on. My father's body has disappeared and I think there's a plot to kill Pyrgus. Pyrgus sent me to find Mr Fogarty – we need him.' She hesitated, then added, 'It would be nice to have you as well.'

Henry felt a flush begin to crawl along the back of his neck. 'Do what I can,' he mumbled, wondering just what he might mean by *that*. He looked about him in a moment of confusion and saw the police station down a side street. 'Oh, there it is!' he said brightly; and the words were swiftly followed by the thought, *What are we going to do now?*

'Henry,' Blue said, 'what exactly *is* a police station?'

Henry looked at her, then realised there was no way she could know. 'It's … it's sort of, like police headquarters. I mean, not the overall police headquarters – that's in Scotland Yard or somewhere. It's sort of headquarters for a *district*.'

'And all the police live there?'

'I don't think they actually *live* there. It's more like an office they come into.'

'And your police are like our police in the Realm?' Blue said. 'They flog you if you do something wrong and cut off your hand if you're caught stealing? Unless you're a noble, of course.'

'No, I don't think they do that,' Henry said uncertainly.

'Why not? It's pretty silly not to, isn't it?' Blue said. She set off down the side street.

Henry realised he was standing on his own and ran down the side street after her. He caught Blue by the elbow. 'What are you going to do?' he asked urgently. 'You can't just swan in and order them to let Mr Fogarty go.' He caught the expression on her face and stopped himself adding, *You're not Princess Royal here, you know.*

'I wasn't planning to *swan* anywhere,' Blue said coldly. She looked into his face and relented, giving a little smile. 'It's all right, Henry – I have some cones with me.'

'Cones?' All he could think of was ice cream, but somehow he didn't believe that was what she meant.

'Spell cones,' Blue said.

Henry felt his jaw drop. 'You're not going to ... you're not going to ... ?'

'Use magic?' Blue prompted. 'Yes, I am.'

'You can't!'

'Why not?'

Why not? Why not? Henry cast around for a reason and couldn't think of one, except that using magic in a police station was probably illegal. Or would be if the police believed in it. Magic was all very well in the Realm where everybody used it, but using magic here – on *anybody*, let alone a policeman – was just something you didn't –

'What sort of magic?' he asked in a small voice.

Sixteen

Henry felt peculiar. In fact he thought he might be going to be sick. Everything around him looked swimmy and when he moved it was like trying to push against treacle.

'I don't feel so good,' he said. His voice echoed in his head like a hollow gong.

'You'll get used to it,' Blue told him briskly. 'Just follow me.' She moved to the front door of the police station and pushed it firmly. When nothing happened, she turned to look accusingly at Henry. 'This door's locked.'

Henry was trying to remember the last thing he'd eaten. He had an idea he might be about to see it again quite soon. 'They do that now,' he said, 'because of terrorists or something. You can't just walk in. You have to ring the bell and speak into that grille thing when they answer.'

'But if I speak into the grille thing won't they know somebody's here?'

Henry looked at her, wondering if he was going to be able to stand upright much longer. 'That's the whole point,' he said. 'So they can let you in.'

'But I don't want them to know I'm here,' Blue said.

It was all getting too much. Henry's brain described a slow, liquid circle inside his skull. 'Then how are we going to get in?' he managed.

The door opened and a man walked through without glancing at either Blue or Henry. Blue stuck out her foot to stop the door. 'Come on!' she hissed and slipped inside. Henry stared after her stupidly for a moment, then followed as the door began to close.

They were in a waiting area with lino on the floor, chairs at one end and a counter at the other. A uniformed sergeant was standing behind the counter. Behind him a young woman with very short black hair was typing at a desk. Three of the chairs were occupied – two by an elderly couple, the third by a middle-aged man trying unsuccessfully to look like Elvis Presley. Nobody paid the slightest attention to Blue or Henry.

'Right,' Blue said briskly. 'We'd better try to find Mr Fogarty.'

'We can ask the Desk Sergeant,' Henry suggested. All he really wanted was to get out, go home and – hopefully – die.

Blue looked at him strangely through the fog that was swirling round him. 'Are you trying to be funny?'

Henry shook his head. 'No. Why?' He reached out and gripped the back of a chair. The head shake had been a *big* mistake.

'What's the point of being invisible if we just walk up to the desk and *ask*?'

The fog cleared a little. Henry stared at her, open-mouthed. 'Invisible?' he echoed.

'What do you think that cone was for?'

'We can't be invisible,' Henry said. 'I can see you perfectly.' The *perfectly* bit wasn't quite true since his vision was still swimming, but he could certainly see her.

'Well, of *course* you can see me. I can see you and you can see your hands and I can see my feet because we're

72

both invisible,' Blue said in the tone of one talking to an idiot child, 'and try to keep your voice down – the spell dampens sound, but if you make too much noise they'll hear you. You might try not to break wind again either – people will wonder where the smell is coming from.'

'I didn't break wind!' said Henry hotly. He realised he was speaking loudly and dropped his voice. 'I didn't,' he whispered.

'Well, someone did,' Blue said dismissively. She lost interest in breaking wind and asked, 'Where will they be holding Mr Fogarty?'

'*I* don't know,' Henry said a little crossly. The only other time he'd ever been inside a police station was because of a missing tail-light on his bike.

'Well, would it be in the back, or through that door? Or do they have a separate building?' Blue asked.

'I don't *know*!' Henry said.

Behind them the door opened and two constables came in gripping the arms of a surly youth in a cracked leather jacket. The sergeant opened up the counter-top without a word and the constables escorted the boy through a door in the back.

'That was a prisoner,' Blue said. 'I'm sure that was a prisoner. They must have cells through that door.'

She might be right, but Henry couldn't see what good it would do them. The sergeant had closed the counter back down, and even if he hadn't done, the two constables had shut the door behind them. Invisibility sounded great, but you couldn't actually *go* anywhere without making it look as if doors kept opening of their own accord. He started to say something, then stopped as his stomach churned.

Blue said, 'Come on!'

To his utter horror, she skipped forward and vaulted over the counter, landing nimbly – and silently – to one side of the sergeant. He didn't so much as cast a glance in her direction. 'Come on,' she said again, waving encouragingly to Henry.

Henry's heart sank. He'd never been much of an athletic type, even when he was feeling well. If he tried to do what Blue'd just done, he was sure to trip up and fall in a heap.

'Henry –' Blue called impatiently.

Henry trudged shamefully over to the counter. Nothing ever seemed to go smoothly. He couldn't vault, but it was unthinkable to let Blue rescue Mr Fogarty on her own. He looked away so he wouldn't have to meet her eye and cautiously climbed up on to the counter, holding his breath so as to make as little noise as possible. There wasn't much room and he knew he was going to knock the mug of tea over and he knew Blue must think he was a complete wimp compared to all the athletic boys she fancied, but he didn't know of any other way to do it safely.

He was straddling the counter when the sergeant reached out for his tea. Henry flattened himself against the surface and prayed. The phone rang and the sergeant set his mug down to pick it up. The flex trailed over Henry's invisible bottom, forming a delicate curve, but for the moment the sergeant didn't seem to notice.

'No, that's Rosewood Street, isn't it?' he said into the phone.

Henry started to wriggle out from under the flex, but before he could complete the manoeuvre, the sergeant cradled the phone again. Henry slid gratefully over the counter to stand beside Blue, who was looking at him curiously. The woman typing was only a few feet away, the sergeant closer still. Was it really safe to say anything? He decided he'd have to risk it and whispered, 'What do we do now?'

'Wait and watch,' Blue said. 'We'll slip through the door when everybody's distracted.'

It sounded a straightforward game plan, except that the two constables emerged from the back (closing the door firmly behind them). A three-way conversation started about somebody called Jackie Knox. Then the typist said, 'You boys want a coffee? I'm making one for myself.' She got up from her desk and suddenly everybody was milling about behind the counter.

Out of the corner of his eye, Henry could see Blue moving gracefully in what looked like a sinuous dance as she skilfully avoided body contact: she was obviously well used to being invisible. But Henry wasn't. He dodged and ducked like a rhino and every movement increased the sickness in his stomach.

The woman finished handing out coffee, thank God, and went back to her desk. A door opened in the waiting area and Mr Fogarty came in with a young uniformed policeman by his side. They walked together to the front door.

'Thank you for your cooperation, sir,' the young policeman said. 'Sorry to have troubled you.'

Mr Fogarty grunted and walked out into the street.

'Did you see that?' Blue hissed delightedly. 'They've let him go.'

The phone rang on the counter and the sergeant reached for it again. 'Nutgrove Station,' he said pleasantly. Another phone rang, this time beside the woman who was typing. She picked it up while moving the mouse of her computer with her other hand. 'That'll be Tom,' remarked one of the constables behind the counter. The girl covered the mouthpiece and called across to the man who didn't look like Elvis, 'Can you come over to the counter a minute, Mr Robson?' The female half of the old couple said sharply, 'What about us? Haven't got all day, you know.' One of the constables said, 'It really shouldn't be much longer, love.' Blue said urgently, 'Come on, Henry.' She swarmed over the counter like a rhesus monkey. The sergeant suddenly exploded, 'Yuuuck!' and dropped the phone. He stared down towards the floor, his eyes wide with astonishment. 'Where did that come from?' he demanded. The two constables turned to look with a mixture of revulsion and amazement. Henry had thrown up on the sergeant's trousers. The results were all too visible.

They steamed a little.

It was weird the way Mr Fogarty kept looking at a spot above his left ear when they talked, but Henry supposed that's what happened when somebody couldn't see you.

'Mistaken identity,' Mr Fogarty said irritably. 'Bank clerk picked out somebody else in the identity parade.'

'Why do you think Henry got so sick?' Blue asked. She was visible again, but Henry had only just started to flicker.

'It'll be his shirt,' Mr Fogarty said firmly.

'What's wrong with my shirt?' Henry demanded. They were back in Mr Fogarty's home and the nausea, thankfully, was dying down a little.

'Synthetic fibres,' Mr Fogarty told him in sepulchral tones. 'They conflict with the energy the spell cone released. Get a resonance going and you're sick as a parrot.'

'You mean he's going to be ill any time he uses magic?' Blue put in.

'Only if he wears that shirt. Get him to take off all synthetics and try another cone. If I'm right, he should be fine.'

'Just a minute –' Henry said. It wasn't just his shirt. His trousers were synthetic too. And he didn't even want to think about his boxer shorts.

But Blue mercifully cut in. 'We'll have to experiment some other time, Gatekeeper. I think it's important you and I get back to the Realm as soon as possible.'

'What's happened?' Fogarty asked.

'My father's body has disappeared,' Blue told him tightly. 'And there's a plot to assassinate Pyrgus.'

Fogarty looked pained. 'Not another one.' He took a deep breath and blew it out vigorously. 'You're right, we'd better go. You got an open portal?' When Blue nodded, he glanced across at Henry. 'You coming?'

Henry blinked. 'I'd have to sort stuff out at home first.' He had to get some dried food to leave for Hodge, but what he really meant was that he needed to sort out his mother, figure out an excuse for leaving home for a while.

Fogarty said, 'You do that, then join us fast as you can. You can use the transporter I left you.'

Blue and Mr Fogarty headed for the door, but when they reached it, Mr Fogarty turned back. He took a small box from his pocket and pressed it into Henry's hand. 'Just get dressed in natural fibres before you use them.'

'What's this?'

Mr Fogarty gave one of his rare grins. 'Little present for your mother.'

Seventeen

There was something wrong with Pyrgus. He was skulking in his quarters when they found him and Fogarty had seen healthier-looking corpses.

'You OK?' Fogarty asked at once.

Pyrgus looked at him with dark-rimmed eyes. 'Yes.'

'Sure?'

Pyrgus nodded. 'Yes.'

Fogarty sniffed. 'Don't look it.'

Blue said, 'He's right, Pyrgus – you look awful.'

Pyrgus shrugged. 'Didn't get much sleep last night. Look, can we talk about important things? Have you told the Gatekeeper what's happening?'

'About our father's body and the assassination plot? Yes.'

Pyrgus glanced behind them. 'Didn't Henry come with you?'

'He's following on,' Fogarty said. 'Any developments?'

Pyrgus licked his lips nervously. 'I questioned the guards. They saw nothing to account for the disappearance of my father – nothing. At one inspection the body was there, at the next it wasn't.'

'Magic?' Fogarty asked.

'Don't see how,' Blue said. 'I've never heard of anything that would spirit away a body.'

'Neither have I,' Pyrgus said. 'But we're not wizards, so there could be a spell we don't know about – maybe something recently developed. I think we should assume it's something of that sort, some unknown magical intervention, and since there's nothing we can do about that at the moment, I don't think we should waste any more time investigating. I think we should wait until whoever did it shows their hand.'

'You think whoever did it might want a ransom for the body?' Blue said.

Pyrgus nodded. 'Probably.'

He was lying. Fogarty was sure of it. What he didn't know was why.

'I think we should concentrate on this assassination story,' Pyrgus said. 'I hope you don't mind, Blue – I've asked your friend Madame Cardui to brief the Gatekeeper directly.'

'No, of course I don't mind,' Blue said. 'Is she here or do you want Mr Fogarty –'

'She's waiting in the anteroom. I asked her to join us as soon as Mr Fogarty arrived. I'll – ah, here she is now.'

Fogarty turned as the door beside him opened. Something struck him like a thunderbolt.

Eighteen

Henry opened the box in his bedroom. Six rust-coloured cones nestled on a bed of cotton wool. He stared at them nervously.

There was writing on the inside of the lid in the curious faerie script that looked like Arabic. But as he glanced at it, some layered magic must have triggered since the shapes began to re-form into English.

LETHE ® BRAND RUSSET SPELL CONES

'Forget You Ever Read This.'

Six (6) *Lethe*® self-igniting spell cones, single usage.

Instructions:
1. Visualise effect required (i.e. who or what to forget).
2. Hold under nose and snap off disposable peak.

DISCLAIMER

Lethe ® spell cones are sold *for personal use only*, as a therapeutic aid for the prompt relief of painful memories. It is an offence to use these cones on another person without their prior consent in writing.

No responsibility will be accepted by the manufacturers for any misuse of these spell cones or any injury or damage caused thereby to any person or persons whatsoever. Lethe® is the registered trademark of Memory Magic plc, a member of the Ethical Spells League. No refunds.

Henry's heart leaped. These were the things Mr Fogarty had told him about – the spells that made people forget. Now he didn't have to make up some stupid story for his mother. All he had to do was use a cone on her and Aisling and he could disappear for as long as he liked without their ever noticing he was gone. They'd remember nothing about him until he came home again. He could join Blue in the Realm and maybe help save Pyrgus for a second time and impress her so much that maybe, just maybe ... Thank you, Mr Fogarty – it was perfect!

Except it wasn't *quite* perfect. He was allergic to magic.

Henry set the box down carefully on the bedside table and went over to his wardrobe. Stuff avalanched out when he opened the door. He poked through it listlessly, trying to find natural fibres.

He unbuttoned his synthetic shirt and replaced it with a cotton T-shirt that said *BABE MAGNET* on the front. It was a present from an aunt who should have known better and it wouldn't have been Henry's first choice, but it was all he could find that smelled clean. He stripped off his trousers and boxers and replaced them with cotton Y-fronts and a pair of baggy combat jeans. He'd never worn the jeans before – they were a present from the same Babe Magnet aunt and quite hideous – but at least denim was a natural fabric and he could always change back into something a bit less startling after he'd zapped Mum and Aisling.

There were voices in the kitchen and when he went in he found his mother and Aisling sitting at the breakfast bar drinking tea. They had their heads close together, but whatever they'd been talking about stopped suddenly when Henry entered.

'Why are you wearing that dreadful T-shirt?' Aisling asked at once. 'It's perfectly vulgar and an insult to women.' She turned to their mother and said seriously, 'Make him change it, Mummy.'

Henry narrowed his eyes, visualised himself, then reached across and cracked a *lethe* cone beneath his sister's nose. A swirl of dusty smoke curled round her head. She jerked back in sudden alarm, but then her face went blank.

His mother was staring at him with a stricken look. 'Is that a drug?' she gasped, wide-eyed. Panic set in. 'It's amyl nitrite. Good God, Henry, what have you done to your sister?'

'Sorry, Mum,' Henry murmured. He visualised himself again, then cracked the second cone beneath her nose.

He had a moment of panic when she went blank too. Aisling was still sitting frozen, her mouth slightly open, her chest unmoving as if she'd stopped breathing. Now his mum had turned into a statue as well. He couldn't have killed them, could he? He wasn't used to working magic – in fact this was the first time he'd actually done it himself. Maybe he'd done something wrong.

He reached out cautiously and touched her arm. 'Mum ... ?'

She *couldn't* be dead. Not even Mr Fogarty would give him a box of cones that *killed* people.

Or would he? Mr Fogarty did strange things sometimes.

Suddenly they were talking again, his mother and Aisling, something about Aisling's ghastly Pony Club. They ignored Henry, as if he wasn't even in the room.

Or as if … as if they'd forgotten him completely.

Cautiously, Henry began to back out of the kitchen. An unfamiliar feeling was bubbling in his stomach and after a moment he recognised it as joy. He'd done it! He'd worked the magic. He was a forgotten man and that meant he was *free*! He could go to the Realm. He could see Blue again. He could go to the Realm *now*!

He took the stairs two at a time. Mr Fogarty's portal control was in a shoebox pushed back on the top shelf of his wardrobe, along with the ornamental dagger he'd been given when Pyrgus had made him Iron Prominent, Knight Commander of the Grey Dagger.

He pulled the shoebox down and opened it. The portal control was no longer there.

It was Aisling! It had to be Aisling! She was the only one who'd sneak into his room and steal something. His mother was perfectly capable of going through his things – she had no sense of private property except when it came to herself – but she wouldn't have taken the control: it looked innocent enough for her to think it was something to do with his computer. Besides, if it had been his mother, she'd have found the dagger, and that was still there. It had to be Aisling, little *cow*!

Henry stormed down the stairs, but neither his mother nor his sister was in the kitchen now. He turned, heading for her room and bumped into Aisling coming out of the downstairs loo.

'You stole my control!' he shouted furiously.

Aisling blinked. 'Who are you?' she asked dreamily.

Nineteen

Hamearis Lucina, the Duke of Burgundy, was a big man who liked to accentuate his bulk by wearing padded armour and, in the winter, furs. In place of a sword, he habitually carried a war axe with an inlaid silver handle, the sort of weapon that was too heavy for a lesser man to wield.

The ferrymen kept giving him curious, furtive glances. He was well known throughout the Realm, and not just in his native Yammeth Cretch, but beyond that he was an individual with presence, a type who oozed charisma as well as strength – characteristics that had helped make him Black Hairstreak's closest ally. He would have attracted attention even as a complete unknown.

He stepped off carelessly as the ferry docked on the Imperial Island. Belatedly, one of the sailors moved to help him, then pulled back. They were wondering, he knew, why he travelled without an entourage, but the move was deliberate. Lesser men would have needed a host of followers to impress. Hamearis, on this occasion, was accompanied by a single cloaked and hooded servant. But he knew his message would have all the more impact for that.

There were no guards on the torchlit pathway that

took him to the Purple Palace and he expected none. He had been questioned and searched thoroughly (twice!) on the river bank before being permitted to enter the ferry. He had been allowed to retain his axe, a badge of rank as much as a weapon, only after it had been clipped and sealed to his belt so that he could not draw it easily. But he gained a little satisfaction from the fact that both searches had missed his assassin's dagger strapped to the inside of his left leg – an elaborate misdirection spell had diverted the attention of the probing hands: the same spell that ensured his cloaked companion was not searched at all. Not that he planned to assassinate anyone today, but it was always nice to know Imperial security could be beaten.

The path curved, emerged from a screening belt of ornamental trees and the Purple Palace swung into view, illuminated from the base of its walls by enormous, half-buried glowglobes. It was a forbidding building, raised in the old cyclopean style and designed as a massive fortress rather than an aesthetically pleasing residence. The ancient purple stone had weathered almost to black (although he was told it still shone purple in certain lights) and crouched like some great squat beast on the little hilltop in the centre of the island. Hamearis approved. Such a fortress was designed to strike terror into an enemy, and he admired good military psychology wherever he happened to find it.

As he expected, guards emerged to meet him once he approached the entrance gate to the garden surround. It was a guard's duty to be suspicious at any time, but especially after dark. Their Captain recognised him, of course, but treated him no differently from any other visitor.

'Your business, sir?'

'To meet with the Purple Emperor Elect.'

'To what end, sir?'

'I carry a message for him from Lord Hairstreak.'

'In written form or verbal?'

'Verbal.'

'May I convey this message for you?'

Hamearis said, 'It is for the ears of Prince Pyrgus alone.'

The Captain shrugged, as if this was no more than he'd expected. 'Are you armed, Your Grace?'

Hamearis gestured towards his captive axe. 'As you see.'

The Captain leaned over to inspect the seal, then took a small device from his pocket and added a second seal of his own. 'Please remove your belt and walk through the archway to the left side of the main gateway, sir.'

Removing his belt meant removing his weapon. 'I am the Duke of Burgundy,' he said formally and firmly. 'I may not be deprived of my axe without due cause.'

'You'll get it back once you're inside,' the Captain said mildly.

Glowering, Hamearis wondered what was going on, but this was not an occasion to make trouble. He unbuckled his belt, complete with the sealed axe, and handed it across.

'Are you carrying any other weapons, Your Grace?'

'No,' Hamearis lied.

'Through the archway, sir.'

Hamearis strode through the archway. A howling alarm sounded at once. In seconds he was surrounded by soldiers, their swords drawn. Hamearis raised his hands and backed off, smiling. His instinct told him what had happened, and if he was right it was truly remarkable. He knew of absolutely no magic that would produce such a result.

The Captain approached him again. 'Perhaps Your Grace has forgotten a weapon … ?' he said politely.

It was exactly as he'd suspected: some sorcerous coating on the archway had detected his dagger. He unfastened the hidden buckle and handed the dagger across.

'Thank you, sir,' the Captain said. 'This will be returned to you when you leave. Your servant now, please.'

The hooded man walked through the arch without triggering the alarm. Hamearis smiled slightly to himself, then walked towards the palace. He suspected the enchanted archway had been created by young Malvae's new Gatekeeper, the Analogue World wizard Fogarty. If so, the man had proven his worth with a single invention. Weapon-detecting magic was an incredible development, something of inestimable value. Perhaps it was something he would not mention to his old friend Hairstreak. Hamearis might see if he could keep the new technology for himself when the Faeries of the Night took over the Purple Palace.

And see if Wizard Fogarty might be persuaded to work for House Lucina.

Twenty

Fogarty held his right hand out in front of him, palm downwards, and noted it was trembling. What a pain that was! Even when his arthritic fingers were playing hell he'd always prided himself that he could hold it steady as a rock. It was ridiculous to start shaking at his age when it wasn't even his age that had caused the shake.

He didn't know what had caused the shake.

Except he did know what had caused the shake. It was just that what had caused the shake was impossible at his age.

He hadn't felt this confused since he was an adolescent.

Which was how he felt generally – like an adolescent. He wanted to hum a little tune and go out and pick flowers and all that sort of damn-fool nonsense. A thought struck him. Maybe it was the start of senile dementia. They used to call that 'second childhood'. You ended up drooling like a baby and wetting yourself, but maybe you went through an adolescent phase first. At eighty-seven, he was certainly old enough for senile dementia.

He wondered if the healing wizards might have a cure.

The trouble was he didn't *want* a cure. Apart from the shaking hand, he felt wonderful. He felt excited and strong and confident and full of energy. He felt like going to a concert and ripping up the seats. He'd never heard dementia made you feel like this. Nobody ever told him senility made you want to see *Led Zeppelin*.

It couldn't be senile dementia.

But if it wasn't senile dementia, it had to be ... Fogarty shook his head. It couldn't be *that* either!

He walked from the master bedroom of his Gatekeeper's lodge into the bathroom, where there was a full-length mirror. His reflection didn't look like him at all. It looked like his grandfather. The odd thing was he didn't *feel* old. He'd never felt old, not even when the arthritis burned in his hands and he discovered he couldn't run any more without his chest paining and his lungs heaving. But he'd never felt this young either. Most of the time he thought of himself, inside, as somewhere around thirty-five – maybe forty on a bad day. That was a long way from feeling seventeen, which was the way he felt just now.

The weird thing was the way it had happened. One minute he was worrying about Pyrgus, listening to Blue, trying to figure what might be going on. The next, there was a claw gripping his guts, his heart was pounding and his brain had turned to mush. All because Madame Cardui walked in.

He'd heard about Madame Cardui, of course – she was one of Blue's agents – but nothing had prepared him for the reality. She was the most exotic creature he'd ever seen – tall for a woman, nearly as tall as he was, in fact. She dressed in shudderingly flamboyant gear – a matching gown and headdress in bright, ever-changing colours with jewelled floaters on her feet that held her an inch or more above the floor and made her even taller.

They called her the Painted Lady, he seemed to recall, and he could see why. She was heavily, almost theatrically, made-up: had she once been on stage? He thought he'd heard that about her too. She was accompanied by an orange dwarf, who carried a fat, translucent Persian cat asleep in a gilded cage. But for all the trappings, the most striking thing about her was her eyes – dark, liquid and penetrating.

Those eyes transfixed him like javelins as Blue made the introductions. Madame Cardui reached out a slim hand writhing with serpent rings, smiled to show fine scarlet teeth, gripped his hand firmly and said, 'It is *such* a pleasure to meet you, Gatekeeper Fogarty. Deeah Princess Blue has told me much about you. May I present my servant Kitterick?' She nodded benignly towards the orange dwarf.

Fogarty, thunderstruck, said nothing. And continued to say nothing as she repeated the story she'd told Blue about the threat of assassination facing someone in the royal household. In fact, the only thing he did say before she swept out of the room at the end of the audience was, 'Madame Cardui, what is your given name?'

She had fixed him again with those wonderful eyes and said in that wonderful voice, 'Cynthia, Gatekeeper Fogarty. My given name is Cynthia.'

Then she was gone and Fogarty stood trembling in her wake. Thank God he'd hidden that from Blue and Pyrgus.

It was ludicrous to have that sort of reaction to a woman at his age. It was ludicrous to have that sort of reaction to a woman at *any* age. He didn't recall having had it before. Not when he was a kid mooning over some pimply first love he couldn't even remember now. He didn't have it when he met Miriam, the woman he married in his twenties. Admittedly Miriam had been a bit of a moo, but still ...

The question was what was he going to do about it?

He knew what he'd have done about it when he was really the age he felt right now. He'd have climbed on the hog and rode out after her like the Lone Bloody Ranger. He'd have grabbed her and kissed her till her ears dropped off. And if she was seeing someone else he'd have beaten him to a pulp.

Wouldn't do now, of course. He was Gatekeeper now, the most respectable, responsible job he'd ever held. Couldn't just take off chasing skirt. More to the point, he was eighty-seven and his days of beating rivals to a pulp were long gone. Unless, of course, he used a cricket bat. Idly he wondered if she had anything going with the dwarf.

He was coming out of the bathroom when somebody started hammering on his front door. Fogarty froze. Nobody was supposed to get anywhere near his home without triggering the security system. There were guards as well – Pyrgus had insisted on that – but even if somebody managed to slip past them, the devices he'd set up would have alerted him long ago. But somebody had got past his guards and his security and was at his door now, in the middle of the night.

Fogarty walked to the bank of viewscreens he'd installed in his living quarters. The remote periphery looked clear, except for his cloaked guards who showed up as reassuring green shapes. The middle ground was clear as well – a few foxes and rabbits (or what passed for foxes and rabbits in the Realm) but nothing to worry about – so it wasn't any sort of mass attack.

His eyes flickered to the screens that showed his front porch. A tall, hooded figure was reaching out a gloved hand to knock again. There was no obvious sign of weaponry (although the cloak could have hidden anything) but at least the figure was alone. All the same, not even a lone visitor should have passed the guards unnoticed. And nobody, but nobody, should have beaten his security devices. The expected assassination attempt? Blue thought the target must be Pyrgus, but word was the victim would be someone in the royal *household*. That could still be Pyrgus, but it could also be Blue herself or any one of a dozen senior servants and advisors, including himself.

Would an assassin knock on your front door?

Fogarty's eyes narrowed as he tried to think it through. Everybody knew assassins didn't just come calling at your door: they snuck in the back or through your window or down your chimney. Or they used a transformation spell to disguise their appearance, make them look like a friend or somebody harmless. The clown outside didn't look like a friend, he looked like an assassin. The hood hid the face, the cloak hid the weapons. But why would an assassin want to look like an assassin and walk right up to your front door? Unless he was an extremely *cunning* assassin who knew that nobody would believe somebody who looked like an assassin and came knocking at your door could possibly really *be* an assassin. Except that –

Fogarty gave up the attempt and took a cricket bat

from the cupboard beside the front door. He'd have preferred his old shotgun, but since he'd used it to kill the Purple Emperor, he thought it was undiplomatic to keep carrying it. What was he going to do – keep explaining he'd been possessed by a demon at the time? Besides, a cricket bat didn't often kill people if you knew what you were doing; and you could use it to break their fingers during the interrogation afterwards. The interrogation afterwards was important. You could find out who sent them and if there was anybody else after you. He hefted the bat and opened the door.

'Good evening, Alan,' said Madame Cardui. 'I thought at our age it might be best to dispense with the preliminaries.' She glanced at the bat as she swept past him. 'Oh, good – shall we be playing games?'

Blue awoke sleepily to find someone was shaking her. Blearily she focused beyond the lamp he was carrying. 'Pyrgus, what are you doing?'

'Hairstreak's sent the Duke of Burgundy to see me,' Pyrgus hissed urgently. 'I need you to tell me what to do.'

twenty-one

Henry had an utterly, totally brilliant idea, one so obvious he wondered why he hadn't thought of it before. Since he couldn't find where Aisling had hidden his portal control, he could at least go and see if Mr Fogarty had another one! It was night now and his mother would have gone ballistic if she'd thought he was visiting Mr Fogarty's home *after dark*. But his mother could no more remember who he was than could his sister, so there didn't seem a lot to stop him.

He pulled on a mac since it had started to rain and caught the last bus out. If he didn't find another control, he could always stay the night and catch the first bus home tomorrow. For all his problems with them, lethe cones had their advantages. And he still had four left.

By the time he was walking down Mr Fogarty's road, a lot of his confidence had evaporated. The trouble was, all he could think about was Blue and how she had to be wondering why he wasn't with her now she needed him. With his luck, there would be no second control and it would be *months* before he got to the Faerie Realm.

His luck turned out to be exactly as he has expected. He searched Mr Fogarty's house from top to bottom without finding so much as a hint of a portal control. He was wondering if he should bang his head against a wall when he had his second utterly, totally, wonderfully brilliant idea within three hours.

He went straight to the desk in the bedroom and rooted till he found Mr Fogarty's notebook.

The notebook was fascinating. There were technical sketches for all sorts of devices – including something called a Wishing Machine – all labelled in Mr Fogarty's small, neat hand. Many of them were clearly unfinished, some were jottings for machine parts and circuit boards, and quite a few made no sense to Henry whatsoever, although he tried to put *that* little discovery out of his head as soon as it occurred to him. If he couldn't make sense of the plans he was looking for, he was in real trouble. And if he couldn't find the plans at all, he was in bigger trouble still.

About a third of the way through the notebook, Henry found the plans he was looking for.

The drawing wasn't labelled 'portal control'. It was headed 'psychotronic reality disruptor' with the 'disruptor' crossed out and replaced by the word 'realignment'. It was the psychotronic bit that caught Henry's attention. He remembered Mr Fogarty mentioning something about his portals using a psychotronic trigger and pumped electricity. There was nothing about pumped electricity on this page, but the psychotronic bit looked promising.

So did the sketch. The exterior of the box was a lot like the portal control Henry used the first time he translated to the Realm. The drawing of the interior made no sense at all. There was provision for a battery, one of those expensive, long-life little efforts that powered digital watches, but beyond that Henry couldn't follow it at all. He stared for a long time, then decided he didn't have to follow it. All he had to do was make it. It was like a television set. You didn't have to know how it worked, you just had to know how to switch it on. If he followed Mr Fogarty's plans exactly, then the portal should open when he pressed the button.

The problem was Henry had never made an electronic device before. He'd learned a bit about circuit diagrams and components at school, then promptly forgotten most of it and switched class before they got to putting things together. But he had built working model cardboard sculptures – how much more difficult could electronic stuff be?

It turned out not to be difficult at all, but it took more time than Henry had expected. What made it easy was Mr Fogarty's habit of making little doodle sketches of every necessary component. The doodles crawled all over his notes so that even when Henry didn't understand terms like *gate transformer*, he had a picture of what he was looking for.

A lot of the parts he needed were stored in the kitchen drawer, while others were out in Mr Fogarty's shed. Henry felt a twinge of guilt as he collected some of them – they were items he'd stolen from his school for Mr Fogarty when they had been trying to build a portal to get Pyrgus back to the Realm: they'd have to go back again before school opened after the summer break.

It was only when he started to put the pieces together than he discovered there was a component missing.

Henry went on a major search after that, but without result. What he was looking for was labelled 'biofilter' in the notebook: a small, flat disc apparently made by fusing two layers of metal to make a sandwich with a third, then attaching a tiny looped aerial. There was nothing like it in the kitchen drawer, nothing like it in the shed. Henry went on another search of the whole house again before deciding that whatever a biofilter was, Mr Fogarty didn't have one. He leafed through the notebook to see if there were any instructions for making one, but there weren't. What to do now?

Henry pored over the design diagram trying to figure what the bio thing actually did. As far as he could see it did nothing – it didn't even seem to be attached to anything. But then again, a lot of the device was like that. There was even a circuit that wasn't a real circuit, but a drawing of a circuit. Mr Fogarty had labelled that one 'psychotronic pathways' and added a note saying, 'Insert right way up in relation to transistor 8'. Henry decided to leave the bio disc thing out altogether. He wasn't at all sure this was wise, but he didn't see what else he could do.

He started to put the device together using an electric soldering iron he found at the back of the kitchen drawer. It was slow, absorbing work, very much like model-making, and it was dark outside before he realised he was very hungry. He left the half-finished device (which didn't look half as neat as the things Mr Fogarty made, but what the hell – it was his first attempt) and went in search of something to eat. The fridge was empty as usual, except for the familiar pint of curdled milk, but he found a Birds Eye shepherd's pie in the chest freezer in the laundry room. *Cook from frozen in the microwave,* Captain Birds Eye told him cheerfully by means of a cartoon bubble.

Mr Fogarty's microwave was pristine. Somebody had given it to him and he had never used it because of something he called 'radiation leakage'. Henry removed the outer packaging, bunged the shepherd's pie inside and set the timer for seven minutes. Then he took a tin of baked beans from the cupboard (Mr Fogarty always had *plenty* of baked beans) and heated them in a saucepan on the gas stove. By the time the microwave *pinged*, the beans were bubbling merrily. He plogged the lot down on a willow-pattern plate and ate his meal with gusto.

Since it was clear he wouldn't have the device finished in the next hour or so, he decided to stay the night. He felt a wonderful surge of pleasure at the decision. The sense of freedom was astonishing. He didn't have to answer to his mother. He didn't have to listen to his rotten sister. He could stay out all night if he damn well liked. They wouldn't even notice he was missing.

Henry's sense of freedom was gone in the morning, replaced by something close to panic. He'd had the weirdest dream about Pyrgus. They were running from a small army of rotting zombies who loped along a city street with bits falling off them. Blue was in the dream as well. She followed after the zombies with a dustpan and brush, sweeping up the bits. As she worked, she kept calling after them, 'What kept you, Henry? What took you so long?'

Whatever about the zombies, he could believe that

was exactly what Blue must be saying now. There was trouble in the Realm, she'd asked Henry for his help and he'd promised to follow on as quickly as he could. She'd probably expected him within an hour or two at most. He grabbed the soldering iron without even bothering to have breakfast.

He finished the portal control around lunchtime, with one break mid-morning to fry up two hamburgers he found in the deep freeze. It looked a real mess as it sat there on the kitchen table – a rat's nest of terminals and wires with an on/off switch too big for the rest of the components. The control Mr Fogarty made was smaller than a mobile phone. Henry's version would hardly fit into a shoebox. He wondered how he was going to carry it about with him, then decided he didn't have to. If he could open a portal to the Realm, Mr Fogarty could always get him back. Or Pyrgus, come to that – there was a portal in the Purple Palace.

He bit his lip, stared at it for a little while, then decided it was time to try it out. Since he'd learned the hard way not to open portals indoors, he carried the device into the back garden and down to the little area of wasteland and rubbish beyond the buddleia bush. It struck him that if he hesitated he'd never have the courage to do anything, so he threw the monstrous switch right away.

Nothing happened.

It was that biofilter thing! It wouldn't work without the biofilter! He was finished. He'd have to go home and wait for Aisling to get back to normal all because of that stupid biofilter!

Or possibly a battery …

Henry felt like kicking himself. The famous biofilter

might yet be a problem, but meanwhile it would be an excellent idea to put a battery in his device. He ran quickly back into the house and searched the drawer. There were several batteries pushed in at the back, but none was the lithium button he needed. He ran to the shed, but could find no batteries there at all.

Where are you, Henry? Why didn't you follow on like you promised?

He was *so* late! He was *so* long delayed! He glanced at his watch. One twenty-eight. That was nearly – there was a battery in his watch!

Henry ripped the watch from his wrist. He needed a little screwdriver to get the back off, but there were little screwdrivers in the shed. In moments he was looking at a battery that would fit his makeshift portal control to perfection. He prised it out of the watch and carried it quickly outside.

He discovered he was breathing heavily as he pushed the battery into place. He checked the contacts and decided everything was ready. Then he had a small heart-thumping panic: there was no way this thing was going to work without its biofilter. The biofilter just had to be the most important component in the entire thing. Dear heaven, what *was* a biofilter?

One last search, he thought. *One last search*. It was stupid risking everything for the sake of a biofilter. What happened if all his work went into meltdown?

Henry ran back to the house – he seemed to be running everywhere these days – and began a search so thorough that at one point he found himself looking behind the bowl in the loo. The ridiculousness of his situation struck him then. Did he really think Mr Fogarty kept a biofilter in his toilet? It was ludicrous.

He was letting his panic get the better of him. What was such a big deal about testing the device without one tiny little component? Worst-case scenario, the chances were it simply wouldn't work. He'd been willing enough to try it without its biofilter a few minutes ago before he remembered he hadn't put in the battery. Why was he making such a fuss about the damn thing now?

He went back outside again. His electronic rat's nest lay where he'd left it on top of a broken-down old garden table Mr Fogarty had never got around to throwing out. Before he could panic again, Henry threw the switch.

In the middle of the rat's nest, an LED glowed green.

Henry looked around. There was no sign of a portal, no sign of anything at all. It hadn't worked. It was never going to work without a bio—

Behind him, somewhere near the shed, there came an electronic hum. It was so low-pitched at first that he felt it through his feet as much as heard it with his ears. But then it rose higher and began to pulse like the siren of a cardiac ambulance. The volume rose to a painful level. This was nothing at all like what happened when he used the portal control Mr Fogarty made. Something was wrong. Something was badly wrong.

The sounding siren stopped abruptly. There was an unfamiliar popping sound and a portal opened little more than six feet from where he stood. Henry stared at it in astonishment. He'd done it! He'd built a working portal control! What's more, it opened up directly into the Purple Palace – he recognised its corridors at once. How great was that?

He froze. There was a small sizzling sound like frying bacon. A whisp of smoke rose from a junction in his makeshift control. As he watched, sparks began to snake through the wiring of the rat's nest.

The portal flickered.

For an instant, Henry's legs refused to function. He knew beyond a shadow of a doubt the flicker meant the portal was going to close again, but he could do nothing, absolutely nothing about it. Then his paralysis broke and he flung himself forward.

The portal collapsed a second after he passed through it. But it didn't matter. He had made it. He was in the Purple Palace.

And something was very wrong.

twenty-two

The old Purple Emperor would never have seen them in the throne room – serious negotiations with serious enemies took place in private. But Hamearis was not even slightly surprised. The Purple Emperor Elect was young and inexperienced. He would see a formal audience as the only possibility with a ranking Duke. Besides, he wouldn't realise how much trouble he was in.

It was years since Hamearis had entered this chamber. It had been set out for a banquet then and packed with gaudy people. Now it was almost empty and surprisingly gloomy. There seemed to be some sort of glowglobe failure: a brace of sleepy flunkies were setting out banks of lighted candles. The flickering flames caused eerie shadows, which was possibly no bad thing, considering the news he brought.

He let his gaze drift casually, arrogantly, along the forest of pillars and up to the acoustic galleries high above. Those baroque constructions carried every whisper through the great hall and out into the corridors beyond. Which was no bad thing either. If servants overheard, the word would spread like wildfire – and cause just as much panic.

At the far end of the chamber, Crown Prince Pyrgus

and his sister, the Princess Royal, were seated on two huge elevated thrones. They had clearly chosen their positions in order to impress, but managed only to look like nervous children. They both had their father's aspect in them, Pyrgus even more than his sister. Word had it he was a wild one, as young people often were, but there was intelligence in his eyes and given a few years he might even have made quite a decent Emperor. Almost a pity he would never get the chance.

Hamearis began to walk towards them. His cloaked companion moved like a ghost three paces behind.

Blue watched Hamearis stride along the aisle. He walked slowly, almost insultingly so, as if he was on an evening stroll. But that would be deliberate. From everything she had learned, Hamearis Lucina was a master of diplomacy and psychological manipulation, skills that in some ways made him even more dangerous than Lord Hairstreak himself. Although she'd seen many pictures of him and watched some of his viewscreen appearances, the reality was even more impressive than the image. His body was well-muscled, like a warrior, but there was a deceptive sensitivity about his face. He had the handsome looks of a hero, which doubtless contributed to his enormous public following among the Faeries of the Night.

Hamearis bowed. 'Greetings, Prince Pyrgus. I must thank you for granting me an audience at so late an hour.' *Prince Pyrgus,* Blue noticed, not *Emperor Elect.* He had tawny yellow eyes like a haniel, and now they moved to her. 'Your Serene Highness,' he acknowledged.

Blue inclined her head slightly. She was glad Pyrgus

had had the good sense to bring her to this meeting. Hamearis might be handsome, but he was dangerous as a viper and crafty as a rat.

Pyrgus said coolly, 'Since it *is* a late hour, Your Grace, I would appreciate your getting directly to the purpose of your visit.'

'Of course,' Hamearis said mildly. 'But first, with your permission, sir, I am required to present compliments and greetings from my friend and colleague Lord Hairstreak, who has expressly asked me to enquire after your health and that of your sister.'

'My health is fine,' Pyrgus said shortly. 'So's Blue's.'

Her brother would never, ever make a diplomat. 'Please convey our greetings to Lord Hairstreak and express our hopes that he too is fit and well,' Blue put in.

'Now get on with it,' said Pyrgus, spoiling the effect.

If Hamearis took offence, he didn't show it. In fact, he actually began to smile. 'As you wish, Crown Prince,' he said.

Blue had a sudden, gripping intuition that something terrible was coming. It was so strong she wanted to cry out, to stop whatever it was that Hamearis Lucina was about to say. But her terror was so great her tongue refused to function.

Hamearis said formally, 'Crown Prince Pyrgus, your father, the Purple Emperor, has contracted a pact with Lord Hairstreak, acting in his capacity as representative of the Faeries of the Night, whereby henceforth the Purple Emperor agrees that, due to his recent and ongoing illness, the functions of State shall become the responsibility of his son Comma, who shall, until his majority, be advised in all matters by Lord Hairstreak in the capacity of Royal Regent.' Hamearis drew a rolled scroll from the pocket of his tunic and offered it to Pyrgus. 'I am charged, Crown Prince, to present you with a copy of this pact, struck with the Imperial Seal and signed by the hand of your father, the presiding Purple Emperor, in the certain knowledge and expectation that you and all members of the Royal Family and Household will abide by the detailed terms herein and grant such aid and assistance as may become necessary to Prince Comma and Lord Hairstreak in the pursuance of their various duties.' When Pyrgus made no move to take the scroll, Hamearis dropped it at his feet.

'Duke Hamearis,' Blue gasped, 'our father is dead!' What the man had just said was appalling, sick, hurtful, despicable, stupid –

Hamearis licked his lips. 'Your Serene Highness,' he said formally, 'it is my pleasant duty to inform you that your illustrious father is very much alive.' He gestured.

The cloaked figure behind him took three steps forward and threw back his hood.

twenty-three

'That wasn't Daddy!' Blue said wildly.

Pyrgus said nothing.

'It can't have been Daddy – Daddy's dead! I *saw* him dead!' She couldn't stand still. She paced the length of the private antechamber, then paced back again. There were tears in her eyes. 'It wasn't Daddy! It wasn't! It wasn't!' She hesitated. 'It wasn't, was it, Pyrgus?'

'It looked like Daddy,' Pyrgus told her dully.

She could still see every movement of the hood, the fold of the cloth as it slipped back. She could see her father's eyes turning towards her. She could see the hasty repairs done to the ravages the Analogue World weapon had wrought on his face.

'It could be a double,' she said. She was aware of her hands trembling. 'Just somebody who looks like him. Or a magical illusion. Something Hairstreak and Hamearis arranged between them. They'd do that, you know. Hairstreak would stop at nothing to –'

'I don't think it was a double,' Pyrgus said. 'I don't think it was an illusion either.'

Neither did Blue, not really. The moment the figure uncloaked, she'd *known*. It was all there, in the shape of his body, the tilt of his head, even that curious open way he held his left hand. Besides, while an illusion or a double might pass muster for an hour or two, maybe even a day, Hairstreak knew there would be no question of pacts or changes in the way the Realm was run. No fake could possibly stand up to the sort of scrutiny that would bring. What she'd seen had to be real.

The emotion hit her like a tidal wave. Her father was alive again! She could see his face, hear his voice. She could feel the touch of his hand on her cheek. They could walk together, talk together as they once had. It could be as it was before!

Then, as suddenly as it came, the wave ebbed. It was not as it had been before. Their father had refused to talk to them, to approach them, refused even to stay in the throne room. He had showed his face, woodenly confirmed the agreement with Lord Hairstreak, then walked out. It wasn't right. Nothing was right. Softly, without warning, Blue began to cry.

Pyrgus was by her side at once, his arm about her shoulders. 'It's all right, Blue. Everything's going to be all right.'

Empty words, and they both knew it. 'Do you believe Hamearis?' Pyrgus looked at her blankly. Blue blinked back her tears. 'He said Daddy was never really killed, never really dead. He was only in a coma and when Hairstreak took him out of stasis he ... he just sort of woke up. Do you believe that?'

Pyrgus said very carefully, 'I suppose that's possible. I mean, people do go into comas. Sometimes. I mean –'

Blue seized him by the shoulders and shook him. 'Do you *believe* it, Pyrgus? Do you believe that's what happened?'

Miserably, Pyrgus shook his head. 'No.'

Blue stared at him bleakly. 'They must have brought

him back,' she said. Her words were scarcely more than a whisper. They hung in the chamber like a sentinel of doom.

Pyrgus said nothing.

With a huge effort Blue stopped crying and used a corner of her gown to dry her eyes. She shook her head. 'Nothing. Nothing.' For a second she thought the tears might start again, but she forced them back and said briskly, 'Have someone fetch the Gatekeeper.' As an afterthought she added, 'And Madame Cardui. I think we're going to need all the advice we can get.'

Although Madame Cardui was staying at the palace, she was not in her quarters according to the servant sent to fetch her. Fortunately Gatekeeper Fogarty found her somewhere. At least, the two of them arrived together. Blue thought they looked smug about something, but had too much on her mind to find out what. She told them what had happened.

'Hairstreak can resurrect the *dead*?' Mr Fogarty put in the moment she drew breath.

'Necromancers can,' Pyrgus said. He had a shamed look, as if he was talking about an obscenity. 'Some of them. A few of them. Most of them can only talk to the ... to the ... '

'But some of them can?' Fogarty pressed him. 'Some of them can actually do it?' From the intensity of his expression, he seemed to have a personal interest.

'If ... you know, if the ... if the ... if things haven't too far gone.'

'You mean if the corpse hasn't started to rot?'

Pyrgus swallowed painfully. 'Yes.'

'Why didn't you do this right away?' Fogarty asked.

Pyrgus stared at him in astonishment. 'Me?'

'You and Blue. Yes.'

'Resurrect Daddy?' Blue was looking at him wide-eyed. She seemed stunned by his question.

'You liked him, didn't you?' said Fogarty. He looked from one to the other, clearly bewildered by their reactions. 'Come to that, how come everybody isn't resurrected? After battles and so forth?'

After a long moment, Blue said gently, 'It's forbidden, Mr Fogarty.'

'Forbidden by who, for God's sake?'

Blue swallowed. 'Law,' she said. The distress was evident on her face. 'And the Church of Light.'

Frowning, Fogarty asked, 'Is that the only reason?' He sounded incredulous.

Pyrgus was staring at the floor. He looked as if he was going to be sick. Blue shuddered. 'It's just *wrong*, Mr Fogarty!' she blurted.

But Fogarty wouldn't leave it alone. 'Suppose *I* died and you put me in stasis, would you be able to have me resurrected then?'

'It's *forbidden*,' Blue said again.

'By your religion? I'm a Presbyterian.'

Long seconds ticked away. Fogarty thought Blue might be going to cry, but eventually she said almost crisply, 'Gatekeeper, the necromancer would have control of you.'

So that was it! That was why they were so upset. Fogarty leaned forward. 'So it's a zombie deal?' They thought their father had been raised from the dead and now he was some sort of shell commanded by Hairstreak. 'Let me get this straight,' he said. 'Lord Hairstreak stole your father's corpse, then animated it?

And now it's his slave? Doing anything he tells it?'

'Not Hairstreak personally,' Blue said. 'It would have to be a necromancer. Somebody who knows how to do it. But he'd have been working on Hairstreak's orders. Or maybe –' she swallowed again and closed her eyes briefly, '– maybe it was somebody who ... who just did it and *sold* Daddy to Lord Hairstreak afterwards. That's happened sometimes: I read about it in the history books. But it doesn't matter what exactly happened. The thing is, Daddy's soul is trapped and he has to do what Lord Hairstreak tells him. That's why he signed the pact. That's the only way he would have signed that pact.'

Mr Fogarty was frowning fiercely. 'If it's a zombie deal, people will know he didn't sign of his own free will. Nobody will take the pact seriously.'

'Ah,' Pyrgus said, but then looked too close to tears to continue.

'That's why Lord Hairstreak is claiming Daddy was only in a coma,' Blue said. 'If there was no death, there was no resurrection. Hairstreak will say Daddy is acting of his own free will.'

'Is he still here?' Mr Fogarty asked suddenly.

'Who?'

'Your father.'

Blue shook her head. 'No. I don't think so. I don't know. He came with Duke Hamearis, but left after he told us to honour the pact.'

'What about Hairstreak's sidekick? This Duke person?'

Blue glanced at Pyrgus, who shook his head. Pyrgus said, 'He went off half an hour ago.'

'Pity,' Fogarty said. 'We might have kidnapped him.

We need a little leverage over Hairstreak.'

Madame Cardui spoke for the first time. 'I'm afraid this has gone beyond simple solutions, Alan.' Blue glanced at her in surprise. She'd never heard anyone call Mr Fogarty 'Alan' before. 'This is a very emotive issue, my deeahs, and a truly dreadful situation. How long before that wretched little man makes the pact public?'

The wretched little man was clearly Lord Hairstreak. Pyrgus said, 'He wants me to step down as Emperor Elect. The pact will be published as soon as I do so.'

'How long can you stall him?' Fogarty asked.

'It will have to happen before my Coronation.'

Madame Cardui said, 'Then we must draw up our plans without delay.'

Blue nodded. She wished Henry were with her. Why on earth hadn't he followed on as he had promised?

Twenty-four

The Facemaster sighed. 'Mr Chalkhill, will you *please* try to concentrate?'

'But I'm improving,' Chalkhill protested. 'I'm definitely improving.'

They were alone together in the vast Practice Hall of Hairstreak's Assassins' Academy, with its highly-polished oakwood floor and mirrored walls. Their images extended to infinity. The Facemaster was a dark-haired man with a lean, muscular body and a cool, professional air.

'Improving?' he said. 'Yes, slightly. But there is still a way to go, Mr Chalkhill. Frankly, if you were to attempt your mission tomorrow, you would fail. And then where would we be?'

I'd be dead, thought Chalkhill. And you'd be trying to explain to Hairstreak why you failed to knock me into shape. The Facemaster knew all about his mission, only one of four to do so, as far as Chalkhill was aware. The remaining three were Chalkhill himself, Lord Hairstreak and the wizard retained to cast the transformation spell – a Halek-trained ninny called Puderow, Plumduff, Psodos ... something of that sort. Everyone else involved with the Coronation had been told Hairstreak himself would be attending. There was not so much as a hint abroad that Chalkhill would be taking Hairstreak's place. Assuming Chalkhill ever got beyond his basic training.

Of course, if he *didn't* get beyond his basic training, Hairstreak would have him murdered. Something slow and painful, no doubt.

'I don't see why all this is necessary,' he said petulantly. 'The illusion spell will make me look exactly like His Lordship.'

'Yes it will, Mr Chalkhill, but it will not help you move like him, which is what we're working on now. You realise what the problem is, of course – it's your bulk.'

'My bulk?' Chalkhill echoed, appalled. He was a little overweight certainly, perhaps enough overweight to be called cuddly, but he hardly thought anyone in their right mind would refer to him as bulky.

'You're a bigger man than Lord Hairstreak,' the Facemaster frowned, 'so you move differently. I'm not criticising you, but it's something we have to change. I'm bigger than Hairstreak too, but watch –'

It was positively creepy. As the Facemaster set off across the room again, he seemed to shrink. His right shoulder dropped in a characteristic Hairstreak posture. His features composed themselves into a grim, unforgiving mask. But most of all, his walk became an arrogant, insectile scuttle. There was no transformation spell, no physical resemblance at all, but you could almost imagine you were watching Black Hairstreak himself.

'Now you do it,' Facemaster Wainscot told him.

Chalkhill tried. Oh how Chalkhill tried. He dropped his shoulder, scrunched his body and made sortie after sortie across the polished floor. He studied his reflections in the mirrored walls. He tried to *think* himself into Lord Hairstreak like an actor taking on a part. He walked and walked and tried and tried until his feet began to ache.

'It's no good,' the Facemaster said at last. 'We'll have to use the worm.'

twenty-five

Brimstone was puffed by the third circuit of the fire, but thankfully the priest signalled them to stop. 'Stand side by side,' he instructed loudly. Then, dropping his voice, he whispered in Brimstone's ear, 'And try to look as if you're enjoying it.'

Too breathless to answer, Brimstone contented himself with delivering a cutting look. Then he turned to smile briefly and hypocritically at his bride. She smiled back cheerfully. *Five husbands!* If she really did put them all down, she must have a fortune squirrelled away. This wedding could prove an exceptionally profitable enterprise.

'Friends,' announced the priest in the general direction of the down-and-outs who looked as if they hadn't a friend between them, 'we're gathered here for blah-de-blah etcetera rhubarb and etcetera, *ah-hummmm.*'

Brimstone looked at him in astonishment.

'Full ceremony costs extra,' the priest whispered. 'Bride won't pay, but I can charge it on to you if you like.'

Brimstone shook his head firmly. 'Get on with it,' he hissed.

'Having dispensed with the religious introduction

and the blessing,' the priest intoned, 'we move on to the symbolic portion of the rite. The bride, as you can see, is carrying a spiny cactus to symbolise the thorns of adversity experienced by all couples in the course of their life together. I now ask the bride to hand those thorns to her groom who, in accepting the gift, solemnly pledges himself to bear those thorns for her henceforth and for evermore, *ah-hummmm.*'

Fat chance, Brimstone thought, but he reached for the cactus anyway, taking care to grip it by the pot. The down-and-outs applauded listlessly.

'Hold it up!' the priest whispered.

Brimstone held the succulent above his head. This time it was the Widow Mormo who applauded. *Five husbands!* That had to be some sort of record; and if it wasn't, it was certainly worthy of admiration.

One of the nymphs tripped forward and relieved Brimstone of his cactus. She had the wasted body and blank stare of a simbala music addict, but she wasn't so far out of it as to forget to ask him for a coin to mark her part in the ceremony. Brimstone gave her a groat and she danced away looking cross.

'Just the impediments now,' whispered the priest. 'Then I can make it legal.' He raised his voice to fill the church. 'I now call on any here present with a prior claim to this woman to enunciate such claim clearly and fully as an impediment to the Holy Ceremony of Marriage we are here to undertake; and I further call on any here present who knows of this or any other impediment to come forward now and so enunciate or henceforth keep shut his mouth.'

This should tell us if any of the last five has survived, thought Brimstone in a moment of rare whimsy. The priest studied the ceiling of his church for a long moment, but nobody piped up to protest.

The priest hitched up his robe as if preparing for a quick exit now the rite was nearly done. 'I now call on any here present,' he repeated, 'with a prior claim to this man to enunciate such claim clearly and fully as an impediment to the Holy Ceremony of Marriage we are here to undertake; and I further call on any here present who knows of this or any other impediment to come forward now and so enunciate or henceforth keep shut his mouth.'

This time it was Brimstone who looked up at the ceiling. A decent pause, the final legalities, then off to the woods to kill her.

It was a very happy wedding day.

twenty-six

The worm was more like an eel or a snake, except it was segmented and protected by a natural, glistening armoured shell. It stared at Chalkhill with black, beady eyes from the bottom of a heated glass tank. There was a sandy floor to replicate the desert of its natural environment and a few desiccated plants to keep it company. Slices of ordle had been scattered on a flat-topped rock.

Chalkhill looked at the Facemaster.

'It's a symbiote,' Facemaster Wainscot explained. He clearly caught Chalkhill's blank look for he added, 'A creature that works in cooperation with another creature to mutual benefit.' He sounded as if he were reading from a reference book. 'It will assist you to walk properly.' He blinked, then clarified, 'So you look like Lord Hairstreak.'

Chalkhill peered at the worm. It was nearly seven inches long and exuded some sort of foul-smelling slime over its armoured scales. 'Let's get this straight,' Chalkhill said. 'This thing is going to help me walk like Hairstreak?'

The Facemaster nodded soberly. 'Yes.'

'And what do I do for it?'

'Pardon?'

'You said it was a symbiote. Mutual admiration society. Tit for tat. You scratch my back, I scratch yours.' Chalkhill understood *symbiote* all right – it was the way he'd functioned most of his life. 'What's the quid pro quo?'

'The worm takes a little of your pigmentation to use in its mating ritual.' He caught Chalkhill's expression again. 'Apparently female worms prefer male worms to have white spots. This one doesn't, so it will extract some of your skin colour to make them.'

'What effect does that have on me?' Chalkhill asked suspiciously.

'You'll look a little pale.'

'Is it painful?'

'Not even slightly.'

It didn't sound too bad to Chalkhill. 'What do I do? Keep the worm with me in my pocket? Something of that sort?'

The Facemaster hesitated. 'Ah … not exactly. The symbiote must be absorbed into your body.'

Chalkhill's jaw dropped. 'I have to *swallow* it?'

The Facemaster shook his head. 'Human saliva is toxic to the species, I'm afraid. Consequently the insertion must be made in one nostril. The worm slides down your throat, crawls through the stomach into the large intestine, thence to the small intestine and, ultimately, the bowel, where it takes up permanent residence in your bottom.'

Chalkhill stared at him in horror. 'Are you out of your mind?' he asked incredulously. 'You want me to stuff that thing up my nose and let it crawl down through my guts?'

'It's no fun for me either,' said the worm.

Twenty-seven

Despite everything, Pyrgus slept late next morning. The others must have been exhausted too, for none of them came to wake him. He woke to sunshine and a feeling of dread. After a moment he knuckled the sleep from his eyes and climbed out from under the layer of woolly endolgs who acted as both inner guards and eiderdown. 'Morning, Boss,' they chorused cheerfully.

'Morning,' Pyrgus grunted. He grabbed the towels someone had laid out for him and headed for the cleansing cubicle. He was never very good first thing in the morning, but this morning was much worse than usual. Last night's discussions had lasted almost until dawn and produced nothing in the way of a solution.

'Good morning, Your Royal Highness,' purred the soft, spell-driven voice of the cleansing cubicle. Pyrgus groaned. Even this damn thing must have heard the latest developments: it had been calling him *Emperor Elect* since his father's murder. The news had to be all over the palace by now.

The cubicle filled with hot mist as he stepped inside and pseudopods extended to scrape sweat and impurities off his back. Small streams of perfumed water oozed up around his feet, insinuated themselves between his toes and began to curl around his legs.

Soothing music crept along the edge of audibility, extracting stress from his shoulders and neck.

What to do? There was another meeting scheduled in –

'Seventeen minutes and thirty-eight seconds,' the cubicle told him. It wasn't sentient or even really telepathic, just expensive. He often felt guilty just using it. Life was hugely simpler when he had hidden among the people and had nothing more to worry about than fights with his father.

– seventeen minutes and thirty-eight seconds and something had to be sorted soon. There was no way he was going to let Lord Hairstreak get away with this, not now, not ever, even if he had to ... had to ... had to what? It was no use waiting for the others to supply him with a plan. He had to come up with one himself. Something swift, decisive and utterly ruthless. *He had to take the initiative!*

The trouble was his mind just wouldn't function.

The cubicle sensed his dilemma and slammed a blast of ice-cold water against his naked body. Pyrgus yelped and leaped outside. But as he reached for the towels to dry himself off, he had to admit his head was clearer now. Perhaps he could refuse to acknowledge the pact, claim his father was still dead and Hairstreak had forged his seal and signature. What could Hairstreak do about it?

He could produce the Purple Emperor, Pyrgus thought. His father was a slave to Lord Hairstreak now.

He dressed slowly as depression seeped over him like grey-black ooze. In situations like this, there was only one consolation:

Things couldn't get any worse.

Pyrgus walked into the meeting to discover things were getting worse.

'What are you doing here?' he asked at once.

It was Gatekeeper Fogarty who answered. 'Your half-brother has something to tell you.'

Blue said, 'I explained you had important things to do, but he insisted. He won't tell us what it is.'

Pyrgus glared at Comma, who seemed to be growing fatter lately. 'Well, what is it?' He noticed Madame Cardui wasn't present. Perhaps Blue had sent her off somewhere. And there was still no sign of Henry. He'd have liked Henry to have been here. Somehow he felt better with Henry around.

Comma said, 'That's no way to talk to your Emperor Elect.'

'Apparently I'm not Emperor Elect any longer,' Pyrgus told him drily. 'That's why I don't have time –'

'I know you're not Emperor Elect,' Comma said. '*I'm* Emperor Elect – that's what I just said.' He glared at Pyrgus as fiercely as Pyrgus had glared at him. 'You never told me Father was still alive, you big *pig!*'

'Comma –' Blue tried to put in. Suddenly she was looking at Comma more sympathetically than she had done in months.

But Comma was not to be diverted. He looked angry and tearful at the same time. 'You pretended to me he was dead. So did you, Blue. You ganged up on me and told me my father was *dead!*'

'Nobody ganged up on you, Comma –' Fogarty began.

Comma ignored him. 'Well, he *isn't* dead!' he shouted at Pyrgus. 'He was *never* dead. And now he wants me to be Emperor.'

For a long moment Pyrgus could do no more than look at him. Then he said, 'So you've been told already.'

'He wants me to be the next Emperor. Not you, Pyrgus – me! Father doesn't want to be Emperor any more because of his deformity. He wants *me*!'

Suddenly there was too much going round in Pyrgus's head. How had Comma found out so soon? The Duke of Burgundy had undertaken there would be no announcement until Pyrgus formally stepped down. And beyond the immediate questions there were others. What was he, Pyrgus, going to do about it? What was he going to do about – ? He couldn't even think about it properly.

It was Blue who asked, quite gently, 'Who told you about Daddy, Comma?'

And Comma said triumphantly, 'Lord Hairstreak!'

Mr Fogarty tried to rescue the situation. 'This isn't the way you think it is,' he said. He glanced across at Pyrgus as if wanting him to explain.

But Pyrgus couldn't explain, not properly. How could he explain a spiritual abomination to somebody Comma's age? How could he explain the animated shell that was now controlled by Lord Hairstreak? How could he explain all that to a boy who just wanted his father to be alive? After all, it was what Pyrgus wanted too.

Blue said, 'Lord Hairstreak tells lies.'

Comma rounded on her, eyes blazing. 'Is he telling lies about Father being alive?'

Blue shook her head. 'Not exactly. What he –'

'What do you mean, *Not exactly*? Father's either alive or dead. He can't be *not exactly* alive. I used to think you were better than Pyrgus, Blue, but you're not. You're just as bad as he is. Father *is* alive. You didn't want me to know that because you didn't want me to be Emperor. But your rotten scheme didn't work. You're not my friends. You've never been my friends. But Lord Hairstreak's my friend now.'

'Hairstreak isn't your friend,' Mr Fogarty said shortly. 'Hairstreak isn't *anybody's* friend.'

But Comma ignored him. 'Look,' he said excitedly. 'Look at this!' He pulled a parchment scroll from the pocket of his jerkin. It looked eerily like the scroll the Duke of Burgundy had carried with the details of the pact. Comma pushed it towards Pyrgus, waving it underneath his nose.

Pyrgus took the document with a heavy heart. Somehow he knew, he just *knew*, what it would contain. He looked at Comma for a moment longer, then glanced down at the parchment. His eyes skimmed the writing with a sense of horrid expectation.

'What's it say?' Blue asked quietly.

Pyrgus took a deep, rattling breath. 'It's an official authorisation for Comma to become next Purple Emperor with Lord Hairstreak acting as Regent until he comes of age.'

'Little git!' Mr Fogarty grunted explosively. Presumably he meant Lord Hairstreak.

'See who signed it?' Comma shouted. 'Read out who signed it, Pyrgus!'

Pyrgus said quietly, 'It was signed by our father.'

'You see? You see?' Comma asked no one in particular. He looked shrewdly at Pyrgus. 'It's no good tearing it up, Pyrgus – I have other copies and so does Lord Hairstreak.'

Pyrgus dropped the paper to the floor.

Blue said, 'Comma, Daddy doesn't know what he's signing now. This is all Lord Hairstreak's doing and he only wants you to be Emperor so he will become Regent.'

A thought occurred to Pyrgus. Hairstreak could *kill* Comma before he came of age. Certainly Hairstreak would never relinquish the throne once he became Regent.

'He told me you'd say that,' Comma said. 'He told me you'd try to stop me becoming Emperor.'

'Of course you can't become Emperor,' Blue said firmly. 'There's no question of your becoming Emperor. Can't you *see* what Hairstreak is up to? Can't you –'

'He told me you'd say that as well, Blue,' Comma said. 'And he told me what to do about it. Are you going to let me be Emperor, Pyrgus?'

Pyrgus started to shake his head. 'Comma –'

Comma darted to the door and jerked it open. 'Quickly!' he called excitedly.

General Ovard stepped into the room. Behind him marched a full contingent of Palace Guards. Pyrgus noticed Ovard was wearing formal uniform as if dressed for a State occasion. The old General looked pained but determined. He glanced sternly from one face to another.

'They won't let me be Emperor,' Comma shouted, his voice high. 'I showed them the Order. Pyrgus just threw it on the floor!'

General Ovard focused on Pyrgus. 'It's a properly executed Order, Crown Prince. Signed by your father, stamped with the Imperial Seal.'

'It's a plot by Hairstreak,' Mr Fogarty sniffed.

'I don't like the bit about Hairstreak becoming Regent any more than you do, Gatekeeper,' the General said. 'But I swore an oath, and if that's what my Purple Emperor has ordered, that's what's going to happen.'

'The Purple Emperor is dead, Ovard. You saw the body.'

'I saw a body in stasis,' Ovard said. 'Alive or dead, they all look much the same like that. But he looked alive enough to me when he handed me the Order.'

'Daddy's still here?' Blue exploded. 'Here in the palace?'

'He was at the barracks. Lord Hairstreak was with him. I don't know where they are now, but I do know this is a legal Order, Serenity.' Ovard seemed troubled, despite his words, but determined.

'I don't want any more talking!' Comma shouted suddenly. 'No more talking, any of you. You have to listen to me now, and do what I say!'

Pyrgus glanced at the ranks of soldiers lined up behind Ovard.

Comma caught the look and started to smile slyly. 'I'm Emperor Elect now and this is my first proclamation. Lord Hairstreak said if you tried to stop me, I was to put you all in prison and have you executed. But I'm not going to do that. You're my half-brother and half-sister. You're my *family*. So I'm not going to do that, whatever Lord Hairstreak says. But I can't have you making trouble and arguing with everything I say, so I *am* going to send you into exile. All of you – Pyrgus, Blue and you, Gatekeeper. I'm going to give you half an hour to get your things and leave the palace. General Ovard, I order you to see they do!' He tossed his head grandly and marched from the room.

There was a long, grim silence. Eventually Mr Fogarty said, 'Can he do that, General?'

'He just has, Gatekeeper,' said General Ovard.

twenty-eight

'Perfect!' called the Facemaster excitedly. 'Look, look, look at yourself in the mirrors!'

Chalkhill didn't have to. He *knew* he was walking like Lord Hairstreak now. Not just walking, but carrying himself like Hairstreak, making gestures like Hairstreak, even sounding like Hairstreak when he spoke. But there was a price.

His bottom was on fire, for one thing. His nose itched perpetually. His limbs were stiff and out of control, as if he were a puppet pulling its own strings.

But the worst of it was the voice in his head.

'*Strictly speaking,*' it was saying in a grating, high-pitched tone that was irritating beyond belief, '*we are no longer separate entities, but a fusion. Yes, a fusion of body and mind, some would say of spirit as well, spirit or soul, if those two are different, but here we enter into the realm of theology, don't we, since there are those – the Halek Clans, for example – who deny the spiritual dimension altogether. Thus we –*' And on and on and on interminably.

Do be quiet, be quiet, be quiet! Chalkhill screamed inside his skull. The worm had talked non-stop from the moment it was inserted. If it went on very much longer, he was going to go mad. 'Why won't this thing *shut up?*' he asked the Facemaster.

'The worm? They do that, I'm afraid. Most people get used to it eventually.'

'*Most* people?' Chalkhill echoed. 'What about the ones who don't?'

'They usually hang themselves.'

'*Which creates an interesting legal dilemma,*' said the worm in Chalkhill's mind, having clearly eavesdropped on the spoken conversation. '*Should one bring a charge of suicide or murder? There are those lawyers who hold that the symbiotic relationship creates, in effect, a new entity, in which case hanging must be deemed an act of suicide. But there are others who would argue that the two sentient entities – wangaramas wyrm and faerie – remain distinct, if interlinked, in which case the suicide of one involves the murder of the other. In Jessup v. Trentonelf, however, Lord Justice Bedstraw ruled on the possibility of collusion by the wangaramas, which raises the spectre of assisted suicide, an offence in itself which, while carrying a lesser penalty than first degree murder, will nonetheless –*'

'Can't they just have the worm removed?' asked Chalkhill, desperately ignoring the inner monologue. 'Can't *I* just have the worm removed?' He could just possibly survive until he slaughtered Pyrgus at his Coronation, but after that he wanted the worm out again within the hour.

'I'm afraid removal is a little more tricky than insertion. The procedure takes about six months.'

'Six months?' Chalkhill exploded. 'I can't have this thing rabbitting inside my head for *six months*!'

There was a small commotion at the door of the Practice Hall as a messenger in Hairstreak livery pushed arrogantly past the guards.

'*All this, of course, represents the situation from the faerie perspective,*' the worm was saying, '*but we may gain fresh insights by examining the other side of the equation, so to speak. At the recent Wangaramas Grand Convention, or WGC as it is more conveniently known, there was a fascinating debate –*'

Facemaster Wainscot contrived to look sympathetic. 'Six months is actually a conservative estimate,' he told Chalkhill. 'But the only viable alternative is surgery, which I'm afraid kills one host in three. Not something to be recommended.'

'Which one of you is Chalkhill?' asked the messenger loudly.

'He is.'

'*A simplistic question, but one which opens up what we wangarami refer to as a "can of men". What is at stake here is the necessity of defining identity, which may appear straightforward at first blush, but –*'

'I am.' What now, Chalkhill wondered. What else had Hairstreak got in store for him?

'Lord Hairstreak presents his compliments,' said the messenger stiffly, 'and begs me to inform you that he shall no longer be requiring your services in the capacity he discussed with you due to a sudden fortuitous change in circumstance. In short, the operation's off.'

Chalkhill stared at the man in horrified bewilderment.

Twenty-nine

This wasn't the palace. It had been the palace when he looked into the portal and it seemed like the palace when he threw himself through, but it wasn't the palace now. Henry was standing on a vast, level plain with really weird maroon-coloured grass growing up around his ankles. Henry kept thinking about Pyrgus, who had used one of Mr Fogarty's portal controls and ended up in Hell. Was this Hell? Henry looked around. It didn't seem hot enough, but what did he know? He'd never been in Hell before.

But he'd never been anywhere like this before either. The grass was freaky. It grew in tufts and each blade wasn't a blade at all, but a thin strand. And it was far tougher than ordinary grass. He couldn't uproot it or break it or anything. It didn't smell like grass either. If anything, it smelled like wool, which probably meant there had been sheep this way lately. Did sheep go to Hell?

The plain went on and on, but there was something wrong with the horizon. Henry found his distance vision wasn't too good – which was something else he didn't understand – but the plain didn't curve against the sky, it just sort of … stopped. Actually he wasn't sure he was looking at a horizon at all. It was almost like a sheer cliff, except *huge*. It was just about the highest cliff he'd ever seen, so high he couldn't really see the top.

The sky was weird as well. It was blue all right, but that was the only familiar thing about it. No clouds and, to be honest, it looked like a rigid dome, like those old medieval paintings of the vault of heaven. But that was probably his eyes as well. He just couldn't seem to get them to focus properly.

Which might account for the look of the trees. There were trees scattered across the plain, growing in oddly geometrical groups of four. Four here ... four there ... four over there ... Nothing in between, no undergrowth, just straight, round trunks with not a branch or leaf. He'd never seen trees grow like that before. But then he'd never seen trees that sort of ... sort of ... sort of grew together at the top to make a wooden roof before. What was wrong with his eyes? Where on earth was he? This definitely, positively, was *not* the Purple Palace.

He glanced behind him, more in vague hope than any solid expectation. The portal was no longer there. Which was really how he'd thought it would be. It had started to collapse as he jumped through. Henry's heart suddenly started to race. What would have happened if it had collapsed exactly when he was passing through it? Would it have killed him? Would it have cut him in half, leaving his head and torso bleeding in the Faerie Realm while the bottom bit kicked and writhed in Mr Fogarty's back garden?

Henry took a couple of deep breaths to pull himself together. The fact was it *hadn't* killed him. He was alive and well and in one piece with nothing to worry about.

Except he didn't have a portal control. The one he'd made was lying in another world now, probably burned out if all that sparking was anything to go by. Which was no big deal if he'd reached the Purple Palace, which had a portal of its own to get him back. But he *hadn't* reached the Purple Palace. He'd reached somewhere else with stupid-looking grass *and he had no way back*!

Don't panic, Henry told himself. There's no need to panic. All he had to do was walk until he found a village or a town. Or even a farmstead. This wasn't Hell – he was sure of that now. No heat, no demons, nobody with pitchforks. So it had to be just a peculiar area of the Faerie Realm. Once he found people, he'd just ask them to direct him to the Purple Palace. He might even cadge a lift, but if not he could walk there. Didn't matter how long it took. Well, it did – Blue would still be wondering what had happened to him – but that couldn't be helped. All he had to do was find some people. If he followed the sun he could be sure of always walking in the same direction. He wouldn't get lost. Nothing to it.

He couldn't see the sun.

He had to be able to see the sun. The vault of the sky was a cloudless blue, but there was no sun. There was light – it was like daylight – but he couldn't see the sun. This wasn't his eyes, although his eyes were still having trouble focusing – the sun simply wasn't there!

Henry pulled himself together with an effort. He didn't *need* to navigate. Since he didn't know where he was going, navigation didn't matter. He was as likely to find people in one direction as another. The thing to do was to stop wimping and get *started*.

Henry began to trudge across the open plain.

There was something on his back! The moment he moved, he could feel it. It was gripping him around the shoulder blades and flapping loosely in a truly horrible, awful, nightmarish way. Without thought he reached round and his hands gripped something ghastly and fragile and insectile and –

And ticklish.

In a moment of pure wonder, Henry discovered he'd grown wings.

Thirty

He'd got all excited about his prospects for the future, wasted hours of effort, and endured the huge indignity of having a worm inside his bottom. All for nothing! Why had Hairstreak called off the mission? Chalkhill wondered furiously.

'*I can help you there,*' the wangaramas wyrm told him.

'*Can you?*' Chalkhill thought at it. He had managed to tune out some of the incessant chatter, but the wyrm was still capable of attracting his attention when it wanted to.

'*Course I can,*' the wyrm assured him. '*All I have to do is poll the Network.*'

'*What's the Network?*' Chalkhill asked, frowning.

'*The wangarami are telepathic,*' the wyrm explained inside his head. '*Amongst ourselves, that is, not with other species, except during an actual symbiosis, of course, such as we have now. I've always believed the characteristic speaks of a certain superiority, but that is, of course, a matter of philosophical discussion among wangarami wise wyrms, so that –*'

'*What's the Network?*' Chalkhill repeated mentally to shut it up.

'*The telepathic Web. Every wangaramas is plugged*

into it. Which means that any given wyrm – myself for example – has access to the knowledge, information, belief and memory structures of every other wyrm.'

'What they know, you know?' Chalkhill ventured uncertainly.

'Potentially, yes.'

'So if any other worm happens to know why Hairstreak called off my mission, you could tune in and find out?'

'As you say,' the wangaramas wyrm confirmed. 'And I would prefer you didn't use that word.'

'What word?' Chalkhill asked aloud, forgetting again.

'"Worm",' said the wyrm. 'The correct term is "wyrm." Or better yet, "wangaramas".'

Chalkhill couldn't hear much difference between 'worm' and 'wyrm' but he thought it best to humour the creature. 'Sorry,' he said. Then to make amends added, 'What should I call you? As an individual?'

'Cyril,' said the wangaramas wyrm inside his head.

Since the messenger had delivered his message, the Facemaster had disappeared to instruct some other unfortunate and Chalkhill had taken the opportunity to make himself scarce. He was now in the grounds of the Assassins' Academy, casually strolling towards the gate. He was far from certain whether the news the messenger had brought was good or bad. If Hairstreak no longer needed him, it could mean he was free to go his own way, do what he liked so long as he kept clear of the Imperial Authorities, which would be easy enough to do if he set himself up in Yammeth Cretch. On the other hand, it could mean that Hairstreak would have him killed, in which case he had to get out of Yammeth Cretch as fast as possible. It was a difficult dilemma. What he needed was more information.

'*Would you do that for me ... Cyril?*' he asked ingratiatingly. '*Would you plug into your Network and find out what Lord Hairstreak is really up to?*'

'*Of course I would, Jasper,*' the wyrm said warmly. '*If the data is there, I shall obtain it for you.*'

Without warning, it was quiet in his head. Chalkhill experienced a wave of relief so extreme he felt quite faint. Then suddenly it was bedlam. A thousand voices, a hundred thousand voices were wittering full blast. The volume level rose until he thought his skull must burst. He felt his vision fading and sank to his knees, clutching his temples.

'Are you all right?' a voice asked from outside him somewhere, but he could not work out who it belonged to.

The inner voices stopped. In the blessed mental silence, he felt Cyril stir. '*Well, that didn't take too long,*' the wangaramas said. '*And it's good news, Jasper. Lord Hairstreak no longer needs you to kill Prince Pyrgus while he's being crowned Purple Emperor because Prince Pyrgus will never be crowned Purple Emperor. Lord Hairstreak has pulled off an early coup. Prince Pyrgus and his supporters have been exiled. The Realm is now ruled by Lord Hairstreak acting as Regent for Prince Comma. It will all be public knowledge soon.*'

For a long moment Chalkhill simply couldn't believe it. The entire Realm ruled by Hairstreak? That meant the Faeries of the Night had triumphed. It was incredible. It was wonderful. It was the opportunity of a lifetime. '*Are you sure about all this?*' he asked.

'I got it from a wyrm named Wilhelm in the bottom of one of Hairstreak's PR advisors,' Cyril assured him.

'Are you all right?' the voice from outside asked again.

Chalkhill blinked. It was a young woman, one of the Academy servants by her uniform. He smiled at her. 'Never better,' he said warmly. 'Never better.'

thirty-one

It was really peculiar. If he tried and thought about it, nothing happened. But if he didn't think about it and just *did it,* the wings moved. Not a lot, admittedly, but some. The trouble was they didn't move together. Sometimes one twitched, sometimes the other waved about a little. But there was no question of coordination, or any real strength.

As he tried to move the wings, Henry discovered he had a brand new slab of muscle. It stretched between his shoulder blades and the wings were rooted in it like a tree. He could move the muscle too, if he wriggled about a bit, but again only weakly. He stood in the middle of the maroon plain, totally absorbed. It was scary, but the wing business was still the most exciting thing that had happened to him in years.

The wings suddenly unfolded and stretched out behind him like a ... like a ... He couldn't think like a what, but he could see himself in his mind's eye as an incredible winged boy, standing statuesque and proud on the edge of unexplored terrain. It made him feel heroic and confident. But it would be a lot better if he could use the wings.

Henry twisted his head to look at them. They hung behind him, large and marvellous. They weren't the wings of a bird, more like the wings of a butterfly or moth – a rusty iron colour with some patchy, muted markings. He'd seen more spectacular butterflies, but his wings were still beautiful. Beautiful! He had wings! He was a winged boy! It was just too wonderful for words.

Henry began to run. He thought that if he ran, his wings might make him fly.

His wings stretched out behind him and he could feel the lift of air beneath them. That was really freaky. There was sensation in the wings, a straining in the new muscles between his shoulder blades while the air itself took on a squishy-pillow feeling. He thought he might lift off, but it didn't happen. He tried again, running harder. His wings vibrated and flapped uncontrollably, but nothing else.

It occurred to him that since he couldn't really move his wings, the next best thing might be to hold them rigid. He ran again, experimentally. His wings locked easily into one position and there was a slight, reassuring sense of upward pull. Maybe he was on the right track.

Near one of the quadruped trees, Henry found a small, spongy hillock. On the far side was a gentle downward slope that ended in a sheer drop of several feet. It was a perfect launching pad.

He could spread and furl his wings now, more or less to order, and while he couldn't move them otherwise, he thought this might be enough. He spread his wings, locked them open, then began to run down the slope towards the drop.

He began to feel the lift on the slope. The locked

wings tugged at him, affecting his balance and almost causing him to veer off to the right. He gritted his teeth, compensated and managed to head straight. Even before he reached the edge, he knew it was going to work.

The edge was rushing towards him faster than he would ever have believed possible. At the last possible moment, he began to doubt. This was stupid. The wings would never work. He was running down a weird hill on a weird plain in some weird world and the chances were when he went off the edge he would end up breaking his neck.

Henry ran off the edge.

And flew.

Henry soared. It was fantastic. It was as if a giant hand had pulled him upwards. It was like nothing he'd ever experienced before, not like running, not like swimming, but a magnificent, wonderful, delightful, joyous *something else*.

The strange thing, the great thing, was how natural it felt. Henry had never had much of a head for heights, but now he didn't care. It was as if he *lived* in the air, as if he'd lived in the air all his life. It felt as safe as walking.

Within seconds he discovered he was in control. He didn't quite know how, but it was happening. If he wanted to turn right, he turned right, banking like a glider with his right wing tipping downwards. He wheeled and plunged and soared and fell and soared again. It was utterly, totally and completely wonderful.

Henry flew higher and higher. He felt the wind on his face and the elation in his heart. He flew until he thought he soon must touch the sky.

His hand reached out and *really* touched the sky. The blue dome wasn't sky at all – it was ceiling. The realisation struck him like a thunderbolt. He was in a giant room. What he had thought were tree trunks were the legs of chairs. The horizon was a wall. That strange formation to the south was actually a bed. There was a dressing table, a cupboard, a wardrobe. The 'hill' he'd used as a launch pad was a crumpled garment somebody had left lying on the floor.

Not a giant room. Not a giant room at all! Henry had shrunk. It all came together now. The strange perspectives. The missing biofilter on the portal control. He had reached the palace all right – he was in somebody's bedroom – but he had undergone a transformation in the process.

He fluttered down to the dressing table and examined himself in the towering mirror. He was a fairy creature. Except for the patterns on his wings, he looked like Pyrgus had looked the first time they met. He was a fairy creature who could fly! He felt like dancing with delight.

Then he saw the spider.

Thirty-two

There were rows of Palace Guards standing in formation on the palace lawn. Pyrgus walked between them with as much dignity as he could muster. Blue was at his side. Mr Fogarty walked three ceremonial steps behind, his features set. They had all taken the short time allowed them to change into official robes, giving the whole nasty affair the feel of a State occasion.

Comma was standing by the main gates, smiling smugly. 'I don't want you to give me any trouble, dear half-brother,' he said as Pyrgus reached him. 'If you try to come back again or interfere in any way, Lord Hairstreak will insist I have you killed. I wouldn't want to, you know that, but it's only fair. We have a Realm to run and there can't be any interference. Besides, I shall be Emperor and any opposition to the Emperor's will is *treason*.' The smile left his face and was replaced by a curious, almost sympathetic expression. He dropped his voice. 'You can keep all your money, Pyrgus, and if you need any more send word and I'll give you more. If you stay away and don't make any trouble, I'll let you come to my Coronation. Lord Hairstreak won't like it, but I shall overrule him.'

'You'll pay for this, Comma!' Blue hissed. Pyrgus said nothing.

'Escort them off the island!' Comma called grandly. 'Then have them transported to the Haleklind border. When they leave the Realm they must not return except on my invitation.' He tilted his head back and struck a pose, then added, 'In writing. And stamped with the Imperial Seal.'

'Where's Lord Hairstreak, Comma?' Mr Fogarty asked in a conversational tone. He managed to sound as if he was going for an afternoon's stroll.

'It's *Prince* Comma, Gatekeeper,' Comma told him crossly. 'And you aren't Gatekeeper any more. I've fired you. I'm going to appoint another Gatekeeper, a Faerie of the Night. Lord Hairstreak says that's more ecumenical.'

'I'm sorry, *Prince* Comma,' Mr Fogarty said mildly. 'I was just wondering where Lord Hairstreak was. After all, he's Regent now.'

'You'd best be glad Lord Hairstreak isn't here,' Comma said, 'otherwise you'd be in jail instead of leaving for a nice comfortable exile. But he's coming soon, once he finishes off some business or something. He'll be living in the palace from now on. With Father.'

'That's what I thought,' said Mr Fogarty.

'Well, you'd better hurry and get out before he does come, and get away while you still can.' Comma moved to one side and the escort fell in behind Pyrgus and his little party.

As Pyrgus stepped through the gate, he allowed himself a backward glance. He wasn't certain, but he thought he saw his father standing at an upper window of the palace.

* * *

'I'm going to kill him!' Blue hissed the moment they were all alone.

'He's only a child,' Mr Fogarty said unexpectedly. 'He thinks being Emperor will make him something special.'

'I'm worried Lord Hairstreak may kill him when he comes of age,' Pyrgus said, echoing an earlier thought. 'Hairstreak will never give up power once he becomes Regent.'

'He's already become Regent,' Blue said sourly. 'He's already put everything in place ready for the official announcement.'

Pyrgus shrugged. 'You know what I mean.'

They were seated together in one of the palace ouklos, an enormous golden carriage with plush purple seating. It floated at a stately pace that ate up miles with a deceptive speed. Through the window they could see the uniformed outriders on their individual floater pods – fiercely helmeted and armed men whose duty it was to ensure they left the Realm.

'This Haleklind,' Fogarty said. 'Have either of you ever been there?'

Pyrgus was staring out the window. 'I have. I lived there for a bit.'

'What's it like?'

'Hilly. Rocky. Barren. Quite primitive, really. There are parts of it where people still live in caves. But our father had excellent relations with the ruling House, so we should be given somewhere comfortable to stay.'

'We're not staying,' Blue said.

'No,' Pyrgus said. 'No, of course not.' His mind seemed on other things.

'Who is the ruling House?' Fogarty asked.

'Of the Halek? House Halek. There is only one House, really.'

'Would they help us take back the Realm?'

'I doubt it,' Pyrgus said. 'But even if they did, they'd be no match for the Imperial Army.'

'It's a backwater,' Blue put in. 'That's why Daddy never bothered bringing it into the Realm – not worth the trouble.'

'Why did you live there, Pyrgus?' Mr Fogarty asked.

'I wanted to get a Halek blade,' Pyrgus said a little sheepishly.

'It's a knife that always kills,' Blue explained to Mr Fogarty, with an expression on her face that suggested she had no time for knives that always killed.

'Couldn't you just buy one?'

Pyrgus said, 'Didn't have enough money. Besides, a Halek blade takes time to make. And you're dealing with Halek wizards. They're the best in the world, but they're tricky and they won't hurry for anybody.'

Mr Fogarty glanced at Blue. 'Could *they* help with our predicament?'

'The wizards?' Blue said. 'They might. Pyrgus is right – they have extremely powerful magical techniques. But we'd have to come up with a plan.'

Fogarty nodded, then sank back in his seat and closed his eyes.

thirty-three

'Gone?' roared Lord Hairstreak. He was dressed head to toe in black velvet and looked like an apoplectic imp. Comma had insisted on their meeting in the throne room, apparently because he wanted to sit on the throne.

'Into exile,' Comma said, emphasising the second word slightly, as if to stress its importance, or possibly just to show he knew what it meant. He had changed into State robes, several sizes too large for him, in imperial purple. From his high vantage point on the Peacock Throne he chose to study the backs of his hands casually.

'I told you to have them imprisoned,' Hairstreak snapped. 'Actually I told you to have them *executed*!'

'I decided to send them into exile instead,' Comma said, then added petulantly, 'Nobody tells the *Purple Emperor* what to do.'

The child was a nightmare and always had been, just like his mother. Hairstreak said bluntly, 'You're not Purple Emperor yet. And until you are, you'll do well to remember that your *Regent* holds the reins.'

Comma glared at him sulkily. 'Well, it's done now.'

'Where have you sent them?'

For a second Comma looked as if he wasn't going to

tell, then he muttered, 'Haleklind.'

Hairstreak swore under his breath. It was one of the few countries that had resisted infiltration by his agents. Particularly galling in such an ignorant backwater. Most of the inhabitants were scarcely down from the trees. But their wizards were something else. Would it be possible to mount a raid? The price was bound to be enormous – Halek magic was weapons magic and the wizards could decimate an army if they dug in … one reason why their country had been left so long alone. Better to try to stop Pyrgus and his sister before they reached the border. Or arrange an assassination if that didn't work.

'When did they leave?' he asked sharply.

'A little while before you came,' Comma told him vaguely.

'How are they travelling?'

'By ouklo. By *imperial* ouklo – they're still members of the royal family, you know,' Comma said.

It could have been worse. Ouklos were not exactly fast and it was probably a day's, two days' journey to Haleklind under the best conditions. There was still time to do something. 'Which route did they take?'

'I'm sure I don't know,' Comma said airily. 'I leave those sort of arrangements to my *minions*.'

Hairstreak fought hard to replace his fury with an icy calm. It would be simple enough to find out what route had been taken. Even Comma wasn't stupid enough to send them off without an escort. Once he knew the road, he could dispatch a party of his best men. The guards would not be expecting an attack – why should they? Pyrgus would be dead before they had time to react. So would anybody else travelling with him.

Hairstreak narrowed his eyes. 'It is foolish for your future to allow your half-brother and half-sister to live,' he said firmly. 'But you may safely leave that to me. Meanwhile, Comma, let me tell you this. If you ever, *ever*, countermand an order of mine again, I shall see that you regret it deeply. You seem to forget I have the full authority of your sainted father.'

The change in Comma was astonishing, but not the change Hairstreak had expected. The boy swung round, eyes blazing. 'That thing you call my father is an empty shell that only walks because of your black magic! You think I'm a fool? Better think again, *dear uncle*!'

Hairstreak turned and stamped out of the throne room. There was no time to lose in mounting the pursuit of Pyrgus and Blue.

He could deal with Comma later.

Thirty-four

Henry found he was thinking two things at once. One was that he knew this room. He'd been here before – it was Blue's bedroom in the palace. The other was, *Yeoooow!* He was afraid of spiders even when they were smaller than his thumb. This spider stood taller than his head.

He recognised it as well. It was the thing Blue kept in her jewel box, some sort of pet. But pet or not, it was a monster that could eat him now he'd shrunk.

Except for one thing, of course. He could fly and the spider couldn't.

Henry turned to launch himself off the edge of the dressing table and found he couldn't move a muscle.

It was the most horrible sensation he'd experienced in his entire life. It was as if something had wrapped filaments around his mind, binding him so tightly he could scarcely think. His whole body felt chill and life-less, like meat. Henry froze on the edge of the dressing table and watched with terror as the spider crawled towards him.

Its eyes were huge, featureless ovoids, black as the depths of Space, liquid and hideously wise. They stared at Henry without emotion.

The creature moved with great deliberation, legs

lifting high, feet placed carefully, almost delicately, as if feeling out the high-grained wooden surface. There was a soft, gentle *click* with each contact and Henry noticed for the first time the spider had claws.

There was a jerk in time, like missing frames in an old movie reel, and suddenly the spider was no more than a yard away from him. The smell was overpowering now, alien and rank. He could hear a tiny hissing, crackling sound like bacon frying.

The spider reached out with one foreleg, as if gently probing. Henry fought his paralysis like a mad thing, but still failed to move. The claw at the end of the leg was embedded in a tuft of yellow fur. It was curved as a sabre is curved, but little longer than a dagger and, like the eyes, completely black. The surface had the polish of horn. It moved with great deliberation towards his eye.

Suddenly the spider slashed him.

The claw missed his eye, but ripped a gash in his cheek, opening it to the bone beneath. Amazingly there was no pain, but blood spurted like a fountain, spattering both eyes and blinding him. At the same time his paralysis broke. Henry jerked backwards in a reflex action, stepped into space and found himself falling. Desperately he knuckled his eyes. Sight returned slowly through a red, stinging haze that cleared as he blinked. He was dropping like a stone. The floor beneath rushed up to meet him.

Henry found his wings again and flew.

His heart was pounding, his whole body trembling, his mind frozen in the shock of his experience. There was a sticky warmth across his cheek, which was beginning to hurt now – a deep, hot throb that spread to take over almost the whole of his face. Yet the wings took him and held him, as if of their own accord. He rose easily and safely until, high above the dressing table and its nightmare, he was able to hover far from danger while his breathing slowed and calm gradually returned.

The spider was drinking his blood.

Henry fluttered down a little closer to make sure, but there was no mistake. Blood from the wound on his cheek had pooled on the surface of the dressing table and the spider was bending to it now, extruding a fleshy tube with which to feed.

For a moment he simply watched, his thoughts tumbling in confusion. Something began scratching at the edges of his mind, like a dog at a door. The sensation was so sinister Henry froze again and it was only when he began to drop directly down towards the spider that he remembered to use his wings. In his anxiety to get away, he found himself fluttering in circles like a wounded moth. But he couldn't get away – the scratching thing was inside his head.

Henry almost lost it then. He wanted to scream and scream and flail about and curl up into a ball and hide and never, never come back out again so long as there were things like –

The spider stopped. It hung there, at the edge of his mind, alert but cautious. Below him, the spider suddenly looked up and watched him with its huge, black eyes. Two spiders, but the same spider. The creature below was just a thought away. The creature below … A stupid, stupid, stupid idea occurred to Henry. The creature below just wanted to make friends.

The thing had ripped his face apart and drunk his

blood! It was about as friendly as a viper!

All the same, he turned his mind towards it and watched carefully. It stayed quite still, waiting. *I have to be mad,* Henry thought. *I have to be nuts even thinking I should do this.* The spider waited. Henry hovered and the spider waited. Henry couldn't stop thinking the spider only wanted to make friends.

The thing below him trilled with pleasure.

He could stroke it like a kitten. If he wanted to, he could just reach out and stroke it. It was crazy, but he could. The spider below was the ugliest thing he'd ever seen, but the spider as it hung at the edge of his mind was somehow ... different. It looked the same to his mind's eye, but ...

The spider moved deeper into his mind. He was reminded irresistibly of a puppy wriggling forward on its stomach, wanting to be stroked and petted, but still a little frightened.

This monster was no puppy. This was the most dangerous, terrible –

Henry reached out with his mind and stroked the spider.

thirty-five

Mr Fogarty opened his eyes. He had a premonition something was wrong seconds before it happened. But when it happened, he didn't realise just at first that it was happening.

Through the window of the ouklo he could see one of the outriders – a big, burly man with a habit of pulling close to the carriage and staring in, as if to make sure Prince Pyrgus and his little party were still inside. He was doing that now, and as he caught Mr Fogarty's eye, he gave a broad, unpleasant smile.

Then he disappeared. One second he was there astride his floater pod, the next he was gone. Fogarty moved in his seat. The riderless pod was still there, pacing the ouklo perhaps four feet above the ground. Then, devoid of any hand at the controls, it veered away wildly, following an erratic course. There were shouts, barked orders and a single scream.

'We're under attack,' Fogarty said quietly.

Pyrgus, who had been deep in conversation with Blue, broke off and stood up. He grasped the window of the ouklo as if to open it.

'Pyrgus!' Blue shouted in warning.

'Might be an idea to keep away from the window,' Fogarty said.

But the window was open now and Pyrgus had his head out. There was another scream and another pod overtook the carriage, tumbling fore over aft, with no sign of its rider. 'You're right,' Pyrgus said. He pulled his head back like a turtle. 'Any ideas?'

'You can start by closing the window,' Fogarty said drily. 'Are either of you armed?'

'Ceremonial dagger,' Pyrgus murmured, pushing the window back up.

'I have a steen,' Blue said a little sheepishly.

Mr Fogarty glanced at her admiringly. 'That's what I call firepower. Surprised you didn't use it on Prince Comma.'

Blue grinned at him.

Mr Fogarty said, 'Any idea who might be behind the attack?'

'Hairstreak?' Pyrgus ventured.

'That would be my guess. You know him better than I do – what's his style?'

'Stealth. Surprise. Likes to outnumber the enemy, but will rely more on speed than weight of numbers.'

'It's him all right,' Fogarty said, looking past Pyrgus through the window. 'They're using unmarked foo discs. Think he wants to kill us?'

'Yes,' Blue said simply.

'Then we'd better try to disappoint him. Did you notice how many were flying this carriage?'

'Just a footman,' Pyrgus said. 'The spell's set to take us direct to Haleklind – it's a known route. Not much for the driver to do but admire the scenery. The out-riders are there to make sure we don't jump out.'

'The outriders look pretty busy to me – those that are left,' Mr Fogarty said. 'Think you can tackle the footman? Do it myself except I'm getting a bit old to climb out of moving carriages.'

Pyrgus nodded.

'I think we'll hold back on the steen,' Mr Fogarty said to Blue, smiling a little. She grinned at him again. Used inside the carriage, a steen would have killed them all. Even used above on the coachman, it could have caused them considerable damage.

Pyrgus said, 'We won't outrun them even if we get control. Not in an ouklo.'

'Send it over open water,' Fogarty said shortly. 'Foo discs can't handle open water. Isn't there a lake around here somewhere?'

'Think so,' Pyrgus nodded. He glanced round at the sound of a loud crash outside.

'Use the window,' Fogarty said. Then, as Pyrgus moved, 'The other one – too much action that side.'

Pyrgus moved fast. He pulled down the window and swung out in a single movement.

'Good luck,' Blue whispered.

It was a war zone outside. A huge fight was going on between the ouklo escort and a band of green-uniformed attackers. The air was full of elf-bolts, humming like enraged bees. Pyrgus flattened himself against the side of the ouklo, then pulled himself up on to the roof, keeping his head low.

The driving cabin of the ouklo was an ornate affair set near the front of the carriage. It was high-backed with ceremonial wings so that the driver had no chance of spotting Pyrgus as he crawled along the roof behind him. But at the same time, both back and wings were reinforced with adamantine silver so the man was safe from any attack except a frontal assault. To reach him,

Pyrgus would have to climb over the top of the cabin, then drop down. He didn't want to kill the man – he was a palace servant, after all, and only doing his duty – so he would have to wrestle him out of the control seat and, hopefully, push him off the carriage altogether. None of it was going to be easy.

An elf-bolt shaved skin off his earlobe.

Pyrgus moved. The less time he spent exposed like this, the safer he would be. Bent double, he ran along the roof of the carriage and scrambled on top of the cabin. To his right he could see a pod rider locked in a vicious, hacking swordfight with one of the green attackers on a foo disc. They swung close to the ouklo itself, which reacted by jerking away from the weapons as its security system cut in. Pyrgus was half thrown from the cabin, but managed to grip the roof felt with his fingernails. For a moment he was convinced he was going to fall, but somehow pulled himself back. In a moment more, he was dropping down at the front of the cabin, ready to grab the driver.

The driver was dead. He sat in the control seat, eyes wide and staring, a trickle of blood dribbling from the left side of his mouth. There was no obvious wound, but the expression on his face was one of intense surprise.

For a moment Pyrgus couldn't quite take it in, but the man was dead all right. There was nothing Pyrgus could do for him now and he had to get the ouklo away from the fight. He grabbed the man's arms and tried to pull the body from its seat. The head seemed to be stuck to the back of the chair.

It was an elf-bolt! It had penetrated the back of the cabin and skewered the driver from behind. But it was impossible for an elf-bolt – or anything else for that matter – to penetrate adamantine silver. The material was spell-woven to resist attack in any form. Pyrgus jerked the body and the head came away, tearing the elf-bolt with it. Pyrgus muttered an apology, then pushed the corpse off the ouklo and slammed himself into the driver's seat.

There were no controls. The ouklo responded to spoken commands from anyone in the driving seat so long as he first gave the password. Fortunately the password for all ceremonial ouklos was the same and Pyrgus knew it – it was the name of his paternal grandfather, a beloved Emperor now long dead. 'Dispar,' he murmured, then, 'Turn right!'

The ouklo maintained its course as if he hadn't spoken.

'Dispar!' Pyrgus said again, then swore quietly. Comma had changed the password! Of course he had, the sneaky little twit. This ouklo was headed for Haleklind by the shortest route and nothing in the Realm was going to stop it. What now? What to do now?

There was a brakeword for the ouklo. He was sure of it. It didn't give you control of the vehicle, but it stopped you in an emergency. And it was built into the fabric of the carriage, so it couldn't be changed. He glanced round the edge of the cabin and a thrown knife missed him by inches. Fierce fighting was still underway. If he stopped the carriage now, two things would happen. The first was that both pods and foo discs would sweep past as they continued their aerial battle. The second was that Blue, Mr Fogarty and he could make a break for it on foot. They were passing through wild terrain with plenty of hiding places. In the confusion there was a chance – maybe even a good chance – they might get away.

What was the brakeword? He couldn't remember the brakeword!

There was a scraping sound behind him. Pyrgus looked round the edge of the cabin again to discover that one of Hairstreak's green-uniformed men had jumped from his foo disc and clambered on to the roof of the ouklo. He was on his feet now and making his way carefully towards Pyrgus.

If Pyrgus was reluctant to harm palace staff, he had no such reservations about Hairstreak's men. He grabbed the dagger from his belt, clambered out of the cabin and threw himself on his attacker.

His attacker was a girl!

Pyrgus was so surprised he almost dropped the dagger. The green-uniformed soldier was a slender girl and a pretty one at that. He hadn't known Hairstreak used girls in his military. He had gripped her jerkin and his dagger was raised to strike, but she had beautiful violet eyes. He was still admiring them when she kneed him between the legs.

The pain was unbelievable. Pyrgus felt the dagger slipping from his nerveless hands and knew he had to hold it, had to hold his attacker, knew he was dead if he didn't somehow dispatch this soldier and dispatch her fast. He knew what he had to do, but what he did do was drop the dagger and fold forward with a howl of agony.

The girl pressed a neat little weapon wand behind his left ear and Pyrgus tumbled into darkness.

thirty-six

Henry fell into light.

It was an incredible sensation. As he touched the spider with his mind it scuttled forward and embraced him. That should have been terrifying, but somehow wasn't, partly because everything happened so suddenly. The effect was almost indescribable. A window opened and pure, dazzling light flooded through to swallow him.

Henry gasped as his perceptions expanded. He was aware of his physical body fluttering down to land beside the physical spider, but he knew now he was in no danger. As his body slumped, his mind enlarged. He was aware of the whole of Blue's bedroom, then the suite of rooms that composed her quarters, then the corridors outside and the whole upper storey of the palace, then the entire palace.

But it didn't end there. His perceptions continued to expand to take in the river island where the palace stood, then the river, then, incredibly, the city beyond. It was so weird, so cool. He saw busy thoroughfares. He saw a dimly-lit simbala parlour and tasted the music writhing in it. He saw a strolling player strumming on a lute. He saw an alleycat chewing on a mouse.

Henry continued to expand and the sensation was pure ecstasy. Tendrils of his mind reached out to every corner of the Realm. He felt the pulsing heart of reality itself and saw the filaments that joined all things. He wanted to expand until he ate up the whole world and worlds beyond. He thought he might reach out and take in the entire universe. It occurred to him that he was God.

It occurred to him he could find Blue.

The thought halted his expansion, gave him focus. He saw Blue at once, but in a strange way. He saw the winding pathway of her life, moving through Space and Time, visiting differing locations of her Realm and once, disturbingly, penetrating the very fabric of reality as she disappeared from the Realm altogether. But she returned again, close to the point of exit, and continued as before.

Where was she now? It was difficult to see, yet the very question helped him. It was as if he stepped out of his body and stepped into a forest glade. Blue was there, and Pyrgus too, and, a little beyond them both, Mr Fogarty in dirty, crumpled formal robes. All three were lying on the forest floor.

All three seemed to be dead.

'Blue!!' Henry shouted in sudden agony. He lost focus, then control. His mind expanded to infinity and his consciousness exploded.

Henry felt as if somebody had put his head through a mincer, then followed up by crushing his whole body in a vice. Every limb ached and he felt weak as a lamb. Movement seemed impossible. Even opening his eyes was an effort and the lids scratched his eyeballs like coarse sandpaper.

He was lying on a floor somewhere, curled into a foetal position, both hands between his knees.

He was not sure who he was.

Or where.

The inside of his mouth tasted like a sewer and his tongue seemed swollen to twice its normal size. There was a distant ringing in his ears.

He moved cautiously. The aches throughout his body peaked, then died a little. He'd had the feeling before when he got a leg cramp playing football. But now the cramps were in every muscle. All the same, they might be bearable. He moved again and this time the pain didn't peak as high. Gradually he straightened out and clambered slowly to his feet.

There was something wrong with the room. He tried to figure what it was, but his head wouldn't function right.

He felt dizzy and reached out for a nearby chair.

That's what it was! Blue's room was its normal size. *He* was his normal size. And there was something wrong with his back. It felt ... it felt ... this was stupid, but it felt sort of *empty*.

His wings were gone!

As he stood there, unsteadily holding the chair, it occurred to him that this was what had happened to Pyrgus. When the House Iris portal had been sabotaged and Pyrgus had become a tiny fairy figure with butterfly wings, the effect had worn off completely and his wings had disappeared. But it had only happened after several days. Had Henry been unconscious that long? His heart dropped to his boots. How was he going to explain all this to Blue? How could he explain losing his portal control and turning up so late? The emergency was probably over by now and he'd done nothing at all to help. It was mortifying.

What was it she'd said? Her father's body had disappeared and there was some plot to assassinate Pyrgus? A horrid thought struck him. What if the plot had succeeded? What if Pyrgus was dead now? Henry would never forgive himself and he didn't think Blue would either.

He was feeling stronger by the minute, but as his brain began to focus he was certainly not feeling any better. Suddenly, out of nowhere, came a mental picture of Pyrgus, Blue and Mr Fogarty lying dead on a forest floor. He'd seen that. He knew he'd seen that. But where?

He tried to tell himself the whole thing was no more important than a dream. For heaven's sake, it probably just *was* a dream! Except he didn't believe that, not for a minute. He had to find out what had happened to Pyrgus and Blue. He had to find out this minute!

Henry began to stumble from the room. As he reached the door he realised there was someone watching him.

Thirty-seven

It was pleasant to be free again. Not just free from prison, although that was a definite bonus, but free from responsibilities. With any amount of luck, Hairstreak would forget about him now – heaven knew the little turd would have enough on his plate just running the Realm. Chalkhill scratched his ear. It might be useful to change his name as a precautionary measure, perhaps adopt something heroic like Lime Hawk, but that apart he could go where he wished, do what he wanted. He'd sell the estate, of course, use the cash to make a new start, possibly look up his old partner Brimstone – dreadful creature, but one had to admit he had a talent for business. The world, as the old saying went, was his chrysalis.

But first he had to get rid of the worm.

The brass plaque said simply *Dr Vapourer* and was as discreet as everything else about the clinic. Chalkhill had used the place before to rid himself of that embarrassing little problem he'd picked up at the tattoo parlour. Expensive, but circumspect and extremely skilful in certain areas. He was fairly sure they could have the creature removed – and painlessly – in a fraction of the time mentioned by the Facemaster.

He reached out to ring the bell and the worm froze

his arm.

'What do you think you're doing?' Chalkhill asked crossly. He was actually more than a little taken aback – he hadn't realised how much control the worm had over his body. But perhaps it was temporary, or perhaps with an effort he could overcome the vermicular influence. Cautiously he tried to move the arm again, but it remained frozen.

'*You don't want to do that,*' the worm said crisply inside his mind.

'*Don't I?*'

'*No, you don't,*' the worm insisted. '*Not until you've heard what I have to say.*'

Chalkhill groaned silently. The creature was about to embark on one of its interminable philosophical debates, he was sure of it. '*Cyril,*' he said patiently, '*it has been a pleasure to make your acquaintance, but the time has come for us to go our separate ways.*' An elderly couple passing in the street glanced at him strangely, but Chalkhill ignored them. '*I'm sure you appreciate –*'

'*I've been instructed to recruit you,*' Cyril interrupted him.

Chalkhill blinked. '*Recruit me?*'

'*You're an intelligent man,*' the worm said smoothly. '*I'm sure it won't have escaped your notice that the Realm is in a mess. Faeries at each other's throats over nothing more substantial than the shape of their eyes or the nature of their beliefs. One Emperor assassinated, the next replaced before he can be even crowned. The constant threat of war. The failing economy. Greed and hedonism everywhere. Complete failure of old family values. The entire Empire would be going to* hell in a handcart if the portals weren't closed.'

'Well, clearly things aren't perfect,' Chalkhill agreed, wishing the worm would release his arm. It was beginning to ache quite badly. 'But they're no worse than they've ever been and there's not a lot that anyone can do about it, so if you'd just let go of my ar—'

'There is something we can do about it,' Cyril said earnestly. 'Specifically, there's something you can do about it. I'm inviting you to join the Wangaramas Revolution.'

Chalkhill suddenly found his arm was free. He flexed the fingers to relieve the ache, then slowly withdrew it from the bell. 'What's the Wangaramas Revolution?'

Thirty-eight

Pyrgus climbed sluggishly out of a deep, black pit to find himself watched by the most beautiful pair of violet eyes he'd ever seen. The girl, he thought, was absolutely gorgeous. His heart was racing and his body trembled uncontrollably. He wondered in passing if he might be in love, but decided it was far more likely he was dying. His head felt as if there were bits missing inside, like a cheese with holes in it. His eyes kept slipping out of focus and recurring bouts of nausea threatened to make him throw up.

The girl must have noticed his eyes were open because she leaned forward and said quietly, 'I'm sorry, but I was worried you might use that dagger. It was only a stun wand.'

He allowed his eyes to roam around without moving his head and discovered he was surrounded by trees. He seemed to be lying on a bed of pine needles in some forest clearing. There were green-uniformed figures swimming out of focus beyond the beautiful girl. For a moment he was too fuzzy to figure out what had happened, then it hit him like an avalanche – he'd been captured by Hairstreak's forces!

Pyrgus closed his eyes again and concentrated on pulling himself together. He wondered if Blue and Mr

Fogarty were still alive, but there was nothing he could do about them for the moment. He was weak as a kitten, but he noticed his arms were free, which was a huge mistake on Hairstreak's part – the man must have thought he was dead. He gave a theatrical groan. If they believed him to be more badly hurt than he actually was, he might be able to take them by surprise when his strength returned.

Could he attack such a beautiful girl? Pyrgus thought about it for a moment, then decided he could. If it was to save Blue and Mr Fogarty he definitely could. What was the girl doing working for Hairstreak anyway? He opened his eyes a slit to find she was still bent over him, a look of concern on her sweet, delicious features. Pyrgus groaned again and this time it was more heartfelt. Of all the luck to meet the first girl he really fancied and find she was working for the most dangerous –

'I think he's coming round,' the girl said. She had a cool, clear voice, like temple bells.

Maybe he'd overdone the groaning – he didn't want to attract too much attention yet. Maybe he could pretend to faint. Maybe –

There was something wrong with the girl's violet eyes. He couldn't quite work out what it was, but something wasn't as it should be ...

He could see other figures gathering around him. One was cloaked and hooded all in black and he knew from the man's size it had to be Lord Hairstreak. The hooded man leaned over him and suddenly Pyrgus realised he was being presented with the opportunity of a lifetime. If he could just make his body obey his will, he could have Hairstreak by the throat in seconds.

With any luck at all he could strangle him, or break his neck before his troops could intervene. It was perfect. It was better than perfect – Hairstreak had committed an unlawful act by attacking Pyrgus and his party when they'd been ordered into exile by the Emperor Elect. If Hairstreak died at Pyrgus's hand, there wouldn't even be serious political repercussions.

But would his body obey him?

Pyrgus gathered his reserves. A part of his mind was vaguely aware that this could well be a suicide action. Even if he managed to kill Hairstreak his chances of getting away were slim. Hairstreak's men would cut him down in an instant. At the same time, if he *did* get away – chance in a thousand though it might be – he would have changed the whole balance of power in the Realm.

The thought galvanised him. Pyrgus exploded into action. He jackknifed upwards, lips drawn back in an unconscious snarl. His hands caught Black Hairstreak by the throat. Hairstreak jerked and his hood fell back.

'My deeah, where are your *manners*!' a shocked voice gasped.

'Oh my God!' Pyrgus exclaimed. 'I'm so sorry, Madame Cardui.'

Thirty-nine

The woman was slim and very dark, and Henry could see she was quite good-looking, except for her eyes which had very funny pupils. She was seated in a chair to one side of the door and there was a patient stillness about her that was positively creepy. She must have been sitting there the whole time, watching him while he was unconscious, watching him as he came to, watching him as he stood up and swayed and tried to keep his balance. She was watching him now, her eyes like sloes, and he was irresistibly reminded of a snake watching a bird.

Then she smiled and the whole sinister quality disappeared. Her face lit up with a delight he could almost taste. 'You must be one of Blue's young friends,' she said.

'Is she all right?' Henry asked at once.

'She should be safe in Haleklind by now,' the woman told him dreamily. 'You must be a very *close* friend for me to find you in her room.'

Henry flushed crimson. 'I'm really a friend of Pyrgus,' he said quickly. Which was true. He wondered if he should try to explain about the portal and the missing filter and the spider, but decided against it. Better to keep things simple. 'I, ah, I wanted to go to *his* room and I got ... lost.' Which was nearly true and sort of true and not actually a lie.

'Why don't I take you to Pyrgus's room?' the woman said. 'It's just a little way away, not far. Not far at all.' She stood and waited, watching him.

'Yes. Thank you. Yes, that would be ... good.' He was trying to figure out who the woman was. She might be a maid or a Lady-in-Waiting – Blue had lots of servants, he knew – but the way she was dressed she didn't look much like a maid, or a Lady-in-Waiting for that matter. Her gown looked like silk, probably awfully expensive, and it was purple coloured. He wasn't absolutely sure, but he thought purple was reserved for members of the royal family. On inspiration he said, 'I don't think we've met. I'm Henry Atherton.' He stuck out his hand and waited.

'I am Quercusia,' the woman said. She took him by the hand and began to lead him gently from the room. 'Queen of the Faerie.'

Henry hadn't known there *was* a Queen of the Faerie. And even now he couldn't make her fit. Pyrgus and Blue's mother was dead, he knew that, so she couldn't be the wife of the old Emperor, and she certainly wasn't old enough to be his mother. So where did this woman fit in? Perhaps she was an aunt, who ruled over some *part* of the kingdom. Or perhaps it was some sort of honorary title that had nothing to do with anything very much.

He felt silly being led by the hand.

Quercusia's own hand was small and slim and very, very cool. In fact it was quite cold, as if she'd come in from a snowstorm.

They passed beneath an archway where two glum guards snapped smartly to attention and saluted Quercusia. Wherever the title came from, she was familiar in the palace. Henry glanced back at the guards and caught a strange expression on their faces. If he hadn't known better, he'd have sworn it was fear.

Pyrgus now used the quarters that had been occupied by his father before the murder. They were guarded as well, but while the men on duty saluted just as smartly, their faces were expressionless. Quercusia pushed through the door and led him inside. Henry looked around for Pyrgus, but there was no sign of him.

Henry extracted his hand and walked over to the mantle where he pretended to examine the ornaments. There was a small, framed miniature of a bee, so cleverly done he could have sworn it was tattooed on human skin. He was glad to have moved away from Quercusia. For some reason she made him feel uneasy.

He looked around and found her smiling benignly at him.

'Do you think he'll be long?' Henry asked.

'Who?'

'Pyrgus.'

'Pyrgus isn't here.'

'He isn't?'

'Of course not.'

Henry blinked. 'Then why did you bring me here?'

Quercusia looked up and studied a corner of the chamber near the ceiling. 'You said you wanted to go to his room.'

Henry's unease increased. He frowned, then gave a small nervous smile. 'Actually, what I meant was I wanted to see Pyrgus. I'm sorry.'

The sloe-black eyes were back on him again. 'You can't do that. Pyrgus is in exile.' A look of pride crossed her features. 'My son is the Emperor now.' She blinked several times like someone waking from a deep sleep. Her face was suddenly very sober. 'I think I'll have you put in jail. You're such a *horrid* boy.'

Henry felt a sudden chill. He swallowed and began to edge towards the door. 'Your Majesty –' he said to humour her.

She rang no bell nor made no sign he was aware of, yet suddenly the room was full of burly men.

'Lock him in the dungeons!' Quercusia screamed. Her eyes were wide and flecks of spittle rimmed her lips. 'Lock him in the dungeons *and throw away the key!*'

forty

Since the ouklo had clapped out completely and refused to leave the graveyard, the Brimstones left for their honeymoon in a two-seater skim. It was an uncomfortable, ill-sprung craft, but cheap and surprisingly fast in open country – or so the man from the hiring company assured them. For Brimstone, the main problem was its size. There was no room to get away from Madame Brimstone, who clung to his arm and made satisfied trilling noises as he stared stonily straight ahead through the open window.

The skim's built-in navigation system had been created for the city and handled the winding streets of Cheapside with ease. It even managed to negotiate Westgate, a notoriously difficult area for precision magic on account of the quartz content in the local bedrock. But once it left the urban confines, it ground to a halt and hung there, awaiting further instructions.

'The lodge coordinates, Dearest Heart?' said Brimstone, forcing a smile.

Madame Brimstone smiled back. '80-42,' she murmured.

'Really?' Brimstone said. 'As deep in as that?' He leaned forward and repeated the numbers to the dashboard of the skim, which absorbed them for a moment, then moved off in a north-westerly direction towards the woodlands. Brimstone leaned back and admired the scenery while trying to ignore the pressure of Madame Brimstone's hand on his knee.

They reached the lodge in something under ninety minutes. Brimstone felt a little better when they emerged in the clearing. He'd expected a log cabin, probably comfortable enough, but small. Instead he was facing an opulent house, wood-built to be sure, but architect-designed and spacious. A lot of money had been spent here and, without the need for illusion spells in so secluded a spot, it all showed.

'Do you like my little place?' asked Madame Brimstone as she climbed down from the skim.

Brimstone didn't answer. He was too busy calculating how much the building would be worth after he'd paid off the death duties on his late lamented wife.

Despite a display cabinet full of elemental servants in pristine brass bottles, Madame Brimstone insisted on cooking supper personally. Brimstone was suspicious at once. It hadn't occurred to him that she might try to poison him on their wedding night – the usual thing was to wait a few weeks so it wouldn't seem too obvious – but he didn't like the look of this at all.

Minutes after she disappeared into the kitchen, he strolled innocently after her in the hope of catching her out, but she shooed him away at once.

'Not a man's place,' she cackled. 'Not *my* man's place, to be sure. You take yourself off and read an edifying book. There's a copy of *The Knicker Ripper* in the living room. You just leave it to me to serve up something delicious. No more bone gruel, Silas – no more bone gruel!'

Brimstone went out again reluctantly. He wasn't quite ready to kill her yet – she had a brother so he'd have to make it look like an accident and that required a little planning – which meant he was going to have to risk the meal. Fortunately, really subtle poisons were expensive, so she probably wouldn't use them, the miserly old hag. With luck and good judgement he could probably spot the cheap ones she was likely to buy. The trick would be to avoid them without making her suspicious.

He found the book and pretended to read. After a while, Madame Brimstone stuck her head around the door. 'All ready,' she trilled. 'I've laid us places in the dining room.'

He walked through to the dining room and found that not only were places laid, but the appetiser was already on the table.

'Sit. Sit,' said Madame Brimstone eagerly. She was looking at him strangely, with a glint of anticipation in her eye.

Brimstone sat down and stared at his appetiser. It was some sort of grey, jelly-like substance flecked with curdled bits of white flesh. The old bat might be making an effort, but this dish hadn't turned out much better than her bone gruel. It looked as if a cat had been sick on a lettuce leaf.

'What is it?' he asked.

'Fish mousse,' said Madame Brimstone, sitting down. 'I leave the skins on for economy.'

It might make him ill, but would it poison him? Brimstone glanced across at her plate. 'You've only given yourself a small helping,' he said.

'Woman's helping, woman's place,' said Madame Brimstone, quoting an old faerie proverb.

'But my dear, we can't have that!' said Brimstone heartily. 'You cooked the meal. You deserve the larger portion.' He forced his features to contort into something she might take for a smile.

Still smiling, he switched his plate for hers. Let's see if she eats it now, he thought.

Madame Brimstone stared down at the plate. Was it a look of dismay? Did she realise she'd been hoisted with her own petard? But then she looked up to give him a dazzling smile. 'Why, thank you, Silas. How very thoughtful of you.' She picked up her fork and began to shovel fish mousse into her mouth.

Brimstone followed suit. To his surprise, it tasted good.

The second course was roast pork and, despite himself, he found his mouth watering as she carried the joint to the table. It was done exactly as he liked it, with crispy crackling, stuffing, and a boat of aromatic gravy.

Madame Brimstone was suddenly holding a vicious-looking knife. 'How would you like it?' she asked menacingly.

Brimstone half-started from his seat, then realised she meant the pork. He opened his mouth to answer, but she went on brightly, 'A slice or two from *here* perhaps?' She pointed with the tip of the knife, then, without waiting for an answer, began to carve.

The poison would only be in part of the joint, so she could calm his suspicions by having her share from somewhere else. 'No, no,' said Brimstone quickly. 'Not there. I'd like some from *here*.' He pointed.

She didn't seem in the least perturbed, but dropped

the slices on to her own plate and began at once to carve where he had indicated. So the joint itself was not poisoned.

'Crackling?' asked Madame Brimstone. 'I expect you like a nice bit of crackling. Can't have it myself – plays hell with my digestion.'

It was in the crackling! It had to be in the crackling! He was supposed to eat it while she did not. What cunning! He *loved* crackling!

'Can't have it either,' he said quickly. 'Gives me gout.'

If she was disappointed, it didn't show. 'Stuffing?'

'If you're having some.'

'I surely am,' said Madame Brimstone. 'And potatoes, carrots, minted sinderack and peas. Always believed in eating well, me.'

Brimstone stared at his laden plate. Perhaps he had misjudged her. No poison here, unless she was prepared to swallow it as well. A thought struck him. Suppose she was using a special poison. Suppose she had already taken the antidote. Suppose ...

It was rubbish. He was letting his imagination get the better of him. The old bat was too stupid and too mean for anything of that sort. Anyway, it made no sense for her to poison him on their wedding night. Not with five notches already on the bed-post. Far too suspicious. She would surely wait a month or two before making her move. But by a month or two, it would be too late.

'I'm sorry, My Dear?' Brimstone murmured. She'd said something he hadn't caught.

'A toast!' Madame Brimstone repeated.

He realised to his horror there was a full glass of wine in front of him. He hadn't even seen her pour it. That's where the poison had to be! She'd have added it to his glass while he was distracted. How was he going to get out of this one without showing her he knew what she was up to?

'Here's to us and those like us,' said Madame Brimstone cheerfully. She raised her glass and waited expectantly for him to drink.

Brimstone scowled. What sort of toast was that? And where had that glass of wine come from?

'What sort of toast is that?' he asked, desperately playing for time. A heavy cut-glass claret decanter had appeared on the table and he assumed this was where the wine came from.

'Do you have a better one?' demanded Madame Brimstone irritably. She was staring at his glass.

Brimstone leaped to his feet. 'Why, *To happy married life,* of course!' he exclaimed. He waved his arms about excitedly and contrived to knock over his glass. The wine flowed across the table like a river of blood. 'Dear me,' shrieked Brimstone, 'how very clumsy of me. Never mind, my dear, I'll pour myself another glass.' As he reached for the decanter he noticed the tablecloth begin to smoke and fall in shreds.

Madame Brimstone pushed her chair back hurriedly and stood up before the liquid could splash on to her lap. 'I'll get a cloth to wipe that up,' she said shrilly.

'In a moment, Dearest Heart!' squeaked Brimstone, pretending not to notice his wine was now burning through the table. 'First our toast, our wonderful toast!' He poured himself a second glass and skipped around the table to link arms with her. 'To happy married life!' he said again, then hit her with the glass decanter.

Madame Brimstone went down like a stone.

forty-one

The tree was very peculiar. It had the huge trunk of an ancient oak, but the branches were twisted like a monkey puzzle. Fogarty walked around it twice, tapping the bole, but could find no opening, which ruled out an illusion spell. And maybe it wasn't a spell at all. At the atomic level, matter was largely empty space, and the only thing that stopped the matter of your backside passing through the matter of your chair was an electrical field. So possibly they'd interfered with the field potential of the tree so the soldier's body could penetrate it. Which would explain the *how* but not the *why*. Why would anybody want to interpenetrate a tree?

'You now,' said another green-uniformed soldier, nodding encouragingly to Fogarty.

Fogarty didn't hesitate – he was far too curious to learn the secret of the tree. He stepped quickly towards the massive trunk, headed for the point the soldier had indicated, reached it, felt the wood rough and solid, yet somehow passed right through it. The sensation, oddly enough, was of sliding sideways.

He was in a shaft. It was metal-lined and wide enough for him to stand, both arms outstretched, without touching the sides. There had to be some sort of dimensional shift. Probably not much, but enough to move the shaft out of phase and allow the tree to keep its heart. Fascinating technology. These people were a lot more sophisticated than they looked.

He felt himself beginning to float upwards and recognised the familiar sensation of suspensor spells at work. In a moment he emerged on to a broad wooden platform high up in the branches of the tree. The young soldier who'd gone ahead – with a start Fogarty realised it was a woman – took his hand to steady him. He looked around and gaped in sheer amazement.

There was an entire roadway system in the upper reaches of the forest.

It was absolutely invisible from the ground, but here it snaked from tree to tree, its main arteries as broad as any motorway and served by scores of side roads, loading bays, parking bays, promenades and avenues. It was a monumental feat of engineering, created from a mix of wood and metal along with something else he didn't even recognise.

Blue was already on the platform, staring around her with studied nonchalance. Madame Cardui and Pyrgus emerged a few seconds later, apparently none the worse for their little disagreement.

'Did you know this was here?' Fogarty asked her at once. You could move an army down those roadways. He tried to calculate how far the forest stretched, but his Realm geography was still too weak to make the estimate.

Madame Cardui nodded. 'Oh yes. I've known about it for some time.'

'You never told me,' Blue said, with just the barest hint of sharpness in her voice.

'Need to know, my deeah,' said Madame Cardui,

voicing one of the basic principles of espionage. 'You didn't need to know.' She flashed a tiny smile at Fogarty. 'Besides, at our age one must always keep a little something back. As insurance, you appreciate.'

Fogarty doubted if Blue did, but he appreciated the principle all right. 'Who *are* these people?' he asked Madame Cardui.

'My deeah, they're called the Feral Faerie – can you imagine it? We've always believed they were primitives. Primitive forest-dwellers. What a camouflage! They have their own culture, their own social structures, their own governing system, their own defence forces. I was astonished when I learned about them.'

'Are they Lighters or Nighters?' Fogarty asked.

'Not relevant,' Madame Cardui said. 'They don't hold allegiance to either side. Sorry, Pyrgus.'

Pyrgus, who was staring along one of the great tree-top roadways, hardly seemed to hear her. 'You could move an army down here,' he murmured, echoing Fogarty's earlier thought.

'Do they have treetop cities?' Fogarty frowned.

Madame Cardui shook her head. 'Just this commu-nications network. They're nomads – urban life would stifle them. They congregate in small communities actually within the living trees.'

One of the green-uniformed soldiers now swarming on the platform murmured something in her ear.

'They want us to move out now, deeahs,' she announced.

'Where are we going?' Fogarty asked.

Madame Cardui smiled broadly. 'To meet the Faerie Queen.'

* * *

The transporter was a large wooden raft that floated some six inches above the surface of the roadway. It bobbed slightly, like a boat at sea, as Pyrgus stepped aboard. A green-uniformed soldier manned the single control, a large joystick set near the front. The craft was big enough to take almost the whole contingent, but by the time it was full, they were pressed shoulder to shoulder except for a small courtesy space around the pilot.

'Brace!' the pilot called.

Pyrgus was wondering what that meant when the raft jerked forward and sped off at a furious rate. He was thrown backwards and would have fallen were it not for the pressure of those around him. He noticed that everyone in green uniform was leaning forward to counteract the motion of the raft.

He found his own balance in a moment and watched the upper branches of the trees flash by. He was finding it difficult to gather his thoughts. Too much had happened in the last few hours. The coup by Hairstreak. Comma on the throne. His exile along with Blue and Gatekeeper Fogarty. The attack on the ouklo, which everyone had thought was carried out by Hairstreak's men, but which turned out to be the work of the Forest Faerie. And now rescue. At least he supposed it was rescue. He needed to talk to Madame Cardui.

Pyrgus half turned to find someone at his shoulder. It was the girl who had stunned him during the fight.

'I want to apologise,' she said quietly. 'I didn't know you were the Crown Prince.'

'It's all right,' Pyrgus said. For some reason he felt embarrassed.

'Well, I'm not sure it is,' the girl said. 'But when you came at me with a dagger, I had to do *something*.'

'Unh,' Pyrgus nodded. He wanted to talk to her properly, but something was making him converse in grunts.

The girl stared into his face for a moment, then gave a little resigned shrug. 'Well, that's all I wanted to say.' She turned away.

'What's your name?' Pyrgus asked quickly, his vocal paralysis breaking at last.

She turned back again and her expression was pleased. 'Nymphalis,' she said. 'Nymphalis Antiopa.' She hesitated, then added almost shyly, 'My friends call me Nymph.'

'I'm Pyrgus Malvae,' Pyrgus said because he couldn't think of anything else.

'Yes, I know.'

The green uniform suited her, even though it was cut for a man. It certainly didn't make her look like a man. He couldn't imagine anything that would make her look like a man. It made her look … it made her look *elegant*. But then she had the sort of figure that would look elegant in a sack.

'The, ah, the business with the, ah, wand in the ear and knee in the – the knee … and the knee: that really is all right, you know. I mean, I understand. Heat of battle and all that.' She just stood there, smiling at him. He wondered if she was a professional soldier. He wondered if she had a boyfriend. 'Do you ha— do, did, wha—' He started again. 'I was wondering why you attacked the ouklo?'

Nymphalis looked surprised. 'You don't believe all that nonsense about the Forest Faerie being brigands, do you?'

'No, no,' Pyrgus said hastily. 'Actually I thought you were Hairstreak's men.' It occurred to him she mightn't know who Hairstreak was, but pressed on. 'No, but I was really wondering why. Why you attacked us?'

The platform lurched beneath their feet.

'Ah,' said Nymphalis, 'we're here already.'

forty-two

Henry had been in the palace dungeons once before –
briefly – when he had tried to rescue Mr Fogarty,
who'd been thrown in jail when everybody had
believed he'd murdered the Purple Emperor. But that
experience had been civilised compared to this. Now
they'd thrown him into a dank, subterranean cell that
smelled of someone else's pee and had no facilities for
his own except a small grating set into the worn,
cracked flagstones on the floor. The walls were stone as
well, and the whole chamber had an ancient feel, as if
it had been built at the same time as the original palace
Keep. There were no windows. The only light came
from a single rush taper that looked in danger of flickering out with every errant draft.

The door was extraordinary. It was nearly a foot
thick and banded in metal for extra strength as if the
designers had expected to lock up a dinosaur. It had
some sort of spell coating that made a sound like
fingernails across a blackboard every time he went near
it. He didn't think the guards had literally thrown
away the key, but he suspected he might be here for a
very long time indeed.

Henry set his back against the wall and slid down to
the floor to think. What had happened to Blue? What

had happened to Pyrgus? And who on earth was Quercusia?

He had to find Blue and Pyrgus, had to find out what had happened. He had to get out of here.

Henry looked around his cell. There must be something he could use to escape, something he could break apart for digging or picking the lock or beating up the guard like they did in the movies. But the chamber was empty. No furnishings. No table, no chairs. Not even a mattress on the floor. Nothing but a moth-eaten rug thrown into one corner.

He stopped his eyes roaming and stared. Why would they give him a rug and nothing else?

Henry pushed himself abruptly to his feet. That was no rug!

'You can stop skulking in the corner now,' he called.

'I'm not skulking,' said the endolg. 'I was asleep. You woke me from a lovely dream.' It started to crawl towards him. 'Oh, it's Henry. Hello, Henry – or do you prefer "Iron Prominent" these days?'

Henry frowned. 'Do I know you?'

'Sure you do. I was the one shopped you to the guard upstairs. Fat lot of good it did me.'

For a moment Henry continued to stare at the creature. Then it came to him. The endolg was referring to Henry's attempt to free Mr Fogarty from the dungeons on their first visit to the Realm. Henry had tried lying to the guard and an endolg in the outer office had spotted it at once.

'That was you?' he asked.

'In the fur.'

'They sent you here to spy on me?' He couldn't imagine why. But then he couldn't imagine why he was here in the first place.

'Ah, the self-centred certainties of youth!' the endolg exclaimed philosophically. 'It's nothing to do with you. That loony old plud had me jailed.'

Somehow Henry knew the loony old plud was Quercusia. 'Why?'

'Why did she have me jailed? Didn't like the look of my pelt. Didn't like the colour of my eyes. Who knows why that barm-brack does anything? She'll have the dungeons full in a month – and Asloght Jail as well, if she keeps on the way she's going. It was a bad day for the Realm when Comma let her out.'

Comma let her out? The endolg mightn't be much use in smashing out of here, but it suddenly occurred to Henry that it could give him an awful lot of much-needed information. 'I've been away for weeks,' he said. 'What's been happening?'

For a horrible moment he thought the endolg wasn't going to answer, but then it sighed deeply. 'Where to begin? You know Prince Pyrgus has been sent into exile?'

Henry nodded. 'Is Blue with him? Princess Blue?'

'Princess Blue and Gatekeeper Fogarty. All history now.' The endolg sighed again.

'How did this happen?' Henry asked. He could hardly believe it. The last thing he'd heard was that Pyrgus was getting ready for his Coronation.

'Orders of his father,' the endolg said.

Henry stared at it. 'His father's dead,' he blurted.

'He was alive and kicking last time I saw him,' said the endolg. 'Well, alive, anyway: he didn't look so good.'

'Last time you saw him? When was that?'

'Couple of days. Before the loony old plud had me

thrown down here.'

'Are you sure?'

'You don't know much about endolgs, do you?' remarked the endolg. 'We can't lie.' It wriggled slightly as if it had an itch. 'Seventy-eight brain cells missing. Doesn't sound like much, but it means we just can't do it. Any time an endolg says something definite, you can take it that's the truth. If we're not sure about something, we say "maybe" or "perhaps" or "somebody told me" or whatever. I saw the Purple Emperor alive, couple of days ago, in this palace. I'm sure. You can believe it.'

Henry couldn't believe it. Pyrgus's father had been shot at close range with a shotgun. But maybe the blast really hadn't killed him. Even in his own world there were people who fell into a coma and the doctors thought they were dead.

'Comma's on the throne now – or will be when he's crowned and confirmed. Purple Emperor Elect and Royal Pain in the Ass. Comma. Can you imagine it? First thing he did was let his mother out.'

'Out of where?' Comma's mother had to be the old Emperor's second wife. Henry had vaguely thought she was dead.

'The West Wing. They kept her locked up there for years.'

It suddenly struck Henry who the endolg must be talking about. 'Comma's mother is Quercusia, isn't she? Why was she locked up?'

'Because she's mad, of course. You know that. They're all mad in her family.'

'Who's her family?' Henry asked curiously.

'Quercusia is Lord Hairstreak's sister,' said the endolg.

forty-three

Pyrgus was finding it difficult to believe what he was seeing.

Close on a thousand faeries had poured into the forest clearing and more were joining them at every minute. They seemed to be emerging out of the very trees, as Pyrgus himself had emerged from a tree only moments before, along with Nymph and others on the transporter. The spells that allowed them to do so had to be related to the portal technology that translated you to another dimension, but he'd never seen anything like this before. The thing was, you *didn't* translate to another dimension. You went into a hollow shaft in the tree. At least that's what he'd done. But to do that, you passed through the solid trunk of the tree itself. Which was some spell. He'd never even heard of a Halek wizard who could do it. He wondered how the Forest Faerie managed it.

An errant thought occurred to him. With a spell like that, no castle was safe. You could take an army right through its walls.

The Forest Faerie were organising themselves in ranks even though not all of them were wearing the green military uniform. Perhaps the rest were off-duty soldiers, or perhaps they were just naturally disciplined. He looked round for Nymph to ask her, but she was nowhere in sight now. Nor was Madame Cardui. He felt a flash of embarrassment at his attempt to strangle her.

Blue emerged from the tree trunk frowning a little. Mr Fogarty came out behind her and turned at once to look at the tree.

'Do you know how they do that?' Pyrgus asked him quietly.

'No, but I'd like to,' Mr Fogarty said.

Blue said, 'Pyrgus, what's happened to –' Then stopped as the entire throng in the clearing suddenly went quiet. Heads began to turn in the direction of a forest path. Distantly, Pyrgus could hear a sound like the tinkling of temple bells.

Two horsemen rode into the clearing and separated either side of the path. Although nobody said anything, the crowd flowed – there was no other word for it – to make space, then flowed again to open up an empty circle in the middle of the clearing. Pyrgus found himself on its edge, along with Blue and Mr Fogarty, isolated from the main body of Forest Faerie. He wondered if he should step back, but decided against it. At least he'd have a good view here of whatever might be going on, and if anybody wanted him to move, they could tell him. He noticed neither Blue nor Mr Fogarty looked much like moving either.

A party of mounted archers was approaching down the path. The armament looked primitive to Pyrgus, but he was quickly learning not to underestimate these people. Their elf-bolts had proven capable of piercing the adamantine silver armour of the ouklo cabin, so perhaps their arrows had special spell coatings as well.

An arrow might not be the latest in weapons technology, but if –

A thought struck him. The elf-bolts must have made use of the same magic that allowed Forest Faerie to pass into their own trees. If their arrows had the same coating, there was no armour in the world that would protect against them. They might even be able to shoot through solid stone!

The sound of bells came nearer. Pyrgus turned his attention back to the path. There was an even larger mounted party following the archers. 'They use horses,' he murmured to himself, frowning. It was clear from their overhead transporter – and their foo discs – that they had levitation spells. Why not use them here?

'More efficient among trees,' Gatekeeper Fogarty murmured back. 'You don't have to guide a good horse – it finds its own way around obstacles. Lot safer than a flying disc, and probably faster when you take everything into consideration.'

The second party had a ceremonial look about it – something in the stately way it moved. Pyrgus craned his neck to try to catch more details, but the forest surrounding the clearing was dense and a leafy canopy arched over the path, leaving it in gloom.

The archers entered the clearing and followed the example of the first two horsemen, splitting apart to form a mounted circle. To Pyrgus's surprise, and just a little alarm, they rode behind him, leaving him isolated with Blue and Mr Fogarty inside the circle. He glanced behind, decided there was nothing he could do, and waited.

A weird processional came into view. Riders on horseback were attended by runners who gambolled and leaped and waved their arms like madmen, keeping apace with the horses with no apparent difficulty. Both riders and footmen were costumed, wearing a curious assortment of clothes that were a full five hundred years behind the current fashions. There was a preponderance of pointed hats and soft, velvet pointed slippers.

'Good God,' said Mr Fogarty abruptly, 'it's the Wild Hunt!'

Pyrgus glanced at him.

'Old folk superstition in my world,' Mr Fogarty explained. 'At least I thought it was a superstition until now. Back in the Middle Ages, they used to believe that on certain nights of the year witches and other supernatural beings rode through the forest hunting for ... I don't know ... souls, I suppose. It was called the Wild Hunt, and sometimes the Faerie Hunt. The myth must have been based on this – look at those costumes, the descriptions are identical: pointed hats, archers, horses, and the woman leading them.'

Pyrgus suddenly noticed there *was* a woman leading them and wondered how he had missed her before. She was the strangest creature he'd ever seen. She was not merely dressed in green – a fur-trimmed cloak over a loose shirt and tight knee-britches – but her skin colouring was green as well, enhancing her enormous golden eyes.

'What *is* she?' he whispered. He couldn't take his eyes off the woman. Even her hair was green, interwoven with a garland of tiny forest flowers. There was a green man riding a little behind her, naked to the waist beneath his cloak, powerfully muscled, a strung bow carried across his back. But his eyes were almost black and his hair was a golden blond.

The woman rode directly towards Pyrgus, then reined in a few feet away and slid gracefully from her horse. Close up, her colouring was even more disconcerting than it had been at a distance. She stared into Pyrgus's eyes as if attempting to read his thoughts, then said soberly, 'Crown Prince Pyrgus Malvae, I am Queen Cleopatra.' She half turned and gestured towards the green man, who had remained mounted. 'This is my Consort, Gonepterix.' Gonepterix nodded a brief acknowledgement. He had an open face, but his expression was wary.

'Queen Cleopatra?' frowned Gatekeeper Fogarty. 'Did you say *Cleopatra*?'

The woman favoured him with a slow, sidelong look. Her face took on an expression of mild amusement. 'That is my name. And you are the Gatekeeper from another world – the Painted Lady told me of you.'

Queen Cleopatra? Queen of what? Or where? It was dawning on Pyrgus that Forest Faerie were not at all what everybody thought them to be. They were very skilled at hiding themselves – and hiding what they had achieved. These were people who could live inside trees. They were practically a separate kingdom within his kingdom.

Queen Cleopatra turned those disquieting gold eyes back on to Pyrgus. 'I wish to bid you welcome – and meet with your sister. Is she with you?'

'I'm Princess Blue,' Blue said, stepping out. She'd been masked to some degree by Mr Fogarty.

Cleopatra smiled at her warmly. 'The Painted Lady has told me a *very* great deal about you – more even than about the Gatekeeper here.'

It seemed a warm enough welcome, but there were a great many questions Pyrgus needed answered. Before he could ask any of them, Blue said, 'Where is Madame Cardui? She was with us a little while ago, but she seems to have disappeared.'

'She went ahead,' the Queen told her. 'She will be waiting for us in the Great Hall. We should go there now – there is much we need to talk about.'

'I don't do horses,' Mr Fogarty said at once. He looked at the Queen's own horse sourly.

Cleopatra glanced at him again. She looked puzzled, but her face cleared almost at once. 'Oh, for the journey?' She smiled. 'Gatekeeper, the Great Hall is closer than you think.'

forty-four

'Hairstreak's *sister*?' Henry exclaimed. 'Why would the Purple Emperor go off and marry Hairstreak's sister?' Quercusia was quite good-looking for an older woman, but not *that* good-looking. A thought struck him. 'She's a Faerie of the Night, for heaven's sake.'

The endolg made that curious rippling movement that seemed to be a shrug. 'That's exactly why he married her – because she was a Faerie of the Night. And Hairstreak's sister. Politics, pure and simple. Apatura Iris thought an arranged marriage with somebody in Hairstreak's family might help bring the Faeries of the Night and the Faeries of the Light closer together. She might be a bit of a wagon, but it was better than civil war. Besides, he didn't know she was bonkers when he married her.'

This was bad. This was very bad. This was very, very bad. Things had happened in the Realm that were almost impossible to believe, all of them bad for Pyrgus, all of them bad for Blue. (And all of them bad for Mr Fogarty, now Henry thought of it.) But at least they were still alive, although it sounded as if they'd only just survived; and if there was ever a time they needed him it was now. He couldn't quite get out of his head the vision he'd seen of them lying on a forest floor.

'There must be some way out of this cell,' Henry moaned helplessly.

'Oh, there is,' said the endolg.

The creature had climbed halfway up one of the walls and was clinging there like a tapestry. Henry looked across at it. 'Pardon?'

'There's a way out,' the endolg repeated.

Henry sniffed. 'Yes, through the door, except they forgot to leave us a key.'

'I don't know why you're taking that sarcastic attitude,' said the endolg airily. 'I assumed it was a straightforward question and I gave you a straightforward answer.' It anchored itself more firmly to the wall and closed its eyes.

'I'm sorry,' Henry said at once. 'Is there really a way out? Where? How?'

'I don't think I'll tell you,' said the endolg. 'I don't react well to sarcasm.'

If it had had a throat, Henry would have strangled it. 'Sorry,' he said again. 'No, honestly, I'm sorry. I didn't mean to upset you. I'm sorry. Sorry. It's just – well, you were here before me. I'd have thought if there was some way out, you'd have taken it, that's all. Sorry.'

'I said there was a way out. I didn't say I could use it. I'm not strong enough. But you are. At least I think you are – you look a sturdy boy to me. Sturdy and sarcastic.'

Henry contained himself with a superhuman effort. 'Won't you please tell me? You've been a huge help up to now.' A thought occurred to him and he added, 'If I get out, I'll take you with me. If it's somewhere you can't go, I'll carry you.'

The endolg's eyes opened again. 'This is one of the

oldest dungeons in the palace,' it said. 'Hasn't been repaired for centuries and wasn't all that well-made to begin with. See that little grating in the middle of the floor ...?'

The grating was the one prisoners peed into. There was a smallish, brown-stained hole beside it. Henry's nose wrinkled involuntarily. 'Yes ...'

'Comes up if you pull it hard enough.'

Henry stared at the grating. It was six inches across at most. 'I couldn't get through that.'

'The flagstone comes up with it,' said the endolg patiently.

'What's underneath?' Henry felt the first hint of a mounting excitement. He didn't want to get his hopes up, but ...

'There's a drain. It's a bit mucky and it'll be a tight fit for somebody your size, but you'll probably get through.'

'Probably?' Henry echoed.

'Well, if you lift the flagstone, you can judge for yourself,' the endolg said. 'If you're not prepared to take my word for it.'

'OK, OK, you think I should manage it. Where does the drain lead?'

'My guess would be the palace sewers,' the endolg said. 'Don't take that as truthspeak, but I once saw a map that showed the whole underground system. I think that must be where it drains to.'

'What about the sewers?' Henry asked. 'Could I get through them all right?'

The endolg snorted. 'Get through them? You could hold a party in them if it wasn't for the smell. They're enormous.'

'What happens if I can't find my way out? Out of the sewers?'

'Oh, come on!' said the endolg. 'I'm telling you how we can get out of here – you want a scale map and a signed guarantee as well?'

'Sorry,' Henry said again.

'If it makes you feel any better, I'll be sticking with you. Don't fancy facing the bilgerats on my own.'

'There are bilgerats down there?' Henry shuddered. He'd only ever seen a live rat once, but they gave him the creeps.

'Big as horses, according to some reports. But I wouldn't take that as truthspeak either.' The endolg started to climb down slowly off the wall. 'With luck we won't meet any, but if we do, it's still better than rotting in here, isn't it?'

'Yes,' Henry said uncertainly.

'Well, what are you waiting for? Get the grille up.'

Henry walked hesitantly to the middle of the floor. The stench seemed stronger than it had been, and not just the smell of pee now either. The grating was stained by years of use and had some unpleasant encrustations. 'Are you sure you couldn't get this up yourself?'

'Definite. Endolgs are smart, but we're not that strong. You should do it easily.'

Henry looked at the grille. 'I don't have any gloves.'

'Just my luck,' sighed the endolg. 'Twenty million people in the Realm and I get locked up with a wuss.'

Henry took a deep breath, reached down to grip the grille (with his bare hand – yuk!) and pulled. He felt it move slightly and discovered the endolg was right – the surrounding flag moved too. But it was a long way off coming up easily.

'Use both hands and brace yourself,' the endolg suggested.

'What's your name?' Henry asked it quietly.

'Flapwazzle,' said the endolg. 'Why?'

'Shut up, Flapwazzle,' Henry said. He reached down with both hands and braced himself.

'Use your legs,' Flapwazzle told him. 'Your legs are stronger than your arms.'

Henry locked his grip and pushed hard to straighten his legs. For a moment he was certain nothing was going to happen, then the flagstone came up smoothly and fell over with a crash on the floor.

Henry peered into the foul-smelling hole below. 'I'll never fit into that,' he said.

'I'll go first in case you get stuck,' Flapwazzle volunteered. 'That way, at least one of us will escape.'

forty-five

Henry had an unhappy decision to make. He didn't fancy getting stuck head first down a narrow drain, especially one that people had peed in … and worse. But if he went down feet first and *didn't* get stuck, he was going to have to negotiate backwards all the way to the main sewers with nothing better to guide him than touchy Flapwazzle, who might, or might not, decide to go off on his own at any time. So which was it to be – head first or feet first into the dark?

'Hurry up!' called Flapwazzle, who had already plunged into the pipe. 'I can't hang about all day – it's smelly down here.'

Henry took his second deep breath of the afternoon and plunged head first through the opening left by the uprooted flagstone.

He got stuck almost at once.

'Push hard,' suggested Flapwazzle.

Henry was loath to take the advice. He could still wriggle backwards and return to the comparatively fresh air of the cell, but each time he pushed forwards, he jammed solid. Pushing harder might get him stuck completely. Even a few feet in, the smell was appalling. He could think of absolutely nothing worse than starving to death while stuck in this ghastly puke-pong of a drain.

'Stop holding your breath!' Flapwazzle advised. 'You're all swole up – no wonder you get stuck.'

'It's my shoulders!' Henry hissed into the foul-smelling darkness. 'It's my shoulders that are stuck. They're not all swole – swollen up.' All the same he released his breath and tried, tentatively, to push forward again. There was a tiny movement, then he stopped.

Somewhere deep in his heart he knew he wasn't pushing hard enough; or at least wasn't pushing as hard as he could. He was terrified of getting stuck fast, but on the other hand the endolg was quite right: there was absolutely no point in wriggling back to rot in a gloomy cell at the mercy of the lunatic Queen.

The thought of the cell gave him an idea. 'I'll just go back and get the taper,' he said. 'We could do with a bit of light down here.'

'Bring a flame into the sewers and you'll set off the methane,' said Flapwazzle calmly. 'Probably take out half the palace.'

'All right,' Henry said sourly. Since he couldn't put off the moment any longer, he pushed forward with all his strength. And was stuck fast, stuck for ever, doomed, choking on the fumes, already dying in the darkness, before he suddenly shot forward like a cork popped from a bottle and found he had actually enough room to work his elbows and propel himself slowly forward.

'Gets wider down here,' said Flapwazzle's voice encouragingly.

'Glad to hear it,' Henry muttered. 'Any idea where we're going?' He'd only moved a yard or two and already it was so dark he could almost touch it.

'Just follow my voice,' said Flapwazzle. 'I'll keep talking.'

Henry frowned. 'Can you see in the dark?'

'No, but I can whistle,' Flapwazzle said bewilderingly. 'It'll be all right in the main tunnels. There's a luminous fungus grows on the crust of you know what. It's dim, but your eyes get used to it.'

'How do you know all this?'

'Been down here before.'

Henry wondered why, but before he could ask, Flapwazzle said, 'Here we are. Corner coming up, Henry.'

Henry had already discovered it by crawling into a wall. He rubbed his head. There was a faint glow to his right. He crawled quickly towards it and fell nearly four feet into a main tunnel just as Flapwazzle said, 'Careful!'

He fell face down in water – at least he hoped it was water – and scrambled to his feet, coughing and spitting wildly. The endolg was right: the tunnel was huge and he had no trouble standing upright. Flapwazzle was also right about the fungus. It grew in bilious green patches on the roof, casting an eerie glow that allowed him to see a yard or two ahead.

'Where are you?' he asked, and listened to his words echo far into the distance.

'Ahead and a little to your right,' Flapwazzle said. 'I'm floating. Try not to step on me.'

Henry peered into the gloom. There was something dark floating on the water that might have been Flapwazzle or might have been something a lot less edifying. 'Are you sure you can find our way out of here?'

'Fairly sure. I've a good memory for maps. Thing is, there are lots of ways out of sewers – garderobes, privies, drains. And if you miss them all, you just follow the flow and you come out in the river. The whole system drains into the river. Which would probably be our best bet for getting away from the plud. You can swim, can't you?'

'Not very well,' Henry said.

'Mmm,' said Flapwazzle thoughtfully. 'That could be a problem *before* we reach the river.'

There was something in his tone that stopped Henry dead. 'Why *before* we reach the river?'

'They flush the system every sixteen hours. Seven billion gallons of recycled water under pressure. Even strong swimmers don't usually survive that. In fact, I can't remember hearing *anybody's* ever survived that.'

'Yes, but if it's only once in sixteen hours, we've lots of time to get out before it happens,' Henry protested.

'Depends when they last did it,' said the endolg.

forty-six

'The Wangaramas Revolution,' wyrm Cyril announced inside the mind of Jasper Chalkhill, 'is potentially the most important political development within the Realm in the past five hundred years; indeed –'

'Can't we just cut to the chase?' Chalkhill asked a little desperately. It was curiously companionable sharing one's mind with a worm, but the creature did tend to drone on.

'Yes, perhaps that would be best, since time is of the essence. If we're agreed the Realm is in a mess – and from a glance at your thoughts I can see we are – then the Wangaramas Revolution is the way to clean it up.'

'Doesn't tell me what it is, Cyril.'

'I was coming to that – you're extraordinarily impatient. You've no doubt heard of the world-famous Wangaramas political theorist Munchen – ?'

Chalkhill reached tiredly for the clinic's bell.

'Wait! Wait!' shrieked the worm. 'I have to tell you this so you'll understand our offer. I'll be quick, I promise. We Wangarami have been the superior species on this planet for more than two point eight million years. Wangaramas philosophers have struggled with this question for generations, creating, examining and dismissing one theory after – DON'T TOUCH THE

BELL! *The thing is, a contemporary Wangaramas philosopher –'*

'Look,' said Chalkhill, *'I'm sure this is all very interesting, but frankly, my dear Cyril, I have better things to do just now, like getting on with the rest of my life, which does not, however, include any input from you whatsoever. So if you'll excuse me, I'll just set up the operation and get our little divorce underway. I'll try to see that you're not harmed, of course, and since you seem to have managed your life perfectly well without me in the past, I imagine you –'*

'We'll make you *Purple Emperor!*' Cyril shouted.

forty-seven

The Great Hall was huge and Fogarty had not the least idea how they'd reached it. He was beginning to feel real admiration for these Forest Faerie: they had tricks up their sleeves nobody else seemed to have dreamed of. Besides, you had to admire a tribe that could hide away for generations without anybody suspecting they existed. Anybody except Cynthia, that was. He threw a fond glance in the direction of Madame Cardui, who was seated almost opposite him across the conference table. She threw a fond glance back.

To the right of the Painted Lady sat Cleopatra, the Faerie Queen. Pyrgus was seated on the Queen's right, the traditional place of honour. To his right was Blue, her face expressionless. Then a pale Forest Faerie named Limenitis, who'd been introduced as Queen's Counsel, then Fogarty himself and finally the muscular Porcellus Hawkmoth, who'd led the assault on the ouklo and was obviously a military man. Fogarty noticed with some surprise that the Queen's Consort, Gonepterix, had no place at the table at all, although he *was* in the room. He stood near a window that presented an illusory view of an angry sea and was the only person in the room permitted to bear arms – the familiar hunting bow of the forest people. He was watching the Queen intently and, from his expression, warmly. Fogarty guessed they had a good relationship, although there was no doubt who was boss.

'What now?' asked the Queen, to no one in particular. It was an interesting opening, Fogarty thought.

'Ma'am,' asked Pyrgus quietly, 'are we your guests or your prisoners?'

The tone was polite, but the question unexpected. Fogarty glanced across at him in surprise. The boy hadn't talked to Cynthia yet, so he didn't know. All the same, it was an intelligent opening that went right to the heart of things. Maybe Pyrgus had more political *nous* than he got credit for.

The Queen smiled.

Madame Cardui put in a little hoarsely, 'My deeahs, Queen Cleopatra ordered your rescue at my request.'

'You are our guests,' the Queen said.

Fogarty had a lot of other questions he wanted answered. Who exactly were these Forest Faerie who'd managed to stay hidden for so long? How had Cynthia known about them? And how was it she had persuaded the Queen to risk her subjects' lives – and, more importantly, the secret of their very existence – in a rescue bid?

'The question we must decide now,' Madame Cardui was saying, 'is what to do next.' She was looking at Blue rather than at Pyrgus, but it was Pyrgus who answered.

'What made you think we needed rescuing, Madame?'

Fogarty suppressed a grin. The operation had been harder on Pyrgus than the rest of them. He'd been knocked out cold by one of the forest soldiers.

Madame Cardui's eyes swung back towards him. She'd changed out of the hooded cloak into one of her more flamboyant gowns. The spell coating of rainbow serpents was in huge contrast with the sober outfits elsewhere in the room. 'Hairstreak did not intend to let you live, whatever your poor deluded half-brother may have wished. He sent soldiers after you.' She looked soberly from one face to the other. 'If the Forest Faerie hadn't acted, you would all have been dead within the hour.'

Pyrgus's head was whirling. Not for the first time he felt swamped by the situation he was in. But the Forest Queen was right. The question was *what now*? Before he could speak, the Queen said, 'Our friend the Painted Lady has explained your situation. My people are willing to help.'

Why? Pyrgus wondered.

'How?' Mr Fogarty asked.

The Queen gave him that odd sidelong glance of hers. 'In any way necessary, Gatekeeper. Up to and including military assistance.'

Pyrgus felt himself stiffen. Military assistance? The Realm had only recently avoided civil war. Now they were talking about another one. He couldn't allow it. But he couldn't allow the present situation either. He'd known that all along, however little he wanted to face it. Even as Comma had sent them into exile with their father's authority, he'd known he must do something. But he had assumed he would have time to make his plans in Haleklind.

'Why?' asked Mr Fogarty, echoing Pyrgus's earlier thought.

'Why?' repeated the Queen. She sighed and her gaze moved from Mr Fogarty to Pyrgus. 'Crown Prince Pyrgus, for generations my people have cared nothing, nothing at all, for the conflict between your Lighters and Nighters. We have used our arts to remain hidden. And most successfully. The deep forest is a dangerous place – few from the outside venture far into it. Any who did saw only what we wanted them to see – a handful of Forest Faerie living rough, surviving as brigands.' The smile came again, tinged with a steely glint in the eye. 'We became known as *feral faerie*, little better than the other wild animals of the forest.'

'Queen Cleopatra, no –'

She waved Blue's words away. 'No offence was meant – I understand. It is of no consequence. These ideas suited our purpose. They meant no one knew the truth, no one envied us, no one investigated us, no one made war on us. We were *left alone* – a precious gift indeed; at least a gift my people hold precious. But we will not be left alone much longer. One of your nobles has recently built himself a forest estate. We tried to discourage the move, but there was a limit to what we could do without revealing our presence. The estate is extensive, but might have been tolerated – there is still a very great deal of forest for us to hide in – but this noble has opened up hell pits beneath his new home, and that we cannot permit.'

'Hell pits?' This from Blue, leaning forward, frowning.

The Queen's voice grew heavy with disgust. 'Some form of entertainment.' She shook her head. 'The forest cannot tolerate demons. They would wreak havoc in our living space. We have guarded the periphery for centuries, but this … creature has introduced the possibility of an invasion from within.'

'The Hael portals are closed down,' Blue murmured.

The Queen nodded. 'Yes, and this has given us a little time to make our plans. But they will not remain closed for ever and when they reopen, we fear for our ancient habitat.' She glanced at Limenitis. 'My Counsel and I were discussing what to do when Madame Cardui approached us with a possible solution.'

'You want us to help you destroy the hell pits in return for your help in restoring Prince Pyrgus to his throne?' Mr Fogarty suggested.

'Both objectives seem to be the same,' the Queen told him bluntly. 'The noble with the hell pits is Lord Hairstreak.'

' "The enemy of my enemy is my friend",' quoted Mr Fogarty and grinned.

Pyrgus said carefully, 'Why don't you simply attack the Hairstreak estate yourself? From what I've seen of your army, you would have little problem razing the place to the ground.'

The Queen's expression did not change. 'Two reasons. The first, as I've said, is that we prefer to show ourselves as little as possible. If we are to help you, you will be under *geis* to tell no one of our origins. The second is that my advisors and I do not believe our security can best be assured simply by attacking Hairstreak's forest estate and closing the pits. We have to remove Hairstreak from the picture altogether. That can only be achieved through an alliance with you.'

Mr Fogarty nodded. 'Makes sense.'

For the first time since they had left the palace, Blue actually began to smile. She glanced appreciatively at

Madame Cardui, then looked back at the Queen. 'Your Majesty,' she said formally, 'your offer of help could not be better timed. I think you can take it that my brother and I –'

But Pyrgus was already on his feet. 'Thank you for your offer, Forest Queen,' he said shortly. 'But a joint attack on Lord Hairstreak is out of the question.'

forty-eight

The body looked like a heap of discarded rags and didn't weigh much more as he dragged it outside. Perfect place for a murder. Not a soul about and the crows would give him warning if anybody approached, although that was unlikely.

Brimstone looked around. It was his first chance to examine his new property properly. He could go through the inside later, but just now what he needed was a toolshed. If there'd been more wine, he could have dissolved her in the bath, but the dregs in the decanter didn't look enough. (The table had fallen to pieces, though.) What he needed was a hidden grave and a stake through the heart to make sure no interfering busybody brought her back before she rotted.

He found a spade in the shed outside, grabbed his late wife by the hair and dragged her into the woods.

Light though she was, he began to tire after a few hundred yards, but fortunately found a spot beyond an ancient oak where the ground looked reasonably soft and began methodically to dig.

As the grave took shape, he let his mind turn towards the future. He was fairly sure her rotten brother would come looking for her eventually, but not before the honeymoon was supposed to be over, and probably not for a week or so after that. By then Brimstone could have the cabin looted and sold, with himself set up in a small country estate somewhere in Yammeth Cretch where he wouldn't attract too much attention from the new Emperor Pyrgus. Perfect ending to a marriage.

When the hole was deep enough, Brimstone glanced briefly down, then threw Maura in. 'So long, my dear,' he told her cheerfully. 'Don't think it hasn't been wonderful.'

He was about to fill in the grave when the crows exploded from the trees.

forty-nine

Chalkhill found a simbala parlour with a trendy out-door terrace and ordered himself a thimble-sized shot. He sipped the liquid music gratefully, listening as it slid gently down his throat to expand into a fiery symphony that drained the tensions from his body.

'*Can I talk now?*' the wangaramas wyrm Cyril asked inside his mind.

'*No*,' Chalkhill said.

He allowed the music to wash over him, creating heroic visions. He saw himself in robes of imperial purple (rather more stylishly-cut, of course, than the sort of thing the old Emperor used to wear) dispensing justice, winning wars, counting his gold and, above all, telling people what to do. Jasper, the Purple Emperor – how proudly the words rolled off his subjects' tongues.

'*Can I talk now?*' Cyril asked again.

The symphony was dying back, and while there was still some music in the glass, Chalkhill set it to one side and let his visions fade. '*All right,*' he said, '*I'm willing to discuss it. But I don't want any of your lectures, Cyril. I know it goes against your nature, but let's keep this brief.*'

After a strangulated pause, the wyrm said, '*Yes, OK.*'

'*You're offering to make me Purple Emperor? I didn't misunderstand that?*'

'No.'

'How?' Chalkhill asked bluntly. 'How are you going to make me Purple Emperor? The short version, please.'

It wasn't all that short, but it was a lot more interesting than most of Cyril's waffle. The wyrms, who seemed to have developed some sort of collective consciousness since they established their mental Net, had formed more symbiotic relationships in the last year than in the whole of their recorded history.

Not only that, but the nature of the symbiosis had undergone a striking change. In the old days, the wyrms linked with their hosts more or less at random. Now the links were carefully selected. With a rising mixture of delight and alarm, Chalkhill learned the wyrms had infiltrated the highest councils in the land.

'I volunteered to join with you because of your political connections,' Cyril said. 'You've worked for Lord Hairstreak, you've met Prince Pyrgus and Princess Blue, you're a wealthy man who moves in high social circles. You can get us places no one else could.'

Chalkhill wasn't so sure of that, but he carefully shielded his thoughts from the wyrm. 'Do the others you've linked with know about your plans for revolution?'

There was a long pause before Cyril said, 'Not all of them ...'

'How many of them?'

There was another long pause. 'Just a few. We have to pick them carefully. It's a matter of trust.'

'Why pick me, then?' Chalkhill asked suspiciously. He couldn't imagine why anybody in their right mind would decide to trust him, given his track record.

'You're one of the few we've found who hasn't any scruples whatsoever,' Cyril told him cheerfully.

fifty

The endolg Flapwazzle climbed a smooth sewer wall to peer into a drainage passage. 'Know what?' he said. 'I think we're lost.'

'I thought you remembered the map,' Henry said accusingly.

'I do, but this part of the system doesn't seem to be *on* the map. I think we're lost.'

Henry said, 'Doesn't matter – we're trying to get to the river anyway. We'll just do what you said and follow the flow until we reach the outlet.'

Flapwazzle slid back down again to floor level. 'I like you, Henry,' he said. 'I thought you were a nice-enough sort the first time I met you, even if you were a dreadful liar. But now I've got to know you better, I think you're even nicer. Not many people would take getting lost so calmly. They'd scream and shout and try to blame me for everything. You know we endolgs have a proverb – *Blame the endolg*. Three of the truest words ever spoken. Everybody blames the endolg. But not you, Henry. You stay calm and never lose your common sense and take things as they come. I really like you, Henry. I think you and I could be good friends.'

'Well, I like you too, Flapwazzle,' Henry said, which

was actually true. They'd been wandering in the sewers for over an hour now and his companion had been unfailingly cheerful and entertaining. He could see why so many faeries took to keeping endolgs. Their truth-sense was useful, but their personalities were great.

'Look down before you say that,' Flapwazzle told him in a comic drawl that suggested he was imitating some Realm celebrity Henry didn't know.

'Pardon?'

'Look down,' Flapwazzle said in his normal voice. 'Then tell me if you still like me.'

Henry looked down. 'What am I looking for?'

'Something that isn't there,' Flapwazzle said. 'The flow we've been following.'

'It's dried up!' Henry said. 'What do we do now?'

'Keep moving,' Flapwazzle said. 'Hopefully we'll soon find somewhere that looks familiar.'

They moved forward together. The tunnel loomed endlessly before them. After a few hundred yards, Henry said, 'Why do you think it dried up?' The liquid flow had been pointing their way to the river since they entered the main tunnels.

'That's what I don't like,' Flapwazzle said. 'Only time the water withdraws is when they're about to do a flush.'

Henry stopped, his heart suddenly thumping. 'You mean you think they're about to flush the system *now*?'

'I can't tell a lie – I think they may be.'

From somewhere behind them, Henry heard a distant rumbling sound. 'What are we going to do?' he asked in sudden panic.

'Get out of the main tunnels,' Flapwazzle said, swivelling his eyes to look behind. He'd obviously heard the same sound Henry had. 'We've *some* chance if we're in a drain or something.'

Henry looked around him wildly. 'I don't see any drains.'

Flapwazzle said, 'Neither do I.'

The roaring sound was getting louder.

'So what do we do now?'

'Run,' suggested Flapwazzle.

Henry ran. The echo of his footsteps was swallowed by the roaring noise behind.

He'd covered several hundred yards before he realised he was alone. He stopped. 'Flapwazzle?' he whispered.

There was no sign of Flapwazzle.

'Flapwazzle!' he called, loudly this time. But with a mounting sense of horror he knew there would be no answer. Stupid! Stupid! Stupid! He should have realised endolgs couldn't move nearly as fast as human beings. They had no feet. They crawled along by wriggling their whole flat little bodies like a snake. He should have picked Flapwazzle up and carried him. With a surge of guilt he realised it would have been so easy: Flapwazzle couldn't weigh much more than a few pounds. But Henry had been so concerned about his own safety he hadn't even thought of it. He'd taken off like a frightened rabbit and left Flapwazzle to ... to ...

'Flapwazzle!' he screamed, and began to run back down the tunnel.

Then he saw the wall of water rushing towards him.

fifty-one

'What do you think you're playing at?' Blue hissed furiously.

They were alone together in a small, insulated antechamber off the Great Hall. The Queen had assured them their privacy was guaranteed.

'We can't attack Lord Hairstreak,' Pyrgus said. 'He's … he's …' He shook his head helplessly.

'He's what?' Blue snapped. 'Come on, Pyrgus, pull yourself together.'

'He's working with our father now!' Pyrgus blurted. He actually looked as if he might be about to cry.

'He's *not* working with our father!' Blue snapped. 'Our father is under his influence – it's not the same thing. This is a great opportunity, can't you see? If the Forest Faerie help us, we can put paid to Lord Hairstreak once and for all. Didn't you notice what those elf-bolts can do? Once we have Hairstreak out of the way, we'll have Daddy back. We can nurse him back to health, get him the best medical treatment. He can take the throne again – Comma will step aside, you know he will, and if he doesn't we'll make him, or Daddy will make him. Daddy will be Purple Emperor again, just like he was before. It'll *all* be like what it was before; only better, because nobody will have

Hairstreak to worry about.'

Suddenly Pyrgus seemed to collapse in on himself. He looked grey and small. 'It won't be like it was before,' he said quietly. 'It *can't* be like it was before, not now, not ever.'

'Pyrgus, it *can*! We'll make plans. We'll call on the whole forest army if need be. We'll –'

'Blue, Daddy isn't ill – he's *dead*. It's not nursing or medical attention –' Pyrgus waved his hands helplessly. 'He's *dead*! That's why Hairstreak can control him. Whatever we do, it won't make any difference – he's still *dead*.'

After a moment, Blue said, 'It's going to be all right, Pyrgus. We'll *make* it all right. We'll get Daddy away from Hairstreak – that's obviously the first step. We'll bring him back here – here to the forest. We can hide him here and take however long it needs to get him back to normal. Queen Cleopatra will help.'

She climbed to her feet and there was a steely glint in her eye. 'It's time we went back to the others,' she said.

fifty-two

Henry flattened himself against the wall of the side drain and waited. He'd no idea if he was going to survive the next few minutes and part of him hardly cared: he felt so guilty about what he'd done to Flapwazzle. But another part, a greater part, cared very much indeed. More than anything else, he wanted to get out of these filthy sewers alive so he could find Blue and help Pyrgus out of the mess he was obviously in.

The rush of approaching water was so loud now it was almost deafening. The entrance to the main sewer tunnel was more than thirty feet away – far enough, he hoped, to keep him clear of any backwash. If he was right and he was lucky – if he was very, *very* lucky – the main force of water would sweep past so quickly that the side drain, which was on a higher level, might stay dry. But if he was wrong, he was dead.

Soon know, he thought. Poor Flapwazzle.

Suddenly he could see a roiling, surging force of water filling the entrance of the side drain like a manic tide. Astonishingly, he felt completely calm. He might be about to die, but there was absolutely nothing he could do.

Then, like a tide, the water retreated. The great flush still roared through the main sewer, but it had drained away from the side tunnel completely. Henry realised he was holding his breath, and released it explosively. He was safe! It was going to be all right!

Then suddenly he was being dragged towards the tunnel mouth.

There was nothing to hold on to. The walls of the side drain were wet with slime. His feet could get no purchase on the floor. There was a whistling of wind in his ears as if he were being buffeted by a storm. As he slid towards the entrance and that boiling mass of water, he realised what had happened. The sweep of water in the main tunnel was so great it was creating a vacuum in the side drains. As air rushed in to fill the vacuum, he was being swept towards the deadly torrent. The elemental noise of wind and water rose until it filled his universe.

Then stopped.

He could hear the roar of water receding distantly, but the vacuum popped and the wind noise died at once. He climbed unsteadily to his feet, gasping for breath. There were scratches on his arms and legs, but otherwise he was just fine; and he was no longer being sucked towards the main sewer. The flush was over. He'd survived.

Although it would be hours before the next torrent, Henry decided he wasn't going to stay inside the sewers a minute longer than he had to. Not that he was certain he'd have been prepared to risk the river anyway. In his last swimming lesson he'd managed only half a length of the pool before floundering. Now he was alone, it felt far more secure to stay on dry land if he possibly could.

Over the next hour, he investigated four side drains, one of them so confined he had to crawl along it on all fours. Three of them ended in gratings so firmly fixed he couldn't move them. The fourth seemed to be a ridiculous dead-end until he noticed the pipes that drained into it from the ceiling. None of them was big enough for him to insert anything bigger than his arm.

He was beginning to wonder if he might have to risk the river after all when the main tunnel forked and he saw distant daylight in the passage to his right.

For a moment he wondered if it might be wishful thinking, but the light in the distance was nothing like the green glow of the fungus closer by. It was the bluish white of a bright, cloudy day. He could almost taste it streaming down into the sewer. He turned into the right-hand tunnel, increased his pace, then started to run. He felt an elation out of all proportion. The light might be nothing, nothing at all, unreachable perhaps, but it was still light and he was still alive – he'd survived.

It was unbelievable. He'd found an inspection trap! Henry stared and, while he'd never been much for religion, he found himself offering up a little mental prayer. It couldn't be better. What he was looking at was a large metal grille set into the ceiling with daylight (no doubt at all about that now) streaming through. The grille was hinged, so it was clearly meant to be opened. But best of all, it hung above an alcoved terrace with a flight of broad stone steps leading up to it. He could reach it easily.

Henry ran up the steps, almost tripping on his feet in his haste. There was a small observation platform at the top and he stepped on to it, heart pounding. He reached up to push the grating, then stopped. It had one of those peculiar little box locks they used here in place of padlocks. The damn things usually had a magical charge and he had no idea at all how to open them. His heart dropped to the bottom of his stomach. It couldn't be locked, it couldn't be. But he knew with his luck it definitely could.

He pushed the grille anyway. It rolled aside smoothly at the first touch. Henry stared at it. The lock was either broken or someone had left it open. Daylight beckoned. He moved back on to the broad stone steps and took the last three at a run.

He was free!

fifty-three

Chalkhill drained the last of his glass and felt the music wind itself around his brain as a pleasing backdrop to Cyril's words. He held up a mental hand to stem the wangaramas's flow. (He was getting good at this.) *'You say you've infiltrated all the important power centres in the Realm?'*

'Most of them. Some of Hairstreak's household. The Imperial Court, although that's getting turned around a bit now. The Council of –'

'So you're linked with some important people?'

'Oh yes. Oh yes indeed.'

'Then why pick me for Purple Emperor?'

He thought there would be a hesitation, then possibly some judicious flattery and enough waffle for him to extract the real reason. But the wyrm answered at once. *'Because you're perfectly placed for the job.'*

Perfectly placed? *'Perfectly placed?'* Chalkhill asked.

'Our philosophers say we need an easy transition for the revolution to succeed, a smooth transfer of power between the existing legislation and our chosen host. In other words, the mass of common people must accept their new ruler. They won't know he has a wyrm inside him, of course.'

'That's what I was asking,' Chalkhill said. *'Why on*

earth should anybody accept me? I'm not of royal blood, I'm not even noble except in the broadest sense of the word.'

'But you won't become Emperor as you. You'll become the first Emperor Hairstreak.'

There was a huge silence, as if the inside of Chalkhill's head had turned into a vast, empty cathedral. The wyrm's last words floated down like gentle snowflakes and suddenly he knew exactly what they meant. 'You want me to go on with the impersonation!' he exclaimed excitedly. 'When Comma is to be crowned, you want me to go as Hairstreak, but when I assassinate Comma – it'll be Comma I assassinate now, of course, not Pyrgus – you want me to take his place. As Hairstreak.'

'Exactly,' said Cyril smugly. 'You're thinking like a wangaramas already.'

It was the most peculiar plan he'd ever heard, but it might work. Hairstreak was a member of a noble house, related to the old Emperor by marriage. More to the point, he had the support of half the Realm – he was the acknowledged leader of the Faeries of the Night. Coups had succeeded with a lot less going for them.

Except for one thing, of course.

Chalkhill frowned. 'What about the real Hairstreak? He's not going to sit around and watch me take the kingdom wearing his face.'

'The real Hairstreak won't be at the Coronation – he told you that himself.'

'No, wait a minute – he told me he wouldn't be at the Coronation when Pyrgus was going to be crowned. There's no reason for him to stay away from Comma's

Coronation. Comma is his puppet.'

'That's true, but he doesn't plan to go to Comma's Coronation either. He thinks the Faeries of the Light might accept the situation more easily if he keeps a low profile for a while.'

It made sense. All the same ... *'How do you know this?'*

'We have it from his Gatekeeper.'

Chalkhill blinked. *'You have a worm in Cossus Cossus?!'* he asked incredulously. It was just too delicious to be true. *'I always thought he had a funny walk.'*

'Cossus is one of our more important symbiotes. So you can take it our friend will not be at the Coronation. Once you kill Comma and proclaim yourself Emperor, you can denounce the real Hairstreak as an imposter, and have him arrested and hung.'

'But won't he tell everybody he's the real Hairstreak?'

'Of course he will, but who's going to believe him over the new Emperor? Besides, we've infiltrated his personal bodyguard as well as Cossus Cossus. With the wangarami helping, it'll be a piece of cake – all you have to do is find somewhere to lie low until we need you.'

Lying low was the least of his concerns. Chalkhill already knew exactly who could sort that out for him. There was only one other thing he could think of to worry about. *'I don't have the illusion spell we were going to use – Hairstreak was going to supply that.'*

'Oh, come on, Jasper,' the wyrm said exasperatedly. *'You think the entire resources of the Wangarami Nation can't stretch to a simple spell? Except it won't*

be an illusion spell – it'll be a permanent transformation.'

'You mean I'll look like Hairstreak for the rest of my life?'

'Exactly.'

'Cool!' Chalkhill exclaimed aloud. Everybody was afraid of Hairstreak, and the man was worth an absolute fortune. Power! Wealth! Fame! All in a single transformation spell!

A passing waiter brought him another glass of the intoxicating music.

fifty-four

Waiting in the Great Hall, Fogarty wondered what had happened to Henry. Wasn't like the boy not to tip up when he said. Especially when he was so obviously sweet on Blue.

He pushed himself out of his chair and walked stiffly to stand beside Gonepterix at the window. After a silent moment he suddenly realised that the view through the window was no illusion spell. He really *was* looking at a rocky shoreline and an angry sea.

'Where the hell are we?' he asked.

'Off world,' Gonepterix said. He looked a little startled.

'Off *world*?'

'For security,' Gonepterix explained.

These faeries could move you *off planet*? Fogarty frowned. It had to be portal technology of some sort. Except he'd seen no portal. But however they did it, the logistics were mind-boggling. You had to find the right sort of planet for a start – somewhere you could breathe where the sun didn't fry you and the gravity didn't crush you. Then you had to target its coordinates. Then you had to open up a space–time doorway, something like a wormhole, only bigger. Then –

It was slipping away from him. The whole thing was

incredible, yet they'd done it so casually. Thank God all they wanted was to be left alone. With technologies like this, they could take over the entire Realm in a fortnight, then swallow up Hael and the Analogue World for dessert.

'How far are we from the forest?' he asked Gonepterix.

To his astonishment Gonepterix didn't hesitate. 'Thirty-eight thousand light years.'

Fogarty blinked. Maybe it wasn't just the pretty face that made him Consort. Fogarty was about to push things further when Blue and Pyrgus walked back into the Hall.

Fogarty caught Pyrgus's expression at once. The boy looked almost ill, and it was Blue who turned to Queen Cleopatra and said decisively, 'Your Majesty, my brother and I want to thank you for your offer of help and accept it gratefully.' She looked from one face to the other as if challenging anyone to disagree. 'Now perhaps we can discuss our plans.'

fifty-five

It was very, very cold. At first, Henry thought it might just be the contrast with the sewers, which had been hot as well as smelly, but his breath was steaming from his mouth now and there was a rime of frost on one wall near a door. Where was this place? He was obviously in the lower reaches of the palace, but where exactly? Some sort of food store? The room above the sewer inspection trap was a stone-lined chamber with two doorways and a window so high on one wall that it touched a corner with the ceiling. Otherwise it was empty. No cupboards, no tables, no shelves, no hooks or rails; nowhere you would store food.

Why so cold? A temperature this low could not be natural. He couldn't see any coolant pipes, but the Realm might have some sort of magically-based refrigeration – a special spell-coating maybe.

Henry's fingers started to go numb and he realised he could freeze to death while he was trying to work out why he was so cold.

He made for the nearest doorway. The door wasn't locked. But his breath still frosted in the next chamber, which was just as cold and much more gloomy: the only illumination came from a dim, cobweb-encrusted glowglobe at the bottom of a flight of steep stone steps leading upwards.

Those steps intrigued him. He might be in the palace cellars – a likely place to be in the circumstances – and if so, the only way to go was up. He could get out of the palace and –

And what? Follow Blue and Pyrgus to Haleklind? He didn't even know where Haleklind was, but he'd worry about that once he had managed to get away from the palace and the loony old plud.

Henry climbed the steps. The door at the top was firmly locked.

Henry sat down on the steps to think. Why hadn't he brought something useful with him? There was a tool-kit in the house with a large wooden hammer (languishing on a shelf in the garage). There was ... but what was the use? Even a penknife would have come in handy, but he no more had a penknife than he had a key.

The door behind him opened.

Henry twisted round to find himself looking at a group of women wearing the most fantastic gowns that shimmered and clung as they moved.

'Hello,' Henry said, scrambling to his feet. He felt suddenly embarrassed. He was wearing combat trousers and his *BABE MAGNET* T-shirt and every-thing, including his face, was filthy from the sewers. He stared at the women, wondering if they worked for Queen Quercusia, wondering if they'd guess he was an escaped prisoner. Eventually he swallowed and said stupidly, 'I'm a bit lost.'

'Then we'd better help you find yourself again,' one of them smiled at him.

fifty-six

It was embarrassing, but very nice. The women brought him to a little room with a huge sunken tub filled with lovely foamy steaming scented water and insisted he have a bath. They didn't leave the room while he took his clothes off, although they *did* turn their backs and, as he slid beneath the foam, he wondered, hoped, was terrified they might actually help him. But all they actually did was take his smelly clothes away.

Henry lay in the tub and realised how exhausted he was. There was something in the water – some herbal additive maybe – that soaked the stress from his muscles. He noticed some of them were paining him, which wasn't surprising considering he'd been shrunk to the size of a butterfly and nearly been drowned in a sewer, but the pain gradually soaked away as well. He wiggled his toes and thought of Blue. Funny thing was, she'd been in a bath like this the first time he'd seen her. Attended by her hand-maidens. His bath was a lot more private, but he had hand-maidens too, of a sort. He wondered who they were.

He sank down quickly when one of them came in carrying towels with something colourful on top. They were very different, these women, different ages, different sizes, different looks, but they all walked the same way, really gracefully, and they all wore these amazing dresses – gowns, he supposed you'd call them – absolutely amazing the way they ... sort of ... clung and moved. The women were very nice too. They'd all been very nice to him, although they didn't have much idea about privacy.

'Brought you fresh clothes,' the woman said, leaving the little pile at the edge of the tub. She smiled at him. 'Come through when you've finished. We might even manage something for you to eat.'

Henry watched her as she left, riveted by the last thing she'd said. A minute ago he'd been seriously contemplating resting his head against the side of the tub and letting himself drift off to sleep. Now he realised he was absolutely ravenous.

He climbed out of the tub and dried himself quickly. There must have been something in the water – or possibly sprinkled on the towels – because the exhaustion left him at once. The hunger stayed, though.

They hadn't brought back his clothes. They'd left a colourful silk outfit comprising matching blouse, britches and socks that looked as if they'd come off a gipsy. He scrabbled around for underwear, but there was none. Since it was the gipsy gear or nothing, he pulled on the britches, feeling most peculiar about the underwear, then the blouse. As he was reaching for the socks, he had a sudden surge of confidence.

It was a peculiar feeling for Henry, but it was very definite. The clothes were nothing like he usually wore – too brightly coloured and a bit girly – but somehow he felt really good in them. (He pulled on the right sock.) Macho and heroic. Well, sort of ... (He pulled on the left sock.) He liked the way the material moved when he moved. Somehow he thought it made him look good. Well, better than the old *BABE MAGNET* anyway, although he fancied he might really be a bit of a babe magnet in this gear.

The boots were the strangest part of the whole outfit. They were dark brown, just short of knee-length, but made entirely of the same silk as his blouse and britches. Even the sole was no more than a few extra layers of silk to give a cushioning effect. They wouldn't last five minutes on stony ground, but he'd worry about that later. For the moment, they moulded to his feet and legs as comfortably as slippers.

He was still feeling good as he walked from the bathroom.

The women were waiting for him. With his newfound confidence, Henry smiled and said, 'I don't know your names, but I'd like to thank you.'

'My name is Peach Blossom,' the nearest woman said. She smiled back at Henry, without making any attempt to introduce the others. 'Thank us for what?'

They were putting food on a little table. Some of it looked unfamiliar, but all of it smelled delicious. 'I don't know – the bath.' And the food, he thought, except that they hadn't actually offered it to him yet. He remembered his manners and added belatedly, 'My name's Henry.'

'We know who you are.'

Henry didn't know what to say to that. What he did say eventually was, 'Who are you?'

'Silk Mistresses,' Peach Blossom said. 'We're Sisters of the Silk Guild.'

*   *   *

He was eating something called ordle which had a smoky flavour and was absolutely delicious. Without thinking, he said, 'Will you get in trouble for this?'

'Why should we get in trouble?' Peach Blossom asked quickly.

Uh-oh. He was sorry he'd said it now. There was no reason for them to know he'd just broken out of the palace dungeons or any of that. If he'd kept his mouth shut, he could have pretended he was just a casual visitor who'd got lost and strayed into somewhere he shouldn't. Maybe he could still convince them that was all he was. Except when he'd told her his name she'd said, *We know who you are.* How did she know who he was? But if she did know who he was, did she know it wasn't all that long since he'd been thrown into the dungeons?

Henry decided to feel his way around it. With luck he might not have to give himself away. 'The new Queen's not too happy with me,' he said as casually as he could. If he played it cool enough, he might find out subtly what they felt about the Queen before he had to commit himself.

'The new Queen's loony as a Border Redcap,' Peach Blossom said.

fifty-seven

He *knew* there was something he should have done. He'd thrown her in without staking her heart. Brimstone looked up at the crows circling overhead and making such a racket. Too late now. There was somebody coming and he didn't know how much time he had before they got here. Whoever was approaching was close and there was no way Brimstone could afford to be found beside an open hole with his wife's body at the bottom. Especially with her skull smashed in and her stupid wizened little brain oozing out of her nose.

He grabbed the spade and set to filling in the grave.

It was hard work, but he couldn't afford to slow. The crows were going berserk now, stupid birds, and he even fancied he could hear somebody stomping through the undergrowth. Fortunately filling a grave with loose earth was a lot faster than digging it in the first place. He flung the last spadeful and glanced around desperately. The whole place looked what it was – freshly-dug earth. He might as well have put up a notice: *New Grave Here.*

Dead leaves!

That was it – dead leaves! Dead leaves for a dead wife. If he could just get the body covered up loosely now, he could divert whoever was coming and get back later to finish the job. He began to strew armfuls of dead leaves across the newly-dug grave. But he was nowhere nearly finished when he was transfixed by a bright blue light and something tall and hideous stepped into the clearing. Brimstone dropped the rest of the leaves. He felt his heart stop and his face go pale.

No more than five yards away loomed Beleth, Prince of Darkness.

Beleth looked awful.

He'd appeared in his gigantic demon form, but one of his horns was crumpled, two of his fangs were broken and he had an ear missing. There was a fading bruise under his right eye, a pulsating lump on his head and a hideous scar that ran all the way down his left cheek, over his jaw and across his throat. Brimstone had always been terrified of the Infernal Prince, but at the moment the creature hardly looked capable of chewing off a baby's leg. His heart restarted and the colour flooded back into his face.

'What happened to you?' he asked.

Beleth scowled. 'That's not important.'

'No, really,' Brimstone said. 'I'm concerned.'

'A bomb blew up in my face,' Beleth said shortly. 'Fortunately this form is virtually indestructible. But what's important –'

'How come all the Hael portals are closed?' Brimstone asked curiously. Beleth must have come by vimana: it was the only way. And since a transport vimana trip would take years, he had to have come alone in one of the fast single-seater saucers, which he'd never, ever done before.

Beleth covered the distance between them in three massive strides and caught him by the throat. Brimstone felt himself lifted up as if he were thistle-down. '*Gaah!*' he choked. '*Gaah!*'

'What's important,' Beleth repeated quietly, his face close to Brimstone's own, 'is that the rest of the Hael Realm wasn't as fortunate as I was.' He released Brimstone, who dropped back to the ground with a spine-jarring thud.

'The Hael Realm was destroyed?' Brimstone gasped, massaging his throat.

'Don't be stupid. But it's in serious need of recon-struction.' He glared at Brimstone with blood-red eyes. 'The cost will run to billions.'

Brimstone swallowed painfully. 'Bit strapped at the moment, I'm afraid. I –' He caught Beleth's expression and ground to a halt. 'That's not what it's about, is it?' He wondered what it *was* about, but one thing was for certain: this had to be good news. If the Hael Realm lay in ruins, then Beleth would have more on his mind than a broken contract. Besides, that whole silly business about sacrificing Pyrgus was old news now, hardly worth even think—

'What it's about,' growled Beleth, 'is treachery! What it's about is ingratitude! What it's about is broken agreements, welching on bargains, turn-coating scumbags!'

Perhaps it *was* worth thinking about after all. 'I'm sorry about that contract business,' Brimstone said hurriedly. 'Circumstances beyond my –'

'Not you, you imbecile!' Beleth roared. 'That mealy-mouthed cretinous little upstart Hairstreak!'

Brimstone blinked. 'Hairstreak? *Lord* Hairstreak?'

Beleth and Lord Hairstreak had been allies in the last attempt to overthrow the Faeries of the Light.

'Yes. *Lord* Hairstreak! Crapulous crud-faced puke-mouthed sewage-headed little ... little ... little ... '

Beleth was losing it. His eyes were flashing seven colours and flecks of spittle were flying from his mouth. The bump on his head had started to pulsate and the scar across his throat seemed to be opening up to show a row of straining stitches. Brimstone wondered if he might actually have had to sew his head back on after the bomb exploded. But this was clearly no time for speculation.

'I thought you and Hairstreak were allies?' he said quickly.

'*Were*,' said Beleth sourly. 'Operative word. Past tense. Hairstreak was happy to accept my help when he thought it would put him on the Peacock Throne. Now I need his, he doesn't want to know.'

'That's dreadful,' Brimstone said sympathetically, wondering what Beleth had expected from a Faerie of the Night. 'He's betrayed you in your hour of need, is that it?'

'Exactly!' Beleth said.

Seemed like a good idea to Brimstone. Beleth was clearly weak now. On his knees, in fact. Perfect time to kick him. Except that demon princes always had their resources – they commanded some very nasty magic. Besides, Beleth now knew Brimstone had been burying a body. Perhaps it was safest to be more subtle.

'So,' he said cautiously, 'what do you want from me?'

Beleth told him.

fifty-eight

It was weird to approach the Purple Palace as an enemy might, examining the terrain for cover, checking points of vulnerability, looking out for guard patrols. Pyrgus felt a mixture of nervous excitement and nausea. It was all so familiar – the river, the island, the palace itself.

He glanced at his companions. Blue, of course. Dearest Blue. He didn't think he'd have got through any of this without her. He'd always been better at doing than planning and since he ... since his fa— and now he could hardly think straight any more. It was thanks to Blue they had a plan in place now. And it was thanks to Blue that with just a little luck, they might clear up this mess.

Next to Blue was a wizard engineer named Ziczac – a tiny, bearded Forest Faerie with brown eyes in a wizened face that made him look like a little woodland animal peering through a bush. He had the technical skills to penetrate walls.

Pyrgus remembered how lost he'd felt during that little discussion, although Mr Fogarty had obviously followed it. The bottom line seemed to be that while Forest Faerie were able to phase-shift into solid surfaces once the necessary magic was in place, setting it up for the first time was something that needed specialist skills. (And testing the set-up was always dangerous, Queen Cleopatra warned. It took only a small misjudgement and you could find yourself trapped in the middle of a solid rock, suffocating to death.) Ziczac was one of the few who had the skills. He carried the necessary equipment in a small backpack.

Protecting Ziczac, Blue and himself were three Forest Faerie soldiers. One of them, to Pyrgus's secret delight, was Nymph.

That was it. There'd been a brief discussion about sending more troops but Blue had overruled the idea without even bothering to consult Pyrgus. She said a full-scale attack might precipitate just the sort of civil war that had been so narrowly averted only weeks before. Far better to stage a small-scale commando raid and simply rescue their father. Once he was removed from Hairstreak's influence, they could decide what would happen next.

Pyrgus hoped they'd be able to find their father quickly – the operation relied on the element of surprise. But he felt fairly confident he could still command the loyalty of many in the palace building. They should have help once they were safely inside.

There was no question of using the ferry to get across to the palace. Neither Pyrgus nor Blue trusted personal illusion spells, and without them their faces were far too easily recognised for them to approach the island openly. Consequently they were now crouched in the shelter of reeds nearly two hundred yards downstream of the official crossing.

Pyrgus glanced at Nymph. 'Do I take your Queen at her word, or should we all get ready to swim?'

Nymph gave Pyrgus a basilisk look, softened by the hint of a grin. 'Today you keep your feet dry, Crown Prince,' she told him. He noticed she never used his given name, and his title was always granted with a tiny emphasis as if she found it ironic. She had really nice legs. The uniform of the forest army ended in green tights that showed them off wonderfully.

Pyrgus reluctantly dragged his gaze upwards. Nymph was pulling some sort of net from the pouch around her waist. As she drew it clear, she cast it outwards over the river as if trying to catch a fish. But somewhere between the movement of her wrist and striking the surface of the water, the net transformed into a smaller version of the raft-like transport the Forest Faerie used on their overhead roadways. It should have been swept away by the current at once, but instead remained as firmly in place as if it had been anchored.

Pyrgus blinked and tried not to show he was impressed. The Forest Faerie kept producing spell technology like nothing he'd ever seen before. Transforming the appearance of something was easy enough: all you had to do was coat it with an illusion spell. Changing what it did was more difficult, but still possible if you had the money for expensive magic. But nothing he'd ever seen changed the essential nature of anything. You could make a pandatherium look and act like an endolg, but it would still have the weight and mass of a pandatherium. Yet this raft, in different form, could be rolled up small enough and light enough to be carried in a slim girl's pouch. That simply wasn't possible, except that he'd seen it for himself.

'On to the raft!' Nymph hissed. 'I have to get us cloaked.'

There was something about her that reminded Pyrgus of Blue. Not that they looked alike, and Nymph was older, of course, but now he was getting to know her better he noticed a bossy streak emerging. Certainly she was a take-charge sort of girl. He wondered what she meant by getting them cloaked, but decided to trust she knew what she was doing.

Blue was less trusting. 'What do you mean, *get us cloaked*?'

'Hide us so we shall not be seen by anyone in the palace,' Nymph said.

'Invisibility?'

Nymph shook her head. 'With invisibility you're still there.'

Which, as an answer, made no sense at all to Pyrgus. But he was anxious to get on. 'I think we should climb on, Blue,' he said softly. She glared at him, but stepped at once on to the raft.

Both Blue and the raft disappeared.

'It *is* invisibility,' Pyrgus said.

But Nymph was shaking her head again. 'Cloaking,' she insisted. 'You cannot feel the vessel or your sister unless I deactivate.' She caught the look on his face and added, 'Go on – try: we have time.'

Pyrgus stretched out his hands to the spot where Blue had been before she vanished. They encountered nothing. 'Blue?' he whispered.

'She can see you and hear you,' Nymph said. 'But you cannot sense her in any way. Nor our transport. Feel.'

Pyrgus knelt down and swept his hand along the

segment of water in front of him. There was no invisible raft. Blue might have stepped out of reach, but the raft had been solidly moored, or so it seemed. Except now it was gone.

Nymph, who was clearly enjoying this, said, 'Now step on board, please.'

Pyrgus straightened up, frowning. 'It's not there any more.'

Nymph actually grinned. 'Just take a pace forward, Crown Prince. Did I not promise you would not get wet today?'

He knew it was a challenge and took it up without a second's hesitation. He stepped forward into what looked like the surface of the swiftly running river.

He was on the raft with Blue. The others were lined up on the river bank.

'What was all that about?' Blue asked.

'Could you see me?'

'Pefectly,' Blue sniffed.

'You could see what I was doing?'

'Right down to your simpering at little Miss Nymph Know-it-all,' Blue said.

Although there was no sign of a propulsion system and no distinctive scent of magic, the raft cut directly across the current.

'What's driving us?' Pyrgus asked quietly.

'No need to whisper,' Nymph told him. 'We can't be heard outside the cloak.' She glanced around as if to emphasise the fact there was nobody to hear them in the middle of the river anyway. She looked back at Pyrgus and smiled slightly. 'We have a standard magical drive. Forward thrust, directional controls, low-grade levitation to reduce the friction.'

'There's no smell,' Pyrgus said.

'Not much point in cloaking if they could still smell us,' Nymph said, without explaining how the Forest Faerie managed it.

Pyrgus was about to press the point when he noticed they were approaching their destination already. The Old Keep of the palace, built in deep prehistory using stones so large that modern technology could no longer handle them, hung over the rearward cliff edge of the island. The Keep itself was largely used for storage now, but it remained attached to the main body of the building. Guard posts were minimal, since it had long been believed that the Keep could not be breached from the river – an idea Pyrgus promised himself would be quickly laid to rest if their present mission succeeded.

The raft docked quietly within a tiny inlet beside some rocks. There was a narrow stretch of stony beach, then the low, sheer cliff topped by the towering walls of the Keep. Pyrgus allowed his eyes to drift upwards, then froze. There were guards on the battlements. Even at this distance he could see they were armed with lethal *kris* wands.

He became aware of Blue at his shoulder, also looking upwards. 'Hairstreak's taking no chances,' she said.

'There are guards,' Pyrgus called over his shoulder.

Nymph moved to stand beside him on the other side from Blue. 'We're safe so long as we stay on the raft,' she said, 'but to get in we will have to cross that beach. Once we do that the cliff will shelter us – they can't see much looking straight down – but if they spot us crossing, they can pick us off like flies.' She'd clearly noticed the guards' weapons as well.

Blue turned to the wizard. 'Can you make us invisible?'

Ziczac shrugged. 'I'm a specialist. I don't do invisibility.'

Pyrgus said, 'What about this cloaking business? Can you extend that? Maybe take the raft across the beach?'

It was Nymph who answered. 'The vehicle is only designed for water usage. And there's no way to extend the cloak beyond it.'

Blue glanced at Pyrgus. 'Is there another inlet that would take us closer to the walls?'

'Not that I know of.'

'So we have to risk the beach,' Blue said thoughtfully.

Nymph said firmly, 'We soldiers will take the Wizard Ziczac and protect him while he does his work. You will remain on the vehicle where you will be safe. When all is ready, you may dash across the beach to join us.'

Blue gave her a look that would have shattered glass. 'We all cross together. Two crossings double the chance of being seen. It's a small distance and the overhang will protect us once we reach the cliff.'

Nymph turned to Pyrgus. 'Is this your wish, Crown Prince?'

'Yes,' Pyrgus said promptly. He fancied Nymph a lot, but long experience had taught him not to get on the wrong side of Blue when she was in this mood.

The plan was a simple one. They would wait until the guards were looking the other way, then make a run for it. The trouble was, the guards never seemed to look the other way at the same time. Some would stare out across the water, some to their left, some to their right, but there was always at least one watching the narrow stretch of beach. They all wore palace uniforms, but Pyrgus was firmly convinced these were Faeries of the Night: they had the jerky, paranoid look that made them such excellent watchdogs.

After a while Nymph said, 'We need a diversion.' She glanced across at Ziczac, who nodded slightly.

'What did you have in mind?' Blue asked. To Pyrgus there was almost a hint of suspicion in her tone.

Nymph shrugged. She turned her head to look out across the expanse of water. The river was particularly wide here, but they could still see the encroaching city suburbs on the further bank. A few of the houses had their own jetties and personal boats.

Ziczac squatted nimbly on the floor of the raft, adjusting his robe to cover his knees. He began to hum quietly to himself.

'What's he doing?' Pyrgus asked no one in particular.

'Wizard's work,' Nymph said. 'Don't you have hummers in your Court?'

Pyrgus didn't. He'd never even heard the word *hummer* used in magic before. But Blue said, 'Illusion, isn't it? Sort of.'

Nymph looked at her with just the barest hint of admiration. 'That's right. Sort of.'

One of the guards on the ramparts suddenly shouted. Pyrgus looked up in time to see him point to something in the water. In seconds the remaining guards were running to join him.

'What are they seeing?' Blue asked.

'Dragon, probably,' Nymph said. 'He likes to do

dragons. Or a sea serpent, since it's in the water. Or it could be naked mermaids – he's got a bit of a naughty streak.' She glanced fondly at Ziczac, then archly at Pyrgus.

'Let's go,' Blue said tightly. She looked at Ziczac without the fondness. 'Can he hum and run at the same time?'

Ziczac waved a dismissive hand in her direction.

It took them less than a minute to cross the narrow stretch of beach. Ziczac stopped humming once they reached the shelter of the cliff face. He grinned at Blue and Pyrgus. 'Giant fireball,' he said. 'I made them see a giant fireball – very bright. Thing is, it leaves an impression on the retina, just like the real thing. I think those boys up there are Nighters, so they're particularly light-sensitive. They'll be seeing spots for the next five minutes. Keep them occupied. Give us time to get inside.'

Pyrgus looked at him gratefully. It meant a lot to have a skilled wizard along on a mission. He began to think they might have a real chance of reaching his father after all.

fifty-nine

'There are those in the Realm,' Peach Blossom said, 'who will not rest until Prince Pyrgus is restored to his rightful place. Prince Comma might as well be a full-bred Nighter now. Everybody knows it's Black Hairstreak who rules. The old Queen, Comma's mother, is dangerous as a slith, but her brother is the one who holds the reins of power. It cannot be allowed to continue.'

From her expression and those of the women around her, Henry had no doubt at all that the Silken Sisterhood counted themselves among those who wanted Pyrgus back. He wondered briefly if they were doing anything about it. From the war movies he watched on television, resistance movements sprang up like mushrooms in times of trouble. 'Do you know where they've gone?' he asked. 'Pyrgus and Blue – the Crown Prince and his sister? Is it true they're in Haleklind?'

Peach Blossom nodded. 'Yes.'

Henry blinked at her. 'I don't suppose you know where that is?'

'It's a bordering country, outside the Empire. That's why Hairstreak sent them there.'

Henry felt his heart sink. 'Is it far?'

'You want to go to them?'

Henry didn't answer at once. He was out of his depth here and had been since he arrived back in the Realm. He'd translated to help Blue – and Pyrgus – but he'd never expected to be involved in a crisis anything like this. Did he want to go to them, to join them in exile? Was there anything he could really do to help? There would probably be fighting sooner or later and he was no soldier. And everything was going to take far longer than he had thought. How long would the lethe spell continue to work on his mother and Aisling? All the same ... He blinked.

'Yes,' he said. 'Yes, I do.'

'We may be able to help you,' Peach Blossom said. She glanced at him sideways. 'And do something about that gash on your face.' She frowned a little. 'If I didn't know better, I'd have thought it looked like a spinner slash.'

The women weren't like any others Henry had ever known, although there was a ruthlessness about them that reminded him a little of his mother. He found himself being told what to do. There was no discussion about anything.

The bright clothes that had made him feel so good about himself were gone now, replaced by well-cut homespun of rough silk that he'd only just stopped the Sisters helping him to put on.

'You don't want to be noticed,' Peach Blossom said. 'But on the other hand, you don't want to be dressed in rags either. You need to be taken seriously, especially in Haleklind. The wizards lay much store by appearances. Nothing flashy, but the proper cut will help get you access anywhere.'

'Thank you,' Henry said, wondering what on earth she was talking about.

'You'll need that to find the Crown Prince,' Peach Blossom said, as if reading his thoughts. 'Now –' She handed him a pouch made from thin, shiny material that looked both waterproof and tough. 'This is your map and some gold.'

Henry blinked. 'Gold?'

'You can't possibly set out for Haleklind on foot. Much too far. You'll be little use to our royals if you take a month to reach them. The gold is to buy passage on public transports.'

Public transports? What public transports? Henry was as lost in the Realm as if he'd been dumped in the middle of the Sahara Desert. How could he take a public transport if he didn't know where to find one, didn't even know what they looked like? But despite his deepening confusion, he said, 'Gold? I really can't accept –'

'You don't have any option,' Peach Blossom cut him off. 'Believe me, you will not survive without coin. If it makes you feel any better, consider yourself in the employ of the Sisterhood. We wish you to carry a message to Prince Pyrgus and Princess Blue.'

'Is that in the pouch as well?' Henry asked.

Peach Blossom shook her head. 'Not that sort of message,' she said. 'We wish you only to tell them that the Sisters of the Silk Guild remain loyal to their rightful ruler and will fight to the death to restore him to the throne.' She hesitated. 'And correct the abomination of Lord Hairstreak in what he has done to the former Emperor.'

Henry murmured, 'I'll tell them.' He felt real admiration for these women. Even from the little he'd seen of the Realm since his return, he was sure they were risking their lives.

'One of the Sisters will take you into the city,' Peach Blossom said. 'Hairstreak does not yet suspect the Guild. But you must –' She broke off. 'What was that?'

That's trouble, Henry thought. There were sounds in the corridor outside and a woman's scream. Then the door of the chamber slammed open. Henry caught the barest glimpse of soldiers in black uniforms and dark shades before a ball of flame roared across the room to catch him in the chest. The impact was so violent it lifted him completely off his feet and slammed him back against one wall. His head struck stone in a sunburst of agony. He felt himself sliding down the wall and clung desperately to consciousness.

But by the time he reached the floor his limbs were folding like a rag doll and everything had turned to black.

Sixty

The last time Pyrgus had been in the Keep he was only four years old. The experience had frightened him so much he'd burst into tears and wailed until his father picked him up. Afterwards, when Apatura Iris asked him why he'd been so scared, little Pyrgus told him firmly there were ghosts in the Keep.

The place still felt haunted. Pyrgus found himself in the middle of a stone-flagged floor waiting for the others to materialise. The chambers of the Keep were enormous – so enormous they dwarfed the stacks of storage crates pushed against the walls. They were also gloomy. Light filtered through slit windows, but was absorbed by the grey stone walls. The architecture was like nothing in the rest of the palace – there were levels upon levels, joined by wide, short flights of shallow steps. It gave the whole place the look of a three-dimensional maze.

Blue appeared, stepping out of a solid wall. She looked around and shivered.

'Have you been in here before?' Pyrgus asked.

She shook her head. 'Never. Do you know the way out?'

'I'm not sure. It's a long time since I've been here.' He decided not to tell her quite how long.

Nymph and her soldiers came through in a bunch. The two others were tough, silent men whose eyes darted round habitually as if watching for the possibility of an attack. Then Ziczac appeared, a bemused expression on his face. He stared at the multi-level chamber.

'Archaic engineering,' he murmured. 'I've never seen it before.'

Nymph said to Pyrgus, 'Can you lead us into the main palace, or should Ziczac ...?'

Pyrgus was looking from one level to the other, trying to remember. 'I think so. I mean I think so. These are stores now, so the doors will be locked, but they should all recognise me – or Blue, come to that. With luck it'll be too early for Hairstreak to have changed the spell, even if he thought we might come back.' He hesitated. 'If we *are* in problems, can Ziczac get us in anywhere?'

He asked the question of Nymph, but Ziczac answered directly. 'Not exactly.'

'What do you mean, *not exactly*?' Blue demanded.

The wizard grinned benignly. 'We can only penetrate thick surfaces. A thin wall or door will stop us dead.'

'That doesn't make sense,' Pyrgus frowned.

'No, it doesn't, does it?' Ziczac agreed. 'I've never really followed it myself, but that's the way the magic works. You need to move inside something that's bigger than you are. The outer walls are enormous: the old cultures always built that way. But inside walls could be a different matter. I suppose we might risk it in an emergency, but ...'

'There's a chance of getting stuck,' Nymph said.

'Which usually proves lethal,' Ziczac frowned. 'In fact, I've never heard of anyone who survived it.'

In the event, they managed quite well. The different levels were confusing and there were times when Pyrgus was a lot less certain than he tried to appear, but the lock spells recognised him without a problem so that they passed quickly through door after door. They reached an archway that looked decidedly familiar.

Pyrgus released a sigh of relief. 'That's it,' he said, pointing to the corridor beyond. 'That will take us into the lower reaches of the palace.' He stepped through the arch and Hairstreak's guards fell on him like an avalanche.

Stupidly, all he could think of was that he didn't have a weapon ready. He was armed with a short sword and fire wand supplied by the Forest Queen and his own Halek blade, overlooked by Hairstreak's men when they set him on the ouklo into exile. But the sword was in its scabbard, the wand in his belt and the Halek blade hidden in his boot. In short, he was helpless as an idiot. He spun and drove his elbow into the stomach of the nearest attacker and had the satisfaction of seeing the man double up and drop his sword. But there were others grinning evilly and *they* hadn't forgotten their weapons. He would be dead in seconds.

Then Nymph was at his side and she was utterly amazing. She moved faster than he would have believed possible, sometimes even blurring. She was carrying some sort of forest weapon, a triangular blade that was too short for a sword, too long for a dagger and left a silver energy-trail much like a Halek knife. She kicked the guard nearest him and killed him when he doubled up. Then she moved protectively in front of

Pyrgus and launched herself savagely at two of the dead man's companions.

Pyrgus drew his own sword and spun to face another of their attackers. From the corner of his eye, he could see the forest soldiers hurl themselves into the fray. They had abandoned their bows for hand weapons, presumably to avoid injuring their own people in the close-pressed combat, but they moved almost as quickly as Nymph. As he parried a thrust from his opponent, Pyrgus realised suddenly how lucky he had been when he faced Nymph himself. The kick to the groin was obviously a favourite move, but at least in his case she'd not followed it up by cutting his throat.

It was over in minutes. Two of the guards were dead, the remaining three dying from multiple wounds. Now the heat of battle was over and he had a chance to remove the guards' dark glasses, Pyrgus could see from their eyes they were all Nighters – Hairstreak's men without a doubt. Even the black uniforms carried the House Hairstreak crest. Clearly Hairstreak did not trust the existing palace military, however firmly Comma was under his thumb; he had lost no time in moving in his own people.

'A thought occurs to me,' said Ziczac, staring at the bodies. 'If we wore black uniforms and glasses, we may find ourselves less liable to attack. At least if *you* wore black uniforms – most of these are too big for me.'

For a moment Pyrgus didn't follow, then it hit him. 'Great idea, Ziczac! Doesn't matter about your uniform. If anybody asks we'll just say… well …'

'Say I'm your prisoner. Say I'm personal wizard to Lord Hairstreak. Say –'

But Pyrgus was already stripping the nearest body.

Ziczac's ruse worked well. As a disciplined party of House Hairstreak guards, they entered the main body of the palace and passed two black-uniformed sentry posts unchallenged. As they marched along a gloomy corridor, Pyrgus took the opportunity to say quietly to Nymph, 'I think you saved my life back there.'

'I think perhaps you were not ready for the attack.'

Pyrgus suppressed a grin. 'Definitely not.' He stared into her eyes. 'I want to thank you.'

To his surprise she blushed, then covered her embarrassment by shrugging. 'It is nothing.'

It was the first sign of weakness he'd seen in her. 'You think saving my life is nothing?' He let the tease show in his voice.

Her colour rose another notch. 'I didn't mean that,' she said hurriedly. 'I –'

But he never found out what she did mean because suddenly they were under attack again. An arm circled his neck and a slim, stiletto blade plunged towards his heart. Before he had time to react, the blade stopped short of his skin and his assailant gasped. He twisted and found he had been seized by a woman. She stared at him open-mouthed. Pyrgus hesitated for a fraction of a second, then kicked out to sweep her feet from under her. She went down badly and struck her head against the wall. Her eyes rolled back, then slowly closed.

There were others attacking, all of them women and two of them almost as fast in their movements as Nymph and her companions. But their weapons were no match for those of Pyrgus's party. The Forest Faeries pointed fire wands.

'No!' Pyrgus shouted.

Nymph glanced at him in surprise.

'No killing!' Pyrgus screamed. These were Faeries of the Light – his own people. They'd attacked what they thought to be a party of Hairstreak's guards. There was resistance in the palace, maybe even an early revolt. These women were on his side! 'Don't you know me?' he called to them.

But the women had seen the wands now and were already running down the corridor. 'Leave them!' Blue shouted, having obviously reached the same conclusion as Pyrgus. Both calls came too late. The Forest Faeries were already racing after them. Even Ziczac joined the chase. 'Your new girlfriend is a menace!' Blue hissed as she ran to follow.

Pyrgus thundered after her, screaming 'Stop!' The women went through a doorway. Ziczac hurled some sort of fireball after them. Then Pyrgus caught up and fought his way through his own party. 'Leave them! Leave them!' He grabbed Nymph's arm as she was about to stab –

To one side came Blue's shocked whisper: 'My God, it's the Silk Mistresses!' Then she shouted, 'Stop it, all of you!'

Nymph pulled back, but in the general melee Pyrgus couldn't see what was happening with the others. He pushed forward frantically. They mustn't harm their own people.

Beyond the group of women, there was a body crumpled on the floor. Blue was right behind him now and she saw it a split second after he did. He heard her gasp, then she pushed him aside and ran forward wailing, 'Henry! Noooo!'

Sixty-one

'*Are you sure you know what you're doing?*' Chalkhill asked nervously. He was back at Hairstreak's mansion in the forest after an even more nerve-wracking trip than the last time. Cyril had guided him through an ill-marked winding trail that smelled of sliths and now they'd emerged between some densely-planted rose bushes on the edge of that palatial lawn.

Chalkhill stared across the vast expanse of green, very well aware that crossing it would leave him totally exposed every inch of the way. He looked round for haniels in the surrounding trees, but his real worry was Hairstreak's guards, who had a well-deserved reputation of shooting first and asking questions afterwards. He could be a pin-cushion of arrows before he took three steps.

'*Of course I know what I'm doing,*' the wyrm said testily. '*Cossus Cossus is expecting you.*'

'*Yes, you said that. But what happens if Hairstreak sees me?*'

The wangaramas gave the mental equivalent of an impatient grunt. '*What do you think happens if Lord Hairstreak sees you? He doesn't know what we're planning, does he? As far as he's concerned, you're still a loyal servant. If you do bump into him – which you*' won't – you can simply say you came back for fresh instructions.'

It made sense, but Chalkhill was still terrified of Lord Hairstreak. In desperation he went back to an argument he'd already lost several times. '*Why can't we just go somewhere else? All I have to do is wait until Comma's Coronation.*'

Cyril gave the mental equivalent of an exhausted sigh. '*That* isn't *all you have to do. I've told you ten thousand times already: you have to be able to pass for Lord Hairstreak. You weren't exactly a star pupil when he sent you to the Facemaster, were you?*'

'*It was just the walk,*' said Chalkhill testily. '*But I've got you to help me with that now. That's why we were introduced in the first place.*'

'*I can only help you with the walk,*' Cyril said. '*There are all sorts of other things. You have to know the people he knows, greet them by name. This isn't like it was before. Hairstreak attending Pyrgus's Coronation could have got away with being introverted and grumpy – people would expect that since he didn't like Pyrgus. But everybody knows Comma is just a figurehead. They'll expect Lord Hairstreak to be strutting round like a turkey-cock. And don't forget you'll still be playing Hairstreak afterwards. This isn't a few hours with a Facemaster – you're going to need every minute we have left to prepare you for the part. Cossus himself will be coaching you. You'll need practice. Ordering servants around, that sort of thing.*'

'*I know how to order servants around,*' Chalkhill said sourly.

'*And you'll be dealing with high-class demons,*' the wyrm said, ignoring him. '*I know the portals are shut just now, but Hairstreak has his demon pits so you can get used to whipping the silly creatures before the portals open again. Then there's the question of –'*

Chalkhill felt worn out, as he always did by this stage of the mental conversation. 'All right,' he said aloud. 'You win.'

If a haniel ate him on his way across the lawn, it would be a blessed relief.

Sixty-two

Henry's head hurt, but not half as much as his hands and chest. He had trouble focusing his eyes, but even so he could see his upturned palms had turned to raw meat. He tried to move and his body protested with a howl of agony.

Henry groaned but no sound came.

There were people around him, but he couldn't remember who they were. They swam into his field of vision, then out again, their voices rising and falling, approaching and fading. One of them looked like Blue. He hoped it was Blue because that would mean she wasn't dead in the forest. He couldn't see whether she was cross with him for being late.

'He's still alive. I think he's still alive.'

'Can you see breathing?'

'No.'

'I thought I saw him open his eyes.'

'Reflex. You often get that with a fireball.'

'The body reacts for hours after the heart stops. Energies keep working on the nerves.'

'I saw one walk five paces once, dead as a coffin nail.'

'He's alive, you stupid cow!' This from Blue. He was sure he recognised her voice.

Henry tried to say 'Hello, Blue', but no sound came. His eyes were closing again, all of their own accord, so that he lay in the red, pain-filled darkness. It occurred to him that he was dying and he didn't care.

'He's alive!' Blue said again. 'He's breathing!'

'I can't see him breathing.'

Somebody was taking his shirt off, the one the Silk Mistresses had given him. He heard a gasp of shock.

'It always does that,' said a cool female voice. 'If he hadn't been wearing spinner silk it would have burned through to remove his heart.'

'It's bubbling ... Yuk, it's oozing blood.'

'Blisters. The skin is just blistering.'

'It's bubbling!'

'I don't like the look of this.'

Henry felt something inside him relax. The pain seemed far away as he sank softly into darkness.

'Do something!' Blue hissed fiercely. She felt a terror welling up inside her. Her father had died like this. One day he was healthy and hearty, the next he was dead; and now it was happening again with Henry.

Nymph frowned. 'He needs new skin. It's the only thing, really.'

'Then get it for him!' Pyrgus ordered.

'We don't have it. We're not equipped.'

Blue rounded on Ziczac. 'You did this!' she shouted. 'Can't you fix it?'

The little wizard looked genuinely desolate. He started to shake his head.

'Blue ...' Pyrgus said.

'You threw the damn thing! You must be able to do something. Reverse the spell. Heal –'

'Blue ...'

'I'm not a healer,' Ziczac said. 'I don't even know much about military spells.'

'Blue,' Pyrgus said gently. 'I think he's gone.'

Sixty-three

It was great to be back in the city. The countryside was too empty for Brimstone, too silent at night, even though he'd only been away for a short period of time. He waved cheerily at the guards on Cripple's Gate and walked on a few steps before he realised they were Faeries of the Night. Well, well, well. Black Hairstreak was moving fast. There hadn't been a Nighter guarding any of the city's gates for the past five hundred years.

He stopped and breathed deeply. He'd always liked the smell of the city – a mix of sweat and dirty laundry with a delicate counterpoint of sewage. Three hundred and twenty-two thousand seven hundred souls packed in a delightful labyrinth of alleyways and slums. There was nowhere like it in the whole world.

A dancing procession wound sinuously past and he stopped to look at the jugglers. With a shock of delight he realised it was a celebration of the Night. Processions like this never used to take place outside of Nighter districts. Extraordinary how things had changed.

The warren of alleyways that was Sailor's Haven led him to the river. He walked slowly along the towpath, examining each set of wooden steps that reached down to the water. Eventually he found one with a hireboat at the end of it. The poleman was an unshaven ruffian, but Brimstone was wearing his demonologist's shawl with the horned insignia, so he expected no trouble.

'Twenty-seven groats,' said the man, trying it on, but pushed the craft off without complaint when Brimstone handed him six.

The river had always been the easiest way to get around the city. Brimstone took a seat in the prow and watched contentedly as the rows of warehouses gave way to office buildings, then looming residential houses. He was feeling ... how was he feeling?... he was feeling *good*. He'd made his peace (and his new bargain!) with Beleth. Pyrgus was no longer headed for the throne. Hairstreak had taken over. The Faeries of the Night were now in charge. Life was sweet. The future, once so confined to Widow Mormo's grubby lodgings, opened up to panoramic vistas.

'Few changes lately,' he ventured smugly.

The poleman looked like one of the few products of Lighter–Nighter interbreeding. But even without that, his occupation meant his loyalties lay with the highest bidder. 'Reckon,' he said laconically.

Brimstone looked around him. There were changes on the river too. General traffic seemed heavier and several of the boats were sporting pennants, indicating a tendency towards piracy. Time was when the water police would have sunk them without trace (sensibly only asking questions afterwards) but there they were, bold as brass. There was even a big pleasure vessel – or at least something he thought had to be a pleasure vessel: there was a multicoloured walrus on its flag. If he was right, it was the first time the trulls had taken to the water in four decades.

The houses on the river bank opened up on to a

broad, stone-paved piazza leading to the ancient Church of Saint Batwits. Batwits was a Lighter saint, much venerated for eating wasps, but now there was a bustling market right outside the church door! A small group of white-robed pilgrims was trying to push through the throng, bemused looks on their faces. They were halted by a fire-eater who declined to stop his act to let them past. In the old days, the Churchwardens would have swarmed out to beat him with their sticks, but today nothing happened. The new dispensation was taking hold everywhere.

The boat pulled in at the Cheapside docks. 'This do?' asked the poleman, reaching for a rope.

'Admirably,' said Brimstone cheerily. He even considered giving the man a small tip, but decided that would be pushing a good mood too far.

Cheapside was busy as ever and there seemed to be even more low-life about than usual – especially fizz-heads for some reason. Brimstone drew the shawl a little closer round his shoulders and stepped into the throng, immediately and immensely pleased with the way people gave him space. The insignia did it, of course. Even with the Hael portals closed, people respected anyone who commanded the infernal hierarchies. Most of them probably suspected the portals would not stay closed for ever.

By the time he reached Seething Lane, Brimstone's mood was bordering on the ecstatic. There was no reason why he should not take up his old lodgings. The old Emperor was dead, Prince Pyrgus was in exile, Beleth was placated – what had Brimstone got to fear? He could move back in and start some very pleasant wheels in motion. Like selling off his late wife's property. Milking some more money out of Chalkhill. Taking up his old position at the glue factory. Searching for –

There was something wrong. Seething Lane didn't *smell* right.

Silas Brimstone stopped, appalled. Chalkhill and Brimstone's Miracle Glue Factory had disappeared! The end of Seething Lane was no more than a pile of rubble: he could see the twisted iron gates from here. An errant breeze from Wildmoor Broads carried in the citrus scent of prickleweed.

Brimstone glared down Seething Lane. Somebody had destroyed one of the most profitable businesses he'd ever had.

And that meant somebody would pay.

Sixty-four

Peach Blossom said, 'We might be able to use silk.'

Pyrgus was leaning over Henry's body, his fingers gently probing one side of his neck. He looked stunned. 'I think it's too late,' he said. 'I can't find any pulse.'

Blue said, 'How can we use silk?'

'It's too late,' Pyrgus said again. He looked round at Blue, then Nymph, his eyes brimming.

'I think he's right, Blue,' Nymph said.

Blue said, 'Shut up, both of you.' To Peach Blossom she repeated, 'How can we use silk?'

Peach Blossom licked her lips thoughtfully. 'We can fuse it to living tissue. We do it sometimes over a small area to make a garment hang properly. Temporarily, of course, but there's no reason why it shouldn't be permanent. Or cover his entire chest,' she added as an afterthought.

'*Living* tissue,' Nymph emphasised quietly. She looked compassionately at Blue.

'Do it!' Blue said.

Peach Blossom was staring down at Henry's ruined body. 'If he does survive, he's going to look strange ... '

'How strange?'

Peach Blossom frowned. 'Fusion silk is multicoloured. You can never tell the exact hue or pattern until the process is finished. We'd have to wrap his entire torso. Thank heavens his face hasn't been burned, but if he ever takes his shirt off his chest will be like a rainbow tattoo. And look at his hands. We'll have to make him fusion gloves. The silk becomes his new skin. He'll have hands that reflect the sun like oil. They won't be covered. Everyone will see them.'

'Oh, for God's sake!' Blue snapped testily. 'If you don't do it, he's going to *die*!'

'If he isn't dead already,' Nymph murmured, staring at the body.

Blue rounded on her in a fury. 'Another word and *you'll* be dead! It was your wizard who did this – don't think I'm going to forget that. Now shut your mouth and see if you can help.'

Nymph said nothing. When Blue turned back, two Sisters of the Silk Guild were bending over Henry unwrapping a bolt of silk so fine it floated towards him like thistledown.

Sixty-five

'These people are dangerous,' Fogarty murmured quietly.

'Why do you say that?' asked Madame Cardui.

They were back in the forest, seated together on a mossy bank beneath the bole of a great tree. Beyond them, in a clearing, Forest Faerie were dancing by a curious bonfire to the hauntingly hypnotic music of drum and pipes.

'I don't like their spell technology,' Fogarty said soberly. 'Portals to other planets ... weapons that can pierce any armour ... ability to pass through solid walls ... Put those together and nothing in the Realm can stand against them.'

'They are our friends,' said Madame Cardui mildly. 'They have *proven* themselves to be our friends.'

'They are now,' Fogarty sniffed. 'But can you guarantee they'll stay that way?'

Madame Cardui said nothing.

'And just look at that bonfire,' Fogarty said. 'Heat to keep them warm, but black flames. Can you believe that – black flames!? Hardly any light emission so their enemies won't find them, won't even suspect they're here. We could never duplicate that sort of magic.'

'It won't burn greenwood,' said Madame Cardui.

'What?'

'The bonfire, my deeah – the black flames aren't so you

274

can't see them, they're so the bonfire won't burn green-wood. So it can't set fire to the trees.'

'Bully for them,' said Fogarty, frowning. 'But what's that got to do with anything?'

Madame Cardui shrugged. 'They love their forest.'

After a moment Fogarty said, 'Ah, I see what you're getting at. You think they have no *interest* in moving against us.'

'Alan,' Madame Cardui said, 'I've known these people for years. They have no interest in moving against *any-body*. All they want is to be left alone. The only reason they're helping us attack Lord Hairstreak is because his stupid demon pits have threatened their forest. If we leave them alone, they'll leave us alone.'

Fogarty looked unconvinced. 'Maybe.' After a moment he said, 'I wonder how they're getting on?'

'Blue and Pyrgus? You wish you were with them, don't you?'

'Of course I do. Growing old's no fun.'

They sat in silence for a while, listening to the plaintive music.

Madame Cardui said, 'Tell me how you got here — what ... *fate* ... led you to the Realm?'

'Thought you'd know that already, Cynthia. From your *sources*.'

Madame Cardui smiled slightly. 'I'd like to hear it in your own words.'

Fogarty stared into the middle distance and smiled a little too. 'Damnedst thing,' he said. 'Once I passed eighty, I started to let things go: well, you do, don't you? House turned into a tip. So I thought I'd better get a housekeeper before the Health Authorities had me condemned. Except I didn't want some old char three times a week poking about in my stuff ...' He shrugged. 'Anyway, I met this kid. Henry, his name was – Henry Atherton. Looking for his sister in the mall. Got sidetracked at one of those computer shops: I found him looking at some sort of music machine. Attention span of a gnat – you know what teenagers are like – but something about him ... sort of likeable. And he looked sturdy, hard work wouldn't kill him. Struck me he was exactly what I needed. Kids that age only ever think about two things – sex and pop music. He'd never have any interest in what I was doing. So I offered him a job.'

'And what happened?'

'Took it, of course. He was saving up for something called an MP3 Player – some sort of game thing I think – so he needed the money. I put him on trial and he was perfect. Arrived on time, did his work, shut his mouth and never tried to jerk me around. Then one day, damn me if he didn't walk in with a fairy in a jam jar.'

Madame Cardui smiled broadly. 'Pyrgus, of course.'

Fogarty grinned. 'Oh, yes. Didn't know it at the time, but that's where it all started. Funny old life.'

'He came over to the Realm as well, didn't he?'

'Who?'

'Henry. I believe Pyrgus made him Knight Commander of the Grey Dagger.'

'Not sure that was legal,' Fogarty said thoughtfully. 'Pyrgus was only Emperor Elect at the time. But he was grateful to Henry. Henry got him out of Hell. I suppose he thought he'd confirm the appointment after his Coronation. Didn't expect the present trouble. None of us did.' He stared out towards the black flames of the bonfire. 'I hope he's all right. Henry's a decent kid – he doesn't deserve to have anything bad happen to him.'

Sixty-six

Henry swam up slowly from the warm, dark depths. His chest no longer pained him quite so much, but it felt tight so that he had difficulty breathing. He could see light, then shapes, but his eyes would not focus properly so he couldn't tell what they were.

'I think he's opening his eyes again.'

'Are you sure?'

'No. I thought I saw –'

'Try for a pulse again, Prince Pyrgus.'

Pyrgus was here! This was great. Pyrgus was here. Henry tried to say *Hello, Pyrgus,* but could not take enough breath in to form the words. He felt something brush against his neck, like the touch of a butterfly's wing.

'No – nothing.' Was that Pyrgus's voice? It didn't sound like Pyrgus's voice, but then everything was echoey and boomy.

'Is the silk working?'

'The fusion's taken, Serenity, but that doesn't necessarily mean ...'

Serenity? Did that mean Blue was here? Henry made a massive effort and opened his eyes. The light blinded him.

'We're fitting the gloves now. His hands are in a

much worse state than his chest. He must have tried to protect himself.'

'Fusion is automatic – it's a property of the silk. It doesn't mean there's healing.'

'Healing is a property of the body.'

'Although a silk fusion will promote healing in some circumstances.'

'Providing the body can support it.'

'If the body can support it, healing can be quite rapid.'

It wasn't Blue. There was a woman bending over him, but it wasn't Blue. It occurred to Henry he was ill. He couldn't see properly, he couldn't hear properly, he couldn't breathe properly, his skin felt tight and there were stabbing pains in his hands and chest. That couldn't be right. He wondered if he was coming down with flu.

To one side of the woman he saw Pyrgus and tried to smile at him. But his face wouldn't work either.

A soft female voice said, 'His eyes are open, Highness.'

That was quite true – his eyes *were* open. Things were coming slowly into focus as well.

Pyrgus reached out to touch him on the neck. 'Henry,' he said. 'Can you hear me?'

I can hear you, Pyrgus, Henry thought. *I just can't tell you I can hear you.*

'There's a pulse,' Pyrgus said. 'Quite strong too.'

'That cinnamon scent means –'

Someone pushed Pyrgus and the woman rudely aside and bent over Henry. His eyes grew misty. It was Blue. It was definitely Blue.

'Oh, Henry!' Blue exclaimed and kissed him on the mouth.

The pain was just as bad and he still couldn't move, but Henry suddenly felt a whole lot better.

Henry pushed himself to his feet. He could see clearly now, could even remember – more or less – what had happened, although what had happened didn't make a lot of sense. He thought perhaps he'd been struck by lightning: a huge fireball had rushed towards him just before he blacked out. But if it was lightning, he'd somehow survived.

Amazingly, his chest had stopped hurting. Even the tightness was easing now, so he could breathe properly. He remembered the Silk Mistresses and how they'd tried to help him, but now Blue was here as well, and Pyrgus. He wondered what was going on.

He smiled at Blue who'd just kissed him. (She'd just kissed him!!) 'Hello, Blue.'

'Hello, Henry,' Blue said.

'Hello, Henry,' Pyrgus said.

There was a pretty girl in a black uniform standing to Pyrgus's right and two others in black behind her. Both Pyrgus and Blue seemed to be wearing black as well, for some reason. They were all carrying weapons and had that nervous, alert look you used to see in television reports of occupying soldiers.

Henry took a deep breath. He no longer felt he might fall down at any minute. He no longer felt shaky at all. There was a pleasant warmth in his chest and it seemed to be giving him energy.

'Hello, Pyrgus,' he said. 'What's happening?'

The girl beside Pyrgus said, 'Prince Pyrgus, time is short. We need to be moving on.'

'Henry comes with us!' Blue said fiercely.

'This is Nymphalis,' Pyrgus said, gesturing towards the girl in black.

Nymphalis said, 'If he's able. Of course he –'

Blue said, 'Henry's coming, whether he's able or not.'

Henry felt pretty able. His whole body was warm now and he was experiencing a remarkable surge of energy. He reached out his hand and said, 'Nice to meet you, Nymphalis.'

'We have to find my father,' Pyrgus said. 'I'll explain as we go along.' He glanced at Nymphalis. 'Of course Henry's coming.'

'Are you all right?' Nymphalis asked Henry, frowning.

But Henry was frozen, staring in astonishment. He had multicoloured hands.

Sixty-seven

Cossus Cossus met Chalkhill at the steps to the main doorway. 'Nice to see you again, Jasper,' he said tightly.

'*He wants you to behave normally,*' said the wangaramas Cyril. '*No mention of wyrms. Hairstreak has listening devices throughout the mansion.*'

'*How do you know?*' Chalkhill asked mentally.

'*Had it from Bernadette, of course.*'

'*Who's Bernadette?*'

'*The wangaramas in Cossus Cossus's bottom.*'

'And you,' Chalkhill said to Cossus, following the instruction to behave normally.

'*You've come to report to Lord Hairstreak,*' Cyril prompted.

'I've come to report to Lord Hairstreak, Cossus,' Chalkhill said.

'His Lordship is not currently in residence,' said Cossus woodenly. 'I would suggest you come inside and wait.'

He followed Hairstreak's Gatekeeper up the steps and into the mansion. Cossus strode off down a corridor, setting such a brisk pace that Chalkhill found himself struggling to keep up. He was relieved when a suspensor tube finally carried them into a comfortable open-plan suite furnished in the old-fashioned Nighter style, complete with closed shutters and low-level lighting.

'My private quarters,' Cossus said. 'You can speak freely here. I have programmed a golem to feed random conversations into the listening devices, otherwise they broadcast as if in an empty room.'

Chalkhill blinked. 'A golem? Isn't that illegal?'

'Yes,' said Cossus shortly.

'And hideously dangerous?' He looked around, half hoping to see the creature, half fearing he actually might.

'Would you like a drink?' Cossus asked.

'I think I would,' said Chalkhill.

He was admiring an admirable picture when Cossus approached him with a silver tray and two glasses. Behind each glass was a hypodermic needle.

'What are those for?' Chalkhill asked, frowning.

'Hold out your arm,' Cossus ordered.

Suddenly Cyril was thrashing about inside his bottom and his mind. *'Don't let him do it!'* the wyrm screamed.

But Cossus already had one of the hypodermics in his hand. He moved with extraordinary speed and Chalkhill felt a painful prick as the needle entered his arm, followed by a sudden surge of warmth as the plunger was pressed.

The room began to revolve slowly around him and his eyes lost focus. 'What have you done to me?' he yelled.

Cossus smiled grimly and picked up the second hypodermic.

Cossus plunged the needle into his own arm.

'What are you doing?' Chalkhill shrieked. He watched, fascinated, as the liquid emptied into Cossus's veins. Cyril, the wangaramas, had stopped thrashing about, thank heavens, so Chalkhill no longer desperately needed a loo. The momentary dizziness was gone as well, but it was replaced by a weird sort of ... emptiness, as if there was a hole in his head.

Cossus withdrew the needle and dabbed at a tiny, welling drop of blood at the site of the puncture. 'I'm ensuring we can talk privately. How's your bottom?'

Chalkhill bristled. 'I'll thank you to keep your nose out of my bottom.'

Cossus closed his eyes momentarily and sighed. 'I merely meant to ascertain whether your wyrm has ceased to function.'

'It has, as a matter of fact,' Chalkhill said, frowning. 'But I'm answering no more personal questions until you tell me what's going on.'

'I need to talk to you,' Cossus sighed, 'so I've put our worms to sleep. They'll be out cold for an hour or more, which should be ample. I've put a little *lethe* in the mix, so they won't even remember anything untoward has happened to them.'

Chalkhill stared at him suspiciously. 'What do you want to talk to me about?'

'Perhaps I should answer that,' said a familiar voice behind him.

Chalkhill's heart rocketed into his throat, his scrotum tightened alarmingly and a wave of icy chills passed through his body. He didn't want to move, didn't want to see who was standing behind him, but his feet moved anyway, turning him slowly of their own accord. He gave a sickly little smile.

'How nice to see you again, Lord Hairstreak,' he said.

Sixty-eight

'Where are we going?' Henry asked. He was stunned by what Pyrgus and Blue had just told him – particularly the fact that you could bring people back from the dead.

'We have to get my father out of Hairstreak's clutches,' Blue said soberly.

'He's here in the palace? Your father? With Hairstreak?'

'They were both here when Comma sent us away.'

Henry had only met Comma once, briefly, and disliked him on sight. Now Hairstreak had put him in charge of the whole Realm. Or at least had made him a figurehead.

'There may be fighting,' Blue said. 'It would be safest if you stayed at the back.'

Henry blinked. He'd never been one for fighting with anybody very much, except possibly his sister, but he realised things were different in the Realm. There was no way he was going to skulk like a wimp at the back of any party that had Blue in it. 'I'd prefer to stay at the front,' he said. Then risked adding, 'With you.' He gave a small, shy smile.

Nymphalis said, 'You have no weapon.'

Both Henry and Blue glared at her, but Pyrgus put in

mildly, 'Better give him one.'

Nymphalis shrugged and handed Henry her sword.
It was a lot heavier than it looked and his arm dipped
suddenly. To cover his embarrassment, he said quickly,
'Won't you need it?'

Nymphalis looked at him without expression. 'I am
trained in open-hand combat. Besides, I have my elf-
darts.' Her eyes dropped to the dangling sword. 'Do
you know how to use it?'

'Yes,' said Henry promptly. 'I'm an expert.'

They were moving fast through the palace corridors
without, as yet, any opposition. Several Sisters of the
Silk Guild had joined with Pyrgus's small party. None
of them was carrying any obvious weapons, but Henry
had learned not to underestimate the Mistresses.

Blue said, 'Henry, I think –' Then stopped. They had
turned a corner. Walking towards them, flanked by an
escort of seven tall guards, was Comma.

Both parties stopped abruptly. Pyrgus moved his hand
in a subtle hold-back signal to Nymph. Apart from the
Silk Mistresses, who were supposed to be in the palace
anyway, they were all in Hairstreak uniforms. There
was a faint chance they might not be recognised, at
least not right away, which could be to their advantage.

Comma looked right at him without a flicker of
recognition. Pyrgus felt, rather than saw, Nymph move
defensively closer. He had a slight advantage in numbers, but he didn't want Comma hurt. For all his faults,
the boy was still his half-brother.

One of Comma's guards leaned down to whisper in
his ear. Something in the man's expression told Pyrgus
this was it – they'd been recognised and any decision

that might avoid a fight was about to be taken from him. The guard straightened and snapped an order to his colleagues: 'To arms!' Blue stepped in front of Henry. The Forest Faeries reached for their weapons.

Comma shouted firmly, 'No!'

The guard beside him looked astonished. 'Sire?'

Comma said, 'At ease, men!'

'Sire, this is Prince —'

'Shut up!' Comma said petulantly. 'Shut up! Shut up! You men, you take your orders from me, and I say *stand at ease*!' He looked across, still with the same half-frozen expression on his face. 'Pyrgus, tell your people not to attack us.'

Pyrgus looked at Blue, who shrugged, watching Comma intently. 'Hold fast,' Pyrgus said quietly.

'Are those really Lord Hairstreak's soldiers with you?' Comma asked, frowning.

'Of course they are,' Pyrgus said, his eyes on his half-brother.

Comma turned to his guards. 'You see?' he said. He turned back to Pyrgus, who caught a pleading look of desperation in his eyes. 'I want you and your people to come with me.' He licked his lips. 'To our father's quarters.'

Blue said, 'We're not going any—'

Pyrgus interrupted her. There was something about Comma's look, his whole stance. 'We'll come,' Pyrgus said.

Blue shot him a sharp glance. 'Pyrgus —'

'Trust me, Blue,' Pyrgus whispered. But he made the old superstitious Sign of the Light behind his back. He wasn't at all sure he trusted himself.

The Emperor's quarters were only minutes away.

Black-uniformed guards stood on either side of the door. Comma walked up to them without hesitation. 'Open the doors for us!' he ordered shrilly. 'You know who I am.' He turned to his personal escort. 'You stay here and guard the doors. All of you. No slacking, mind. Make sure nobody comes in or goes out. Nobody. Without my orders, of course. You understand that?'

It occurred to Pyrgus they might all be a lot safer with Hairstreak's men out of the way completely. 'Dismiss them, Comma.'

Comma rounded on him. 'You be quiet, Pyrgus. My men must guard the door!'

It was back down or fight. Pyrgus said, 'Whatever.' He gave Comma an intense stare. 'But *my* people come inside with me.'

To his surprise, Comma said, 'Yes, Pyrgus. Yes, they must.'

The Emperor's main living quarters were surprisingly modest in size, so that it felt almost crowded when the whole party moved inside. Pyrgus noted the sudden stiffness in Blue's body. This was where she'd seen their father's body less than an hour after he'd been murdered. Pyrgus wanted to slip his arm around her shoulder to comfort her, but the beastly Comma was actually tugging at his sleeve.

'Pyrgus, I daren't send them away. The Captain knew who you were – you and Blue. If I send them away, they'll get word to Lord Hairstreak. But they aren't allowed to disobey a direct order.' He caught Pyrgus's expression. 'My guards,' he said. 'If they all stay at the door we know where they are.'

'Oh yes,' Pyrgus said vaguely. 'Listen, Comma –'

But Comma, still clinging to his arm, began to burble. 'Besides, I've told them to let nobody in. They'll keep my mother out.'

It hit Pyrgus like a douse of iced water. 'Your mother?'

'Your mother?' Blue echoed.

'They let her out,' Comma said. 'Just after you left. She's – you know, she's *free*.' He blinked. 'In the palace ... somewhere.'

'*Who* let her out?' Blue demanded.

Comma looked at her, then looked at Pyrgus, then looked down at his feet. 'I did.'

'Are you out of your mind?' Blue exploded.

'I didn't know ... I didn't know she'd be –'

'Of course you knew!' Blue snapped. 'We *all* knew!'

Henry, who was always uncomfortable in the middle of a family row, asked, 'Is this Quercusia?' He thought the question might somehow calm them down.

Blue rounded on him, surprised. 'How do you know about Quercusia?'

'I met her,' Henry said. 'I ... you know ... talked to her.'

Blue closed her eyes. 'My God, and you survived!?'

'Well, sort of,' Henry said. 'She had me thrown into a dungeon.' He remembered Flapwazzle suddenly with a huge pang of guilty sorrow.

But Comma ignored them both. He was still clinging to Pyrgus's sleeve. 'I'm so sorry, Pyrgus. I never thought it would turn out like this. Uncle Hairstreak said I should be Emperor, but he promised he wouldn't hurt you. He said he would give you a new house and you didn't want to be Emperor anyway and we all knew that and he said I could do anything I wanted and give orders and people would have to do what I said. But then when I sent you and Blue away, it was all different. He –'

Pyrgus cut him short. 'Comma, you know our father is alive again.'

Comma blinked. 'Yes.'

'Is he still here? Can you take us to him?'

Comma shook his head. 'No.'

'Where is he?' Blue put in.

'Uncle Hairstreak took him away.'

Blue looked exasperated, so Pyrgus said quickly, 'Where did he take him, Comma?'

'To Uncle Hairstreak's new mansion in the forest.'

Pyrgus looked at Nymph, then Blue. 'Back where we came from!' He turned to Comma. 'You'll have to call your guards off the door.'

But Comma shook his head. 'If I send them away they'll know you've gone and they'll probably guess *where* you've gone and then they'll send word to Lord Hairstreak.'

'But if you don't send them away, we're stuck here,' Blue said patiently.

'No you're not!' said Comma quickly. 'You can leave by the secret passage.'

Pyrgus blinked. 'Secret passage? There's no secret passage here.' He'd been using the Emperor's quarters for weeks now and thought he knew every inch of it.

'Oh yes there is!' Comma told him smugly. 'Look –' He ran over to the mantle and twisted an inlaid decoration. The whole fireplace moved to one side with a slight grinding sound. Behind it was a small chamber with stone steps leading downwards. 'There's a passage at the end of the stairs. It comes out on the edge of the woods at the far end of the island. There's even an old rowboat if you want it.'

Pyrgus looked at Comma with new eyes. The obnoxious little toad had come up trumps for once. 'This is brilliant, Comma,' he said sincerely. 'If you close the entrance after us and keep quiet, we can be off the island before the guards know we're even missing.'

'We'll close the entrance from the inside,' Comma said. 'I'm coming with you.'

Sixty-nine

Somebody had snapped the hinges of the door to Brimstone's old lodgings in Seething Lane. Brimstone kicked aside the charred remains as he mounted the stairs, making a mental note to have the door repaired as soon as possible. His magical securities would keep out intruders, of course, but a damaged door was an open invitation.

He checked his living quarters off the first landing and found his illusion spells intact. The place looked like a doss-house: nothing to attract a would-be thief. He went up another flight and his goblin guard met him, gibbering and prancing, in the library. Brimstone silenced them with a gesture, then set out on a full inspection of every room.

It was not until he was certain all traps and triggers were intact, nothing was missing, all as it should be, that he walked into the wardrobe of his bedroom and closed the door behind him.

A glowglobe sensed his presence and cast a soft illumination on the controls for the hidden stairway. Brimstone pressed a button, pulled a lever and the false back of the wardrobe slid away. He climbed the stairway to his secret attic.

The remains of his last operation were still strewn

about – the dried-up circle of guts and goat skin, the broken trapped-lightning machinery, the cold charcoal, the toppled brazier.

He picked his way across the debris and opened the wall cupboard that held his magical equipment.

The phial was there, exactly as Beleth had promised. He could see the glowing green slime roiling within. There was history trapped inside that glass, Brimstone thought. A near-unique substance, more precious than gold. No use to a demon, but most effective when used by a faerie. And the side effects were quite delightful.

He could hardly keep his hands off it, but he knew he needed to prepare. Beleth had let him off the hook once, but a second failure would mean his life and soul for sure. It took him no more than minutes to find the other items Beleth had left for him. He felt oddly excited, like a child about to go on holiday.

He flicked the cork out of the phial with his thumb and drank down the writhing slime.

For a moment he glowed green, then Brimstone disappeared.

Seventy

They were seated around an oval table in a corner of the living quarters. Chalkhill was keeping a wary eye on Cossus Cossus's golem, which was clumping around serving drinks. He'd never seen anything so frightening in his life. The creature stood nearly seven feet tall and its skin was as grey as the clay Cossus had used to make it. Chalkhill didn't like its teeth – God alone knew what Cossus had used to make *them*: they glinted like obsidian spires.

But the teeth weren't the worst of it. Every so often the golem twitched. That was a fearfully bad sign. Chalkhill avoided black magic whenever he could, but he'd read in a magazine somewhere that a twitching golem was usually on the point of going berserk. Golems frequently went berserk and strangled their creators – one reason why making them had been illegal for five hundred years. Once freed from their creator, they typically went on a blood rampage, killing anything they could get their enormous hands on. The same magazine had claimed their favourite form of attack was dismemberment – tearing people limb from limb.

Cossus had dressed *his* golem in a frilly apron. The man was clinically insane.

The creature served Hairstreak first, of course. His Lordship drank pimento juice, as, in imitation, did his Gatekeeper. Chalkhill needed something stronger and had asked for gin. The golem set a brimming half-pint glass in front of him, stared into his eyes and twitched.

The truly dreadful thing was, Chalkhill knew the golem was not the most dangerous entity in the room. He took a gulp of his gin and turned his eyes on Lord Hairstreak. The little creep smiled at him, his teeth stained by the pimento juice, then lifted the glass in a toast and said, to Chalkhill's horror, 'Here's to the Wangaramas Revolution!'

Nymph, who was lying beside Pyrgus, wriggled closer to him, then leaned across to hiss in his ear, 'I still think we should have stopped off for reinforcements, Crown Prince!'

Pyrgus turned his head. Nymph had a charming little nose, tilted upwards at the end. He came within a fraction of brushing his lips across her cheek as he placed them beside her ear. She had a very nice cheek, very smooth and inviting.

'Element of surprise,' he whispered back. 'We agreed about that, right at the start.'

She pulled her head away, waited until he turned his, then put her lips back to his ear again. 'That was a different situation. You might expect to have help at the palace – from friends, people who know you. This is Lord Hairstreak's mansion. All enemies here. And you don't know your way around it like the palace. We've no idea what we might find.'

'We're all wearing Hairstreak uniform,' Pyrgus said. 'Except Ziczac and Comma, and we can pretend they're our prisoners if we have to.' The Silk Mistresses had stayed back at the palace on Pyrgus's order. They weren't fighters, and besides, he liked the idea that they might stir up some trouble for Hairstreak's people. Everyone else had travelled directly to Hairstreak's mansion.

'We could have stopped on the way,' Nymph said, ignoring him. 'We practically *walked through* Queen Cleopatra's camp.'

It was news to Pyrgus, who still couldn't spot the Forest Faerie if they didn't want to be spotted. 'Too late now,' he said, a little gracelessly. The trouble was, Nymph was distracting him. He needed to keep his mind firmly focused on the job ahead. He didn't even want to think about it, but he was terrified of what was going to happen once Blue and he found their father.

'I could go back,' Nymph offered promptly. 'It's not far. The rest of you could stay here, keep an eye on what's happening. I could bring back enough people for a frontal attack if you want. I know the Queen would agree – she wants those pits closed.'

For a moment Pyrgus was tempted, although not by the prospect of a frontal attack. He had his own agenda here and it was different from that of the Forest Faerie. But if Nymph did go back to her people, he could send Comma with her. Pyrgus suspected he would be much happier with Comma out of the way, preferably under lock and key. And they could certainly do with *some* reinforcements: not for a frontal attack, but simply because they were heading into *real* enemy territory now.

He opened his mouth to put it to her about Comma, then shut it again abruptly. Hairstreak's guards were marching off towards their barracks in fine order. Within a moment all of them disappeared, leaving the way to the mansion clear. Pyrgus made a snap decision.

'No time!' he hissed. 'We go now!'

Then, without waiting for her reaction, Pyrgus rose and, bent double, raced towards the mansion.

Chalkhill suddenly stopped worrying about the golem. He swallowed, tried to stop himself speaking, then heard his voice gulp, 'You know about the Revolution?'

Black Hairstreak shrugged and grinned a little. 'The worms have been revolting for years. Every generation their stupid plan gets more desperate.'

'Every generation?'

'Short-lived species,' Hairstreak said, smiling now. 'As soon as they get anything in place, half of them die off and they have to start again.' His smile disappeared abruptly and he looked shrewdly at Chalkhill. 'You didn't take it seriously, did you, Jasper?'

'Not for a moment,' Chalkhill told him.

Seventy-one

It was nice to be back in New York. Brimstone looked up at the Church of the Transfiguration, marvelling at how accurately the potion had translated him to this spot. There was a woman screaming a few yards away from him, presumably because she'd witnessed his sudden appearance. Brimstone shouldered his bag and smiled at her. Thank God for New Yorkers. They thronged past, ignoring the screaming woman, ignoring him, ignoring the green-domed architecture of this delightful church, avoiding eye contact, locked in their own beleaguered worlds. If the woman told what she'd just seen, they'd think she was mad. But if they didn't, they still wouldn't care.

There'd been some massive renovation on the church since the last time he'd translated, but the people streaming in suggested they were still holding a daily Mass. For a moment he was tempted to slip inside – the quaint attempt at white magic always entertained him – but decided to get business finished with before he took in any of the city's fine diversions. Besides, he still hadn't quite decided how he would carry out his mission.

In the old days he would probably have walked north on Mott Street, then turned right into the

Bowery. But the Bowery wasn't what it used to be. There were still lots of down-and-outs, of course, but it might be difficult to find two he could actually use. The trouble was even the worst scumbags were better off these days. They had cheap wine in their paper bags. None of them touched the metholated spirit that thinned the blood so beautifully. He could spend all day taking samples before he found anybody suitable. And after that, there was the whole nuisance of killing them. No, best to spend a little of Beleth's funny money, put in an order and do it all the easy way.

He crossed the road and headed into Doyers Street, the dear old Bloody Angle. There were fewer people here, as if people somehow scented the horrors of its past. Brimstone plodded along, a benign expression on his wrinkled face, sniffing the air – such wonderful air, so full of fumes.

Moments later he had vanished into the lattice of streets and alleys beyond Doyers.

'You shouldn't have done that!' Nymph said sharply. 'You could have got yourself killed.' She was the first to join him.

'We had to make a move sometime,' Pyrgus said reasonably. The others were piling in at a run, led by Blue. He glanced at Henry, who seemed to be holding up all right, despite his recent brush with death.

They moved as a group round the side of the mansion, well away from the barrack wing where Hairstreak's soldiers had just disappeared. As they reached the rear, their luck still held – still no sign of any more guards. But perhaps that wasn't surprising: the wall was of smooth, massive stone and toweringly high. Hairstreak must have thought he was impervious to attack.

Pyrgus waited for Ziczac to catch up. 'What do you think?'

The little wizard looked around. There was a rocky outcrop that came close to the wall itself. 'That looks interesting.'

'It does?' Pyrgus frowned.

Ziczac chewed his lip. 'Typical formation,' he said, without explaining typical of what. 'Does anybody know if Lord Hairstreak built cellars?'

'Yes, of course he did,' Nymph said a little impatiently. 'Cellars and demon pits. That's why Her Majesty wants us to help Prince Pyrgus.'

'You don't know if he made them from a natural cavern, do you?'

Nymph looked at him blankly and Pyrgus shook his head. Blue said, 'You think there's a natural cavern underneath?' She glanced at the outcrop as well. 'It's the right geology ...'

'Yes,' Ziczac said eagerly. 'Yes, it is.'

'What are you thinking of?' Pyrgus asked.

Blue smiled suddenly. 'He's thinking of taking us *underneath* the building! Aren't you, Ziczac?'

The little wizard nodded. 'Yes. Yes, I am.'

'Can you do that?' Henry asked.

'Oh, yes. Oh, yes indeed. We'll have to penetrate on a vertical axis rather than lateral, then move horizontally. It's a bit tricky, but I can do it. Provided you all keep still, of course. In fact, I think I'd like you all to link arms and stay together until we break through.'

'That means we can't use our weapons if we're attacked,' Nymph said sternly.

'This way, hopefully, we *won't be* attacked,' Ziczac told her patiently.

'What do you think, Prince Pyrgus?'

Pyrgus hadn't the least idea what the wizard was talking about, but he'd got them into the palace safely, so presumably he'd be able to do the same here. 'I think we should do what Ziczac says.'

Nymph shrugged resignedly.

Henry moved quickly beside Blue and waited for everybody to start to link arms. Blue gave him a fond look and said quietly, 'You all right?'

'Never better,' Henry said. He wanted to ask her what exactly was happening, but wondered if that would make him sound like a wimp. Or stupid. Or both.

It almost seemed as if Blue caught the thought because she said, 'Ziczac can get us through walls.'

'With magic?'

Blue nodded.

'Cool!' Henry exclaimed.

'Well, we'd better do it then,' Pyrgus remarked to no one in particular.

Ziczac did something and they all dropped into darkness.

Seventy-two

They stepped into a roofless corridor. High walls and floor seemed to be made from obsidian blocks, but beyond where the ceiling might have been there was a vast open space, then, in the gloom, a vaulting dome of rock, as if the corridor had been constructed on the floor of a gigantic cavern.

'I don't like the look of this,' Pyrgus said at once.

The others said nothing. They stood without moving, looking around to get their bearings. The corridor ran straight in both directions, turned right at one end, turned left at the other. Floating high above them was some sort of platform, walled with opaque black glass.

'I don't have much sense of direction,' Henry said. And what little he did have had been completely confused by the passage downwards through apparently solid rock. But at least he didn't want to throw up.

'That's north,' said Ziczac confidently, pointing.

'Is that a suspensor spell?' Pyrgus asked, his eyes on the floating platform.

Ziczac glanced up. 'Yes.'

There was a light source, although it wasn't obvious. They could see each other quite plainly, yet there were no glowglobes, no ornamental torches on the walls.

Blue said, 'I agree with Pyrgus – this place is creepy.'

She half turned. 'You can let go now, Henry.'

Henry released her arm sheepishly. To cover his embarrassment, he said, 'Can you hear something?'

They all stopped for a moment, listening.

'Like running water?'

Henry nodded. 'Yes. There may be an underground stream.'

Nymph said to Ziczac, 'Where are we? Do you know?'

'Under the mansion,' Ziczac said. 'We were right about the cavern.'

'Why are we walled in? I mean, why would Hairstreak build an open corridor on the floor of the cavern?'

'Maybe it's not finished,' Blue suggested, frowning.

'Looks finished to me,' Pyrgus said. He hesitated. 'There's something not right here. Can you take us through these walls, Ziczac?'

'Not sure,' Ziczac said. 'Depends on their thickness.'

'So we're trapped here?'

'Oh, no, Princess Blue,' Ziczac said. 'I can always take us down again and across. But I'd prefer a more direct route.'

'Through the walls?'

'Yes. I think I might try to find out how thick they are.'

'Nymph's right,' Blue said. 'I'd like to know why Hairstreak built this sort of structure on the floor of a cavern. And why use volcanic glass?'

'There's something about volcanic glass ...' Pyrgus murmured. He looked at Ziczac. 'I think I'd better try to find out the thickness of the walls.' He drew his Halek blade.

'Can you do a mystical triangulation?' Ziczac asked. Pyrgus shook his head. 'I don't know what that is.'

'Then I'd better do it,' Ziczac said. 'The best place would be at the corner. I think perhaps the rest of you had better stay put.' He began to walk briskly north, but halted abruptly after just four steps. 'There's some sort of forcefield here.' He reached out cautiously with both hands and patted the air in front of him.

'I can't see anything,' Henry said foolishly.

'Neither can I,' Ziczac said, 'but I can feel it.'

'Come away, Ziczac,' Nymph said anxiously.

'It's all right – it's just a barrier. I can get us through it if I have to.' The wizard backed off and turned. 'Let's see if we're trapped the other way.' He walked past them, headed for the southern corner of the corridor.

'The rest of you –' Pyrgus began.

There was a yelp and a peculiar squelching noise. Henry spun round. 'Where's Ziczac?' There was no way he could have reached the corner already.

'Stay back!' Pyrgus snapped. He began to run in the direction Ziczac had taken.

Both Nymph, Comma and Blue all ignored him and started running at the same time. They arrived together at the edge of a narrow pit that had opened in the floor of the corridor. Pyrgus looked down.

Ziczac's body was impaled on seven vicious metal spikes set into the floor of the pit. His eyes were open, but he was clearly dead.

Seventy-three

Brimstone found the narrow stairway between a Buddhist souvenir shop and a tiny store that specialised in selling pickled eggs. The flathead on the first landing was seated on a wooden chair reading the *National Inquirer,* his jacket open to show the shoulder holster.

He recognised Brimstone at once. 'Ho?' he sniffed.

'Yo,' said Brimstone, using one of the dreadful colloquialisms he'd picked up on an earlier visit to Spanish Harlem. Nobody here knew where he really came from and he preferred to keep it that way.

The flathead jerked his thumb towards the next flight and went back to his *National Inquirer.*

Two sweet little girls ushered him into Mr Ho's offices on the first floor, giggling behind their hands. Mr Ho was seated in a cracked leather armchair, smoking something resinous in a long, clay pipe. He had the eye folds of a Faerie of the Night, but not the slitted pupils. He took the pipe from his mouth and favoured Brimstone with a benign smile.

'Mr Brimstone,' he acknowledged.

'Mr Ho,' said Brimstone, nodding. He glanced around the room, pleased to see Mr Ho's shelves were still well-stocked with both books and supplies.

'Excuse it that I do not rise in deference to your hugely advanced ancientness,' Ho said. The benign smile again. 'I am unable to revere you on account of extreme intoxication.'

'Think nothing of it, Mr Ho.'

'Tea, Mr Brimstone? Or a pipe?'

'Neither, thank you, Mr Ho. May I enquire about the health of your granddaughters?'

Mr Ho beamed. 'Excellent, I can report. I note from the ring on your finger that you have recently married, Mr Brimstone. May I, in turn, enquire after the health of your illustrious new wife?'

'Dead,' said Brimstone.

'Ah,' Ho said, nodding. 'Her legacy?'

'Substantial,' Brimstone told him.

Ho took another puff of his pipe and smiled. 'Supplies then, is it, Mr Brimstone? Some items on which to spend your fortuitous substantial legacy?'

'A grimoire, Mr Ho.'

Ho's eyes widened a little. 'The *Lemegeton,* Mr Brimstone? Or the full *Clavicle*? Or perhaps the *Grimoire Verum*? Or shall I have my ladies find you the *Boke of the Mervayles of the World*?'

They both laughed heartily. *Mervayles of the World* was a book of *white* magic. Brimstone shook his head. 'No, no, Mr Ho. I need the *Grimoire of Honorius the Great.*'

Mr Ho stopped laughing at once. 'Are you serious, Mr Brimstone?'

'Deadly, Mr Ho.'

'I do not have it.'

'But can you get it?'

'The cost would be astronomical,' Ho said bluntly.

Brimstone smiled. 'I have American Express platinum.'

Ho's eyes widened again. 'May I see it, Mr Brimstone?'

Brimstone rummaged in his bag and produced the card Beleth had given him. Ho took it, examined the magnetic strip on the back, then bit it carefully.

'This seems to be in order, Mr Brimstone.'

'So you can get the book?'

Mr Ho held up a single finger. 'One hour, Mr Brimstone. Permit me one hour.'

Seventy-four

Blue was standing by his shoulder, staring into the pit. She looked as if she might be sick at any minute. Pyrgus said quietly, 'You know what this place is, don't you?'

Blue nodded. 'An obsidian maze. Hairstreak has built an obsidian maze. Pyrgus, that monster has our father!'

Frowning, Nymph asked, 'What's an obsidian maze?'

'What's an obsidian maze,' Comma echoed. He was staring down at the body with fascination.

'It's a game,' Pyrgus said. 'The maze is filled with lethal tricks and traps, demons, wild animals, that sort of thing. You put somebody in it and the game is to see if they'll survive.'

Nymph stared at him. 'You make a game out of watching somebody fighting for their *life*?'

Pyrgus shook his head. 'We don't. It's illegal. Has been for a long time – centuries. I can't remember when it was made illegal, it was so long ago.'

'Except,' Blue said sourly, 'our friend Hairstreak seems to have built himself one.' She looked at Pyrgus. 'I wonder why there haven't been rumours – I never heard so much as a whisper.'

307

'Obviously has good security,' Pyrgus sniffed. He was staring down at the broken body of the little wizard. 'What are we going to do about Ziczac?'

'He's dead, Pyrgus – there's nothing we *can* do.'

'I meant about the body.'

'Oh,' Blue said. They stared down together.

Nymph said sharply, 'I'll get it if you're squeamish. He was my friend.'

Pyrgus said, 'He was a friend to all of us, Nymph. But most traps in an obsidian maze have double triggers.'

'What's that mean, Crown Prince?' She was looking at him angrily.

Blue said, 'It means that if anybody tries to go down there, it will trigger a second trap, more lethal than the first. It may even seal off this segment of the maze, flood it with poison gas, something like that. Ordinary traps can be avoided if you're careful, but the rules of the game are that secondary traps can be built with no way out.'

'You know a lot about this game, Princess Royal,' Nymph said.

'Blue knows about all sorts of stuff,' Comma said. He was still staring into the pit.

'I studied it in my history lessons,' Blue snapped.

Nymph's face was expressionless, but her voice softened a little. 'We shall have to leave him where he lies – we cannot endanger the party further. It is a warrior's death.'

Henry came up beside them. 'Except he wasn't a warrior.'

'He was our only way out of here,' Blue said.

They all turned to look at her.

Blue said, 'Without Ziczac, we can't pass through walls. We may have to fight our way out of Hairstreak's mansion.' She glanced around.

Comma said quietly, 'If we survive his obsidian maze.'

Brimstone looked at the tome with something close to wonder. It was written on sheepskin and was more than seven hundred and fifty years old. Cautiously he opened it at random.

Trinitas, Sother, Messias, Emmanuel, Sabahot, Adonay, Athanatos ... The words crawled across the page. There was a diagram of a magic circle.

Mr Ho was hovering anxiously by his shoulder. 'Is it what you wish, Mr Brimstone?'

It was what he wished all right. Exactly the grimoire Beleth had told him to find – the ultimate black book of the Analogue Realm, the most diabolical work of dark magic ever circulated. And written by a Pope! He turned another page. He would have to study it very carefully.

'This is perfect, Mr Ho,' he said. 'But in addition, I shall want a large sheet of virgin parchment.'

'I have it,' Ho said. 'You shall have it.'

'And a black cockerel.'

'I can get it,' Ho said. 'You shall get it.'

'Three pints of human blood.'

'Which group, Mr Brimstone?'

Brimstone blinked. 'Group?'

'Which blood group do you need, Mr Brimstone. They will ask me when I buy it for you from the Blood Bank.'

They had Blood Banks in the Analogue Realm? How

very sensible. Saved all the bother of finding a victim. Might be a business worth starting at home.

'Doesn't matter,' he said to Ho, 'so long as it's fresh.'

'Consider it yours, Mr Brimstone! Anything else?'

'A private room to study this fascinating text, Mr Ho.'

'At once, Mr Brimstone.'

'And a place to carry out the working. Say tomorrow, or the day after.'

'An abandoned church, Mr Brimstone, with its graveyard intact? I noticed one for sale in the property section. A short taxi ride from the city.'

'Admirable,' said Brimstone.

Ho waved the card and smiled. 'All on American Express, Mr Brimstone?'

It never ceased to astonish him how people in the Analogue World imagined a ridiculous little bit of plastic had the same value as gold. Brimstone smiled. 'All on American Express, Mr Ho,' he confirmed.

Seventy-five

'I want to show you something, Jasper,' Hairstreak said. He was beaming smugly – one of his least pleasant expressions.

'Yes, of course, Your Lordship,' Chalkhill said, trying desperately to look interested.

Hairstreak stood. 'Come with us, Cossus,' he invited.

The Gatekeeper bowed his head slightly and the three of them left the chamber. Chalkhill's nerves were getting to him badly, but at least they were leaving that ghastly golem behind.

Hairstreak took them down several winding sets of stairs and Chalkhill's nervousness increased as he realised where they were going. This was clearly the dungeon area of the mansion – cells surrounding a central torture chamber in the classical great-house design. You could never tell with Hairstreak. He could be all smiles one minute and the next you were on the rack with a red-hot poker cooling in your –

Hairstreak took a key from a hook on the wall, opened a cell door, then stood back. Chalkhill approached more nervously still. The cell was small, dark and windowless and there was a smell coming out of it as if something had died in there. Was this how it would end? It was his own fault, of course. He never should have listened to that stupid worm.

Chalkhill swallowed. 'Your Lordship –' he began. Then stopped. There was already somebody in the cell, a crumpled figure squatting by one wall. It was, Chalkhill realised, the source of the smell.

'Recognise anyone?' asked Hairstreak cheerfully.

Chalkhill had no idea what he meant, then realised he was talking about the figure in the cell. Chalkhill risked peering a little more closely. It was obviously some elderly derelict, a criminal perhaps, or more likely somebody who had crossed Hairstreak at some point and now faced a daily routine of torture, starvation and sleep deprivation. But *who* it was Chalkhill could not say. He suspected that didn't matter: Hairstreak was probably just showing what happened to anyone who irritated him – a little psychological pressure before the accusation of treachery. Why, oh why, had he listened to the worm?

'No?' asked Hairstreak. 'Hold your head up!'

For a moment Chalkhill thought Hairstreak was talking to him, then the wretched creature in the cell straightened slowly. Chalkhill caught his breath with an audible gasp. He was looking into the pain-soaked eyes of Apatura Iris, the late lamented Purple Emperor.

'Recognise him now?' Hairstreak asked.

Chalkhill nodded wordlessly.

'That's the reason you're here, Jasper. Strange are the ways of fate.'

Chalkhill glanced at Cossus, who stared back at him expressionlessly. He looked down at the floor. He didn't want to look at the Purple Emperor again, who was a truly horrific sight, and he was afraid to look at Hairstreak.

'You understand what's happened here?' Hairstreak said.

Chalkhill shook his head without looking up.

'This is a resurrection!' Hairstreak snapped. 'Any fool can see the signs of a resurrection.'

'Well, yes,' Chalkhill mumbled. 'I mean, I assumed it was a *resurrection* ...' The trouble with Hairstreak was you never knew what he was talking about until it was too late. By that stage you were either in deep trouble or dead. Chalkhill just managed to suppress a desperate little whine.

'That's the problem, isn't it?' Hairstreak said. 'One look and you know.' He pulled a short wand from the inside pocket of his jacket and used it to poke the figure in the cell. The Purple Emperor cringed away from him. 'You see? We're claiming Apatura never died at all. We're saying he went into a coma, but that he's woken up now and he's fit to make decisions on the future of the Realm. We've got away with it so far because we've kept him hidden most of the time, only gave a few people a glimpse of him, but do you think our story will stand up when he has to make a public appearance?'

What did Hairstreak want him to say? The wrong word here could mean jail or death or torture or ... Chalkhill looked desperately at Cossus again, who was still no help. His gaze was drawn to Hairstreak like a songbird fascinated by a snake.

'Yes,' he said. 'And ... no.' He waited, stomach tight and bowels loose.

'No, of course not,' Hairstreak said impatiently.

'He'd be spotted as a resurrection in a trice. And since resurrection is illegal, any proclamation he might make would be illegal too. Let me tell you, Jasper, we of the Night may have made some gains in the last few days, but we shall not hold them unless we do something about this problem.'

'What problem?' Chalkhill asked.

'It would be in your interests to listen more carefully,' Hairstreak said sourly. He stared gloomily at the huddled shape of the Emperor. 'You know there's only one thing that will fix this, of course.'

'I do?'

'A wyrm, you idiot! Specifically a mature wyrm transfer!'

Chalkhill wondered what a mature wyrm transfer was, but thought it safer not to ask. Instead he gave a vacant smile of encouragement to Hairstreak and nodded vigorously.

'Of course,' he said. 'Of course.'

Hairstreak sighed. 'Really, Jasper, if you didn't occasionally prove of some minuscule value, I'd have fed you to the sliths by now.'

'It's just –' Chalkhill hesitated. 'It's just ... well, I don't *quite* see how I ... ah ... actually might, well, fit in, Your Lordship.'

To his astonishment, Hairstreak smiled. 'It's not so much *you* fitting in, Jasper, it's more your wyrm fitting in. Fitting into the Emperor, that is. I've brought you here so we can transplant Cyril, your experienced wangaramas.'

Seventy-six

'We can't go north,' Nymph said. 'Don't you remember Ziczac said there was a forcefield?'

'North's blocked, Blue,' Comma said helpfully. If he was worried about their situation, it didn't show.

'Humour me,' Blue grunted shortly. She led them back along the corridor and they passed without difficulty beyond the point where Ziczac was stopped. Blue turned to face the others. 'The forcefield was just a device to send us south, so someone would trigger the spiked pit. Once the trap was triggered, the forcefield switched off automatically. It's standard game protocol. If you don't know about it, you assume you can't get north, jump the open trap and head south – where there are even more dangerous traps waiting.'

'So north will be easier?'

'Not much,' Blue admitted, 'but according to the rules of the game we're supposed to have *some* chance of surviving this way. South we'd have had no chance at all.'

'How do we know your Lord Hairstreak kept to the rules when he designed the maze?' Nymph asked.

Blue glared. 'We don't. But do you have a better way to play it?'

If this kept going they'd come to blows soon, Pyrgus

thought. He moved to defuse the tension by stepping forward with a smile he didn't feel. 'Look,' he said, 'we're all in this together. We've lost a good man because we didn't know right away what was happening. But we know we're in an obsidian maze now and that gives us a chance. The other thing is that we're a team. These mazes are designed for just one victim. If we pull together and stick together, we can beat this thing.' He looked directly at the two forest soldiers with Nymph and realised he didn't even know their names. 'I'm sorry,' he said. 'I don't know what to call you.'

'Ochlodes,' one told him.

'Palaemon,' said the other.

'Ochlodes, Palaemon,' Pyrgus said, 'you have already proved yourselves fine fighters on this mission. We may well be called on to fight again before we get out of this maze, but it's even more important to use your head and take care – most of the dangers here are from traps.' He looked at Nymph, Blue and Comma. 'That goes for you three as well – think before you do anything, take it slow and never assume anything is what it seems.'

After a moment, Blue said, 'I'd suggest we spread out. Spread out, but keep an eye on each other. That way if one of us does get caught in a trap, the others aren't likely to get caught as well, so we can help one another.'

'That's good strategic thinking, Princess Royal,' Nymph said with sincerity. Blue favoured her with a frosty little smile.

They separated out as far as space would allow, then cautiously began to move north up the corridor. They had gone no more than fifty yards before a swiftly spinning blade emerged from a side wall to slice the lobe from Palaemon's ear.

If he hadn't had the preternatural reflexes of a Forest Faerie, it would have cut his throat.

Seventy-seven

'I'm worried about the kid,' Fogarty said suddenly.

'Henry?'

'No – Pyrgus. I'm worried about him,' Fogarty said. 'It's taking too long.'

'You think so, deeah?'

'The theory was they slip into the palace, grab their father and slip out again. How long does that take?'

'Perhaps longer than one might imagine,' said Madame Cardui. 'The palace is a substantial building. Pyrgus has to *find* his father before he can rescue him.'

'I'm not sure they're still at the palace,' Fogarty said. 'I'm not even sure the Purple Emperor is at the palace.'

'Pyrgus said he saw his father at a window when they were forced to leave.'

'Pyrgus said he *thought* he saw his father at the window,' Fogarty corrected her. 'But even if he was right, that doesn't mean his father stayed there.' He leaned forward. 'In a case like this, you have to figure out what your enemy is thinking. Emperor Apatura isn't himself now. He's under orders from Hairstreak. On his own, the Emperor would stay at the palace. But would Hairstreak want him to stay at the palace?'

'Well, don't keep me in suspense – would he?'

'I don't think he would,' Fogarty said. 'I wouldn't.

I'm trying to tell the world the old Emperor is sound of body and mind, but just happens to want me to take over ruling the empire. People will never buy that if they see Apatura wandering about like a zombie. If I were Hairstreak, I'd hide him away at my own place.'

After a moment, Madame Cardui said, 'Lord Hairstreak has two places: a home in the city and the other –' She stopped, looking at him.

'The other one's somewhere in this forest,' Fogarty finished for her. 'He'd never take the Emperor to the place in the city – far too public.'

They looked at one another.

'Why didn't you say this before?' Madame Cardui asked.

'I didn't think of it before,' Fogarty said sourly.

'What are you going to do about it?'

Fogarty said, 'I think I'll go and talk to the Queen.'

Seventy-eight

The short taxi ride turned out to be a long taxi ride, but the driver took American Express. Brimstone stared up at the church he'd just bought with a rising feeling of delight. It was perfect. Derelict. Isolated. Surrounded by trees to guarantee a little privacy. And, as Mr Ho had promised, an ancient graveyard all around it. One or two of the graves had fresh flowers, which suggested there might be recent corpses available. Not that he was likely to need them. According to his grimoire, you could do without them in the Analogue Realm.

'Be so good as to carry my bags inside,' he told the taxi driver grandly.

'Bug off,' said the taxi driver, scowling. He was sweaty and overweight with an offensive body odour.

Brimstone grinned at him benignly. He opened the bag Beleth had given him and extracted one of the ridiculous pieces of paper that served as coinage in this world. (They passed paper around and pretended it was money! That was even sillier than the little plastic card.) The number 100 was printed on the front, which meant people believed they could exchange it for one hundred ... for one hundred ... for one hundred what? Brimstone actually wasn't sure. Sheep? Cows? Gold bars? The weird thing was it didn't matter. People just kept collecting them to pass around again.

Brimstone waved the paper under the taxi driver's smelly nose. 'Be so good as to carry my bags inside and I shall give you *this*!'

The driver's surly look disappeared and he scrambled from his cab. 'Why didn't you say so?'

The church had been deconsecrated according to Mr Ho, but otherwise left to rot. There were rows of broken woodwormed pews, broken stained-glass windows, broken statuary in mouldy niches, broken floor tiles and, best of all, a dusty altar. There was even a threadbare altar-cloth in silver and gold.

Brimstone dragged his luggage from the vestibule where the driver had left it, locked the front door again and settled down to unpack. The job he had to do for Beleth could take some time, so best to get started as soon as possible. He checked the grimoire, then walked up to the altar. He understood what he had to do. It was a mental preparation, designed to put him in the proper frame of mind.

Standing alone before the altar of the broken-down, deconsecrated church, Silas Brimstone began to confess his sins aloud.

It would, he thought, take quite some time.

They said it was a preparation room, but Chalkhill wasn't fooled for a minute. The furniture was minimal, the door was locked. He was in a holding-pen – a cell by any other name – to keep him safe until the hideous surgery. Worse still, Cyril had woken up again.

The worm was in a frenzy. He knew he'd been chemically sandbagged, but the lethe meant he couldn't remember what had happened. Now, having failed to extract the information directly from Chalkhill's mind, he was trying to nag it out of him.

'*But we're* friends!' Cyril exclaimed mentally. '*At least I thought we were. You know what happened, don't you? Why don't you tell me? I'm the one who's going to make you Purple Emperor. Have you forgotten that? Don't you have any loyalty? To me? To the Revolution?*'

'*Your Revolution's a joke,*' Chalkhill told him sourly. Then, echoing something Hairstreak said, '*You haven't been able to make real headway for centuries.*'

There was a sudden mental silence. Then the wangaramas said, '*How did you find out? Who told you that?*'

'*Not you, anyway.*'

'*It's not relevant any more,*' Cyril shrieked mentally. '*We're not going to fail this time!*'

'*No you're not,*' said Chalkhill tiredly, '*But it doesn't matter. What's happened is that our friend Lord Hairstreak has decided to have you surgically removed from my bottom and transplanted into the body of Emperor Apatura.*'

The wangaramas gave the mental equivalent of a screech. '*The old Purple Emperor? But he's been resurrected!*'

'*That's the whole point,*' Chalkhill said. '*Apparently with you inside him he'll appear a lot more lifelike.*'

'*You know this will kill me, don't you?*' Cyril said.

Like that mattered to anybody. Chalkhill said, '*Don't be silly, Cyril. Of course it won't kill you. You wouldn't be much good to Hairstreak if you're dead.*' A thought struck him and he mused aloud, 'I wonder why he doesn't just stick a new wyrm up the Emperor's nose, though ...'

Cyril picked up on the question. '*Won't work with a resurrected host. Has to be a transplant.*'

'Well,' said Chalkhill piously, '*I feel for you, Cyril, I really do. I think Lord Hairstreak is being beastly and not for the first time, I might add. If it was in my power to help, then help I would, but regrettably it isn't – I'm as much a prisoner of that vile little man as you are.*'

'*Oh, save your sympathy for yourself,*' said Cyril sniffily. '*You probably won't survive the operation either.*'

Seventy-nine

They moved at a crawl through the remainder of the first level. Most of the traps were lethal, but easy to avoid provided you were cautious and kept your wits about you.

Eventually, their nerves stretched to breaking-point, they reached the stairs to Level Two.

Henry hung back feeling cross and frightened at the same time. He was cross because Blue had asked him to stay close to Comma (who liked to lurk at the back of the party for safety) so he couldn't stay close to *her*. He was frightened because this place would frighten Arnie Schwarzenegger. You could be killed here, horribly. One of the party already had been.

They were on a downward flight of broad stone steps, dimly lit by torches set at intervals along the walls. Henry assumed the torches were for atmosphere, to give the stairs a suitably eerie effect. In the Realm, interior light mostly came from softly glowing spheres called glowglobes, but even apart from that these torches didn't look right. They made no smoke stains, for one thing. And their flames all seemed exactly the same size, as if they were generated artificially, like a coal-effect fire or something made by magic. Or maybe, thinking of magic, they weren't really there at all. Maybe they were an illusion, a sort of three-dimensional moving wallpaper.

'Pyrgus ...' Blue said uncertainly.

Pyrgus was in the lead, flanked by Nymph. Pyrgus was always in the lead – he didn't seem to be afraid of anything. Henry thought if they got out of this weird maze alive he'd ask if that was for real or just bluff.

Pyrgus stopped at once. 'Everything all right, Blue?' She was just a step or two behind, on the opposite side of him from Nymph. Then came the soldiers Ochlodes and Palaemon, then Comma and Henry ignominiously bringing up the rear.

Blue said, 'Is there a statue?'

'What?'

'Is there a statue at the bottom of the steps?'

'I can't see to the bottom of the steps yet,' Pyrgus said. 'What's this about, Blue?'

'I want you to tell me if there's a statue at the bottom. When you can see. Tell me at once.'

'Yes, all right, Blue.'

The torches were all the same. Not just the flames, but the torches themselves and the brackets they were in. If you looked at one, it looked old – the iron was sort of rusty and flaky. But then when you looked at the next one, it was rusty and flaky in exactly the same places. That couldn't be natural. Or a coincidence either. There was something fake about these torches, maybe not an illusion spell, but –

'There's a statue, Blue,' Pyrgus said. He was hesitating at a bend in the flight of steps, staring down at something the rest couldn't see.

'Is it pointing?'

'It's got one arm stretched out, yes.'

'I knew it!' Blue hissed.

Pyrgus started to move forward. Blue caught up. Nymph was saying, 'There's a circular chamber at the bottom of the steps and a pointing statue in the middle.'

'I can see it now,' Blue said, then added worriedly, 'We'd better stop for a minute.'

Henry stopped. One of the torches *wasn't* the same as the others. It was similar – very similar – but when you were looking at them as closely as he was, you could see the flaking was in a different place. Why should all the other torches be exactly the same and this one different? With a thought half-formed in his mind, Henry reached up to touch the torch – one way of finding out if it was an illusion. It felt solid and there was heat from the flame. Then he noticed that the bracket was on a pivot. He glanced at the other torches, but no pivots there: they were all firmly fixed. The special torch was some sort of lever! It was a *disguised* lever!

'What is it?' Pyrgus asked.

'Nobody go near the statue!' Blue said urgently. 'Nobody!'

'What's special about the statue, Princess Royal?' Nymph asked.

There was a sudden excitement in Blue's voice. 'I can get us out of here!' she said. 'If you just give me a minute, I'm sure I can get us out safely. Hairstreak's based his design on a historical maze!'

It was Pyrgus who got it first. 'You know where the exits are?'

'I think so,' Blue said. 'I studied this maze at school. I still remember bits of it. I certainly remember the statue. You can move it round. If I'm right, it makes a difference where the statue is pointing. If you turn it the wrong way, you can kill yourself, but there's one setting that opens a way out. If I can remember it, we're free.'

Henry curled his fingers around the torch bracket. If there was a secret lever, it had to open something.

'Be careful,' Pyrgus said to Blue. 'You have to be very careful: this is the second level – you can be attacked.'

'You're all right behind me. If there's any danger, come running. I think I remember what to do. This is our best chance to get out of here.'

'Good luck, Blue,' Pyrgus said softly.

Blue started down.

Henry pulled the lever.

There was a grinding noise of stone on stone. A huge section of the steps fell away beneath their feet, plunging the entire party into an abyss beneath.

Eighty

'– after which I stole her knickers,' Brimstone concluded with a look of satisfaction. The confession had taken longer than he thought, largely due to that business with the seven imps, but the effort would be worth it. Mindset was everything in this sort of magic. You could ditch almost all the other preparations – and even some of the safeguards – once you got it right.

He trotted back down the aisle, picked up the bag containing the black cockerel – parrot, indeed! – and began to wrestle with the drawstring. Once he had bitten the head off the bird, he could use the blood to draw the necessary circle and mark out the protections. The human blood from the Blood Bank would come into the picture a little later.

The bag sprang open suddenly and the cockerel exploded out of it in a frenzy of squawks and feathers. Brimstone grabbed for it and missed. The bird took off across the broken pews. Brimstone hared after it but ran out of breath after several paces. He stopped, panting. He'd have to do without the damn cock. At least he still had the bag of human blood. If he used it properly, it would work almost like a sacrifice.

Brimstone began to shift pews to give himself a clear working space. When he had finished, he took a piece of chalk from his bag and, with the expertise of long practice, drew a large equilateral triangle on the floor, its apex pointing towards the altar. He sketched the symbolic fortifications quickly, then stood with one arm upraised while his free hand held the grimoire.

' "Save us from the fear of Hell",' he intoned, using the orison from the book. ' "Allow not the devils to destroy my soul when I conjure them from the Pit and when I order them to accomplish that which I desire. Let the day be light, let the sun and moon shine, as I call them. They are indeed terrible and of monstrous deformity: but let them be restored to pleasing and familiar forms when they come to do my bidding. Save me from those who have frightful faces and permit them to obey me when I call them from Hell!" '

He put the book to one side – fearfully windy, like most Analogue World grimoires. Who cared what they looked like? Demons were demons and just as dangerous in their spindly little natural form than they were when they took on hideous shapes.

He sighed philosophically, then searched out the bag of blood and set it in the middle of the triangle. Astonishing really: blood-in-a-bag – the Analogue World was a creepy place.

There was an athame somewhere in his standard equipment, useless in the Realm (unless you wanted to stab somebody) but perfect here in the Analogue World. He found it eventually and used it to draw the outlines of the opening sigils in the air above the triangle. At home they would actually have appeared. Here you had to visualise them, imagining a trail of blue fire oozing from the tip of the athame. It was a bit tricky working this way, but he took his time and managed it effectively enough.

As he finished, he stabbed the blood bag through the centre, pinning it to the floor of the church. *'Trinitas,'* he called out loudly, *'Sother, Messias, Sabahot, Athanatos, Pentagna, Agragon –'* The words of power went on and on. Within minutes their vibrations began to strain the fabric of reality beyond the triangle. *'– Ischiros, Otheos, Visio, Flos –'*

The bloodflow from the punctured bag started to crawl across the floor towards the tip of the triangle, then reared up like a snake. Brimstone was chanting now, intoning the words in a steady hammer beat. *' – Origo, Salvator, Novissimus –'* The blood snake began to sway in time to the rhythm.

He was approaching the climax of the operation. He could feel the power like trapped lightning all around him. For the first time he had a twinge of doubt about short-cutting the safeguards and preparations, but there was nothing he could do about that now. *' – Primogenitus, Sapientia, Virtus, Paraclitus –'* The blood snake reared to its fullest extent, then pulled back as if about to strike. The familiar Orchestra of Beleth struck up all around him, quietly at first, then swelling like a symphony to fill the church. *' – Via, Mediator, Medicus, Salus, Agnus, Ovis, Vitulus, Spes!'* Brimstone screamed. The blood snake struck.

With an audible snap, a portal opened up before the altar. Demon forms swarmed through it in a gibbering horde.

Eighty-one

Fogarty found Queen Cleopatra skinning a deer. Her green arms were bloodied to the elbow and there were spatters of blood on her bare legs.

'Don't you have people to do that for you?' Fogarty asked curiously.

She gave him a sidelong glance with those astounding golden eyes. 'That's not the way things are done in the forest, Gatekeeper.' Her hands wielded the knife deftly as she plunged deeper into the carcass. 'We all muck in.' She smiled slightly. 'Isn't this the way it's done in the Analogue World?'

'Can't imagine our own dear Queen with anything between her knees except a horse,' Fogarty muttered dourly. 'Your Majesty, I –'

'Cleopatra will do. Or Cleo. No one stands on ceremony in the forest once they've been introduced.'

Fogarty sat himself down on a tree stump, pleasantly surprised by the lack of stiffness as he bent. 'I think our little party may be in trouble,' he said bluntly.

Cleopatra set down the knife and turned to look at him. No questions: she just waited. Fogarty liked that. 'I don't think the Emperor was at the palace,' he said. 'I think Hairstreak may have taken him to his new mansion right here in the forest. I think our party may be trying to get into Hairstreak's mansion right now.' What he really thought was that the party was probably inside and under attack, but since he couldn't really justify anything he felt it better not to overstate his case.

Oddly enough, Queen Cleopatra didn't ask him why he thought any of it. Instead she said, 'My people would have reported to me if the status of their mission had changed.'

'Mightn't have had the chance,' Fogarty said.

'If they went to Hairstreak's mansion, they would have returned to the forest.'

The implication was clear enough. If they'd passed through the forest, they would have stopped and told her. Fogarty sighed audibly. 'Pyrgus was leading them,' he said. 'You can't tell what that boy would do.'

The trouble was it all sounded lame and Fogarty knew it. Besides which, he wasn't sure what he wanted the Queen to do, even if she believed him. But Cleopatra only said, 'You're worried about the boy.'

'Yes.'

'My daughter's in the party,' Cleopatra said.

Fogarty blinked. 'Your daughter?' He made a rapid calculation. There was only one person it could be. 'Nymphalis is your daughter?'

The Queen nodded. 'Yes.' She pushed herself erect. 'I think I trust your intuition, Gatekeeper.'

'So what are you going to do?'

'Lead my army to Lord Hairstreak's mansion,' the Queen told him soberly. 'If you're right, the time for concealment may have passed us by.'

Eighty-two

'*Tell him no!*' screamed the wyrm desperately.

Chalkhill, who needed no urging, was already shrieking, 'No, I won't do it! Not now. Never. Leave me alone. Get your filthy hands off me. I won't, I won't, I absolutely, positively, simply won't! You can't make me.'

Hairstreak watched him with mild amusement. 'Actually I can,' he said. He nodded at two black-uniformed guards who fell in beside Chalkhill and seized him by the arms.

'*Fight them! I'll help. Head-butt them in the face!*'

'*Will you be* quiet!' Chalkhill hissed mentally. '*I'll never get us out of this if you don't let me think.*'

As the wyrm fell silent, Chalkhill raced through his options and found there weren't any. He could go like a sacrificial lamb and have the lethal operation or he could fight tooth and claw and get dragged away to have the lethal operation. Either way, he had the lethal operation.

'I don't know why you're making such a fuss,' Hairstreak said. 'It's a minor procedure.'

'Which will kill me!' Chalkhill snarled. He was still terrified of Hairstreak, but well beyond being polite to him any more.

Hairstreak raised an eyebrow. 'Who on earth told you that?'

Chalkhill stared at him. It was only Cyril who'd told him the operation was lethal and Cyril hadn't proven all that trustworthy in the past.

'*I don't suppose I could persuade you –*'

'*Shut up!*' Chalkhill growled.

Now he came to think of it, it didn't make a lot of sense for Hairstreak to have him killed – he'd proven himself very valuable in the past. So perhaps the operation *wasn't* dangerous. Perhaps –

'Oh, very well, Lord Hairstreak,' Chalkhill said decisively. 'I'd be delighted to have this operation if it can assist you in any way.' He stood off the restraining hands of the guards and marched smartly towards the open door.

'*Nooooooooooo!*' wailed Cyril inside his head.

It was irritating, but the sweeping exit was spoiled by the fact he didn't know where he was going. Chalkhill stopped at the door and waited until Hairstreak's goons caught up with him.

'Lead on, my good men,' he instructed them grandly.

The guards glanced at Hairstreak, who nodded slightly, then strolled across to join them. 'I'm glad you've seen sense, Jasper,' he said mildly. 'But it really is completely safe.'

To Chalkhill's surprise, there was not so much as a whimper from Cyril.

It was a part of Hairstreak's mansion he hadn't visited before, although he'd heard rumours about it. They marched through some sinister crypts, then down wide stone steps into what looked like a massive natural cavern. Chalkhill spotted the obsidian maze at once, then looked away quickly, pretenting he hadn't. People who learned Hairstreak's darker secrets had a habit of disappearing permanently. He glanced around ostentatiously, trying to find the operating theatre.

A horrid thought struck him. Perhaps all the talk of an operation was just to get him here. Perhaps he was going to be dropped into the maze to face the –

'*That's it!*' said Cyril suddenly. '*That's what he's planning! We have to get out of here. Knee him in the wambles! Stick a –*'

But that couldn't be right. If Hairstreak simply wanted him down here he'd have said so, or had him dragged down by the guards. No need for some elaborate deception.

'Above your head,' said Hairstreak.

'Sorry?'

'You were looking for the operating theatre. It's above your head.'

Chalkhill looked upwards.

Eighty-three

Darkness.

'Are you all right, Pyrgus?' Nymph's voice, concerned but steady. 'Is everybody all right.'

Somebody groaned.

'Blue? Is that you, Blue? What's happened? What's wrong?' Henry's voice, and he sounded on the verge of panic.

Pyrgus said quietly, 'I'm on top of something soft – I think it may be alive.'

'That's me,' said Comma crossly.

'Blue? Where are you?'

'It's all right, Henry – I've hit my head, that's all. Has anybody got a light?'

'I've got a sparker,' Comma said. 'If Pyrgus would get off me.'

But Nymphalis beat him to it. Her face suddenly emerged out of the darkness, illuminated by a portable glowglobe about the size of a hen's egg. It floated gently upwards as she released it, then expanded and brightened until its light picked up them all.

They were in a wide corridor with gleaming metallic piping running down both walls. The heat was appalling and there was a rhythmic pounding in the floor.

Blue said softly, 'Nymph ...'

'I see him,' Nymph said.

Pyrgus turned in the direction of her gaze. Ochlodes was stretched out on the floor, still clutching the remnants of his shattered bow.

From the position of his head, it was clear his neck was broken.

Eighty-four

Brimstone had a moment of funk – he hadn't bothered with a circle and now there were an awful lot of demons to control. He raised his hand and drew a series of command sigils with his finger. They should have appeared in the air, outlined in flame, but nothing happened. He tried again. Still nothing. Then, with a muttered curse, he remembered magic didn't work that way in the Analogue World. You had to earth every visualisation!

The demons were spreading out across the church, hopping across pews and climbing up the walls. One of them started grimly to beat up a statue of a saint. Brimstone grabbed a piece of parchment from his bag and savagely bit the end of his right thumb. As the blood welled up, he drew the sigils roughly on the paper:

' "Give unto this skin power to assume the signs that I have made upon it!" ' he called through pursed lips. (Biting himself on the thumb had proved incredibly painful.) ' "Which signs are inscribed with my blood in order that such inscriptions may be endowed with power to do that which I desire."' Honorius the Great was so *long-winded*. '"And make it so that it will also repel the devilment of demons who shall become afraid when they see these characters, and who will be able only to tremble as they behold them and approach."' That should do it.

He waved the parchment in the air, the inscribed side facing the approaching demons. 'See that?' he shouted. 'Now pull yourselves together and line up in orderly ranks!'

The demons ignored him. Several scampered through the broken window high up in the wall behind the altar and disappeared into the world outside. 'Come back!' Brimstone screamed. They were just a cab ride from New York City: demons could run that distance in no time. There'd be riots if they turned up in Times Square. He waved the paper again. 'If you don't behave, I'll stuff this parchment up –'

The demons stopped skittering abruptly and began to congregate to one side of the altar. Those on the walls slid down sheepishly. 'That's better,' Brimstone began, before realising their behaviour had nothing to do with his command sigils. An enormous horned figure was squeezing awkwardly through the portal.

'You might have made it bigger,' Beleth growled. 'You know I had to set up a special connection from the Faerie Realm.'

The demon prince was looking a lot more together than the last time Brimstone had seen him. His broken horn had regrown and his skin taken on a luminous red tinge that made him look as if his insides were on fire. He also seemed to have grown talons. Or had he always had them? Brimstone shook his head. He was sure he'd have noticed before.

'Honorius didn't know about resizing,' he explained. 'Or if he did, he didn't put it in his grimoire.' He watched Beleth warily, more aware than ever there was no circle of protection, but the prince only stretched luxuriously.

'No matter,' Beleth said. 'You've set up a working portal and that's the main thing.'

'So we're quits?' Brimstone asked quickly. 'I can go now?' He never liked to admit it, but he always felt a little uncomfortable in the Analogue World. Too much of his basic magic didn't work the way it should and a lot of the people here seemed deranged. He'd no idea why Beleth wanted portal access here, but now the demons were through, Brimstone was well content to leave them to get on with whatever damage they planned to inflict on New York.

'Quits?' Beleth echoed, his voice reverberating through the church. He smiled. 'Not quite, Brimstone. Not quite.'

Eighty-five

They took Chalkhill up to the floating platform, where he was faced with the most terrifying sight he'd ever seen. Although it did have some reassuring aspects. It was clean for one thing. All the metal surfaces sparkled, the floor had been recently polished and there was fresh linen on the operating tables.

There were two tables, side by side. Apatura Iris, the Purple Emperor, was strapped naked to one of them. His eyes were open, staring at the ceiling, and, while his face had a flaccid, expressionless look, Chalkhill somehow didn't think he was under the influence of an anaesthetic spell. Although to be fair, Hairstreak would probably use one. He'd want the Emperor fit and well as soon as possible after the operation.

There was a swarthy man in a shaman's loincloth between the two operating tables. His eyes were so dark it was impossible to tell whether he was a Faerie of the Night or some eccentric Lighter. He had very large, powerful hands.

'This is Mountain Clouded Yellow,' Hairstreak said by way of introduction. 'Our psychic surgeon.'

'Pleased to meet you,' Chalkhill said without enthusiasm.

* * *

The scary thing, Chalkhill thought as he climbed on to the operating table, was the equipment. There was a lot of it packed into the theatre and none of it was nice. He recognised an automatic stitcher for treating open wounds, and a weighted scissor blade that amputated any limb poked through an adjustable aperture. There was a glass-fronted cupboard with shelves full of body parts – hands, feet, toes, fingers, ears and, alarmingly, an enormous number of eyeballs laid out in colour-coded batches.

'*I hope they use everything on you,*' Cyril muttered sourly in his mind.

Chalkhill ignored him. They'd taken his clothes off and he was feeling chilled to the bone as he stretched out on the table. Psychic surgeons didn't necessarily use equipment, of course. The good ones just plunged their hands into your body and fiddled with your guts. It sounded hideous, and he'd read in a magazine somewhere that it was seventeen times more painful than having your testicles crushed in a vice unless an anaesthetic spell was used.

He wriggled to try to get comfortable and wished they'd cover him up with something, preferably a heavy blanket. He supposed Mountain Clouded Yellow would plunge his hand in and rummage around in his intestines until he found Cyril. Then he would probably rip the worm out and ram him directly into the abdomen of the Purple Emperor.

Chalkhill wished he hadn't thought of that. He was suddenly feeling so nauseous that his stomach had begun to heave. Worse still, Cyril was feeling nauseous as well, something that gave Chalkhill the sensation of a small dog throwing up on his brain.

Chalkhill closed his eyes and prayed Hairstreak wasn't double-crossing him, prayed that, frightened though he was, this would be started quickly and finished soon, prayed that –

'Just waiting for the anaesthetic wizard,' Hairstreak told him cheerfully.

An elderly wizard tottered into the operating theatre and looked around vaguely.

'Ah, Colias,' Hairstreak said. 'So glad you could make it.'

A look of panic flitted across Colias's face. 'I'm sorry, Your Lordship – I forgot what day it was.' He forced a smile that showed rotted teeth and waved one trembling hand in the air. 'But I'm ready now, Your Lord ... ah ... Your Lord ... ah ... Your Lord ...'

'Ship,' said Hairstreak.

'Ship,' said Colias. 'Ready now, Your Ship. Oh yes indeed.'

'This is your anaesthetist, Jasper,' Hairstreak said.

Chalkhill stared at the walking wreck in horror. The man's eyes were streaming so badly it was odds on he could hardly see. A drop hung at the end of his nose, which probably meant he was suffering from some disease. The tremors in his hands extended to his body at regular intervals, so that he shook uncontrollably all over. His filthy robe hung on his wasted frame like a rag thrown over a tent-pole. This was the *anaesthetist*? He couldn't remember what day it was and his magical skills didn't even extend to preserving his own teeth.

'Oh no,' Chalkhill said and tried to sit up. At once the leather straps on the operating table snapped around him in a series of audible slaps. 'Yipes!' He struggled wildly, but was firmly held.

'They're for your own good, Jasper,' Hairstreak told him, grinning. 'Can't have you moving when the surgeon gets to work, can we?'

'*This will kill you,*' said Cyril smugly. '*I told you so, but would you listen?*'

Chalkhill didn't even bother to tell him to shut up.

Hairstreak looked at Mountain Clouded Yellow. 'Are you ready to begin, Mountain?'

The shaman nodded.

With a sinking sensation, Chalkhill realised he was supremely expendable in this whole ghastly affair. What mattered was Cyril, who would survive since nobody was messing with *his* innards, and the Purple Emperor who, let's face it, was dead already and couldn't be killed a second time unless Mountain Clouded Yellow accidentally staked him through the heart or cut his head off.

Hairstreak turned to the supine Apatura Iris. 'Are you ready, Your Majesty?' he asked with mock deference.

The Purple Emperor said nothing. Chalkhill noticed that while his eyes moved slightly, he did not breathe at all.

Black Hairstreak smiled broadly. 'In that case,' he said, 'we'll begin.'

Eighty-six

'What?' asked Brimstone irritably. 'What? What's not quits? I've opened you a portal into the Analogue World. It works. You've arrived. There are demons heading for New York. You can do anything you want now – idiots here don't believe you exist any more. You could have yourself elected President and three-quarters of them wouldn't know the difference.'

'Don't be a fool!' Beleth bellowed. 'Why would I want to waste time in this miserable little world? Oh, no, it's the Faerie Realm I'm after. Several scores to settle that require full portal access.'

'The portals aren't working any more,' said Brimstone, not without a hint of malice. 'I expect you'd have fixed them by now if you could.'

'The *direct* portals aren't working any more,' Beleth corrected him. 'Demons can no longer reach the Faerie Realm – you're quite correct in that. But what's to stop a two-stage journey?'

It hit Brimstone all at once. Beleth wanted him to open up a second portal! Not between Hael and the Analogue World, but between the Analogue World and the Faerie Realm. Or maybe more than one. Maybe dozens – scores – of portals between the Analogue World and the Faerie Realm; and probably a few more between the Analogue World and Hael.

It was so simple! That way Beleth could invade the Faerie Realm any time he wanted to. All he had to do was send his troops via the Analogue World. And since nobody would suspect the existence of the new portals until they were actually used, Beleth and his demons could lay to waste the entire Realm before anybody even realised what was happening. It would be a disaster of the first magnitude. It would mean the end of the Faerie Realm as they knew it.

'What's in it for me?' Brimstone asked.

Eighty-seven

They stared down at the body.

'We can't just leave him here,' Pyrgus said.

'Yes, we can,' Nymph said firmly. 'Ochlodes was forest-born and soldier-trained. Any soldier who dies in the forest expects to be left where he fell. The trees take care of the body. That way his soul becomes part of the forest itself.'

Henry chewed his upper lip. 'There aren't any trees down here,' he said. He was feeling ill. Ochlodes's death had been his fault.

Nymph glared at him. 'It's still Ochlodes's belief.'

Blue looked at Pyrgus. 'It's not as if we have any option.'

Pyrgus moved away from her and turned to take in his surroundings. 'Is this the second level? Does anybody know how we got here? Did we fall into a trap?'

Henry's mouth had gone dry. 'I think I –' He swallowed.

Blue moved beside her brother and followed his gaze. She shook her head. 'This isn't the second level. It isn't any level.' She blinked. 'At least it doesn't look like a level to me.'

'It's a service tunnel,' Comma said.

They turned to stare at him.

'Well, just look at it,' Comma said defensively. 'Look at the heating pipes on the walls. I bet if we follow this corridor, we'll find machinery that runs bits of the maze. Uncle Hairstreak would do it that way – it's cheaper than using spells all the time.'

Blue glanced at Pyrgus. 'What do you think?' she asked quietly.

'Why aren't there lights?' Pyrgus demanded aggressively. 'You wouldn't have a service tunnel without lights – it doesn't make sense.'

'How should I know?' Comma muttered. 'Maybe this isn't the main service area. Maybe it's just a connecting passage. You wouldn't need lights in a connecting passage.'

'What do you think, Nymph?' Pyrgus asked.

'Does anyone know how we got here?' Nymph asked in her turn.

'I did it,' Henry blurted.

'Henry,' Blue said, 'I don't –'

But Henry was sick to his heart with the need to confess. 'I did it,' he repeated. 'One of the torches – I was fiddling with a lev— Look, when we were coming down the stairs I noticed the torches were fake. I mean, I don't know about this stuff, but I was fiddling with one of them and it turned out to be a lever and I pulled it and the stairs opened up and we all fell through and I killed Ochlodes.' He finished close to tears.

To his astonishment, nobody started shouting blame. Pyrgus said, 'A lever?'

Henry nodded. He was watching Blue out of the corner of his eye, but she didn't seem upset by what he'd done.

Pyrgus said, 'This *must* be a service tunnel. The

engineers would know about the lever, but they wouldn't use it without a ladder or a portable suspensor spell.'

'And a light,' Comma put in brightly.

'But I ki—' Henry bit back the rest. He was learning that life and death were treated very differently in the Faerie Realm to the way they were at home. Ochlodes was just one more bit of guilt to add to his personal store. He thought briefly of Flapwazzle and shuddered.

'OK,' Pyrgus said, 'let's see if Comma's right and this corridor leads to a machinery bay. But be careful. We don't know for sure yet. There could still be traps, so keep your eyes open.' He hesitated. 'But if this really is a service corridor then we've survived the maze and that's something we have Henry to thank for.'

Henry blinked. He'd killed Ochlodes, and Pyrgus was saying he'd saved them all. In the turmoil of his emotions he found himself thinking he didn't belong here, in this Realm. He didn't have the courage or the toughness, or –

Comma said, 'If it's a service tunnel there'll be a way out.' He grinned, happily.

They began to move as a group down the corridor. Without any further discussion, they left Ochlodes's body where it lay.

Eighty-eight

It was incredible. There were Forest Faerie everywhere, swarming in the branches, squeezing in endless files of two or three from the boles of the larger trees. You could hear the tramp of their feet on the overhead roadways.

There were hundreds, then thousands, then tens of thousands, ranging across the forest floor, arranging themselves rank on rank in clearings. All of them were armed: with bows, with javelins, with swords, with their ubiquitous, lethal little elf-bolts and, to Fogarty's great surprise, with ice cannon, disruptors, stone crackers and other heavy magical ordnance he didn't even recognise. It reminded him of the milling crowds at Dunkirk, except the faerie were less noisy. All the same, there was a steady hum throughout the forest, like a giant hive of bees.

'She did this because I told her I had a feeling about Pyrgus,' Fogarty whispered, bemused. There was an army massing in the forest, one big enough to overthrow a kingdom. If these people ever decided to leave their beloved forest, no throne would be safe.

'Don't flatter yourself, my deeah,' said Madame Cardui kindly. 'Queen Cleo has been teetering on the brink of attacking Hairstreak for weeks now. The only thing that's really held her back was the old worry about attracting attention. I expect she hoped Pyrgus might sort things out without any major forest involvement, but she never had much faith in the commando raid. All you did was tip the balance – it would never have taken much. I'm surprised she's held back so long.'

'I'm not,' Fogarty sniffed. 'Her trees are safe unless the Hael portals open again. That may never happen.'

'Oh, it's not just demons that worry her, Alan, whatever she said. She was never happy about Hairstreak building in the forest. He simply commandeered land and cut down trees. She was afraid it might start a fashion – others seizing land and building. She asked my advice about it at the time.'

'What advice did you give her?' Fogarty asked curiously.

'To wait and see.'

Fogarty stared at the massing troops. 'Looks like she got tired of waiting.'

Eighty-nine

Harsh light flared, reducing Nymph's glowglobe to sudden insignificance. Henry started and both Pyrgus and Nymph raised their weapons in alarm, but Comma only crowed, 'I told you so!'

They were in a control room – no doubt about it. The machinery was like nothing Henry had ever seen in his life, but it was definitely machinery. Much of it comprised tangles of transparent piping carrying different-coloured fluids and mists, but there were gleaming metal cabinets as well, some with switches and levers, and a massive semi-circular desk supporting banks of flashing lights. Above the desk was an illuminated plan of the maze flanked by screens showing segments of the structure itself. Henry noticed at once that one of them displayed the open staircase through which they'd fallen when he fiddled with the wall torch.

'You're right,' Pyrgus said to Comma. 'This has to be a service area.'

'A control room,' Blue said, half to herself. 'We could sabotage Hairstreak's whole set-up.'

'Inadvisable,' Nymph said shortly.

Blue rounded on her furiously. 'Why is it every time I say something you contradict me?'

Nymph shrugged. 'I'm not sure I do, but in this instance I don't think your plan is advisable.' She met Blue's glare steadily.

'I think there's something in that corner,' Henry whispered.

There was a movement in the shadows between two cabinets. A hideous thought occurred to him. Supposing, despite all appearances, this *wasn't* a service area? Suppose it was still part of the maze, a cunning, subtle secret level designed to throw people off their guard? The control panel could be booby-trapped. All sorts of monsters could be hiding in the cupboards. More than anything, anything at all, Henry wished he knew how to use the sword they'd given him.

They turned to stare. For the barest embarrassing moment, Henry wondered if he might have imagined it – his nerves were strung out, after all – but then the movement came again.

'There *is* something there!' Blue hissed.

'Yes,' Nymph agreed, stepping a pace to the right so that she was between the dark corner and Pyrgus. Pyrgus quietly moved around her.

'What is it?' Comma asked. He didn't seem the least frightened, but then he'd treated the entire maze as if it were an entertainment.

'It's probably a giant spider,' Henry muttered sourly. It would be just his luck to meet another one.

But the thing that hurled itself from the gloom was not a giant spider.

Ninety

This was fun, Brimstone thought. With Beleth here, the demons did exactly what they were told in order to construct the second portal.

And what a portal it was! In his whole life, Brimstone had never seen anything remotely like it. For a start it was big. Most portals allowed people through one or two at a time. But already there was a vaulting archway in the nave that would allow perhaps ten abreast. Beleth was obviously planning a full-scale invasion.

The demons were working like ... well, like demons. Bizarre wooden structures went up in an eyeblink and were pulled down just as quickly. Brick thudded on brick, stone slammed on stone, metal discs were cemented home and copper wiring snaked through the entire structure. It was a new design. Beleth must have created the prototype in Hael and instructed his team exactly how to build it.

Three demons dragged a cable from outside the church and attached it expertly to the new portal. They scampered across to prostrate themselves at Beleth's feet.

'Finished, Your Gloriousness,' one said.

Beleth reached out to throw a switch. A massive

blue-white bolt of lightning crackled along the cable. As it reached the portal, the wire mesh flared and melted, leaving a shimmering green forcefield between the pillars.

The ranks of armoured demons began to march towards it.

Ninety-one

Palaemon raised his lance and Nymph stepped forward with her bow.

Henry gave a panic-stricken scream. 'Don't shoot! Don't shoot!' But it was already too late to shoot. Flapwazzle was clinging to him like a hairy chest and anything that hit Flapwazzle would hurt Henry too. 'It's Flapwazzle!' Henry shouted, hugging the endolg. 'It's Flapwazzle!'

'Relax,' Pyrgus said. 'It's an endolg.' He grinned. 'Hi, fella!'

Both Palaemon and Nymph reluctantly stood down.

'It's Flapwazzle,' Henry said again, beaming. 'I thought you were dead, Flapwazzle. What are you doing here?'

'Saving your hide as usual,' Flapwazzle told him sourly.

Henry hung on every word as Flapwazzle told them what happened. The tidal wash in the sewers had carried the endolg past Henry's refuge and along the main pipework until the system took a right-hand bend. At that point, Flapwazzle was smashed into the brickwork. When he regained consciousness, he was floating in the river.

'Endolgs are quite difficult to drown,' he told them seriously. 'We don't use much air at the best of times and we can actually extract a little oxygen out of water, like fish. We die underwater eventually, but it takes a while.'

'What did you do then?' Henry asked excitedly. 'After you woke up in the river?'

'Swam for shore,' Flapwazzle told him. 'What do you think I did?'

But the nearest shore, as it happened, was Palace Island. Flapwazzle dried himself out in the sun – endolgs are slow movers when waterlogged – then returned to the palace in the hope of finding Henry.

'That was very brave of you,' Henry said, smiling at Flapwazzle. 'Considering Quercusia wants to lock you up.'

Flapwazzle made the rippling movement Henry took for a shrug. 'She has the attention span of a lettuce. Besides, she's locked up again herself now.'

Comma said, 'Mother's been locked up again?' He looked, if anything, relieved.

'What happened?' Henry asked.

'I'm not sure.' Flapwazzle had slid down from Henry now and was talking to them from the floor. 'Somebody said the order came from Cossus Cossus, Lord Hairstreak's Gatekeeper.'

Pyrgus looked at Blue. 'Hairstreak must have found her more trouble than she was worth.'

'She's mad. She's been mad for years. You can't have a mad woman on the loose, giving orders. I can't *believe* Comma let her out in the first place,' Blue said.

'She's not mad,' Comma said. 'You've always had it in for her.' He sounded sulky, but not altogether convinced.

'Well,' Pyrgus said, 'one less thing to worry about.'

'What happened, Flapwazzle?' Henry asked quickly. 'When you went into the palace to look for me?'

'The Sisters of the Silk Guild told me what had happened to you. I knew you wouldn't find the Purple Emperor in the palace –'

'How did you know?' Pyrgus interrupted Flapwazzle.

'Overheard some guards talking. They'd taken the Emperor to Hairstreak's mansion. I figured you'd find out eventually, so I came here.'

'Yes, but how did you know we were in the maze?'

'I didn't,' Flapwazzle said. 'I got lost and ended up in the ventilation ducts. I was trying to back out again when I saw you on one of the viewscreens.'

Henry couldn't stop grinning. 'That was clever of you, Flapwazzle.'

'Anyway,' Flapwazzle said, 'once I got here and figured out the controls, I tracked you and switched off traps wherever I could.'

Nymph said, 'I don't suppose you know a way out, do you, Flapwazzle?'

And Flapwazzle said, 'Oh, yes – that door there.'

Ninety-two

'*Now* we're quits,' said Beleth.

Brimstone watched the marching soldiers disappear ten abreast through the gigantic portal. This was no commando raid: it was a full-scale demonic invasion. It occurred to him he needed to get back to the Realm as quickly as possible. Apart from anything else, he wanted to watch the fun.

'Can I go now?' he asked Beleth sharply.

Beleth stretched and metamorphosed into his huge, red, muscular, horned form. Presumably he planned to join the fun himself. 'Your work for me is done. Go!'

'Use that?' Brimstone asked, nodding towards the portal.

'If you wish.'

Brimstone gathered his belongings and joined the next rank of marching soldiers. As he reached the portal, he wondered suddenly where it opened in the Faerie Realm.

'This is what I call *style*,' said Fogarty, grinning like a ten-year-old. He was being carried in a sedan chair by two burly Forest Faeries, who must have been using spell assistance to judge from the cracking pace they kept up.

The entire forest floor throbbed beneath the feet of Forest Faerie, thousands upon thousands of them dressed in military green. Every face seemed to hold a look of calm determination. 'I think it's more of an extermination,' Fogarty said.

'A lot of troops ... ' Madame Cardui said, looking around again.

'I think,' said Fogarty, 'the idea is to raze Hairstreak's mansion to the ground.'

'Yes, I know. He has guards, of course, but I'm not sure I understand why we need *quite* so many soldiers. We must outnumber his people several hundred to one.'

Fogarty wrinkled his nose. 'As I understand it, Queen Cleo wants to strike hard and fast, win in as short a time as possible. Then the mansion is demolished brick by brick – she can't burn it down because of the trees – demolished, maybe even buried. Now you see it, now you don't. After that her people melt back into the trees, leaving behind a mystery. She's hoping a disappearing mansion will discourage anybody else from building in her forest.'

'Mmm,' said Madame Cardui. 'Perhaps.'

Fogarty glanced at her sideways. 'What's worrying you, Cynthia?'

'Oh, I'm not exactly worried, deeah. Perhaps ... a little *concerned*. It's just that in my experience, once one sets a force this size marching, one always finds some reason to keep it going.'

Fogarty peered through the trees ahead. 'Well, we'll soon find out,' he said. 'I think we're nearly at the mansion now.'

* * *

Colias, the anaesthetic wizard, dropped two cones and broke a third before he managed the spell. God alone knew what was *wrong* with the man. Anaesthetics weren't exactly rocket science. You cracked a cone – the damn things were self-starting – and aimed it in the right direction. That was it. A trained monkey could do it.

Chalkhill watched the sparkling cloud wind sinuously across the room to descend first upon the Purple Emperor, then on himself. He sighed deeply as the tiny pinpricks of light penetrated his body. In a moment the anaesthetic would kick in, carrying him out of his body on clouds of bliss while the surgery was carried out. Soon it would all be over. He'd be rid of the garrulous Cyril –

'*This will kill you, mark my words,*' Cyril murmured, but without much force or conviction.

– and Hairstreak would once again be in his debt. There were worse places to be in. Much worse. He waited.

He was still in his body.

He waited.

Still no clouds of bliss. But of course time always crawled when you were in a state of anticipation.

He waited.

An errant thought occurred to him. That old idiot, who ruined three spell cones before he even managed to crack one, had probably made the cones in the first place.

'That should do,' said Hairstreak abruptly. He nodded to Mountain Clouded Yellow. 'You can start the operation now.'

Chalkhill pinched himself. It hurt like hell. He tried

to sit up, but the straps restrained him easily. He tried to shout, to warn the surgeon he was nowhere nearly ready, but a sunburst of fear caused the words to gurgle in his throat.

The psychic surgeon, Mountain Clouded Yellow, moved with terrifying speed to plunge his hands into the abdomen of the Purple Emperor and rip the bloody opening that would become the new home of the wyrm.

The Purple Emperor screamed.

They were in the vast natural cavern, but outside the obsidian maze. Pyrgus looked around him with a curious tightness in his stomach. Above him, huge rafts, hung by sensor technology, floated below the ceiling, each accessed by a branching suspensor shaft. One of them supported a vast room with transparent walls: obviously an observation chamber where spectators could watch death stalk the maze. Beside it –

'There's something moving up there,' Blue said quietly.

Pyrgus suddenly realised how vulnerable they were. When the party emerged there had been a general flood of relief that they had escaped from the obsidian maze at last, but now they were exposed – a small, tightly-bunched group on the featureless sweep of the cavern floor. If they were discovered, Hairstreak's men could pick them off in minutes.

Nymph must have had the same thought, for she said, 'Crown Prince, we need cover.'

Pyrgus said, 'We need to get out of here. Hairstreak won't be holding my father underground. It's dangerous to talk to –' He stopped abruptly, licked his lips.

'Can any of you see a way out?'

'I think that's a staircase over there,' Henry said.

He was right. 'Keep low and keep moving!' Pyrgus said. 'Henry, grab Comma's hand. All of you – quietly as possible.'

As a party they made a run for the cut-stone staircase. They had almost reached it when a bloodcurdling scream echoed through the cavern.

'That's Daddy!' Blue exclaimed at once.

Ninety-three

It was hideously dangerous, but they crowded into the suspensor shaft. (Henry spotted the entrance to that one as well: Henry was getting very good at spotting things.) Standard suspensor spells were set to lift a maximum of three people with a ten per cent margin of error, besides which there was the probability of meeting Hairstreak's guards either in the shaft itself or when they stepped out.

But after the single scream no one hesitated. For an instant the spell strained, lifted, trembled, then shot them upwards abruptly. Comma squeaked in alarm, but only seconds later they reached a floating platform that fanned out a network of walkways. One led to an empty observation chamber. Another wound towards an open archway, through which appeared a horrifying scene.

Blue's father lay naked on an operating table, his abdomen open and bloody. A strange, squat Nighter was bent over him, splattered with the Emperor's blood. Beside them, a second man was strapped to another table. With a start Blue recognised him as Jasper Chalkhill, her old nemesis, who was supposed to be in jail. Behind them was an old man in shabby wizard robes, an expression of bewilderment on his face. Watching it all was the familiar slim figure of Lord Hairstreak himself.

There were no guards! There were no guards at all!

'Get Hairstreak!' Pyrgus shouted. 'I'll look after Father!'

A murderous rage descended on Blue like a scarlet mist as she launched herself at Hairstreak.

Nymph drew her bow and calmly shot the man bending over the Purple Emperor. The arrow caught him in the throat and he collapsed with a strangled gurgle, tearing at the shaft. She put two further arrows in his back, but by the time the second hit he was already dead.

Nymph turned to kill Lord Hairstreak, but Princess Blue was in the way.

Henry stood on the edge of the action, his emotions churning. He had no weapon he could actually use! Why had no one given him something sensible like an Ouzi? Why did he have to stand like a wimp while the others got stuck in?

Pyrgus threw himself across the room. He had almost reached his father when, to his astonishment, the elderly wizard in the tatty robe hurled a massive firebolt in his direction.

Pyrgus flung himself to the floor. The flaming mass singed his hair, then struck Palaemon squarely in the chest.

Palaemon fell backwards, his body a smoking crater. He trembled twice on the floor, then lay still, his dead eyes open, staring at the cavern ceiling high above.

The old wizard looked down at Pyrgus on the floor and grinned. 'I won't miss this time,' he cackled.

Nymph put an arrow in his chest and he died with the grin still on his face.

Hairstreak ran.

Blue hared after him, her short sword at the ready. She was going to kill him, once and for all, and hang the political consequences. The man was a slug, a smear of slime on the face of the Realm.

Henry hesitated for no more than half a heartbeat, then ran after Blue. Nymph switched her bow for a vicious-looking knife and ran to join them both.

Hairstreak raced from the operating theatre on to the walkway that led to the observation chamber. He was moving quickly, but Nymph was already ahead of the others and gaining on him.

'Leave him to me!' Blue hissed angrily and increased her pace. But they had him. There was no other walkway from the observation chamber. There was nowhere he could go. Then she saw the suspensor shaft. Unlike the one that had carried them up, this shaft descended direct from the observation chamber. 'Suspensor shaft!' Blue screamed.

'I see it!' Nymph called. She seemed to be running flat out, but somehow increased her pace and reached the observation chamber no more than a pace or two behind Hairstreak. She hurled herself forward and managed, miraculously, to get between Hairstreak and the shaft.

Hairstreak made a sweeping movement with one hand and Nymph staggered backwards, clutching her arm. Blood oozed between her fingers. Hairstreak jumped. Nymph grabbed for him and missed.

Blue and Henry raced into the room. 'Where is he?' Blue gasped, looking around wildly. 'Where's the shaft?'

Nymph turned. 'It's –' Then stopped, bewildered.

'He's cloaked it!' Blue howled.

'Where is he?' Henry asked.

'He's cloaked the shaft!' Blue shouted in frustration. 'He's cloaked the shaft! There must have been an automatic trigger. We can't use it. We can't even see it.'

Henry looked over the edge of the observation raft. Far below, the slim figure of Lord Hairstreak was racing for the cut-stone steps. Nymph must have spotted him as well, for she said quietly, 'Lord Hairstreak will raise an alarm. We must return to Prince Pyrgus.'

'Yes,' Blue agreed.

Yes, Henry thought. *And then we'd better find some way to get out of here.*

They entered the operating theatre at a run. Pyrgus was standing over his father, a stricken look on his face. Blue stopped dead. 'What's wrong? Pyrgus, what's wrong?'

Pyrgus licked dry lips but said nothing. The room was a scene of carnage. Comma was crouched in one corner, curled into a trembling ball.

'*Pyrgus!*' Blue's cry was almost a scream.

'It's –' Pyrgus swallowed and started again. 'Blue, he's ... he's ...' There were tears welling in his eyes. 'I – we – it's too late,' Pyrgus said. 'Daddy's dead.'

Blue started forward like someone sleepwalking.

Pyrgus moved at once to meet her. 'You mustn't look, Blue. He's – it's not –' He reached out for her arm.

Blue shook off the restraining hand and pushed past him, her face set. She looked down at her father stretched out and strapped on the operating table. Blue whispered, 'His head has been cut off.'

Pyrgus said, 'I know, Blue. Come away.'

But Blue would not come away. 'He can never be resurrected again.' She looked at Pyrgus, then, helplessly, at Henry and repeated, 'He can never be resurrected again.'

'Excuse me,' Chalkhill said, 'but would somebody like to release these straps and give me back my clothes?'

Ninety-four

They moved out as a group, trembling with shock and exhaustion, but alert for the guards they knew must appear at any moment. There had been a short, broken discussion between Blue and Pyrgus about taking their father's body, but Nymph had cut it short by pointing out brutally that it would take two of them to carry the corpse and another to carry the head – out of the question since they were going to have to fight their way out of Hairstreak's mansion.

Nymph more or less took charge after that, Henry noticed. Which was probably a good thing. Their party had shrunk to six. Comma, who was hardly more than a child, looked a nervous wreck and wouldn't meet anybody's eye. Henry was armed now – he'd taken a long dagger from the body of the shaman who'd killed the Purple Emperor – but had no illusions about his ability to use it. Both Pyrgus and Blue were functioning like automata and their faces had taken on a weird, jelly-like look. Even Flapwazzle looked subdued.

Nymph found the original suspensor shaft and made Henry wait with Comma while she, Blue and Pyrgus went down. Henry watched them float gently to the ground, then put his arm around Comma's shoulders and stepped into the shaft when Nymph waved.

Comma shook the whole way.

They reached the floor of the cavern and Nymph led them to the staircase. She warned them quietly to have their weapons ready and there was such authority in her voice that even Comma managed to produce some sort of knife, although his hand shook as he held it.

But as they moved upwards into the main body of the mansion, there were no guards, no hint of Hairstreak or any of his staff. The entire building felt deserted. Once they passed an open door which gave a glimpse of a half-eaten meal on the table inside.

They were still creeping through the ground-floor level when they heard the screams outside.

'Good God!' Fogarty exclaimed.

Madame Cardui, normally phlegmatic, snapped an order that brought both their bearers to a halt. She leaned forward in her seat. 'My deeah,' she said, 'this is quite extraordinary.'

There was a massive portal opened on the lawn outside Lord Hairstreak's forest mansion. Demon troops were pouring through it in an orderly stream. A pitched battle was underway between the portal and the house.

'Those are Hairstreak's people,' Fogarty said. 'Fighting the demons.' He started to clamber down from his sedan chair. It wasn't just Hairstreak's armed guards – the whole of his household staff seemed to be outside, as if the mansion was under attack.

'Where are you going, Alan?' Madame Cardui asked sharply.

'To get a closer look.'

'My deeah, you will be careful?'

But Fogarty was already pressing forward through the still ranks of Forest Faerie soldiers. This made no sense. First of all, the Hael portals were closed down. Secondly, he'd never seen a portal anything like this one. It was the wrong colour, there were no cold flames and it was huge. Thirdly, Nighters dealt with demons all the time and Hairstreak in particular was rumoured to have cut some sort of long-term deal with the Demon King or whoever their stupid leader was. Why were the demons attacking his home now?

He caught sight of Queen Cleo at the head of her troops and made his way quickly towards her. 'Do you know what's going on?' he asked breathlessly.

'No, Gatekeeper. But those are demons in my forest, exactly as I feared.'

'They're attacking Hairstreak's men,' Fogarty said. 'Maybe we should let them get on with it before we think of interfering.'

The Queen watched the action thoughtfully. Her troops were massed in the trees, out of sight. Their discipline was absolute. There was not a sound that would draw attention to their presence. 'You think they may do our job for us?'

'Could do.' Hairstreak's people were losing, no doubt about that. Their bodies were strewn everywhere. He'd no idea why this was happening, but given half an hour he was fairly sure it would be a wipeout. With Hairstreak out of the picture, the Forest Faerie could demolish his mansion at their leisure.

Queen Cleo said, 'What do we do with the demons, Gatekeeper?'

Fogarty looked at her. After a moment he said, 'Good point.' It was the possibility of demon portals that had worried the Forest Faerie in the first place. That thing on Hairstreak's lawn must be their worst nightmare. And there were one hell of a lot of demons marching through it.

'It may be a question of timing,' the Queen told him thoughtfully. 'As you say, Gatekeeper, it could be useful that the demons have attacked Lord Hairstreak. But we still cannot permit demons in the forest, not at all. The interests of my people would be best served if Hairstreak was routed, his mansion destroyed, the demons driven back to their own realm and their portal permanently closed. Ideally without revealing the existence of the Forest Faerie to the outside world.'

'Tall order,' Fogarty said.

'Not if we attack now,' the Queen said quietly. 'While we can still contain the situation.'

It made sense. As the Queen turned to signal to her people, Fogarty thought of Blue and Pyrgus. He hoped they'd have the sense to keep their heads down if they were anywhere nearby. There was a major battle coming and it was very easy to get yourself killed in crossfire.

'Those are demons,' Nymph said.

They were standing by an open window in Hairstreak's mansion watching the slaughter outside. Maybe the best thing was simply to stay put, wait for the demons to wipe out Hairstreak's guards and servants – which probably wouldn't take too long by the looks of it.

As against that, there were more and more demons pouring through the portal and, once they had dealt with the defenders, there was every chance they might take over the house. Pyrgus had been captured by demons once before and it was an experience he didn't want to repeat. Maybe they should make a break for it now, try to escape in the confusion.

The one thing he was absolutely certain they *shouldn't* do was get involved in the fight.

'Those are my people!' Nymph exclaimed suddenly.

He followed the direction of her gaze. Forest Faerie were pouring from the trees like a river in spate. Before he had time to react, Nymph had jumped through the window and was running towards the fray.

'Nymph!' Pyrgus shouted desperately, then leaped to follow her.

'Pyrgus!' Blue shouted and launched herself through the window after him.

Henry hesitated for no more than a second before following. Only Comma remained. He stared through the open window with a bleak look on his face.

Fogarty chilled as he watched the Forest Faerie fight. They were the most ruthlessly efficient killing machines he'd ever seen in his life. The odd thing was nobody seemed to give orders, yet everybody clearly knew exactly what to do. The stream of faerie emerging from the forest split in two to circle both the demons and the remaining few of Hairstreak's defenders. But instead of plunging into close combat, they remained at a distance and showered their opponents with arrows and elf-bolts. There was a moment of confusion, then demons began to fall.

For a moment he thought the whole battle might be fought from a distance, but the demons quickly regrouped and turned to face their new attackers. The

Hael troops were like insects, completely without personal fear. They hurled themselves forward, oblivious to the deadly rain of bolts and arrows. At the same instant, a tightly-knit group of Forest Faerie made a lightning sortie towards the open portal.

'A convincing grasp of strategy,' said Madame Cardui. 'Disable the portal and you cut off demonic reinforcements.'

The swelling demon army clearly came to the same conclusion, for a large contingent of Hael troops separated off to stop the sortie. The faerie fighters fell back, then were reinforced in their turn and pushed forward again. New ranks of larger, more heavily armoured demons had begun to emerge from the portal now. One raised a massive fire wand. An elf-bolt sliced through his right eye as he triggered the weapon and the gout of flame passed over heads to set fire to a tree.

'The Queen's not going to like that,' Fogarty said sourly. There was a stirring in his blood. He actually wanted to be out there in the middle of the fight. Which was strange, since when he *had* been a soldier – nearly sixty years ago, could you believe it? – he'd spent his time avoiding battle whenever humanly possible. Old age was a pain. It gave you brave new ideas, then took away the ability to carry them out.

It looked as if he was right about the Queen not liking it. The river of Forest Faerie emerging from the trees abruptly became a flood. Foot soldiers hurled themselves upon the demon horde while archers pounded them with darts and bolts. A team made straight for the burning tree, snapping cones of suffocation spells to extinguish the flames. The party headed for the portal suddenly found itself massively reinforced. Fogarty noticed there was a three-strong team of wizards at its core.

What happened next was almost too fast to follow. The key was a vast, flame-free explosion at the portal. The structure erupted into fragments that showered down like hail, bloodied by the body parts of nearby demons caught in the blast. Starved of their constant reinforcements, the remaining demons fell like chaff beneath the horde of Forest Faerie. It was over in minutes.

As work teams of Forest Faerie moved in to demolish Hairstreak's mansion, Fogarty and Madame Cardui walked on to the battlefield. The dead and dying were everywhere, but already faerie clean-up squads were hard at work destroying the evidence of what had happened here.

'My deeah, isn't that Prince Pyrgus?'

Fogarty followed her gaze and felt a chill claw clutch his stomach. Pyrgus was lying on the grass, his jerkin soaked in blood. Blue and a worried-looking boy were kneeling beside him – with a start, Fogarty recognised him as Henry. Nymph was standing behind them, bow in hand like a guard. For some reason there was an endolg at Henry's feet.

'Pyrgus!' yelled Fogarty as he ran towards the group.

Pyrgus opened his eyes slowly and gave a wan smile. 'It's just a flesh wound, Gatekeeper. I'll be fine.'

'Can you find us a Healer, Mr Fogarty?' Blue asked. 'And tell somebody to get Comma out of the house before they pull it down around his ears.' She hesitated, but only briefly. 'My father's body is in there too. I should like it brought back to the palace for his burial.'

Ninety-five

Blue woke with a start.

There was someone in her room! She could hear the steady breathing. How had they passed the guards?

She scrabbled for a weapon and found instead an emergency moon cone. Pale light flooded her chamber as she cracked it.

Comma was standing at the bottom of her bed.

'What do you think you're doing?' Blue snapped angrily. He was always creeping around where he wasn't wanted, but this was something else.

'Couldn't sleep,' Comma said sulkily. 'I want to talk to you, Blue.'

'I don't care. You can talk to me in the morning. Late in the morning. Or dammit no, you can't. Just leave me alone and talk to somebody else. I'm going back to sleep.' She turned and pulled the blankets over her ear.

Comma moved to sit on the bed. 'They've locked Mummy up again.'

'Yes, I know. And I'm glad. She's –'

'Sometimes I can hear her screaming in the night.'

'No you can't – that's just dreams.'

'I'd have talked to her if they hadn't locked her up. She could tell me what to do about Pyrgus.'

There was something in his tone that stopped her at

once. She sat up, caught Comma looking at her night-gown, and pulled the bedclothes up around her throat. 'What about Pyrgus?' she demanded angrily.

Comma said almost sleepily, 'He killed our father.'

'No he didn't. You know he didn't – it was the demon that possessed Mr Fogarty, you little creep. If you –'

'It was Pyrgus the second time,' Comma said in an oddly singsong voice. 'He thought I wasn't watching and he cut off father's head.'

'That's it!' Blue said. 'Get out!'

'All right, I'm going,' Comma told her hurriedly. He leaped from the bed and scuttled across the room, but paused at the door. 'You ask the other man,' he said. 'He saw it too.' Then he was gone.

Blue lay in bed, fuming. Whatever happened, how-ever bad, you could always rely on Comma to make it worse somehow.

There was no question of sleep now, so she climbed out of bed and pulled on a dressing gown. Why did he do it? Why? Why make up stories at all, let alone in the middle of the night? Their father was already dead when they had reached that ghastly operating room. His stomach was open and his head – his head –

Actually she couldn't remember noticing his head was severed, but it must have been. There was certain-ly that hideous open wound on his stomach. Hairstreak must have – must have –

All the same, Comma was pure evil. Or mad like his mother. Why else would he make up a story about Pyrgus? The thing was, he always messed up on the detail. Ask the other man, he said. But there wasn't any other man. Nymphalis had killed everybody else in the room except Hairstreak, and Hairstreak had run. There was just Comma and Pyrgus and the bod—

There was Chalkhill. They'd left him strapped to the other operating table. They'd walked out and left him hurling abuse, demanding they come back, threatening ... Threatening what? Blue couldn't remember, but it had nothing to do with Pyrgus or her father. Just threatening, that's all – the sort of thing people like Chalkhill did when they couldn't have their own way.

She wondered what had happened to Chalkhill when the Forest Faerie had demolished Hairstreak's mansion.

If Mr Fogarty was surprised to see Blue in the middle of the night, he didn't show it. He stood, dressed in a weird nightcap and gown, looking, she thought, more like a wizard than the wizards of the Realm.

'Yes,' he said in answer to her question. 'The Forest Faerie found him. They released him to my custody and I sent him back to Asloght.'

'The jail?'

'He has the rest of his sentence to serve. Lord Hairstreak sprung him on a ruse.'

She'd never heard the term *sprung him* but decided it must mean that Hairstreak had released Chalkhill illegally. 'I need to see him.'

'Now?'

'Yes.' She waited for him to point out it was the middle of the night.

'Let me get some clothes on and I'll take you,' Mr Fogarty said.

Ninety-six

'Beg pardon, sir,' said Clutterbuck, 'but there's people to see you. I told them you had company.'

They'd given him back his old cell, but despite the comfortable bed, Chalkhill couldn't sleep. He'd been lying looking at the ceiling and talking to Cyril. 'I don't have company,' he said.

'*Liar!*' the wyrm whispered inside his mind.

Clutterbuck looked around. 'So you don't, sir – thought I heard you talking to somebody,' he said easily. 'Shall I show them in?'

Chalkhill pushed himself upright. 'Who is it?' he asked.

'Princess Blue and Gatekeeper Fogarty.'

Chalkhill was on guard at once. It could be his release, but it could just as easily be trouble. He'd have to play this very cautiously indeed.

'Yes, show them in,' he said.

Blue eyed Jasper Chalkhill with distaste. He'd lost a little weight, but apart from that he was the same obnoxious, painted piece of slime he'd always been. 'I've come to ask you a question,' she said without preliminary.

Chalkhill smiled at her. Even in jail he'd managed to

get hold of his ghastly magical mouthpaste so that his teeth flashed and sparkled like tinsel. 'Yes, of course, my dear.'

She bit back the urge to tell him not to call her *my dear*. This was a difficult, delicate mission and there was no sense in antagonising him. 'Dismiss your Trinian,' she said bluntly.

'Clutterbuck is here to protect me in case of attack,' Chalkhill protested.

'Who do you think is going to attack you, Mr Chalkhill? Me?'

Chalkhill's eyes wandered over to Mr Fogarty, who was standing with his back against the door.

Blue said, 'Oh, for heaven's sake!' She turned to Mr Fogarty. 'Would you leave us, Gatekeeper – I'll be fine.'

Mr Fogarty nodded. 'I'll be just outside if you need me.'

Chalkhill's smile returned and this time it actually reached his eyes, which glittered with a sort of pleased malevolence. 'You can go, Clutterbuck,' he said.

As soon as they were alone, Blue said, 'The chances are you'll be a guest of Asloght for a long time, Mr Chalkhill, perhaps even for the rest of your life. But if I were to have a word with my brother, it's possible your term of sentence might be shortened. Do we understand one another, Mr Chalkhill?'

'Perfectly, Serenity,' Chalkhill said with a peculiar flash in his eye. 'What do you want me to do?'

'Just tell me what happened in the operating theatre.' Chalkhill looked at her blankly.

'Why were you there and what happened –' she hesitated, but only for a heartbeat, '– what happened to my father?'

'Ah,' Chalkhill said.

After a moment, Blue said, 'Well ... ?'

Chalkhill licked his lips. 'This, ah, reduction of my sentence ... You say you would be willing to speak to your brother – your brother Pyrgus – about it?'

'Yes.'

'Do you think he would be ... sympathetic?'

'I can't give you guarantees, but I think he might.'

'What happens if he isn't?'

Blue turned and knocked on the door. 'I'm ready to leave!' she called.

'No, just a minute,' Chalkhill said quickly. 'There's no need to be like that. Of course I'll tell you. Why wouldn't I? If I can be of any help, any help at all, to any member of our illustrious royal –'

'Get on with it,' Blue warned.

He seemed to come to a decision. 'Very well. The operation. Lord Hairstreak found he could not control your father as effectively as he wished. The Purple Emperor was – is – was a man of strong and noble will. Even in death he was too much for Lord Hairstreak. The operation was an attempt to increase the level of control by interfering with your father's brain.'

'How?'

Chalkhill licked his lips. 'He was going to – he tried to – to reconnect the neural pathways in a different order.'

Blue stared at him with distaste. 'Why did he cut my father's head off?'

'That was a mistake,' Chalkhill said. 'Entirely a mistake – a ghastly mistake. Lord Hairstreak hired this ... *primitive* to carry out the operation. Mountain Clouded Yellow. Can you imagine a more ridiculous name? Dreadful man, but a very powerful psychic surgeon. I gather he came well recommended, despite his failings. The trouble was, he had too high an opinion of himself – too cocky by half. The most important connections were at the brain stem and he decided to access them through the neck. He believed he could reconnect the head afterwards.' Chalkhill's face took on a sorrowful expression. 'But he couldn't. Lord Hairstreak would have killed him, if your people hadn't done it first.'

'So it was this ... this Mountain Clouded Yellow who cut my father's head off?'

'Yes.'

'No one else?'

'No, Serenity, of course not. Who would want to?'

Blue said, 'One final question. What was your part in the operation? Why were you there, Mr Chalkhill?'

'Blood donor,' Chalkhill told her promptly. 'I happen to be the same blood type as your illustrious father. I was on hand simply in case of an emergency; and delighted to be of any possible help to your father, of course.' He looked at Blue earnestly. 'But in the event he was beyond my help.'

Blue stared at him for a moment, then said, 'Thank you. Thank you, Mr Chalkhill. You've been ... helpful.' She knocked behind her on the door and it opened at once.

As she moved to leave, Chalkhill called out, 'You'll tell your brother what I said, won't you? You'll tell him exactly?'

He was lying. She was certain of it. The question was why? Except she had a feeling she already knew the answer – or at least knew somebody who knew the answer.

Mr Fogarty asked curtly, 'Satisfactory?'

'In a way,' Blue said.

'Where are we going now?'

'Back to the palace,' Blue said. 'I want to talk to Pyrgus.'

Ninety-seven

'Don't lie to me!' Blue screamed. 'I've been up all night and I've talked to that beastly Chalkhill and I can't *take* any more!'

Pyrgus looked a little better. His arm was bandaged and there were more bandages wrapping his chest and stomach underneath his shirt, but his colour was good except for the dark rings around his eyes. Maybe he hadn't had much sleep either.

'Blue, I –' Pyrgus said. 'Listen, it was all very confused. I don't think any of us will ever find out what really –'

'Comma has been making up stories about you,' Blue said. 'I don't believe him, but I don't believe you either. I just want to know the *truth*!'

'What's Comma been saying?' Pyrgus asked sharply.

'That you cut – that you cut off –' She just couldn't finish. Suddenly she was so tired she could scarcely stand up.

Pyrgus turned away from her. 'Do you believe that?'

'No, of course I don't. But I talked to Chalkhill and he lied to me – I know he lied to me. What I don't know is why!'

Pyrgus said very softly, 'He lied to you because I told him I'd arrange his freedom if he did.'

'You told him that? Why would you want to arrange his freedom?'

Pyrgus sighed. 'It was bribe him or kill him, and I couldn't do any more killing.'

Blue was looking at him open-mouthed. 'I don't understand you, Pyrgus. I don't understand any of this.'

Pyrgus said, 'It wasn't Hairstreak who resurrected Father. It was me.'

Blue stared at her brother in stunned disbelief. They had retired to the garden chamber where their father had once tended his orchids and the room was heavy with their scent. Spell reinforcement made it one of the most private places in the Purple Palace. 'You did *what*?' she gasped.

Pyrgus looked physically ill. 'I was afraid to become Emperor,' he said.

'*Afraid*?'

'You know how useless I am at that sort of thing – politics and negotiations and diplomacy. I'd even be useless trying to run the Army. The Realm would fall apart with me as Purple Emperor. Worse, it would fall to the Nighters. There would be wars and chaos and –'

Blue said incredulously, 'So you resurrected our father?'

Pyrgus nodded miserably. 'I didn't know what else to do.'

'Have you any idea how illegal that is? How dreadful that is? How ... how ... *forbidden* that is?'

Pyrgus nodded again. He was seated hunched over on a bench and looked as if he might be sick on the floor.

'How could you?' Blue asked. 'How could you?' A thought occurred to her and she added, 'How *did* you?'

'Went to a necromancer,' Pyrgus muttered.

'A Nighter?' It had to be a Nighter! No Faerie of the Light would touch the dark magic involved in raising the dead.

'Yes.'

'Have you no sense?' Blue demanded. Pyrgus looked almost suicidal and in any other circumstance that would have made her want to comfort him, but there was a feeling of panic in her now that ran away with her tongue. 'Didn't you know a necromancer could *control* anyone he raised? That's what went wrong. It was bound to go wrong. You had to know it would go wrong!'

Pyrgus shook his head helplessly.

Her anger had carried her this far, but now the enormity of what Pyrgus had done was really beginning to dawn on her. She'd never made a profound study of magic, but she knew enough to realise that necromancy – sorceries involving the dead – was something ten times worse than the techniques of demonology that Faeries of the Night employed so often.

'You'd better tell me everything,' she said.

Pyrgus took a deep breath and told her.

Ninety-eight

Pyrgus had slipped away from his royal bodyguards somewhere between Cheapside and Northgate. He entered the teeming warren of narrow alleys that led into Pushorn, a hand on his newly-purchased Halek blade. This was one of the roughest districts in the city and, while he'd never had much concern for his own safety, it would be a nuisance to lose his purse at this point. He'd a feeling he was going to need every scrap of gold he was carrying.

With the long dusk gathering into darkness, the torches were lit in Pushorn. No glowglobe streetlamps here. The local council claimed poverty, but the truth was glowglobes never survived long, even with magical protections. The inhabitants were an opportunist mix of Nighters, the scum of Lighters, Violet Trinians, half-civilised Glaistigs, semi-feral endolgs and a sprinkling of addicted Halek wizards who found simbala music cheaper here than in the licensed parlours of Northgate. Every one of them preferred to hide in shadows than have their activities examined by the lawful authorities.

The smell was distinctive: a mix of sweat and pitch-blende. Pyrgus felt his nose wrinkle as he pushed through the throng that emerged after dark in search of illegal entertainments.

''Oo do you think you're pushing?' growled a bruiser in a cracked leather jerkin.

'Sorry,' Pyrgus muttered, hurrying past. He kept his head down, but at least he hadn't been recognised. A minimal illusion spell distorted his features and changed his hair colouring.

He'd memorised directions, but the narrow streets were confusing and he dared not ask the way, so that it took him almost an hour to find Gruslut Alley. While the rest of Pushorn was dimly lit, Gruslut wasn't lit at all beyond the flickering light that seeped through cracks in shuttered windows. He stopped, allowing time for his eyes to adjust, and after a while was able to see reasonably well.

What he saw was not encouraging. Like much of Pushorn, the houses were three- and four-storey buildings that had seen better days. Now they were all cracked plaster and peeling paint. Some seemed to have shifted foundations: their walls bulged alarmingly as if threatening to fall into the street. He still wasn't absolutely sure he was in the right place – part of the sign-board had rotted so that the first three letters were missing – but he moved into the alley all the same.

Gruslut was known as a street where certain commodities and services might be bought, but there were no shops here. A few of the wooden doors had discreet nameplates, but nothing that gave a clue to what might be on offer. He had almost given up hope when he stumbled on the blue door he'd been told to look for.

Pyrgus licked his lips nervously. As he reached across to knock, he realised what he was about to do wasn't merely illegal, but hideously dangerous. Whatever – he still had to do it. Despite the brave front he put on with Blue and all the rest, Pyrgus knew he could never become Emperor. He wasn't suited and he didn't want the job. He'd never wanted the job. That was why he'd fought with his father so much when he was alive. His father had always insisted he should behave like an Emperor in Waiting when all he'd really wanted to do was lead an ordinary life. Pyrgus knocked.

For a long time nothing happened. He was reaching out to knock again when he heard the first footfalls inside. Someone was approaching at a slow, deliberate pace. Pyrgus withdrew his hand and waited, his heart suddenly pounding. The door swung partly open. Two glittering black eyes stared at him from the gloom.

Pyrgus swallowed. 'Are you –' he began. 'Are you ... Pheosia Gnoma?'

The voice that answered was like the rustling of dead leaves. 'Come in, Your Majesty,' it said. 'We've been expecting you.'

The blue door opened into a narrow corridor that plunged almost at once down a flight of rickety wooden steps. Pyrgus followed the stooped figure into a poorly-lit basement room smelling of dust and mould. There were no glowglobes here either, just rushlights and a smoking, fly-specked lamp. Books of arcane lore lined the whole of one wall. An open cupboard displayed a collection of skulls. There was alchemical equipment on a bench in a corner. Beside it Pyrgus noticed a *kangling* trumpet carved from a human thigh bone.

'You know who I am?' he asked.

'Of course, Majesty. Your illusion spell has all but worn off.'

It was impossible to guess Gnoma's age. He had the eye folds and cat's pupils of a Faerie of the Night. His head was completely shaven and he seemed to have filed two of his front teeth into points, giving his face an odd, vampiric look. He was wearing a tattered brown monk's robe that looked a shade too small for him.

'Who else is here?' Pyrgus asked.

'No one, Majesty.' The soft dry voice scarcely rose above a whisper.

'You said "*We've* been expecting you." Who did you mean by *we*?'

'My spirit helpers,' Gnoma told him.

Gnoma was nothing like Pyrgus had expected. The man had a hungry look that was deeply disturbing. He never took his eyes off Pyrgus's face. Pyrgus pushed his nervousness aside. Best get down to business, then get out of here.

Pyrgus said, 'Pheosia Gnoma, I want you to raise my father from the dead.'

They sat facing one another across a lightweight wooden table. Gnoma placed a small glass before him and filled it with blue liquid from a swan-necked bottle. Pyrgus eyed it uncertainly.

Gnoma smiled, showing his weird serpents' teeth. 'Libatrix wine. A simple herbal tincture that prolongs life and clears the mind.' He produced a second glass, filled it and drank it down in a single swallow. 'See,' he said, 'quite harmless. I have no interest in poisoning my clients.'

Pyrgus watched him for a moment, then took a sip from his own glass. The liquid was cool, sharp and slightly sweet.

Gnoma placed both hands, palms down, on the table. 'Resurrecting your father may prove difficult.'

'I'll pay whatever you want.'

Gnoma smiled coolly. 'It's not a matter of money.'

Pyrgus didn't believe him. With Faeries of the Night it was always a matter of money. After a moment, he said, 'But you *can* resurrect him?'

'Oh yes,' Gnoma said. A drop had been forming on the tip of his nose and he sniffed suddenly to get rid of it. 'There are methods. Unfortunately ...'

'What?' Pyrgus hissed. 'Unfortunately what?'

Silence stretched interminably. Eventually Gnoma said, 'The most reliable method is not lawful.'

'I am Emperor!' Pyrgus told him firmly. 'I'll say what's lawful!'

'You're Emperor Elect,' said Gnoma, 'but I take your point. However, I must warn you the method I have in mind runs contrary to *spiritual* law. That's quite beyond your ruling.'

Pyrgus pushed back his chair so quickly that it toppled over. 'I must speak with my father!' he shouted wildly. 'As your Emperor Elect I order you to raise him!'

Gnoma remained seated. He looked up at Pyrgus and smiled again, slowly. 'Then bring me your father's corpse,' he said.

Ninety-nine

Gnoma's laboratory was a sterile, windowless subterranean cube that smelled of Chinese wash. There was an alchemical furnace in one corner near a blacksmith's anvil and a selection of alembics in an open cupboard. Towards the centre of the room was a six-foot metal gurney underneath a set of high-powered glowglobes. Beside it was an instrument tray that made the Royal Herticord's equipment look like toys.

The crate was on the floor beside the gurney.

'No one knows you brought it here?' Gnoma asked.

Pyrgus shook his head. 'Except the coachman and he doesn't know what's in it.' He was feeling so nervous he could scarcely keep still.

Gnoma said, 'I must ask you again, Pyrgus Malvae, if it is your wish to go through with this operation? Once the work begins, it cannot be stopped.'

Pyrgus licked his lips. 'Let's get it over with.'

Gnoma gave him a glance that might have shown contempt. 'There's a floater on the crate and contents?'

Pyrgus nodded.

'Open it,' Gnoma commanded.

Pyrgus glared at him, but said nothing. He might be Crown Prince and Emperor Elect, but he was engaged in something so forbidden he could scarcely stand on ceremony now. He knelt by the crate and uttered a silent prayer for forgiveness. The lock was keyed to his touch and he pressed his thumb firmly against it. There was an oily click as the bolts slid back. Pyrgus looked up.

'Open it,' Gnoma repeated, more quietly this time. His eyes were gleaming.

Pyrgus discovered he was holding his breath and released it explosively. He pushed back the lid of the crate which fell over on its hinges with an horrific and unseemly crash. His father's body lay inside on a cushion of clean straw.

The stasis spell held corruption at bay, so the only smell was that of fresh, cold meat, but not all the application of the embalmer's art could repair the ravages to the face of Apatura Iris. Henry said the weapon used to kill him was something called a shotgun, which caused an explosive charge to propel several hundred violent beads of lead. It had been used at close range. Merciful tears swam before Pyrgus's eyes to soften the image.

'Place the body on the operating table,' Gnoma said.

He had expected something of the sort. Eyes still streaming, he reached inside the crate. It was the first time in years he'd put his arms around his father and the floater spell rendered him unreal, like thistledown. Pyrgus stood up, the corpse cradled in his arms. Shuddering with sobs, he placed it gently on the gurney.

'Face downwards,' Gnoma said.

'Is that necessary?' Pyrgus asked sharply. It was improper for a Purple Emperor to lie prone.

'We must have access to the luz,' said Gnoma firmly.

Pyrgus turned the body.

'Please stand clear,' Gnoma said. 'Your work is done.'

Pyrgus stepped back. With a massive act of will he held himself steady, but emotions were pouring through him like a torrent. He could no longer understand why he had fought so long and so hard with his father. The disagreements seemed unimportant, even silly. The body on the table was so small, so helpless, so ... empty. But perhaps he could make amends now. Perhaps he could make it all right.

Gnoma took a massive pair of tailor's shears and inserted them into the back of the Emperor's formal purple jacket.

'What are you doing?' Pyrgus demanded in sudden panic.

'Be quiet!' Gnoma hissed. 'You ordered this to be done. Now leave me to do it!' The shears ripped through the material as if it were a cobweb.

The Emperor's naked back came into view. Pyrgus stared at the butterfly tattoos that were now matched by his own.

Gnoma reached for a scalpel.

'What are you going to do?' whispered Pyrgus.

'Remove the luz,' said Gnoma shortly. He plunged the scalpel into the Emperor's spine.

It was a small piece of bone, about the size of a thumb joint, shaped a little like a vertebra, but without the typical protuberances. It gleamed white now that Gnoma had wiped it.

'That's it?' Pyrgus asked in wonderment.

Gnoma held the bone between his thumb and forefinger, eyes gleaming. 'Watch,' he said softly. He took two steps across the room and placed the bone gently on the anvil. Then he opened a drawer in the bottom of the albemic cupboard and drew out a large, short-handled hammer. The metal head writhed with serpentine energies.

Gnoma glanced at Pyrgus, then smashed the hammer down with heart-stopping violence. The sound was like a thunderclap. Trapped lightning exploded from the hammer-head.

'No –' Pyrgus screamed. He moved to grab Gnoma's arm.

The anvil shattered into fragments under the impact of the blow. Gnoma tossed the hammer to one side and reached down casually into the debris. He held up the bone, still in one piece, unharmed. 'The luz is indestructible,' he said.

Pyrgus stepped forward to examine the bone. It was not so much as scratched.

'It is the bone used by God Himself to resurrect a man on Judgement Day,' Gnoma whispered.

Pyrgus closed his eyes.

'It is the bone I shall use,' Gnoma said, 'to resurrect your father.'

Pyrgus heard the distant footsteps and felt very much afraid.

For lack of a chair, he was perched on an old wicker trunk in a room jam-packed with dusty theatrical equipment. Life-sized puppets slumped from their strings like grinning corpses. There were several cabinets displaying crudely-painted flames. Decorative masks watched him blankly from the walls. The room was at street level. Gnoma said it was dangerous to meet the dead underground.

The footsteps reached the stairway and stopped briefly. For just the barest second he felt a flicker of relief, then there was the creak of wood as someone – something? – started to ascend.

What was approaching on the stair?

Gnoma's lodgings were deceptive. As well as the basement living room and the deeper subterranean laboratory, the ground floor of the house was a warren of corridors and chambers, most suspiciously locked. This theatrical storeroom smelt of grime and shimmered behind a watery curtain of tears that would not leave Pyrgus's eyes.

What had he done?

There was less than two weeks to go before the Coronation and after that there could be no going back. Nobody knew how that felt. Not Henry, not Mr Fogarty, not even Blue. Everyone expected him to do his duty. Everyone assumed he would want to be the Emperor. No one knew the fear.

Although that fear felt like nothing set against the terror he felt now.

What had he done?

He couldn't become Emperor. He had no talent for it, none at all. They all thought just because he was his father's son it meant he was equipped to follow in his father's footsteps. But Pyrgus and his father had fought about everything. Everything.

The trouble was he hated politics. He hated the lies and the deceit, the double-dealing and corruption. Yet he knew it was impossible to survive in high office without them. Even his father, an honourable man, had been forced into questionable acts from time to time.

But his father had at least been ruthless enough to undertake them. Pyrgus knew he never would. He would try to hold firm to his principles and ruin the Realm in the process. How could he follow in his father's footsteps?

His father's footsteps were coming closer.

It was peculiar. He believed Gnoma could raise the dead – that's why he was here, that's why he'd subjected his father's body to ... to ... But at the same time he didn't believe, not really. Dead was dead. There was no turning back. Once the stasis spell was removed, his father's body would quickly turn to dust. There was no way to escape, no incantation that could ...

Yet he believed in Gnoma. And something was approaching.

The footsteps had reached the top of the stairway and were now on the corridor outside. Perhaps it was Gnoma himself, come to admit failure. The man would be full of excuses, full of reasons why he should keep his fee.

Why was he moving so slowly? The tread was like a leaden procession. One step ... one step ... one step ... Not halting or feeble or stumbling or ill, but miserably, terrifyingly *slow*.

Slow or not, the footsteps were close now. He could imagine the figure in the corridor and in his mind's eye he knew it was not Gnoma.

What had he done?

A dark shape loomed in the doorway. Apatura Iris stepped into the room.

Apatura, once Head of House Iris, former Purple Emperor of the Realm of Faerie and Lord Protector of the Church of Light, father of Pyrgus Malvae, had been a striking man, not handsome exactly – his features were too coarse for that – but with charisma and appeal. He had carried himself with nobility and grace.

Now he was a monster. His spine was twisted from the removal of the luz. No wonder he walked slowly – he could scarcely hold himself upright and his body seemed wracked by preternatural pain. But the real monstrosity was his face. The wax used by the morticians to reconstruct his features had fallen away once life returned, leaving almost all his head a raw and bloody open wound. One eye remained intact, glittering darkly from the mass of torn flesh. The regal nose was no longer there. The mouth was little more than a gash.

'Father,' Pyrgus whispered. But this creature was no longer his father. It was an animated shell, driven by dark powers.

It moved towards him and suddenly he imagined he could smell the stench of rotting flesh. It reached out a hand, the fingers curled like claws.

What had he done? What had he done?

'Kill me,' Apatura Iris said.

One hundred

'Why didn't you?' Blue demanded. 'If Daddy was so awful, why didn't you kill him there and then?'

'I couldn't,' Pyrgus told her simply.

'But –'

Pyrgus seemed to gather strength from somewhere. 'Look, Blue, he may have been awful, but he was still Daddy. How could I kill him? I'd only just had him resurrected. I didn't know what was going to happen. I didn't know Gnoma would go to Hairstreak or how bad things would get. I thought I could take him home and have him healed – you know, have his face healed and anything else that was wrong – and it would be like it was before. He could be Emperor and it would be like it was before.'

'But you didn't take him home.'

'Gnoma said the process wasn't complete – the resurrection process. He said it would be dangerous to release ... ' Pyrgus took a long, shuddering breath, '... Daddy before everything stabilised. So I left him with Gnoma.'

'And Gnoma took him to Hairstreak.'

Pyrgus nodded miserably. 'Yes.'

After a while Blue said, 'I wonder how they made him look like his old self.'

Pyrgus shrugged. 'Illusion spells. I think there was some healing too. But it wasn't holding. That's why Hairstreak arranged the operation. They were going to transplant a wangaramas.'

Blue stared at him with dawning realisation. The wyrm would have allowed her father's body to function far more effectively, would have created the illusion of health and life, would have allowed Hairstreak to maintain the fiction that the Purple Emperor had never died. 'Chalkhill was carrying the wyrm?'

'Yes.'

'It was Chalkhill who told you what Lord Hairstreak planned to do?'

'Yes.'

'So you cut off Daddy's head.'

'Yes. Yes, yes, yes!'

'What are we going to do?' Blue asked.

Pyrgus looked at her. 'Nothing. It's done now. I should never have brought him back – I know that now. It was horrible for Daddy and a disaster for the Realm. But I've put it right now. Daddy's dead, properly dead. Hairstreak can't bring him back again. Nobody can.' He suddenly moved across to take her hands. 'Blue, I have it all worked out,' he said earnestly. 'We'll use Hairstreak's story against him. He's put it about that Daddy never died, just went into a coma then revived. *We'll* say Daddy never fully recovered, that he hung on for a little then died from his original injuries. Hairstreak won't dare to contradict us – he can't without admitting his involvement. I'll go ahead with the Coronation. When I'm Purple Emperor, I'll tear up the stupid pact Hairstreak made Daddy sign.'

Blue shook her head. 'You can't. The treaty is

binding on Daddy's heir as well as himself. Hairstreak was taking no chances – you're mentioned in the wording by name.'

Pyrgus waved her objection aside. 'I'll think of something. I'll put things back the way they were. Outside of you and I, nobody need know anything illegal happened.'

'Comma knows,' Blue said.

They called a Conference of Friends. Pyrgus didn't want to, but Blue insisted. Mr Fogarty was there. Madame Cardui was there. Henry was there. Pyrgus wanted Nymphalis there too, but Blue vetoed that promptly.

'We don't know her well enough,' she said. 'Besides, she owes her loyalties to the forest, not to House Iris. I'm sure she's wonderful, but this is too delicate to take the slightest risk.'

When they were all in the Orchid Room and the door securely locked and spelled, Blue outlined the problem, holding nothing back. They listened attentively, sober-faced, saying little, nodding occasionally. When she'd finished, Blue said, 'I'd like to know what you think.'

No one spoke until, eventually, Henry said, 'But Hairstreak already knows what you did, Pyrgus – wouldn't Gnoma have told him?'

'Yes. Yes, he did,' Pyrgus said. 'Gnoma definitely told him. But Hairstreak can't admit to that, otherwise everyone will know he was lying about Father never having died and the new agreement and everything.'

Mr Fogarty glanced across at Pyrgus. 'It would nearly be worth owning up to everything. To drop

Hairstreak in it.'

Pyrgus started to say something, but Blue cut in quickly. 'There's no question of Pyrgus owning up.'

'Why not?'

'I told you – resurrection is forbidden.'

'So what are they going to do to him?' Fogarty asked impatiently. 'Have him say five *Hail Marys*?'

'Hang him,' Blue said starkly.

There was a long moment's silence in the room. Then Fogarty said, 'Are you serious?'

'That's the penalty.'

'Even for an Emperor Elect?'

'Only the Emperor is above the law – a properly crowned Emperor. The Emperor Elect can be tried like anybody else.'

Mr Fogarty sniffed. 'Should have waited, shouldn't you?' he said to Pyrgus. He turned back to Blue. 'But would it actually happen – a trial? Who would bring the charges?'

'The priesthood,' Blue told him. 'It's a spiritual issue.'

Henry said, 'What happens if it gets out that Pyrgus, you know, cut his – ah, killed –'

'A resurrected body is an abomination,' Blue said. 'There's no penalty for sending the soul back to its proper home.'

'Except your father's body isn't supposed to have been resurrected,' Henry said gently. 'Hairstreak's story is that the Emperor never died and you've decided to support that, haven't you? If you don't, then Pyrgus will be hung for resurrecting him.'

Blue and Pyrgus looked at one another.

Madame Cardui said, 'He's right, Crown Prince

deeah. But if we stick to Hairstreak's story and Comma tells what he saw, you could be facing a charge of murder in place of a charge of resurrection. I'm afraid that's hanging again.'

'Simple answer,' Fogarty said. 'We bung Comma in solitary until you're made Emperor.'

Madame Cardui raised an eyebrow. 'A little rough on the boy, wouldn't you say, Alan?'

Fogarty shrugged. 'Could have Pyrgus crowned in a week. A week's not too rough in solitary: I've done it my—' He stopped himself and coughed, then added lamely, 'Solves the problem, doesn't it? They're not going to hang their Emperor for murder.'

'Ah,' Blue said.

'Why are you saying *Ah*?' Mr Fogarty asked sourly. 'What's *Ah*?'

Blue looked strained. 'When I said the Emperor is above the law, there's one exception …'

'Murder?'

'Not exactly,' Pyrgus said. 'Just murdering the previous Emperor.'

'That's right,' Blue confirmed. 'Realm Law holds that the Purple Emperor *owns* his subjects and thus can dispose of them as he wills – he can execute someone, which is just another name for murder, or have somebody carry out a murder, or pardon somebody who's committed murder. But the one exception to all of that is the previous Emperor, who is not defined as a – I forget the term, but it means he's not defined as being owned.'

'You can see why,' said Madame Cardui cheerfully. 'It stops the royal family murdering their way to the throne.' She hesitated, smiled, then leaned forward to say quietly to Blue, 'The word is *chattel*, deeah.'

Fogarty said, 'So if Comma talks, Pyrgus hangs – threats may keep him quiet for a while, but if we don't sort out something permanent, we all know Comma *will* talk, sooner or later.'

'I'm not having you kill him,' Blue said sternly. 'He may be a pain in the neck, but he's still our baby brother.'

Fogarty looked at her in mild surprise. 'Actually, I was thinking more of bribery. Offer him something he wants – few toys, money, a fancy title, seat on the Government ... whatever it takes, just so long as he has no real power. Make sure he knows it all disappears if Pyrgus isn't Emperor.'

'Trouble is Pyrgus doesn't *want* to be Emperor,' Blue remarked quietly.

'I think I may have an idea about that,' said Henry.

After he'd told them, Henry looked from one face to the other, waiting for a reaction.

Pyrgus shook his head. 'It's not possible, Henry.' His expression might have been one of regret.

'It's not legal,' Blue echoed.

'Actually it is,' said Madame Cardui. 'The legislation has been in place for a very long time, although you seldom hear about it.' She smiled a little. 'The real problem, Henry, is that it couldn't possibly work.'

'It works in my world,' Henry said. 'All the time.'

'Is that true, Alan?' Madame Cardui asked.

Mr Fogarty shrugged. 'I'm not sure *works* isn't a bit of an exaggeration.'

Henry looked at him in disgust.

One hundred and one

The State Barge pulled away from Palace Island with the pink light of dawn glinting on the golden filaments that were strewn across its surface. The initial movement was matched by the first rumblings of a 101-impact thunderspell salute, the traditional signal to the population of an impending Coronation. It seemed, however, that the population had little need of it: crowds had already begun to line the processional route by midnight.

The barge turned north-west at once to avoid interfering with traffic across the Official Ford (which had been particularly heavy for days) and hugged the northern bank of the Wirmark below Eastgate. At the first cheer of the dockland crowds, wizards on the barge combined their efforts to float up two gigantic illusions, one depicting the Peacock Crown, the other the butterfly emblem of House Iris.

As the illusions flowered, the cheering increased and the spectators were rewarded with an interactive display – the illusions changed colour in response to the pitch and volume of the cheers. Even at this early stage, the people were calling for sight of their new sovereign, but the only figures on deck were barge crew in their neat purple uniforms and the wizards who maintained the spells.

Once clear of the island, the barge began a ponderous, slow zigzag course that ensured no riverside segment of the city was favoured above any other. First south to Merkinstal, a suburb so underdeveloped that it still showed farmland right up to the river's edge. Yet even here the people had turned out in droves to watch the pageantry. Poor but loyal, Pyrgus thought fondly as he watched them through a darkly-tinted porthole. The predominant cloth here was the dun-coloured homespun of the countryfolk. Further in, the silks and satins of the more sophisticated inner-city dwellers would begin to appear.

The state barge turned south-west so that it would enter the central river channel before it reached Lohman Bridge.

Henry was having problems with his britches.

He was no longer Male Companion – his idea about what should happen at the Coronation meant the position was no longer relevant – but he was still Iron Prominent, Knight Commander of the Grey Dagger, and that meant he had to dress up. The blouse and jacket had been bad enough – they were spell-woven to flash a different colour with every change of light – but the cloth-of-gold britches were sheer murder.

The real problem was that they were just too small. Henry had been measured for his Knight Commander gear the day Pyrgus had presented him with his dagger, but the costume had been tailored while he was at home in the Analogue World. Today was the first time he'd tried it on and there was definitely a mistake in the britches. They were too tight across his bottom, too tight around his waist and when he pulled them on eventually by sucking in his gut, they were a good six inches short on both his legs.

Slowly, he forced one button after the other – the Faerie Realm had never taken to zips – his fingers trembling with the effort. With every one he closed, the wedgie pressure at the crotch increased. He suspected walking was going to do him a serious injury and sitting down would likely lead to something worse.

'Better get a move on, Henry,' said Mr Fogarty. 'The Royal Barge has already left.'

'These breeches are too small.'

'Yes,' said Mr Fogarty. 'You look a bit of a prat.'

Although Henry would have amputated his ankles rather than admit it, Mr Fogarty himself looked magnificent. He'd exchanged his Gatekeeper robes for the dress uniform that went with one of his lesser titles – Lamed Wufnik of God and Realm. It was cut from blue velvet and worn with white, knee-length socks and buckled shoes. When he tried on his tricorn hat, Henry thought he was the image of Lord Nelson.

'I'm worried about sitting down,' Henry said.

'Do you have to sit down?'

'I don't know. Nobody told me what happens in the ceremony. Do you know?'

'Like I'd ask you if I knew. How do I look?'

'All right,' said Henry grudgingly.

The Silk Mistresses had made Blue a new gown which they insisted was more appropriate for the occasion – an elaborate creation with an ultra-violet sheen that gave the illusion of folded wings. She stared at her reflection and decided it made her look taller, probably no bad thing in the circumstances, but that it didn't suit her quite as well as the other one. She was about to pull it off when Comma burst in, looking like a moonbeam.

'Don't you ever *knock*?' Blue hissed. 'I could have been naked!'

'Well, you weren't,' Comma muttered, scowling. Then he brightened. 'Can I go on deck, Blue, and wave to the people?'

'Yes,' Blue said.

'Do you think Pyrgus would mind?'

'Why don't you ask him?'

'I don't want to,' Comma said. He caught sight of himself in the mirror behind Blue and preened. He was dressed in white from head to toe – white shoes, white socks, white britches, white shirt, white cap. 'I'm going to wear this all the time,' he said. 'Not just at the cere- mony.' He turned to his left, then turned to his right. 'I think it suits me.'

'You'll never keep it clean,' Blue muttered.

'I'll use spells,' Comma said. 'You can give me the money.'

Blue glared at him. 'Why don't you just go and prance about on deck. I'm not ready yet and we'll be docking in a minute.'

'We won't be docking for *hours*,' Comma said. 'They haven't even opened the bridge for us yet.'

One hundred and two

As the barge approached, the Keeper and his Team marched along the centre of Lohman Bridge in fine order, their way cleared by an escort of purple-liveried Guardsmen. Safety regulations insisted the bridge was out of bounds to the public until the barge passed through, but the public had piled on anyway.

The Keeper stopped before the massive mechanism. At his signal, one of his Team hoisted a plain cyan flag. On the water below, the State Barge stopped dead and hovered like some great, wonderful waiting beast.

'Places,' snapped the Keeper.

His men moved with mechanical precision to the accompaniament of a few ironic cheers. Three went directly to the Great Wheel. All the others manned the network of ropes and cables attached to it.

'Action,' called the Keeper. Like his Team, he was dressed in a style that had gone out of fashion a thousand years ago.

The men on the ropes began to pull while the others strained at the Great Wheel. The watching crowd fell suddenly silent. Tradition was king on the day of a Coronation: ancient machinery, part of the original bridge, had to be used.

The trouble was, despite constant care and attention,

there was no guarantee the ancient machinery would actually work. The Coronation of Good King Glaucopsyche had been delayed for two weeks while mechanics toiled around the clock to get the Great Wheel functioning again.

For a moment it looked as if history might repeat itself, then, with a deep, ominous creaking sound, the Wheel began to turn. The crowd cheered and shouted encouragement to the straining men. The bridge trembled underfoot, then moved.

A momentous cheer erupted.

On the barge below, a white figure emerged on deck and waved. The cheering redoubled. The bridge began to split in two. There was a minor panic as spectators scrabbled to get to one side or the other before the chasm widened, but for once nobody fell into the water. To howls of delight and roars of approval, Lohman Bridge opened.

The Royal Barge resumed its stately pace and passed slowly through.

'Did you see that?' Comma exclaimed excitedly. 'They loved me! They all cheered and waved! This was the best idea I ever had!'

'For heaven's sake!' Blue hissed through gritted teeth. 'Have you no idea, no idea at all, about privacy? And it wasn't your idea, not even slightly.'

Comma said thoughtfully, 'You look nice in that thing.'

'Do I?' Blue asked. 'You don't think it makes me look too old?'

'What are you going to do with that thing during the

ceremony?' Mr Fogarty frowned.

'Are you talking about me?' Flapwazzle asked aggressively.

'Are you talking about Flapwazzle?' Henry asked aggressively. 'He's not a *thing*.'

Mr Fogarty shrugged. 'The endolg. What are you going to do with him during the ceremony?'

'He's not staying behind,' Henry said.

'I'm not staying behind,' Flapwazzle confirmed.

'Did I say you should? It's just –' Mr Fogarty shrugged again, '– he's a bit smelly and you're leaving it a bit late to give him a bath.'

'Good grief,' Flapwazzle exclaimed. 'He's telling the truth – I *am* a bit smelly.' He started to undulate across the floor.

'Where are you going?' Henry asked in alarm.

'I'm perfectly capable of giving myself a bath,' Flapwazzle said.

One hundred and three

The barge was sailing along Cheapside, rather more distant from the river bank now for fear of missiles from the anti-royalist element in the district. But so far as Pyrgus could see, there was no sign of any trouble. The shoreline was a waving mass of miniature House Iris flags and the cheering was so loud it actually echoed back from the massive warehouse buildings on the other side of the river.

Pyrgus wondered if Henry's idea would really work.

'Do you think my idea will really work?' Henry asked. It had all gone so fast and now, suddenly, he needed reassurance.

'Nothing else was going to,' said Mr Fogarty. 'And you have to admit it'll be interesting. Especially when Hairstreak discovers what's happening.'

'Do you think Lord Hairstreak's still alive?'

'I know it. Cynthia's people reported he was in his place at the Cathedral just before first light. Take more than a demon invasion to kill off that little slimeball.'

'What if he tries to cause trouble?' Henry asked.

'You leave Hairstreak to me,' Mr Fogarty growled.

Flapwazzle slid under the door in a perfumed cloud. 'Our ouklo's here,' he said.

'Best go then,' Mr Fogarty said. 'Wouldn't do to get there after the Royal Barge.' He glanced at Henry's britches. 'You'd better travel standing up.'

'Blue,' Comma said, 'why did the demons attack Uncle Hairstreak's house?'

Blue turned on him suspiciously. The trouble with Comma was you never knew what was going on inside his head. After the night he'd come to her bedroom, he'd not mentioned Pyrgus again to anyone. Even when they went to him with Henry's scheme there'd been no trouble. She'd expected him to rant and rave and make demands and threats, but all he did was shrug his agreement, as if their plans had nothing to do with him at all. He hadn't even seemed all *that* interested in Mr Fogarty's bribes of a new title and a trust fund to spend any way he liked. At the time, Blue had wondered if he'd been feeling guilty about the part he'd played in helping Hairstreak make a monster of their father. Whatever it was, he'd said nothing about Pyrgus's actions and there were times when she half wondered if he'd forgotten what he'd seen in Hairstreak's operating theatre. But now he was thinking about the day it happened. Was his question a preliminary to something much more sinister?

She decided to play it straight. 'I think Lord Hairstreak upset the Demon Prince,' she said.

Comma glanced through the expanded porthole. 'We're nearly at the Cathedral,' he told her.

The great riverside tower swung into view, marking the outer boundary of Westgate. They would reach the Cathedral Dock in twenty minutes, half an hour at most. Pyrgus sighed. He'd never felt so nervous in his life. Yet he knew he was doing the right thing. The more he thought about Henry's idea, the more it made sense. He should have thought of it himself, weeks ago, instead of … instead of …

He pushed the thought savagely from his mind and stood up. Best concentrate on getting ready.

The ermine cloak he had to wear throughout the ceremony was hanging in the cabin wardrobe. He took it out and placed it round his shoulders, staring at his reflection in the mirrored door.

He thought of his father, who had worn this same cloak at *his* Coronation. He thought of his mother, who had been Faerie Queen for such a tragically short time. Then he turned and walked up on to the golden deck to let his loyal subjects see him as the barge drew slowly into the Cathedral Dock.

One hundred and four

The ouklo pulled up between ranks of Imperial soldiers and tightly-packed, cheering crowds. As Henry stepped out he was surprised to receive a crisp salute from every man in uniform, then realised the salutes were not for him at all, but for Mr Fogarty, as Gatekeeper, who was in overall charge of security.

Mr Fogarty himself, resplendent in his Lord Nelson gear, returned the salute with a casual wave of his hand, then cornered the nearest Captain.

'Everyone here?'

'Yes, sir.'

'Lord Hairstreak?'

'Yes, sir.'

'Our men in place?'

'Yes, sir.'

'You've moved my nameplate as instructed?'

'Yes, sir, absolutely sir.'

Henry stared at the Cathedral, wondering what the nameplate business was all about. The building was huge, dwarfing St Paul's or Westminster or any cathedral he'd ever seen. But it wasn't the size that was impressive – it was the architecture. The entire structure had a light, lacy, filigree look that was straight out of a fantasy painting. It seemed as if the first strong gust of wind would be enough to blow it down, but somebody had told him the building had stood for seven hundred years and once survived a direct hit from a meteor.

'Crown Prince Pyrgus?' Mr Fogarty asked the Captain.

'The Royal Barge will dock in five minutes,' the Captain said. He pointed. 'If you look through there, sir, you can see it.'

'Excellent,' said Mr Fogarty. He turned to Henry. 'Come on, young Iron Prominent, we'd better take our seats.'

It was the moment Henry had been dreading. His britches were as tight as ever.

Henry actually stopped in astonishment as he stepped into the Cathedral. Tier upon tier of seats were packed with the nobility of the Faerie Realm, each one vying with the other in the opulence and finery of their costumes. He saw colourful blocks of Trinians, stately Halek wizards and representatives of races he had never even heard of. The hum of conversation was like a swarm of giant bees.

'Hello, Henry,' said a soft voice from the aisle to his left.

For a moment he didn't recognise her, then he realised suddenly it was Nymphalis. She had exchanged the familiar green uniform for a fur outfit that made her look like Conan the Barbarian.

'Hello, Nymph,' Henry grinned. 'I like your gear.'

Nymph leaned across and whispered in his ear, 'I wanted to see Prince Pyrgus crowned, but I didn't want anyone to know I came from the forest.'

'They wouldn't guess in a thousand years,' Henry assured her as Mr Fogarty tugged his arm to make him get a move on.

As he moved on to the centre aisle, Henry discovered the Cathedral altar wasn't set in the east like the churches he was used to, but centred in the massive building. It consisted of a golden cube, above which hovered a shimmering sphere of writhing light that drew his eyes hypnotically.

'What's that?' he asked Mr Fogarty.

'Some sort of device that lets God manifest.' He sniffed, then added cynically, 'I gather He doesn't often bother.'

They walked together to the altar and, following Mr Fogarty's lead, Henry bowed to the empty throne. 'Right,' whispered Fogarty, 'we take our seats now – you're with me.'

There was a peculiarly-designed chair that looked like the Gatekeeper's Seat Henry had seen when they made him Iron Prominent, but Mr Fogarty ignored it and led him up steps to the higher tiers. Eventually they found two empty seats directly overlooking the altar. There were brass plaques with their names on each of them.

'Hello, Blackie,' Mr Fogarty said cheerfully. 'So glad you could make it.'

The man beside him scowled, but didn't speak. Henry sat down very, very cautiously and found to his delight that the material of his britches stretched but didn't tear. He wasn't comfortable, but at least he was still decent.

It was only when he settled that he realised the man Mr Fogarty had spoken to was Lord Hairstreak.

Blue joined Pyrgus on the deck of the Royal Barge to tumultuous applause from the dock. 'You all right?' she whispered.

Pyrgus drew a deep breath. 'Yes.'

She hesitated. 'You don't want to change your mind? You still can.'

'I don't think so, Blue,' Pyrgus said soberly. 'But I don't want to anyway.'

'What are you going to do … you know … after?' It was something they hadn't discussed.

'Let's just get today over with,' Pyrgus told her.

There was the tiniest grating sound as the barge docked. A golden walkway extruded smoothly at their feet. They looked at one another.

'This is it,' said Pyrgus. 'We'd better do it.'

They processed slowly down the walkway, side by side.

'Long live King Pyrgus!' someone called from the crowd. 'Long live our Purple Emperor!'

The cry was taken up until it swelled across a thousand voices. 'Long live King Pyrgus! Long live our Purple Emperor!'

Pyrgus adjusted his ermine cloak. With measured tread, he and his sister began the long, slow walk up to the Cathedral.

One hundred and five

A trumpet fanfare jerked Henry's attention off Lord Hairstreak. He leaned forward and turned towards the main door of the Cathedral, certain it must be Blue and Pyrgus, but instead it turned out to be a procession of priests and wizards, each one without exception dressed in flowing spinner silk.

'The clown with the beard is Archimandrake Podalirius,' Mr Fogarty whispered. 'He does the actual Coronation.'

Archimandrake Podalirius was a tall, heavily-built man with so much black hair that his face was almost totally concealed. Henry tore his gaze away as Podalirius took up his place behind the empty throne. His priests fanned out in a semi-circle beyond him. Altar-girls scurried forward with jars of sparkling ointment and small silver ewers of sacred oil. The trumpets sounded a second time and Pyrgus entered the Cathedral, his sister Blue a step behind him. His head was bare and he had removed the special hairpiece so that his shaven tonsure was exposed. Usually Henry couldn't take his eyes off Blue, but on this occasion Pyrgus commanded his entire attention.

He looked every inch the Emperor as he began to walk towards his throne.

'Going to have another try at killing him?' Mr Fogarty asked lightly out of the side of his mouth. 'Illusion spells or worms or something of that sort?'

Hairstreak stared straight ahead. 'Heard that foolish rumour, have you, Gatekeeper.'

'From the horse's mouth,' Fogarty said cheerfully.

'Pity you can't prove it,' Hairstreak said.

'Yes, isn't it? Still, might get the proof if you were to try again.'

'Oh, that's hardly likely,' Hairstreak said, 'so long as I have this ... ' He drew a roll of parchment from the inside of his doublet.

Below them, the priests behind the Archimandrake set up a sonorous chant. Their voices swelled to fill the entire Cathedral.

'What's that?' Fogarty asked.

'Copy of the pact signed by the late lamented Apatura Iris when he recovered from his recent coma. It remains legally binding even though he is no longer with us.'

'I suppose it does,' said Fogarty.

Hairstreak glanced at him suspiciously. 'And binding on his son, Gatekeeper. Remember that. Clause Five, specific. Crown Prince Pyrgus is even named. The moment he becomes Purple Emperor he is legally bound to implement the treaty.'

'Surely not the *very* moment,' Fogarty said. 'Won't you even let him celebrate his Coronation?'

Hairstreak ignored him. He turned to Fogarty and gave a small, bleak smile. 'There are changed times coming, Gatekeeper. Although I very much doubt you will last long enough to see them.'

The chanting stopped abruptly as Pyrgus sat down on the empty throne. Blue moved to stand on his right-hand side. Archimandrake Podàlirius loomed behind the throne.

'No doubt we'll soon find out,' said Fogarty.

The Archimandrake filled a vial from a ewer of sacred oil.

Two priests stepped forward carrying the State Crown between them. It was heavily encrusted with polished amethysts and surrounded by a purple aura.

Archimandrake Podalirius poured oil into the palm of his left hand, dipped his right thumb and used it to trace a mystic sigil on Pyrgus's tonsured scalp. 'I prepare the head that God has called to wear the crown,' he intoned.

Pyrgus looked straight ahead, his face expressionless.

From somewhere in the body of the church a female choir began to sing. Their high, clear voices swooped and dived like birds. Above them, the distinctive tones of an Endolg Chorus began a descant. A slow procession of chanting monks paced through the body of the church towards the altar.

Archimandrake Podalirius took the Purple Crown from the two priests, held it aloft, then set it gently down on Pyrgus's head. Crackling energies flowed down into his body. All sound ceased.

'Behold your Emperor!' the Archimandrake proclaimed in ringing tones.

Henry found he was holding his breath. From the corner of his eye he could see Lord Hairstreak leaning forward slightly, a self-satisfied expression on his face.

'And now the Emperor's first proclamation,' said Mr Fogarty quietly.

Pyrgus stood. The crown must have been enormously heavy, but he wore it well. When he spoke, he spoke quietly, but spell amplification around the throne carried his words to every corner of the Cathedral.

'It is tradition,' he said, 'that an Emperor must make the first official proclamation of his reign here in the Cathedral at the very moment of his Coronation. I hold to that tradition today and herewith proclaim my abdication, effective immediately, in favour of my sister, Her Serene Highness, the Princess Holly Blue, who shall, by this my imperial proclamation, henceforth rule as Faerie Queen and Sovereign Empress of the Realm, Champion of –'

Despite the spell amplification, the remainder of his words were drowned out by the tumult that erupted throughout the entire Cathedral. Hairstreak was on his feet, the parchment treaty crumpled in his fist. 'He can't do that!' he roared.

'He just has,' Mr Fogarty said mildly. Henry's idea and a very neat one. He glanced at the parchment. 'Looks like your treaty's worthless now – I don't recall anything that makes it binding on Blue.'

Hairstreak rounded on him furiously. 'It's not over, Gatekeeper. We both know what Pyrgus did, and believe me, I shall bring the boy to justice for it.'

Mr Fogarty never even blinked. 'I think you'll find the Purple Empress will pardon all her brother's misdemeanours.' He gave one of his most chilling, feral smiles. 'She may even make it her first proclamation.'

Epilogue

Henry wondered why he felt so miserable. Blue was Queen now, which was wonderful. She wouldn't have much time for him, of course, not with her new position and titles and being busy and so forth, but that was all right. The important thing was that she was Queen, which she'd be very good at, and Pyrgus wouldn't have to be Emperor, which he'd been dreading, and she'd pardoned Pyrgus so Hairstreak couldn't make trouble over the things Pyrgus did, which meant everything was all right and everyone was happy and it didn't matter a bit, not a bit, that Blue would never again have time for somebody like Henry who wasn't even a faerie or a hero or a wizard or anything exciting really. It didn't matter at all. It wasn't like they'd been *going out* or anything.

Maybe it was the thought of going home that was depressing him. The lethe cones would help, but there was still the fact that he'd got multicoloured hands, although they were fading a bit now. And there was Mr Fogarty's house to sort out. And Aisling. The thought of Aisling was always depressing. That had to be it. Nothing to do with Blue at all.

He closed the door of his palace quarters and immediately peeled off his golden britches. The relief was astonishing. He was on his way to the wardrobe to find a pair of really baggy trousers when he saw the single rose left on his table. Beside it was a tiny phial of amber liquid. Although the room was warm, the rose had dewdrops on its petals.

Henry picked up the phial and uncorked it. He thought it might be perfume, but the scent, while pleasant, proved far too mild. Cautiously he tilted a single drop on the tip of his tongue.

It was like a silent explosion. His depression disappeared like morning mist and ecstasy crashed over him. The palace dissolved into a pulse of pure white light. His soul burst from his breast to fill the universe. He was all and everything and it was bliss.

The experience lasted a lifetime and ended in a second. His hands were trembling as he pushed the cork back in the phial. As he turned it over, he caught sight of the tiny lettering engraved in the glass:

Essence of Love

Henry wondered who had sent it.

Glossary

Key:

FOL: Faerie of the Light
FON: Faerie of the Night
HMN: Human

Analogue World (a.k.a. the Earth Realm). Names used in the Faerie Realm to denote the mundane world of school and spots and parents who look like they might end up getting divorced.

Apatura Iris. (FOL) Father of Prince Pyrgus, Prince Comma and Princess Blue. Purple Emperor for more than twenty years.

Asloght. The major prison of the Faerie Realm.

Athame. Witch's dagger.

Atherton, Aisling. (HMN) Henry Atherton's younger sister and pain in the ass.

Atherton, Henry. (HMN) A young teenage boy living in England's Home Counties who first made contact with the Faerie Realm when he rescued the faerie prince, Pyrgus Malvae, from a cat. Henry has a portal control, made by his old (i.e. ancient) friend, Mr Fogarty, which allows him to visit the Realm at will.

Atherton, Martha. (HMN) Headmistress of a girls' school in the south of England. Wife of Tim Atherton, mother of Henry and Aisling.

Atherton, Tim. (HMN) Successful business executive. Husband of Martha Atherton, father of Henry and Aisling.

Beleth (a.k.a. the Infernal Prince; the Prince of Darkness). Prince of Hael, an alternative dimension of reality inhabited by demons.

Blue, Princess Holly. (FOL) Younger sister of Prince Pyrgus Malvae and daughter of Purple Emperor Apatura Iris. Blue runs her own private espionage service and keeps an illegal psychotronic spider that enables her to carry out certain difficult spying activities.

Brimstone, Silas. (FON) Elderly demonologist and former glue factory owner.

Bubble wand. Magical wand designed to produce a stream of coloured bubbles. Very popular at weddings and similar occasions.

Cardui, Madame Cynthia (a.k.a. the Painted Lady). (FOL) An elderly eccentric whose extensive contacts have made her one of Princess Blue's most valued agents.

Chalkhill, Jasper. (FON) Business partner of Silas Brimstone and, secretly, former head of Lord Hairstreak's intelligence service.

Cleopatra. Queen of the Feral Faerie.

Clutterbuck. An Orange Trinian hired by Chalkhill during his imprisonment.

Comma, Prince. (FOL/FON) Half-brother of Prince Pyrgus and Princess Blue. (Same father, different mothers.)

Cossus Cossus. (FON) Lord Hairstreak's Gatekeeper.

Demon. Form frequently taken by the shape-shifting alien species inhabiting the Hael Realm when in contact with faeries or humans.

Dingy, Harold. (FON) Bodyguard and general dogsbody of Lord Hairstreak.

Endolg. An intelligent animal that looks much like a woolly rug. Endolgs have a unique ability to sense truth which makes them popular companions in the Faerie Realm.

Faerie of the Light (Lighter). One of the two main faerie types, culturally averse to the use of demons in any circumstances and usually members of the Church of Light.

Faerie of the Night (Nighter). One of the two main faerie types, physically distinguished from Faeries of the Light by light-sensitive cat-like eyes. Make use of demonic servants.

Faerie Realm. A parallel aspect of reality inhabited by various alien species, including Faeries of the Light and Faeries of the Night.

Feral Faerie. A wild, nomadic faerie people who live and hunt in the depths of the great primeval forest that covers much of the Faerie Realm. The Feral Faerie are not known to hold allegiance to either the Faeries of the Light or the Faeries of the Night.

Fogarty, Alan. (HMN) Paranoid ex-physicist and bank robber with an extraordinary talent for engineering gadgets. Fogarty was made Gatekeeper of House Iris in recognition of the help he gave to Prince Pyrgus, even though it was Fogarty's cat which nearly ate Prince Pyrgus in the first place.

Forest Faerie. The way you refer to a Feral Faerie if you don't want to give offence.

Gatekeeper. Ancient title used to describe the chief advisor of a Noble House.

Glaistig. Semi-feral intelligent bipedal blood-feeder, thinner and slightly shorter than the average male faerie. Wild Glaistigs are reputed to kill travellers and drain them of their blood.

Gnoma, Pheosia. (FON) A freelance necromancer.

Golem. A clay figure brought to life by magic.

Gonepterix. Consort of Cleopatra.

Graminis. (FON) Widow Mormo's brother.

Grimoire. Black book of sorcery.

Hael. Polite name for Hell.

Hairstreak, Lord Black. (FON) Noble head of House Hairstreak and leader of the Faeries of the Night.

Halek knife (or blade). A rock-crystal weapon which releases magical energies to kill anything it pierces. Halek knives are prone to shattering occasionally, in which event the energies will kill the person using them.

Halek wizard. Non-human, non-faerie. Reputedly the

most skilful of the magical practitioners in the Faerie Realm. Halek wizards typically specialise in weapons technology.

Haleklind. Homeland of the Halek wizards.

Haniel. Winged lion inhabiting forest areas of the Faerie Realm.

Hodge. Mr Fogarty's tomcat.

House Iris. The Royal House of the Faerie Empire.

Kitterick. An Orange Trinian in the service of Madame Cardui.

Malvae, Crown Prince Pyrgus. (FOL) Teenage heir to the throne of the Purple Emperor. Pyrgus likes animals a lot more than politics and at one time actually ran away from home to live as a commoner because of disagreements with his father.

Mormo, Widow Maura. (FON) Brimstone's temporary landlady and even more temporary wife.

Ouklo. Levitating, spell-driven carriage.

Peacock. Chief Portal Engineer of House Iris.

Portal. Inter-dimensional energy gateway, either naturally occurring, modified or engineered.

Psychotronics. An obscure branch of Earth Realm science which studies the interaction of the human mind with physical reality. The practical application of psychotronics seems indistinguishable from some forms of Faerie Realm magic.

Purple Emperor. Ruler of the Faerie Empire.

Quercusia. (FON) Comma's mother and Apatura Iris's second wife.

Seething Lane. Former site of the Chalkhill and Brimstone Miracle Glue Factory.

Severs, Charlotte (Charlie). (HMN) Henry Atherton's closest friend in the Earth Realm.

Silk Mistress. (FOL) Member of a (exclusively female) Guild trained in the control of spinners and the making of spinner silk into expensive and much-sought-after fashion items.

Simbala. An addictive form of music sold legally in licensed outlets and illegally elsewhere.

Sinderack. A savoury with a naturally smoky flavour, particularly popular among city-dwelling faeries.

Slith. Dangerous grey reptile inhabiting forest areas of the Faerie Realm. Sliths secrete a highly toxic acid which they can spit across considerable distances.

Spell cone. Pocket-sized cones, no more than an inch or so in height, imbued with magical energies directed towards a specific result. The old-style cone had to be lit. The more modern version is self-igniting and is 'cracked' with a fingernail. Both types discharge like fireworks.

Spinner. Giant spider used to manufacture a special silk much prized in the faerie fashion industry.

Steen. Small, easily concealed faerie military field weapon that generates a localised volcanic eruption at point of aim. Not recommened in enclosed spaces because of the danger to the user.

Trinian. Non-human, non-faerie dwarfen race living in the Faerie Realm. Orange Trinians are a breed that dedicate themselves to service, Violet Trinians tend to be warriors while Green Trinians specialise in biological nanotechnology and consequently can create living machines.

Vimana. Sanskrit, Faerie Realm and Hael name for a flying saucer.

Wildmoor Broads. A flat area of thorny shrubland north of the faerie capital much favoured by the wealthy of the Realm for their estates, since the difficulties of travelling through the area go a long way towards ensuring their privacy. The only really viable means of transport is by levitating carriage. Ground transport is attacked by prickleweed, a semi-sentient plant that will typically swarm over any vehicle and bring it to a halt in minutes. Crossing the area on foot is impossible – the prickleweed paralyses pedestrians, then rips them apart for their nutrients.

Yammeth Cretch. Heartland of the Faeries of the Night.